VIOLETTA AND HER SISTERS

Nicholas John has been Dramaturge at English National Opera since 1985, responsible for many publications for the company, including the nightly programme books and the ENO Opera Guides series, published by John Calder. He worked with Jonathan Miller on *The Don Giovanni Book* (Faber, 1990). He is the author of the *Oxford Topic Book on Opera*, and is currently compiling the *Blue Guide to Operatic Europe*.

Violetta and her Sisters

The Lady of the Camellias:
Responses to the Myth

edited by NICHOLAS JOHN

faber and faber
LONDON · BOSTON

First published in 1994
by Faber and Faber Limited
3 Queen Square London WCIN 3AU

Photoset in Sabon by Susan Clarke
Printed in England by Clays Ltd, St Ives plc

A CIP record for this book is available from
the British Library

ISBN 0-571-16665-2

10 9 8 7 6 5 4 3 2 1

Contents

Acknowledgements

This book owes much to the inspirational work of Charles Bernheimer (*Figures of Ill Repute*, Harvard, 1989), Alain Corbin (*Les Filles de noce*, Paris, 1978) and Christiane Issartel (*Les Dames aux camélias*, 1981). My thanks to all those who have contributed to its genesis: the contributors, the translators, the publishers and my colleagues, notably Jennifer Batchelor and David Pountney. I owe an especial debt of gratitude to my parents, who hosted the lunch at which the project was conceived, to Nicholas Cronk and Lindy Grant, also then present, for their unfailing insights and enthusiasm, and to Bill Rafferty and Philip Ward-Jackson for help with the illustrations.

The texts by Simone Benmussa, Béatrice Perregaux and Martine Segalen were translated by Renée Williams. Gautier's *The Camellia and the Daisy* was translated by Liz Heron. Baudelaire's *Comes the Charming Evening* is a translation by David Paul. The extracts from Dumas's play and Flaubert's trial were translated by Jennifer Batchelor. The extracts from the novel *The Lady of the Camellias* are given in the translation by David Coward (World's Classics, OUP, 1986), from *The Wild Ass's Skin* in the translation by Herbert J. Hunt (Penguin, 1977), from Michelet in the versions by Richard Howard (Blackwell, 1987), from *Madame Bovary* in the translation by Gerard Hopkins (World's Classics, OUP, 1981) and from Flaubert's letters to Louise Colet in the translation by Charles Bernheimer given in *Figures of Ill Repute* (Harvard, 1990). The poems associated with Hébert's sculpture were identified by Jeanne Stump, and translated by her. Liane de Pougy's *My Blue Notebooks* was translated by Diana Athill (London, 1979). The other French translations are by the editor working with Liz Heron, Naomi Segal or Renée Williams.

Christine Brückner's monologue was translated by Stewart Spencer, and all rights in this text including those of translation and performance are reserved.

The interview with Irmgard Arnold was translated by Detlef

Sölter. Mieke Kolk's text was translated by Tim Coleman. The interview with Riikka Hakola was translated by Erki Arni.

The article by Peter Brook first appeared in the *Observer* (March, 1963) and the extract by Margot Fonteyn is reproduced from her *Autobiography* (W.H. Allen, 1975). The letters of Verdi and Strepponi were translated by Frank Walker for *The Man Verdi* (London, 1962).

Unless otherwise noted, the illustrations are reproduced by courtesy of the Bibliothèque Nationale, the Conway Library/ Courtauld Institute of Art, the Mander and Mitchenson Theatre Collection, the Metropolitan Museum of Art, the Stuart-Liff Collection, the Trustees of the British Museum, the Trustees of the Theatre Collection of the Victoria and Albert Museum, the Musée Carnavalet (Cliché photothèque de la Ville de Paris, © SPADEM 1993) and the Musée d'Orsay (photo R.M.N.).

Front cover Helen Field as Violetta at English National Opera, 1988 (photo Bill Rafferty)

Back cover The jewel box of Marie Duplessis (collection Mary Jane Phillips-Matz; photo Tom McGovern)

Frontispiece La traviata at English National Opera, 1988 (photo David Scheinmann/Avid Images)

Nicholas John
Introduction

' Another book on the Lady of the Camellias?' people asked
an author earlier this century, and the question deserves a
reply today.

A production of Giuseppe Verdi's *La traviata* at English
National Opera in 1988 was the starting point. Verdi's libretto
(1853) had been fashioned by Francesco Maria Piave from *The
Lady of the Camellias*, a novel (1848) and then a play (1852) by
Alexandre Dumas *fils*. He was the illegitimate son of the flamboy-
ant Alexandre Dumas who had just written *The Three Musketeers*
and *The Count of Monte-Cristo*, and he was inspired to write his
first novel by the death of a famous courtesan, Marie Duplessis,
with whom he had had an affair two years before. Indeed her
death from consumption at the age of twenty-three was the talk of
Paris.

This book was conceived as a collection of short personal
responses by women to a man-made myth and has grown to
include a kaleidoscopic picture of the society from which that
myth emerged. The contributors represent a broad spectrum of
disciplines and cultures, and the book is the richer for the unre-
solved contradictions between them. That contradictions do arise
is not surprising since the contributors include the world's most
published romantic novelist, a psychoanalyst who is also a nun,
North America's most celebrated sex therapist, four opera singers,
a drag artist, a descendant of the husband of the Lady of the
Camellias herself, a Californian grandmother reminiscing about
her career as a high-class hooker in Paris, writers as well as critics
of literature and drama, a composer and a conductor, musicolo-
gists and social historians. For each of these women the legend has
a special meaning. For others – it is perhaps unnecessary to add – it
does not: a Duchess refused, saying she had attended only one
opera and never intended to go to another. Those who did pick up
the gauntlet often responded to a folk-memory of Dumas's original, which is now better known through film versions than the

play – Greta Garbo and Isabelle Huppert rather than Sarah Bernhardt and Eleonora Duse have kept the myth alive. Alessandra Comini's essay offered an inspirational link between the modern reader and Marie Duplessis, and became both the book's keynote and title.

The texts fall naturally into four sequences according to their focus – social, literary, artistic and performance – taking the reader from a discussion of the social realities of the historical figures, through the process of fictionalizing the narrative and its effects on the visual arts, to a sequence devoted to the realities of performing it. Each section opens with a longer essay: Elizabeth Wilson sets the Parisian scene; Lucy Hughes-Hallett offers a challenging interpretation of Dumas's novel; Philip Hook discusses the fallen woman in French nineteenth-century painting; and Mary Jane Phillips-Matz, Verdi's most recent biographer, brings the insights of meticulous research to a fresh account of his personal *traviata* during the composition of the opera.

In different ways these historical and literary studies touch upon the obligation of artists to their work and to society. Operas and plays were not alone in being subject to censorship: every form of artistic creation was debated publicly on grounds of morality, and we reproduce here extracts from the two celebrated prosecutions of Flaubert and Baudelaire in 1857, and from the Salon commentaries of the time. While offence to morality could be used to castigate a great work, in the commercial art world a moral tag or preface could be used to validate a mediocre one. Fallen women were familiar subjects for the stage but always distanced from the audience by historical settings: Victor Hugo's *Marion Delorme* or Donizetti's *La favorite* encountered no such problems. In the same way, as we shall see, the visual arts assumed historicism to avoid reproach. Contemporary life was, on the other hand, the particular concern of the novel, where conventions were less rigid and, incidentally, where women writers could rise to prominence. Dumas *fils*'s novel made little sensation compared to his stage adaptation: it was the topicality of the subject for the stage that upset the censors. With a change of government the censors' ban was lifted and the play, in contemporary dress, ushered in the Second Empire.

Italian opera was even more bound by convention: Verdi's

opera had to be set in the time of Richelieu. Mercedes Viale Ferrero tells us that the prima donna took her own (contemporary) costumes with her from city to city, so that any coherent sense of historical period was unthinkable. In *La traviata* no one could miss the unmistakable tone of Verdi's personal morality, born of a peasant mistrust of the Church and social hypocrisy, and his admiration for spiritual courage and self-sacrifice. Where Bellini and Donizetti had been content to sacrifice their heroines for love alone, Verdi sought redemption and social acceptance for Violetta.

The Lady of the Camellias, in its various treatments, is central to the nineteenth-century debate about the interaction of society and art and, typically, it involves discussion of the representation of woman. To give a vivid picture of the society from which Dumas's fiction emerged, we explore the contemporary attitude towards women, and in particular towards prostitution. Alain Corbin has proposed that the century's need to define and to pictorialize the prostitute sprang from a desire to identify an 'endstop ... of the feminine', as opposed to the icon of the respectable woman, who was mother, sister and daughter. The prostitute embodied a threat to the health, both bodily and moral, of society. Prostitution inspired civil servants, politicians and philosophers as well as artists. Dumas *fils* returned repeatedly to the theme which he had first broached in his play, hammering home his views on the decadence of France. Women also had articulate views about the condition of French society, and much of their writing appears here for the first time in English, a testimony to the neglect of authors of the calibre of Marceline Desbordes-Valmore and George Sand, Louise Colet and Marie d'Agoult.

In 1800, Madame de Staël compared the condition of an intelligent woman in France to that of 'the Pariahs in India'. The most famous French woman writer of the mid-century, George Sand, had the advantages of being, like Mme de Staël, an aristocrat and a 'woman of letters'; yet even she adopted a male pseudonym and masculine clothes to play the role of the eccentric – a saint to some, an abomination to others. What were the roles available to women who sought independence and who were not aristocrats? Constitutional and property laws denied them rights and society tended to define them in relation to their men. The professions were closed to them and even small trades like dressmaking were increasingly dominated by men; domestic service and the stage were options. Marriage and motherhood were what society expected of women, even the 'legalized prostitution' of marriage with no hope of divorce. In 1855, Dumas coined the word 'demimonde' to denote the world in which those who had once been respectable women were condemned to live; and in 1872 he invented the term 'feminist' for the causes for which he battled against prejudice and injustice towards women.

What do men and women still find so sympathetic in a work of his youth which dramatizes the sacrifice of a woman to such a moral code? The novel's conversational style and apparently untidy scrapbook construction have the peculiar merit of engaging the reader as though it were a social document as well as a romance. Moreover, the co-existence of fact and fiction, rather than either element in isolation, intrigues us as it did contemporaries. It continues the process of fictionalizing the life of a courtesan which she had herself begun. Rose Alphonsine Plessis was a Norman peasant girl who changed her name to Marie Duplessis when she came to Paris, and finally assumed the title of Comtesse Édouard de Perregaux by a marriage in the Kensington Register Office in London (and therefore not recognized in France) a year before she died. Transformed into his fictional heroine, she was christened by Dumas the 'Lady of the Camellias', as she has ever since been known. She crossed the Atlantic in 1856 as 'The Lady with the Camellias' and in an 1876 New York translation she became Camille.

According to Mary Jane Phillips-Matz, a family legend says that Verdi attended the first performance of the play. He knew Paris well because, as a young widower, he had lived there on and off for five years. It was in Paris during 1847 (while he was writing *Jérusalem* for the Opéra) that he became intimate with the singer Giuseppina Strepponi. He did not marry her until 1859 but in 1849 they moved together into a property he had bought outside his birthplace of Busseto, near Parma. Local disapproval of the liaison became increasingly vocal and in 1851 they went back to Paris, and Verdi wrote a famous letter to Antonio Barezzi, the father of his first wife, describing Giuseppina: 'In my house there lives a free, independent lady . . . Neither she nor I owes any explanation for our actions to anyone at all . . .' The breach was healed, and they returned to Busseto, where Piave wrote the libretto of *La traviata* and the opera was begun in earnest.

For all the topicality of the barely disguised characters and incidents, audiences also saw that Dumas's book belongs to a theme in French literature going back to *L'Histoire du chevalier des Grieux et de Manon Lescaut* (1731) by the abbé Prévost. That novel is also partly autobiographical, and concerns the adventures of a young seminarian with a loose-living girl who returns to him after many affairs and dies in the odour of sanctity. Nineteenth-century commentators shifted the focus away from des Grieux on to the character of Manon as a woman who led men astray; Barbey d'Aurevilly described her as 'the mother of all fallen women'. It was so popular that it was reprinted as *Manon Lescaut* almost every year and the existence of a copy in Marie Duplessis's library has naturally been supposed to show that it was one of her favourite books. It is the talisman of the love affair in Dumas's novel: the narrator buys it – hardly knowing why – at the auction of Marguerite's goods, and discovers the enigmatic dedication 'Manon to Marguerite, Humility'. It is the intertextual thread by which Dumas leads his readers into and through his story, using it to contrast with the poignant reality of Marguerite's experience.

The moral purpose of the novel was much debated in French literary circles. Dumas, like George Sand – whom by the 1860s he addressed as 'Maman' – came to favour socially committed literature. In *The Lady of the Camellias* he adopts a high moral tone but his drama is played out to the rules of society. He questions whether this society will ever allow a woman who has once transgressed to free herself from sin: the procuress, Prudence, argues that it is rare for such women to reintegrate themselves into society; Armand's father says baldly that it is impossible for a decent family to accept her. Her consumption is associated with the feverish quality of her life in the city, and hence with her transgression. Consequently, Dumas suggests that the possibility of an unclouded future of selfless love is as illusory as her temporary recovery. He implies that her past, like her disease, will catch up with her, however much she may persuade herself that love will cure and save her. Instead society offers her a blessed memory in Armand's family if she will renounce her love and accept the death that fol-

lows as a consequence. Neither father nor son reaches her deathbed, 'which was now nothing less than a holy tabernacle' according to the maid. In the play, Marguerite asks Armand to go with
her to the marriage of one of her friends before she collapses; its
last lines are: 'Sleep in peace, Marguerite. Much will be forgiven
you since you have loved so deeply.' The opera heightens still further the religious aura of reconciliation in Violetta's last moments:
she refers to her confession; she desires to go to church with
Alfredo, and Germont comes in person to beg forgiveness, apparently full of remorse at his cruelty.

Marguerite/Violetta recognizes the roles she plays, and her pro-
ficiency in doing so is an aspect of her brilliance as a professional
performer. This does not mean that she can change them, or
choose not to play them. Her protest at being forced to accept
images of herself that do not suit her is to buy herself a few months
with her lover. Unlike the majority of her contemporaries in fact
and fiction, she has the ability and the independence of means at
least to try to invent an alternative role for herself. A prostitute is a
dangerous performer in a society preoccupied with money and
sex; she holds the trump cards. But when Germont tells
Marguerite, 'I was warned that you were a dangerous person', she
replies, 'Yes, dangerous to myself.' She is an exception – that is
why Dumas claims to be telling the story – and she turns on its
head society's expectation of prostitutes by accepting self-sacrifice
in return for redemption.

The debate about prostitution, and about the containment of
sexuality in an overcrowded city, was – as we have seen – one of
the great issues of the century. The acquisition of money through
commerce or speculation made movement within this society possible, and the prostitute was a prime example of market forces at
work. Parent-Duchâtelet, doyen of municipal investigators of
sewage disposal and prostitution in Paris, likened the influence of
prostitution to the putrefaction of sewers (and he acknowledged
that both were necessary evils). 'Look at the filth of your past,' the
father tells Marguerite, using the word 'fange' (filth) which is the
key to Parent's comparison of prostitutes with rottenness. Parent
admitted, however, that his system of classification could not cope
with the courtesans – the 'femmes galantes', the 'femmes à parties'
and the 'femmes de spectacles et de théâtres' – who infiltrated the

upper echelons of respectable society. Twenty years later, what he most feared had happened, namely that they had become the almost official symbol of Paris, the embodiment of the falsity and rootlessness of the Second Empire. As performers in a world of appearances, they stole the limelight from the respectable women from whom they were indistinguishable in their manners, dress – and male companions.

French art of the mid-century was crowded with representations of courtesans. Although the Academy of Fine Arts was closed to women students, female nudes were everywhere in public and private art, imprisoned or passive in promiscuously vulnerable poses. The models and muses who inspired the male artists did not belong to the ranks of respectable women; it was prostitutes – often of the higher class – who were dressed, or rather undressed, for male fantasies in the fancy-dress of religion, antiquity or the Orient. Manet's *Olympia* (1863–5) caused confusion because her gaze and her pose contradict what people expected: identifiable as a courtesan, she does not pretend to be an allegorical figure or an odalisque, yet she refuses to be an outcast with a sentimental moral tag.

The situation in literature was rather different. There were many women writers (and only a minority adopted male pseudonyms), and countless works in which 'Woman' was discussed. This in turn fed into an aesthetic debate about the nature of creativity and the artist. The historian Jules Michelet proclaimed that Marceline Desbordes-Valmore was 'the greatest love poet of the century'; Verlaine included her in his list of 'poètes maudits'. Michelet wanted to isolate what was specifically female about a woman: 'woman, above man's word and the song of a bird, has an entirely magical language with which she interrupts that word or that song: the sigh, her impassioned breath' (*Love*, 1858). In order to understand the essential otherness of woman he recommended men to act as maid servants to their wives during their menstrual periods. 'Men of letters and artists,' he wrote in an essay (*Woman*, 1859), 'androgynes without knowing it, take part in the specifically feminine dimension of culture.' Flaubert, in the midst of creating his novel of middle-class adultery, *Madame Bovary*, encouraged his mistress Louise Colet to write but deplored the intrusion of her sexuality into her work. He told his 'muse' in

1854: 'I have always tried (but it seems that I have failed) to make you into a sublime hermaphrodite. I want you to be a man down to your stomach. You embarrass me and trouble me and *sully yourself* with your femaleness.'

Other writers attacked the virtual impossibility of divorce, or the different values placed on sexual gratification outside marriage for a man and a woman, but not even George Sand created women characters with an overt political voice. Colet, so frank about her own sexuality, was confused about what was politically appropriate for women: the protagonist of her *Woman of the People* (from *Poem of Woman*, 1854) participates in revolution for personal vengeance, and Colet reproached Sand, who introduced political and moral polemics into her prefaces, for being too masculine in tone. Sand's interventions as a narrator in her controversial first novel *Indiana* (1832) are more direct than anything she gives her heroine to say about politics.

The careers of both Colet and Sand demonstrated that the city could offer women an independence that provincial society did not; both maintained the conventional opposition of the country as a place of health and healing as against the corruption of the city. This twist to the ancient opposition of culture and nature had been influentially articulated by Rousseau's *The New Heloïse* (*La Nouvelle Héloïse*, 1761). From very different viewpoints, they agreed that the natural world was essential for a virtuous family life and that woman was in her natural element there as mother, sister and daughter. A typical instance was Sand's short novel *The Devil's Pond* (*La Mare au diable*, 1846), a celebration of the honesty, sincere emotions and profound kindness of the peasants despite the poverty and physical hardship of their farming life. Dumas almost parodied this convention with the country idyll in *The Lady of the Camellias*. In the book he sets this at Bougival – which was not so far from where his father built his fantastic Château de Monte-Cristo in 1848; in the play, Marguerite and Armand retire to Auteuil, near Passy, where Verdi and Giuseppina lived during the summer of 1847. Either way, this 'country' was a walkable distance from the centre of Paris, which may signify the fragility of Marguerite's new life. For reasons, perhaps, of dramatic intensity, Verdi and Piave further specify that the retreat to the country happens in winter; she dies the following February. Any escape into nature takes place therefore strictly in the mind, or at best in a hothouse.

How unlike the urban desert, where independent beings of either sex sought to survive in new, perhaps more liberal, perhaps more perverse, relationships. Flora Tristan dedicated her polemical *Walks in London* (*Promenades dans Londres*, 1840) to the poor of both sexes as a warning of the depravity inevitable in the vastness of what she called 'the monster town', and there were many who agreed. For male writers, the city also offered the anonymity and darkness necessary to explore the heights and depths of human experience. In many of their texts the prostitute is a key figure: Baudelaire found the inspiration for *The Flowers of Evil* (*Les Fleurs du mal*, 1857) in the slums and brothels. Pre-eminent among evocations of Paris before 1848 is Balzac's *Human Comedy* (*La Comédie humaine*), a series of novels which contain many magnificent passages about this society in turmoil. The description of the orgy in *The Wild Ass's Skin* (*La Peau de chagrin*, 1833) included in Part One captures the spectacular scale of the dissolute life that Violetta Valéry leads in Verdi's opera more evocatively than the more intimate parties of Dumas's novel. *A Harlot High and Low* (*Splendeurs et misères des courtisanes*, 1842–5) hinges upon the self-sacrifice of Esther the courtesan. She earned her nickname of 'the Torpedo', an electric sting-ray, from her beauty's effect on men, and it was especially appropriate because of her dangerous capacity to swim through Parisian society and so to deny the distinctions between her lovers as members of different classes or even as individuals. 'You have all been more or less her lovers,' comments a cynical observer; 'none of you can say she was your mistress; she can always have you, you can never have her.'

Not all the literature featuring Paris was so potent. On the level of melodrama, for instance, Eugène Sue owed a lot to Parent-Duchâtelet's reports which informed *The Mysteries of Paris* (*Les Mystères de Paris*, 1843), a thriller strewn with observation of the most sordid Parisian underworld. A child prostitute, aptly named Fleur-de-Marie, is rescued and brought to a farm rich in milk and religion. Marx and Engels commented in *The Holy Family* (*Die heilige Familie*, 1844) that in the transfer she loses her vitality as a character, and that by imposing bourgeois morality upon her, Sue destroys her. Whereas in her early state she is admirably honest, she is later forced to lie to conceal her origins. Although Dumas's taste for the victims of society was not steeped so deeply in depravity, he enjoyed voyeurism, most obviously at the moment of the exhumation of Marguerite's decaying corpse. And his narrator throughout shares the excitement of the crowd at the auction picking over Marguerite's belongings while professing moral indignation: 'why should we too turn away souls that bleed from wounds oozing with the evil of their past, like infected blood from a sick body, as they wait only for a friendly hand to bind them up and restore them to a convalescent heart?' For him the most thrilling of this courtesan's charms is just that characteristic which Parent-Duchâtelet most feared: her capacity to pass for a respectable woman – 'A Duchess', he says, 'could not have smiled differently.'

Verdi, who had rejected Hugo's romantic historical drama *Marion Delorme* because it was about a whore ('putain'), admired the moral tone of Dumas's play. The music that opens the opera allows no doubt about the purity or the certainty of Violetta's death. Each act turns upon her suffering on the cross of pain and delight ('croce e delizia') involved in the renunciation of love. Two of Verdi's most recent operas, *Luisa Miller* (1850) and *Rigoletto* (1851), had centred upon a father–daughter relationship of exceptional intensity which causes the death of the daughter: in the central scene of *La traviata* Violetta obeys the father-figure and agrees to sacrifice herself for the sake of the pure daughter image. 'God may be merciful,' she cries; 'Man is implacable.' This closely echoes *Stiffelio*, the opera he had based in 1849 on another French play (*Le Pasteur ou L'Évangile et le foyer* by Bourgeois and Sylvestre). In the final scene, the pastor publicly quotes Christ's words to the woman taken in adultery and concludes: 'She rose up pardoned.' We have seen how reconciliation and forgiveness are introduced in the final scene of *La traviata*: the loneliness and agony of Marguerite's death in the novel have been replaced by Violetta's acceptance into the family, and her transfiguration. Is there any place in either operatic ending for ambiguity – does Stiffelio the husband forgive his wife; would Germont *père* accept the fallen woman as his daughter-in-law if she revived?

Death, and the metaphors of consumption, permeate this subject. In the nineteenth century this disease held a particular terror as a fate that could fall upon anyone regardless of class or fault; unlike cholera or typhoid it did not attack a whole community. Consumption singled out its victims, and they acquired an interesting individuality; the decline refined them in suffering, and they suffered the prototype of a passive death, consumed by an inner, unseen passion. Far from the clinical reality of foul breath and emaciation, it was portrayed as a death of aesthetic beauty, directly allied to spiritual innocence. Verdi's first title for *La traviata* was *Amore e morte* (*Love and Death*). Alfredo, as much as Armand, knows that he loves a woman whose days are numbered, and this intensifies his desire. For the healthy, the allure of beauty and youth can be enhanced by the fascination of disease and mortality – infection may be the terrible price to be paid for desire. Such perverse sensuality is present in the early writings of Balzac as well as Théophile Gautier, whose dalliance with death and the supernatural in the ballet *Giselle* (1831) or the prose-poem *The Beautiful Vampire* (*La Morte amoureuse*, 1836) carry premonitions of the decadence of the end of the century. Marie d'Agoult acidly observed that spirituality was back in fashion in the late 1830s, when the Princess Belgiojoso – the doyenne of Italian patriots in Paris – affected the appearance of having one foot in the grave.

The Lady of the Camellias wants to live, she wants to love, and she wants to be an exception to the rules of illness and society. She shows admirable courage to fight these twin antagonists, which seem to her and to us remorseless and unjust. Her submission does not condone the myths and values for which she dies, but Dumas makes her die so that she can win a martyr's crown – and be placed among the works of art in a respectable Second Empire drawing-room.

*Maria Callas as Violetta in Visconti's 1955 production at
La Scala, Milan*

Alessandra Comini
Violetta and her Sisters

*Alessandra Comini is University Distinguished Professor of Art
History at Southern Methodist University, Dallas, Texas, and the
author of* The Changing Image of Beethoven: A Study in
Mythmaking.

I can't remember how old I was when I first realized that the
'celebrated courtesan' heroine of *La traviata* was a prostitute.
How long does it take any child, any adolescent actually, to comprehend what the word prostitute entails? My Italian father, who
taught me his favourite Verdi and Puccini arias when I was still
quite young, would occasionally look mysteriously all-knowing
and tell me that some day he would sing for me the 'other words'
to Violetta's cabaletta 'Sempre libera' – words that (my mother
told me) all Italian men of his generation seemed to know and
chuckle hugely over. Even after I was exposed to the crude *doubles
entendres* of the substitute text my pure, sympathetic view of
Violetta remained unviolated. Never mind that she was a 'fallen
woman', a 'traviata' – a woman led astray. In the opera, as Verdi's
music so clearly suggested, she was glamorous (despite a bad
cough), popular, and big-hearted; she abandoned an exciting life
and friends in Paris to live in isolation with an impetuous, infatuated (to me hair-splitting: 'io vivo *quasi* in ciel' 'I live *almost* in
heaven') young man who was surprised to learn that it cost *money*
– Violetta's money – to live comfortably in the country ('Oh mio
rimorso!'); she was talked into leaving him by an unpleasant
('bella voi siete – ma col tempo' 'You are beautiful – but with
time') old man who claimed Alfredo's angelic sister wouldn't
otherwise be able to marry and who kept (it seemed to me) exhort-
ing her to cry ('Piangi, piangi, piangi, o misera'); back in Paris she
was insulted by a sour-grapes, jealous Alfredo, unaware of her
noble 'sacrifice', in front of all their friends – insulted so vilely that
even party-crashing Papa Germont was horrified; and finally she
still yearned loyally for her Alfredo even as she lay dying of

tuberculosis, fantasizing with him when he made a last-minute appearance in her humble death chamber that they would leave Paris together and her health would reflower ('Parigi, o cara'), only to collapse in death a few moments later.

This tear-jerking story of misunderstood self-sacrifice and ill-fated love, combined with Verdi's beautiful, stirring music, left me enthralled and uncritically content. Certainly I never questioned what a courtesan was; I just knew that Violetta wasn't married and Alfredo wasn't married and that they met, fell in love and began living happily together in the country, with Violetta footing the bills until Alfredo's great pecuniary discovery. Was Alfredo a 'kept' man, then? I didn't know about such things yet and any-how there were other operas with far more disturbing aspects to worry about – how *could* Lieutenant Pinkerton have returned to Japan with a second, 'American' wife on his arm in *Madama Butterfly*, for example? My American mother could never give me a satisfactory explanation; her rational resignation before cultural differences and customs did nothing to soothe my juvenile in-dignation.

Out from under parental wings and learning about The World at Barnard College in the pre-feminist 1950s, I gleaned much that seemed to bear on my accepting, non-judgemental image of Violetta (as portrayed in those happy days by Renata Tebaldi). Of course I was introduced to the Alexandre Dumas *fils* play of 1852, *La Dame aux camélias*, and moved quickly from the fictional Marguerite Gautier to the real-life courtesan Marie Duplessis, with whom Alex Jr had had his stormy eleven-month fling (they were both twenty) before her death from tuberculosis at the age of twenty-three in 1847. According to Dumas the showy, rose-like white camellia was the trademark of Marguerite: camellias filled her sumptuous apartment on the Boulevard de la Madeleine, and she always carried a bouquet of them with her to the Opera (Greta Garbo wasn't exaggerating in the 1936 film version *Camille*). I have never found corroboration in any accounts of Marie Duplessis for the famous detail in the novel: periodically – once a month in fact – she would appear at the Opera with a bouquet of *red* camellias, signalling to interested patrons her temporary non-availability. When I somehow concurrently stumbled across the arcane fact that the dreadless Hell's Angels award each other a special emblem to wear on their leather jackets if they've 'made it' with a menstruating woman – what lubricious courage! – I couldn't help but think of Dumas's picturesque custom whether drawn from life or not.

College also brought me into contact with the nineteenth-century American feminist Tennie C. Claflin (*Constitutional Equality, a Right of Women*, 1871) and her thought-provoking declaration: 'Public prostitution is but nothing to that practised under the cloak of marriage.' Although the implications of that daring pronouncement are different for everyone, I have since thought that it constitutes an interesting preliminary answer to the cigar-fixated Freud's absurdly naive question: 'What do women want?' The simple answer – 'The same advantages as men' – seems never to have occurred to him or his circle. But listen to this rudimentary if materialist answer given by the courtesan Marie Duplessis in Dumas's novel when asked by her close friend the actress Judith Bernat why she had taken up prostitution. 'Why do I sell myself? Because the labour of a working girl would never have brought me the luxury for which I've had such an irresistible craving ... I wanted to know the refinements and leisures of artistic taste, the joy of living in elegant and cultivated society.' Marguerite's *goals* don't seem that different from the professed aims of many of the university students I now teach. Were her means of achieving these goals that different from practices common to present-day society, such as influence-peddling, insider-trading, and complicity between weapons manufacturers and military acquisitions officials?

But to return to Violetta and her sisters. One of them, Flora Bervoix in the opera, seems to have had the best little gambling table in Paris. Along with beauty, charm and wit (Lola Montez was continually amazed at the premium placed on intelligent conversation in women during her siege of Paris), the role of hostess seems to have been a requirement for the successful courtesan (Act I and scene ii of Act II of *La traviata* in fact feature parties given by Violetta and Flora respectively). Like Marie Duplessis, the courtesan was frequently supported by multiple admirers. That word 'support' is exactly what differentiates the salon of a courtesan from that of a mistress like, say Madame de Staël, George Sand, or even Liszt's own Marie d'Agoult. The latter were financially independent, whereas the courtesan/prostitute accrued wealth through her patrons. It was after all by the sale of her jewels (presumably gifts from her former 'professional admirer' Baron Douphol) that Violetta met the expense of cosy country living ('pur tanto lusso') with the carefree Alfredo. On a more grandiose scale, vast sums were spent financing Bonapartist propaganda by Henriette Howard, the London actress turned Saint-Cloud courtesan and mistress to Napoleon III. The most successful courtesans during the Second Empire lived the life of the upper classes. They maintained villas, carriages, horses and boxes at the opera; they held literary salons and vied with one another for publicity and even exchanged or recommended patrons to each other. Alexandre Dumas *père* had a brief fling with Marie Duplessis's new acquaintance Lola Montez just about the same time as his son was commencing the affair that would supply the story-line for his *La Dame aux camélias*. For men of a certain class and wealth the *demi-mondaine* (the expression employed by Dumas *fils* to designate the woman who was morally superior to the prostitute but lower than legal wife) was almost mandatory. She was a status symbol, the displayed index of a man's wealth.

What was and is so compelling about Verdi's *demi-mondaine* is what I would call the *transfiguration motif*. (Not to be confused with that old chestnut, the redemption motif.) Because Violetta chooses to live with Alfredo for love rather than for money she is transformed from *courtesan* to *companion*. She is simultaneously up and downgraded to mistress (able to enter the world of George Sand and Marie d'Agoult on their terms). Illicit love minus the money factor becomes romantic. Unmarried love can even demand the right to be happy. Just listen to Verdi, writing to his former father-in-law in defence not of Violetta but of Giuseppina Strepponi, the ex-singer, successful music teacher, and mother of several illegitimate children (not by him) with whom he had openly been living since 1847.

> In my house there lives a free, independent lady, a lover (as I am) of the solitary life, who has means that cover her every need. Neither she nor I owes any explanation for our actions to anyone at all; but on the other hand, who knows what relationship exists between us? . . . Who knows whether she is or is not my

wife? . . . But I will say that in my house she must command
equal or even greater respect than I myself . . .

(Verdi and Strepponi did finally marry quietly in Savoy in
1859.)

Is Giuseppina Violetta's sister? However little or much bio-
graphical parallel we may wish to see in *La traviata* the larger
question is how Verdi's sympathetic, devastatingly sincere portrayal of the courtesan-turned-companion was in itself a parallel
to the changing mores of the mid-nineteenth century. As we
approach the end of the twentieth century, what for many had
been the compromise ('prostitution' in Claflin's view) of a loveless
marriage is no longer a social commandment. The idea of living
together for love, in or out of wedlock, is the *bella trovata* legit-
imized by Violetta and her sisters. Perhaps my unquestioning
childhood acceptance of Violetta was not so naive after all.

PART ONE
The Woman in the City

Elizabeth Wilson
Bohemians, Grisettes and Demi-mondaines

Elizabeth Wilson is Professor of Social Studies at the Polytechnic of North London and this article summarizes themes dealt with at greater length by her in The Sphinx in The City *(London, 1991) and 'The Invisible Flâneur',* New Left Review *(no. 191, 1992).*

Writing in 1836, Frances Trollope (the novelist Anthony Trollope's mother, and a popular travel writer herself) described Paris in ecstatic terms as 'this gay, bright, noisy, restless city – this city of the living', and decided to think 'only of enjoying myself' during her stay. That all the delights of urban existence appeared at this time to be condensed in the cafés, concerts, theatres and parks of the French capital is due to a set of unique historical circumstances. Industrialization and urbanization occurred later than in Britain, but came rapidly and suddenly. This engendered a changing, diversifying and mobile class structure. The cramped quarters, usually apartments, in which Parisian families lived meant that they spent more time socializing in public places, by contrast with the privacy of the London bourgeoisie capaciously housed in its terraces and squares. Politically, the aftermath of the Revolution brought frustration and recurrent instability. In addition, the French capital was not blighted by the Sabbatarian influences of a puritan or evangelical culture which so stifled public life in London during the nineteenth century. Spain was languishing in feudal backwardness, Italy and Germany were yet to become states in their own right, so Paris had no rival, and became a cultural crucible. The dominant role it played in French life was the outcome of a tradition going back at least to the time of Louis XIV and, as the Goncourt brothers were later to observe in their journals, this made the atmosphere of Paris supercharged and overheated:

> We talked about the absence of intellectual life in the French provinces, compared with all the active literary societies in the English counties and second- or third-class German towns; about the way Paris absorbed everything; and about the future of France which, in the circumstances, seemed destined to die of a cerebral haemorrhage.

One of the most striking figures to emerge from the social melt-down was that of the Bohemian. A Bohemian was either a student or an aspiring artist of some kind – painter, writer, musician – adapting to a new socio-cultural order in which patronage was retreating before the market, and the families from which the Bohemians themselves came – artisans and small shopkeepers – were gradually in the process of being displaced and impoverished by the restructuring of manufacturing and industry.

An illustration by Gavarni for the 1838 edition of
The Wild Ass's Skin *by Balzac*

The Bohemian, named after the gypsies of central Europe – impoverished wanderers – in many cases came from the provinces to Paris to study for the professions or to make his name in the cultural world. This journey was, however, not simply geographical; it was equally important as an interior journey; a cultural and intellectual voyage, the focus of which was rebellion against the bourgeois order, now in the ascendancy. The Bohemians lived out the ideal of the Romantic movement, which set the heroic individual against the constraints of society. In many respects the intellectual was the most romantic hero of all, because his struggle was willed and voluntary. It was more than the defeat of any enemy; it was the insistence on a new way of seeing things, a new morality, a revolution of the spirit and the emotions, and the creation of revolutionary forms in which this new consciousness might be expressed.

Only urban life provided the necessary stimuli – a variety of contacts and spectacles, other budding talents, and the crucially

An illustration by Gavarni for the 1838 edition of
The Wild Ass's Skin *by Balzac*

important commercial opportunities for the development of talent. Paris was particularly rich in all these things.

Urban life also offered a widening of horizons to women, who came to seek their fortunes, or to escape the restrictions of patriarchal peasant life. French divorce statistics at the end of the eighteenth century suggest that divorce was more common in cities because women had a wider choice of alternative sources of financial support (paid work) and independent living arrangements than in the countryside, although they remained badly off by comparison with men of their own class.

They certainly did not participate in the life of the city on the same terms as men. How were they to become part of its artistic life? At the beginning of the century there had still been, for example, a large number of women artists, but the organization of painters into formal associations resulted in the gradual exclusion of women from the professional bodies and to a trivialization of

An illustration by Gavarni for the 1838 edition of
The Wild Ass's Skin *by Balzac*

their work. Indeed, at all levels of society, women's work was marginalized. Women did not have access to the same range of occupations nor the same rates of pay as men. A French study published in 1873 (Paul Leroy-Beaulieu, *Le Travail des femmes au XIX siècle*) suggests that there were sixty per cent more female than male paupers.

There was always one 'profession' open to women: prostitution. The term 'profession' is a misnomer, since prostitution was not necessarily organized or clearly demarcated from less commercial relationships in the eighteenth and early nineteenth century. It was the new industrial society that eventually produced a much greater regulation of prostitution, so that the prostitute did become more rigorously distinguished from other women and thus, in the long run, more stigmatized. This was in part the result of the generally more commercialized nature of life in the metropolis, as industrial capitalism created a society of consumption and commodities, in which sexuality and sexual pleasure could be bought and sold on the open market.

Thus city life was double-edged and highly contradictory for women. It offered new opportunities, but correspondingly greater dangers. While the wives and daughters of the bourgeoisie were allowed less sexual licence than the women of the old aristocracy, women of the working classes, on the margins of the petty bourgeoisie, or on the very lowest rungs of society, might climb the ladder of success by making use of their sexuality. Equally they might fall into a chasm of poverty and disease – propagandists against prostitution painted apocalyptic scenarios of disaster and death.

Either way, women were far more defined and determined by their sexuality than were men. The female counterpart of the Bohemian was not a woman artist or poet but a 'grisette'. The Bohemian's grisette was a young woman of humble origins who, as his mistress, shared his poverty and deprivations; their liaison defied the class structure only temporarily, however, and she was likely in the end to marry a man from her own background. For the Bohemian, sexual rebellion and sexual adventure constituted an important, perhaps even an essential, aspect of his challenge to conventional society and bourgeois customs. Arsène Houssaye, a noted Bohemian of the 1830s and 1840s (but who became successful in worldly terms as director of the Comédie Française under

Napoleon III), described the grisettes as similarly in revolt against convention. They were, he said:

> janitors' daughters in rebellion, dressmakers' apprentices who had snapped their needles, chambermaids who had thrown their bonnets over the rooftops, governesses who had tasted too fully of the tree of knowledge, actresses without a theatre, romantics in search of Prince Charming.

Theirs was a romanticized misconception, for the role of mistress to a struggling artist offered the young women of the Latin Quarter what were, in terms of sexual politics, all-too-well established roles as fallen woman, woman of easy virtue or tragic victim of male lust. At best, the grisette could play the part of muse to the genius of her lover, but at all times extra-marital relationships threatened to make a woman a social outcast where they represented only freedom from responsibility for a man. Another Bohemian writer, Jules Vallès, who was far to the left, politically,

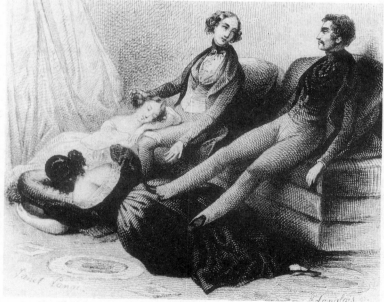

An illustration by Gavarni for the 1838 edition of
The Wild Ass's Skin *by Balzac*

of Houssaye, wrote: 'If [the grisette] flourished in the Latin Quarter it was certainly not in my time,' and he described the tragic life of Pavillon, said to have been mistress to a number of prominent Bohemians, including Henry Murger, author of the novel *Scènes de la vie de bohème*, on which Puccini's opera was based. Pavillon ended her life in an asylum.

If the grisette was a romanticized figure, this was but one aspect of the way in which the atmosphere of gaiety and pleasure that existed in Paris for most of the century relied upon an intimation of sexual licence, which filled the air with the promise of erotic excitement. Here began what has become so pervasive a feature of contemporary life: the sexualization of all relationships and spectacles, the emphasis on bodily provocation and display, on physical beauty, the obsession with sexuality, and our belief that sexual experience represents the ultimate truth of life and of ourselves.

Social life was eroticized. As the Goncourt brothers were to reflect in their description of an evening at the Opéra, during the period of the Second Empire (Napoleon III was declared Emperor in 1852):

> It is wonderful what a centre of debauchery the theatre is. From the stage to the auditorium, from the wings to the stage, from the auditorium to stage and from one side of the auditorium to the other, invisible threads criss-cross between dancers' legs, actresses' smiles and spectators' opera glasses, presenting an overall picture of Pleasure, Orgy and Intrigue. It would be impossible to gather together in a smaller space a greater number of sexual stimulants, of invitations to copulation. It is like a Stock Exchange dealing in women's nights.

This erotic web drew its glamorous veil over many of the public spaces of nineteenth-century Paris, and entangled all who came in contact with it.

During the 1850s and 1860s, sexual relationships became more commercialized than they had been during the heyday of the Bohemians in the 1830s and early 1840s. The grisettes of the Latin Quarter had been superseded by the lorettes, so called because they lived in the district of Notre Dame de Lorette; their sexuality was more clearly for sale than that of the mistresses of the Bohemians. The image of the grisette had been of self-sacrificing devotion, but as sex became commodified the courtesan was more likely to be depicted as a rapacious than as a victimized character.

During the reign of Napoleon III the courtesan became a key figure in the Parisian hierarchy. These courtesans, the *grandes horizontales*, played a special role in a society that was both politically repressive and at the same time unstable, indeed highly volatile, economically and socially. Napoleon III gathered about him a crowd of men and women on the make – and some, such as Houssaye, and Baron Haussmann, who redesigned Paris, were extremely able.

At the Imperial Court, appearance was everything, and the display did not need to be rooted in ancestry, nor even in solid industry or commerce. Rather this was a society based on speculation on the Stock Exchange. The courtesans played an important role as intermediaries in the financial transactions that took place, as well as in many cases being quite prepared to ruin the men who became infatuated with them. Thus the courtesan became a figure of cruelty who exploited men, rather than one who was exploited by them. Yet of course prostitution continued at every level, and many prostitutes were among the most exploited and destitute in the great emporium of luxury, vice and excitement – above all, of traffic in human life – that Paris became.

Marguerite, 'La Dame aux camélias', stands somewhere between the figure of the rapacious, Second Empire courtesan and the devoted grisette of an earlier Bohemia, or rather, she manages to combine both roles. The inner truth of Marguerite none the less, is her devotion to her young lover, Armand; it is only on the surface that she appears as a heartless courtesan, and even in this role she is menaced from the beginning by the romantic nemesis of tuberculosis, known then as consumption. She is consumed by her life of pleasure, and both Verdi, the composer of the opera *La traviata,* and Alexandre Dumas *fils*, author of the book and the play upon which it was based, deployed a well-established contrast between the city of vice and the redemption of rural life to point this up. It is in Paris that Marguerite plays the role of heartless cocotte and ruins men; it is only in the country that her love for Armand is expressed and fully experienced.

In pre-industrial discourse, the city had been seen as a centre of civilization and a pinnacle of refinement; in the nineteenth century the great size and often squalor of the new metropolis, the vast city, came to be experienced rather as infernal. This negative view of urban life was closely associated with the way in which 'normal' patriarchal (as well as class) relationships were disrupted. The city swallowed up the anonymous individual in a terrifying swamp of anomie, promiscuity and miasma. Its swamplike quality was somehow in itself female, and one of the most disturbing aspects of the metropolis to many of the men who wrote about it was the way in which female sexuality flooded it, uncontrolled, disordered, engulfing.

Violetta's fate therefore represents more than that simply of the tragic romantic heroine. Her role as exploitative, yet vulnerable, but – yet again – ultimately diseased, sexual woman living outside marriage constituted a threat that had to be defeated. Like Henry Murger's real-life Pavillon, she must die because the feminine sexual freedom to which she aspires, and which only urban life made even possible, even conceivable, is so dangerous to bourgeois society and so dangerous to men.

Frontispiece by Gavarni for The Wild Ass's Skin

Alfred de Vigny
from Paris – Élévation, *1831*

— Je vois un cercle noir, si large et si profond
Que je n'en aperçois ni le bout ni le fond.
Des collines, au loin, me semblent sa ceinture,
Et pourtant, je ne vois nulle part la nature,
Mais partout la main d'homme et l'angle que sa main
Impose à la matière en tout travail humain.
Je vois ces angles noirs et luisants qui, dans l'ombre,
L'un sur l'autre entassés, sans ordre ni sans nombre
Coupent des murs blanchis pareils à des tombeaux.
— Je vois fumer, brûler, éclater des flambeaux,
Brillant sur cet abîme où l'air pénètre à peine,
Comme des diamants incrustés dans l'ébène.
— Un fleuve y dort sans bruit, replié dans son cours,
Comme dans un buisson, la couleuvre aux cent tours.
Des ombres de palais, de dômes et d'aiguilles,
De tours et de donjons, de clochers, de bastilles,
De châteaux forts, de kiosks et d'aigus minarets;
Des formes de remparts, de jardins, de forêts,
De spirales, d'arceaux, de parcs, de colonnades,
D'obélisques, de ponts, de portes et d'arcades,
Tout fourmille et grandit, se cramponne en montant,
Se courbe, se replie, ou se creuse ou s'étend.
— Dans un brouillard de feu je crois voir ce grand rêve.
La tour où nous voilà dans le cercle s'élève.
En le traçant jadis, c'est ici, n'est-ce pas,
Que Dieu même a posé le centre du compas?
Le vertige m'enivre, et sur mes yeux il pèse.
Vois-je une Roue ardente, ou bien une Fournaise?

— Oui, c'est bien une Roue; et c'est la main de Dieu
Qui tient et fait mouvoir son invisible essieu.
Vers le but inconnu sans cesse elle s'avance.
On la nomme PARIS, le pivot de la France.

from Paris – From a Height, *1831*

— I see a black circle, so broad and profound
that I cannot make out its rim or its depth.
Hills in the distance seem to enclose it,
and yet nowhere do I see nature,
but everywhere the hand of man and the angles that his hand
imposes on matter in every human work.
I see those black shining angles piled
one upon the other, chaotic without number,
cutting across walls whitened like tombs.
— I see torches smoking, flaming, blazing,
glisten above that abyss where air scarcely reaches,
like diamonds encrusted in ebony.
— A river sleeps there, silent, winding in its course
like the hundred coils of a grass-snake in a bush.
Shadows of palaces, domes and spires,
towers and keeps, belfries, bastilles,
fortresses, kiosks, pointed minarets;
the shapes of ramparts, gardens, forests,
spirals, arches, parks, colonnades,
obelisks, bridges, gates and arcades,
all this swarms, expands, clings as it climbs,
crouches, unfolds, hollows out or stretches.
– Through a mist of smoke I see this great dream.
The tower we stand on rises within the circle.
Long ago, when God traced it out, is it not here
that He placed the centre of His compass?
Wild with vertigo, my eyes grow heavy:
Is what I see a Wheel of fire, or is it a Furnace?

— Indeed it is a Wheel; and it is the hand of God
that holds and moves its invisible axle.
It rolls unceasingly towards its unknown goal.
They call it PARIS, the pivot of France.

Grisettes and Lorettes

When Alphonsine Plessis came to Paris, penniless and without contacts, she joined the army of the poor seeking to survive in this chaotic city. Her contemporaries went to astonishing lengths to chart this ever-expanding underworld of poverty, crime and

'Just imagine! My little Emile came for dinner when I was engaged to have supper with fat Mr Thingy!'
   'Silly! You should have dinner with the fat one, and supper with the slim one!'

Above and on following pages: three of The Lorettes *by Gavarni, c. 1840*

degradation, and took particular interest in the classes of girl on the edge of respectability. The subject made good copy. A multitude of picturesque accounts of them survive, penned by poets, novelists and journalists for whom a happy phrase was more important than social demography. Two famous types were the 'grisette', so-called because of the grey cloth commonly used in the clothing trade, and the 'lorette', who owed her name to the cheap and cramped accommodation around Notre Dame de Lorette, where she lived when not enjoying more luxurious quarters. Dumas fils claimed that neither type survived into the Second Empire, when they came in retrospect to epitomize the romantic joys of Bohemian life and be the subject of nostalgic affection.

Théophile Gautier described a grisette as a girl who worked at a humble job six days a week but accepted a student lover on Sundays; in return she took a bonnet or a lemonade and meringues. She kept her independence, feeding herself usually on milk, potatoes and radishes, and professing a virtuous aversion to any financial assistance. Gautier distinguished them from lorettes who resembled the lilies of the field because they 'toil not neither do they spin'. Typically, a lorette had once had pretensions to be on the stage as a dancer, a singer or an actress, and she was no younger than fifteen (these were separately classified as 'rats') and no older than twenty-nine. She lived off admirers 'with butter yellow curls and white waistcoats', careless of the morrow, full of faith in her beauty; she had what Gautier called 'the innocence of vice'.

Charles Baudelaire
from Some French Caricaturists, *1857*

Gavarni created the lorette. She certainly existed a little before him, but he completed her. I believe indeed that he invented the word. The lorette . . . was not a kept woman, which is a thing of the Second Empire, condemned to live in funereal intimacy with the metallic corpse, a general or a banker, off whom she lives. The lorette was a free person. She came and she went. She kept open house. She had no master; she enjoyed the company of artists and journalists. She did what she could to be witty. I said that Gavarni completed her; and in fact, led on by his literary imagination, he invented at least as much as he saw, and, for that reason, he had a great influence on the way people behaved. Paul de Kock created the grisette, and Gavarni the lorette; and several of those girls perfected themselves by adopting his images, just as the young people of the Latin Quarter were affected by his drawings of students, and many people force themselves to look like fashion plates.

'I've had many troubles, dear Henri, since I saw you last: I lost Mr Money-bags!'
  'The father of your little girl?'
  'No, Henri . . . her godfather!'

Théophile Gautier
from a review of Gavarni's Collected Works, *1857–64*

How he understood the Parisienne! That's how she holds her head and her hands, and how she moves her hips; that's her step, her gesture, her look! Her delicate little face, so wide awake, so sharp, so piquant in its irregularity, is framed with hair so gracefully arranged; her eyes do not burn like those of Spain, nor dream like those of Germany, but say everything they mean; her

'At least I'm not registered . . . like a cab!'
    'That's because you run by the month and you're not on the streets!'

half-teasing smile inspired Victor Hugo with the little pout of Esmeralda; there is the ivory chin and the blond nape with stray curls twisting into a knot; her complexion resembles a camellia which has been worn all night dancing, and has a freshness both tired and delicate – who has caught them, if not Gavarni?

Honoré de Balzac
from The Wild Ass's Skin, *1833*

They drained their goblets full of learning, carbonic acid, perfume, poetry and scepticism.

'If the gentlemen would like to move into the drawing room, coffee will be served,' said the maître d'hôtel.

By now almost all the guests were whirling in that delightful

An illustration by Gavarni for the 1838 edition of The Wild Ass's Skin

limbo in which the light of the mind is extinguished and the body, released from the tyranny of its master, gives itself up to the delirious joys of freedom. Some of them, having reached the highest point of intoxication, remained dejected and painfully concerned to snatch at any idea which would convince them of their own existence; others, sunk in a lethargy brought on by the sluggish process of digestion, renounced all movement. Some orators, undaunted, were still uttering vague remarks of whose meaning they themselves were uncertain. A few snatches of song echoed out like the tinkling of a musical box forced to grind out its artificial and soulless tune. Silence and rowdiness had become strange bedfellows.

None the less, on hearing the sonorous voice of the maître d'hôtel who was announcing fresh joys in his master's name, the guests rose to their feet and dragged, supported – even carried – one another along. For a moment the whole troop stood stock still and spellbound on the threshold of the room. The immoderate pleasures of the banquet paled into insignificance before the spectacle prepared by their host to titillate the most voluptuous of their senses. Beneath the sparkling candles of a gold chandelier, around a table laden with silver gilt, a group of women suddenly appeared before the stupefied guests whose eyes began to gleam like so many diamonds. Rich were their adornments, but richer still was their dazzling beauty which far eclipsed all the marvels that this palace contained. These girls had fairy-like charms and passionate eyes, livelier and brighter than the torrents of light which brought out the satin sheen of the hangings, the brilliant whiteness of the marble statues and the delicate curves of the bronzes. The senses were set on fire at the sight of their tossing heads, the contrast presented by their hairstyles and poses, so diverse in charm and character. It was like a hedge of flowers mingled with rubies, sapphires and coral; a girdle of black necklaces on snowy necks, with light sashes playing around them like the flames of beacons; haughty turbans and modestly provocative tunics.

This seraglio offered seductions for every eye and pleasure to suit every whim. Ravishingly posed, a dancer appeared to be nude under the wavy folds of her cashmere. There a diaphanous gauze, here iridescent silk concealed or revealed mysterious perfections. Tiny, slender feet spoke of love while fresh and rosy lips were

An illustration by Gavarni for the 1838 edition of The Wild Ass's Skin

mute. Delicate and decorous-seeming girls, make-believe virgins whose pretty hair breathed out pious innocence, appeared as airy visions that a breath could dissipate. Then there came aristocratic beauties proud of glance but indolent; slim, willowy, graceful; bowing their heads as if they were still in the market for royal protection. An English girl, a white, chaste, ethereal figure wafted down from the clouds of an Ossianic landscape, looked like an angel of melancholy or repentance fleeing before crime. Nor was there lacking in this tempting assembly the woman of Paris, whose whole beauty resides in indescribable gracefulness, vain of her toilet and her wit, armed with her omnipotent fragility, pliant but unyielding, a siren without heart or passion, yet able by artifice to create the treasures of passion and simulate the accents of the heart. The eye was caught too by Italian girls, placid in appearance but conscientious in the felicities they dispense, and richly endowed and magnificently proportioned women from Normandy, and yet others from the south, with dark hair and almond-shaped eyes. Having spent the time since morning furbishing their charms, they reminded you of the beauties that Lebel used to assemble at

An illustration by Gavarni for the 1838 edition of The Wild Ass's Skin

Versailles, and came on the scene like a bevy of eastern slave-girls awakened by the trader for departure at dawn.

They stood there shamefaced and shy, and pressed round the table like bees buzzing inside a hive. This timid embarrassment, at once reproachful and coquettish, was either calculated or involuntary bashfulness. Perhaps a feeling which woman never completely lays aside enjoined them to wrap themselves in a mantle of virtue in order to give greater charm and piquancy to the prodigalities of vice. Thus the plot hatched by old Taillefer seemed likely to fail, for to start with these men, normally uninhibited, were subjugated

An illustration by Gavarni for the 1838 edition of The Wild Ass's Skin

by the daunting power which invests a woman. A murmur of admiration ran through the room like the soft strains of music. Sexual desire had been damped by wine, and instead of being swept up in a whirlwind of passion the guests, caught in a moment of weakness, gave themselves over to the delight of voluptuous ecstasy. The artists among them, at the dictate of the poetry which always holds artists in thrall, were content to contemplate the delicate nuances which distinguished these paragons from one another.

Stirred by a thought perhaps attributable to some emanation of carbonic acid from the champagne he had drunk, a man of philosophic bent shuddered as he imagined the misfortunes that had brought these women, once worthy perhaps of the purest of tributes, to this place. Not one of them, doubtless, but had some painful story to relate. Almost every one brought her own particular hell with her, trailing behind her the memory of some faithless lover, or promises betrayed, of joys which had been paid for with misery.

Marie Duplessis at the theatre: a watercolour by Camille Roqueplan

Alfred de Musset
from Rolla, *1833*

Pauvreté! Pauvreté! c'est toi la courtisane,
C'est toi qui dans ce lit as poussé cette enfant
Que la Grèce eût jeté sur l'autel de Diane!
Regarde, – elle a prié ce soir en s'endormant . . .
Prié! – Qui donc, grand Dieu! C'est toi qu'en cette vie
Il faut qu'à deux genoux elle conjure et prie;
C'est toi qui chuchotant dans le souffle du vent,
Au milieu des sanglots d'une insomnie amère,
Es venue un beau soir murmurer à sa mère:
'Ta fille est belle et vierge, et tout cela se vend!'
Pour aller au sabbat, c'est toi qui l'as lavée,
Comme on lave les morts pour les mettre au tombeau;
C'est toi qui, cette nuit, quand elle est arrivée,
Aux lueurs des éclairs, courais sous son manteau!
Hélas! qui peut savoir pour quelle destinée,
En lui donnant du pain, peut-être elle était née?
D'un être sans pudeur ce n'est pas là le front
Rien d'impur ne germait sous cette fraîche aurore.
Pauvre fille! à quinze ans ses sens dormaient encore,
Son nom était Marie, et non pas Marion.
Ce qui l'a dégradée, hélas! c'est la misère,
Et non l'amour de l'or. – Telle que la voilà
Sous les rideaux honteux de ce hideux repaire,
Dans cet infâme lit, elle donne à sa mère,
En rentrant au logis, ce qu'elle a gagné là.

from Rolla, *1833*

Poverty! Poverty! You are the courtesan.
'Tis you who cast into this bed this child
whom Greece would have thrown upon Diana's altar!
See her – tonight before she slept she prayed . . .
Prayed! – To whom, great God! 'Tis you, in this life,
you whom on her knees she must entreat;
'Tis you who whispering in the breath of wind,
among the bitter sobs of nights unslept,
came one fine evening to murmur to her mother:
'Your child, the lovely maiden, could be sold!'
To send her to the sabbath, you washed her
as corpses are washed before they are put in the tomb;
you, this night, when she arrived here
lit up by lightning, ran wrapped in her cloak!
Alas! Who can tell for what fate
had she had bread, she might not have been born?
This brow is not that of a shameless creature,
and nothing impure waits beneath this dawn.
Poor girl! At fifteen her senses were still asleep,
her name was Marie, never Marion.
She fell alone, alas!, through wretchedness,
and not through love of gold. – So much so that
under the shameful curtains of this hideous hovel,
in this bed of infamy, she gives her mother
what she has earned when she comes home.

Alexandre Parent-Duchâtelet
from Prostitution in the City of Paris, *1836*

Once I was shown the usefulness, I would almost say the necessity, of undertaking this work, I had to undertake it honestly, and that is what I have done. Dealing with a serious subject and addressing myself to serious-minded people, I had to give things their real names and to go straight to the point. As a free man, not bound by ties of office, I will distribute praise and blame impartially; as a religious man, I will not blush at what my pen has written; as a man without prejudices, I will say everything demanded of me by science, by the good of society and of the unfortunate class which has furnished me with so many subjects of study and meditation ...

When a motive as noble as love of the public good inspires our research, we must neglect nothing which might somehow or other throw light on the subject: without this we may make the gravest mistakes and be harmful where we wish to be useful. We discover the vices of a system or a way of preventing serious failings most often by inspecting the most abject subjects, those apparently least important and so most scorned. Here is an example which I may give the more readily because it is a personal one: when I was engaged in my research on the sewers of Paris [1836], everything seemed fine so long as I was content to study them at ground level; but having visited them from within, often with sludge above my knees, it became easy for me to perceive what was wrong with the system in practice until then. I could foresee the serious dangers to which the capital would be exposed, and indicate the means of bringing about a prompt remedy ...

To return to the abject subjects of prostitution, I must reiterate that to study them I needed greater courage than to visit sewers filled with mud and infected air, which could have been detrimental to my health; in this new investigation, I had to gather all my courage and recall the formal commitment I made to myself not to let myself be deterred by the inevitable difficulties. The nature of these difficulties would have made them insurmountable had I been left to myself; but thanks to the intervention of doctors and those in charge at the *Bureau des Moeurs*, I was able to visit brothels at every hour of the day and night, and to garner numerous important observations; doctors accompanied me during the day, a police officer attached to the Bureau took me there at night. I was then able to return ALWAYS IN THE COMPANY OF AN INSPECTOR and do all the necessary verification.

What is the major cause of prostitution?

It may be generally stated that every woman who registers as a public prostitute has lived in a disorderly way for some time. In ten years, only three or four girls have registered themselves at the dispensary before losing their virginity; thus, for a certain type of girl, prostitution is the inevitable result and consequence of a single lapse from the most important of duties; on this point there is no disagreement among those who have done any research on prostitution.

This cause is general and applies to all prostitutes in different ways; but there are secondary, so to say, individual causes, which I will also consider.

Laziness may be placed in the first rank as a cause of prostitution; the desire to obtain pleasures without work motivates many girls not to stay in their jobs or not to look for one; the laziness, nonchalance and weak character of prostitutes have thus become proverbial.

Destitution, often to the most appalling degree, is still one of the most active causes of prostitution. How many girls abandoned by their families, without relatives or friends, unable to find refuge anywhere, are obliged to turn to prostitution so as not to die of starvation! One of these unfortunates, still sensible to feelings of decency, struggled desperately before she took what she considered to be the ultimate step, and when she came to register there was proof that she had not eaten for almost three days.

Vanity and the desire to show off in fine clothes provide, together with laziness, another active cause of prostitution, especially in Paris. In a society where opprobrium is heaped on clothes which are simple or – even more so – in rags, can we be astonished that so many young women allow themselves to be seduced by a dress which they desire, and the more so since it will lift them out of the position in which they were born, and allow them to mix with a class that they thought despised them. Those who know the strength of some women's love of appearances will easily appreciate that in Paris this can be such a cause of prostitution.

For country women there is a particular cause which does not apply to the girls of Paris: namely that they have been abandoned or left by their lovers. Many youths, soldiers, students, commercial travellers and others seduce girls in the provinces, and get involved with them, and they are led to Paris by a deceitful promise of marriage, or some sort of domestic arrangement, or because they need to hide; soon they are abandoned and left to fend for themselves . . .

Not every girl from the country is drawn to Paris in the same way: many come of their own accord after a first seduction; for them the capital represents a refuge where they find the means to hide their dishonour from their relations and neighbours, and a way out of the destitution which threatens and overwhelms them.

Domestic misfortune and the bad treatment which some women receive from inhumane and cruel parents motivate others; if we are

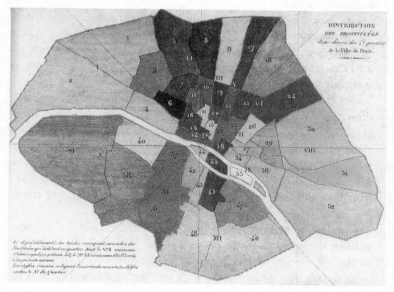

Map showing the density of brothels in Paris in 1836, from Parent-Duchâtelet's De la prostitution dans la ville de Paris. The darker the shading, the more prostitutes: thus there were 316 in No. 6 (Palais Royal) and none in No. 33 (Ile St Louis).

to believe what they say, they often leave home to escape the brutality of a step-father or step-mother; it even appears that a large number are thrown out, and this is probably because of their own behaviour for, while there are some cruel parents, we must believe that their number is happily limited ...

Different classes which we must distinguish among the population of prostitutes:

FEMMES GALANTES Nearly all these women are kept, if not completely, at least in part, and they offer themselves publicly in order to pay for their luxuries and extravagance. They have certain characteristic manners; their every care is to conceal what they are doing from the men with whom they normally have relations; in public places and at receptions, they are indistinguishable from respectable women; but they know how to adopt a tone of voice, an appearance or a look which is meaningful for those who are looking for this type; they allow themselves to be accosted, pursued and escorted, and they usually receive clients at the houses of their friends or in private houses.

Because the price these women attach to their favours is higher, and their behaviour more sophisticated and decorous, it may be understood that they mix only with men of means and education; which enables some of them to acquire the patina of good society.

In general these women are refined and quick-witted; they possess the arts of seduction to a very high degree; and this makes them very dangerous ... The title 'femmes galantes' by which they are known is how they style themselves when speaking to people who know their way of life, and in particular to officials of the administration.

FEMMES À PARTIES They resemble the above, except for the following differences: beauty alone is not sufficient for them; they must add the grace and charms of a cultivated intelligence. In general, to be received by them, one must be introduced by a member of their circle; they play the hostess; they give dinners and evening parties; they ply their charms at private gatherings of renown, where gambling and loose morals attract libertines who come there to lose both their fortune and their health.

FEMMES DE SPECTACLES ET DE THÉÂTRES This numerous class
has special habits and customs, which are not those of the above. I
said 'numerous' for I have found references to three or four hundred in many accounts; but as no one has made a special study
either of them, or of the previous two classes, we remain vague on
this . . .

Prostitutes are as inevitable in a metropolis as sewers, cesspits and
rubbish tips; the civil authority should treat the one as it does the
other – its duty is to supervise them, to reduce the dangers inherent
in them as far as is possible, and to this end to hide them and rele-
gate them to the darkest corners; in short, render their presence as
inconspicuous as possible.

    Prostitution exists and will always exist in cities because, like
begging and gambling, it is a stratagem and a recourse against
hunger – one might even say against dishonour; for to what
extreme will a person not go who is deprived of all support and
sees his or her very life threatened; it is true that this means degradation but it is a way out none the less.

Flora Tristan by Constant, engraving from
Les Belles Femmes de Paris, *1839*

Flora Tristan
from Walks in London, *1840*

Flora Tristan y Moscoso (1803–44) alienated herself from her family with Pérégrinations d'une paria *(1833–4) and from the polite literary world with* Promenades dans Londres *(1840). She died campaigning for the rights of workers, having published the* Union œuvrière, *an overtly political book, in 1843. Herself illegitimate and the partner of a disastrous arranged marriage, which ended in a murder attempt and eventual divorce, she espoused the causes of those on the margins of society – artists, women and workers.*

Since in our societies all passions can be satisfied with money, since there are no obstacles nor any resistance that money cannot overcome; since it takes the place of talent, honour, integrity, and in a word since with it one can do anything, people balk at nothing in order to procure it.

Auguste Barbier
Lazare

Allons, mes soeurs, marchons la nuit comme le jour;
A toute heure, à tout prix, il faut faire l'amour;
Il le faut, ici-bas le destin nous a faites
Pour garder le ménage et les femmes honnêtes.

Lazarus

Let us go, my sisters, let us march night and day;
At all times, at all cost, we must make love;
We must, for here below Fate has made us,
To safeguard home and women's honour.

Marie d'Agoult, writing as Daniel Stern
from Moral Sketches, *1851*

Marie d'Agoult (1805–76) was born of wealthy and aristocratic parents and married a husband fifteen years her senior. From 1835 to 1844, she lived with Liszt, by whom she had three children (the second was Cosima, who would be Wagner's second wife). After the definite break in this relationship, she continued as a prominent literary hostess and a writer using the pen-name of Daniel Stern. Apart from fiction – including Nélida, *a romanticized version of her affair with Liszt – she wrote on matters of social concern; her masterpiece is the* Histoire de la révolution de 1848.

I dislike the copious weeping of women. They are victims, they say; victims of what? Of an ignorance that makes them blind, habits of idleness that make them prey to boredom, a feebleness of spirit that keeps them in chains, a frivolity that will undergo any humiliation for the sake of an ornament, above all a pettiness of mind that limits their sphere of activity to the intrigues of gallantry or domestic worries. Weep less, dear ladies of today! Virtue is not fed on tears. Leave behind the gestures, attitudes and tones of supplicants. Stand up and step forth; walk with a firm step towards the truth. Dare just once to look truth in the face and you will be ashamed of your lamentation. You will understand that Nature is not interested in your sterile sacrifices, for she demands one thing of all her children: the free expansion of their lives. For her, suffering is only useful as a spur to progress. Your passive sorrowing, your vain sighs and futile agonies are entirely contrary to her energetic plans. Once again, dry your tears; take your part in the somewhat bitter knowledge and intricate work of this century. Society is transforming itself; it needs your collaboration. Consider, think, act; and soon you will find that you have no time to bewail your imaginary wrongs or accuse the supposed injustices of fate, which are really nothing but the just punishment for your wilful ignorance.

The woman of today is placed in a false milieu. It is neither the grave household of the Roman matron, nor the merry 'open house' of the Greek courtesan, but something in between known as *society*; that is, a pointless grouping of idle minds, subjected to the artificial conventions of a morality that tries in vain to reconcile the amusements of gallantry with the duties of the family. The result is the loosening of domestic virtues and hypocrisy in social relations. Do not expect of such women either the chastity of Lucretia or the spiritual strength of Cornelia, or the supreme intellectual grace which kept Socrates at Aspasia's banquets. Their feather-brained virtues or slavish graces make them equally unworthy of a husband's respect or a lover's passion. Their youth is sullen and their old age is without nobility. Their faded features, their uncertain gait, their borrowed gestures, all these reveal the deep disharmony between their social position and the laws of nature. This disharmony causes suffering to them, to the family, even to the nation. But custom reigns supreme, blind and pitiless, dominating everything.

Love affairs, even the finest, often fail because of a lack of pride in the woman and a lack of sensitivity in the man. She exceeds the just measure of condescension and becomes boring; he exceeds the just measure of domination and becomes overbearing. A wiser awareness of her own worth in the woman and a less crude awareness of his superiority in the man would preserve the harmony between them and prolong that sentiment which is not so fundamentally inconstant and ephemeral as many people affect hereabouts to believe.

It is a fine thing if a great soul devotes herself to love, but she should do so as a queen not as a slave. Women let devotion become degraded into self-abandonment; and when they complain that they have been abandoned, they are forgetting that they themselves have in a way set the example.

It is strange indeed that the most perfect model, the purest type of female love in all its energy, disinterestedness, greatness and constancy, should have entered our history and our poetry in the person of Héloïse, in a country where the temperament and spirit of women seem to force them rather into a subtle, light-headed, egoistic and calculated coquettishness which is the very obverse of passionate love.

Men of today have such petty souls that if they should happen to inspire one of those heroic passions of which women's hearts are still capable, and which so to speak call up an equivalent greatness in them, they become uncomfortable and embarrassed. They make it their business to diminish it, to debilitate it and bring it down to their own size.

When a flirtatious woman repulses a man's advances, he interprets her action simply as a whim that offends him; he feels irritated and

Marie d'Agoult by Lehmann, 1843

seeks his revenge. When a virtuous woman, on the other hand, refuses to yield to the importunings of an admirer, whether because she wishes to remain chaste, or in order to stay faithful to a prior love, the rejected man feels no slight to his vanity; he respects the reason for the refusal, however it might wound him; for his heart alone has been attacked, and the heart knows how to forgive. It is not uncommon indeed to find such repulsed admirers becoming the most devoted friends of the *belle dame sans merci*.

Modern men know only two kinds of women: the lady of pleasure and the lady of work. The former amuses them after they have drunk, the latter serves them the food they eat. If, against all likelihood, such a man should find a true companion, a wife according to God, love and freedom, would he know what to do with her?

Women who have been unhappily married are demanding divorce; those who love their husbands are in favour of the indissolubility of marriage; this is the whole of their argument. It is inevitable that the liveliness of their sentiments and the weakness of their reason should bring everything back to the individual case. If they will permit me a general reflection: given the inferiority of the woman of today, her limited education and enfeebled character, if she were able to change husbands she would merely be changing masters. What advantage would she gain from it? The satisfaction of her impulsive wishes? That is not the purpose of life. The aim of a free being is to attain the full dignity, the full excellence of his nature. For a woman to reach this goal, one kind of divorce is needful, which I have not yet heard her advocate: that is the divorce from her ignorance, her frivolity, her childish whims. By means of this divorce, which she is free to pronounce this very day, she would come into possession of a moral freedom that would first substitute for, and later necessitate, domestic and civil liberties. Without such a private divorce, the other sort would remain fruitless; the condition of women would be made neither better nor worse.

Motherhood is a revolution in a woman's existence, and it is characteristic of revolutions that they release all the life forces. What utter degeneration one must imagine in a woman if in this painful crisis of creative nature she were not to feel beating in her breast the enthusiasm of a new devotion. The first wailing cry of her child is an oracle sent to announce her own greatness to her; and the blade which cuts from her body an immortal creature in whom she can see herself reborn, divides her at the same stroke from the childishness and selfishness of her solitary girlhood. The harsh clasp of the forces of generation, the extraordinary labour her weakness undertakes; the hopes, terrors and nameless efforts that suffocate her, glorify her, and burst forth in every groan; and then the final convulsion which is followed by the august calm of nature restored to peace, having achieved her greatest task – all this is far from what has traditionally been thought, the punishment or sign of the inferiority of a whole sex. Quite the contrary: the woman's ability to take part thus intimately in the processes of nature, the thrill of life quivering within her, these are a higher initiation bringing her face to face with a divine truth that men may only approach by long circuitous routes, with the help of complicated machines or the dry discipline of science.

The duties of a mother are compatible with great thoughts but they cannot be combined with a taste for frivolity. While she nurses her infant son, a woman may muse with Plato or meditate with Descartes. Her mood will become more serene, the quality of her milk will be in no way spoiled. But let her adorn herself, paint her face, stay up late, go dancing or scheming, and her blood will become heated, her bile irritated, her breasts will dry up and her child will starve; she will become detestable and absurd. Why then are men nowadays so afraid of a female philosopher, but so indulgently tolerant of a coquette?

When an Athenian woman announced that she was pregnant, her house would be carefully adorned with statues and paintings depicting the most pure types of human beauty. The Greeks believed that these noble or graceful images had a beneficial influence on the unborn child. I find it regrettable that such a custom has not been passed down to us by those masters of the art of living. We are too reluctant to take precautions against ugliness. It surrounds us, invades us; today it is everywhere, in places of worship and on the streets; we cannot keep our homes free of it, and I have reason to fear that it may have entered our blood with the barbarous tastes of our mothers. Some of my readers will smile perhaps if I assert that there is a close connection between physical and moral grace, and that the minds of those who live habitually in a world without harmony or beauty will carry the unfortunate traces of it. The aesthetic is sister to the moral. Dignify your dwellings, and your speech and action will the more easily rise to noble heights. Do I hear myself accused of materialism, even of paganism? Let me then take refuge behind a noted authority and invoke the testament of one of the finest luminaries of the Christian Church, whose word is surely above suspicion. I quote from Fénelon's *Treatise on Education*: 'I should like to show our young women the noble simplicity to be found in the statues and other surviving figures of Greek and Roman women; they would see how lovely and majestic is the hair loosely knotted behind and the full simple draped garment falling in long folds. It would be good for them also to listen to painters and other people who understand the exquisite taste of the ancients.'

Marie d'Agoult, writing as Daniel Stern *from* On Liberty, *1847*

We must replace the sceptre of the despots (the authority of father, of husband, of confessor, of lover) with the sole legitimate authority, that of reason ... Do you want to have among us only Sapphos, Catherine the Greats, Semiramises, or Aspasias? No – just strong women [*femmes fortes*], able to police the little states of which they are sovereign rulers.

Louise Colet modelled for Pradier as The City of Strasbourg,
one of the statues in the Place de la Concorde, c. 1850

Louise Colet

Louise Colet (1810–76) came to Paris from Aix-en-Provence with her husband, a flute teacher at the Conservatoire. Her first book of poems caught the attention of the literary world, and she continued to write verse for the next twenty years. A very beautiful woman, she caused a scandal when she knifed Alphonse Karr for implying that her husband was not the father of her daughter. In 1846 she met Flaubert, seven years her junior, in the studio of the sculptor James Pradier and immediately became his mistress and muse. Their tempestuous affair lasted on and off for a decade, and is documented by an extraordinarily powerful correspondence in which Flaubert describes, inter alia, *his progress on* Madame Bovary *and comments on her writing; during that time she also had liaisons with Vigny and Musset. In* Lui *(1859), she gave a fictionalized account of her relationship with Musset and Flaubert, while the poet in* La Servante *is a bitter portrait of Vigny – so transparent that Flaubert urged her to withdraw the poem.*

*De la femme was planned in 1851 to contain six long narrative poems but she completed only three (*La Paysanne, La Servante *and* La Réligieuse*), and they were published with two previously written texts (*La Femme du peuple, La Femme du monde*) as satirical prefaces.* La Servante *traces the fate of two peasant sisters, Thérèson and Mariette, who come separately to Paris: the one falls into prostitution, while the other – inspired by a love of the poet and of the romance of books – is brought to destitution and the madhouse. In the poem following, Thérèson/Thérèse has invited her sister to dinner with 'some friends', and Mariette discovers the truth about her. The reference to Lola is to Lola Montez, the dancer who became the mistress of the King of Bavaria and friend of Marie Duplessis.*

La Servante
from La Poème de la femme, *1854*

'Ah!' dit la femme brune aux yeux noirs et profonds,
'Ne cherche pas ici l'amour, nous l'étouffons
Et nous ne sommes pas comme toi langoureuses.
L'homme est notre ennemi, nous le sentons assez
A ses mépris d'instinct, à ses rigueurs de maître;
Rendons-lui, rendons-lui nos affronts entassés,
Lorsque sa convoitise arrive à le soumettre!
S'il est beau, s'il est jeune et s'il nous plaît, songeons
Qu'on nous dénie à nous l'amour qui refait l'âme;
Que jamais notre amant ne nous prendra pour femme,
Et qu'en l'avilissant de lui nous nous vengeons,
S'il est vieux, s'il est riche, oh! des jours de misère
Souvenons-nous! . . . Alors que quelque impur vieillard
Nous sourit, en songeant au sourire d'un père,
Nous allâmes vers lui des pleurs dans le regard;
Il pouvait nous sauver et nous nommer sa fille,
Cet homme que la mort réclamera demain;
Mais pour nous secourir il a fermé sa main,
Et pour nous acheter son or s'étale et brille.
Punissons-le, joutons avec lui d'impudeur;
Pillons, trompons, raillons cette immonde matière;
Avec notre beauté flagellons sa laideur
Ainsi que fit Lola de son roi de Bavière!'

Comme elle prononçait ces mots avec mépris,
Dans l'élégant boudoir entrèrent les convives.
Elle sourit, Thérèse eut des yeux attendris,
La danseuse étala ses grâces les plus vives.

C'étaient trois financiers ventrus, couperosés,
Chauves, les doigts carrés, le pied osseux et large;
A plusieurs millions on estimait leur charge,
Le monde les traitait en hommes bien posés.
Mais la société d'un moderne prophète

The Servant
from The Poem of Woman, 1854

'Ah no!' said the dark woman with deep black eyes,
'you will find no love here, we stifle it,
we don't languish like you.
Man is our enemy, we sense clearly enough
from his instinctive contempt, from his harshness as our master;
we shall repay, repay those heaps of insults
when his lust shall at last subjugate him!
If he is young and handsome, and we like him, let us not forget
that love, that rebuilder of the soul, is denied us;
that our lover will never make us his wife,
and that in debasing him we avenge ourselves;
if he is old and rich, oh! let us remember
the days of abject poverty! . . . When some lecherous old man
smiled at us and, thinking of the kind smile of a father,
we went to him with tears in our eyes:
he could save us, name us his daughter,
this man whom death will claim tomorrow;
but to come to our aid his hand closes like a fist,
while to buy us his shining gold is thrown around.
Let's punish him, let's vie with his shamelessness;
pillaging, deceiving, mocking that vile stuff;
and let's use our beauty to scourge his ugliness,
just like Lola did with her king of Bavaria!'

As she spoke these contemptuous words,
the dinner guests came into the elegant boudoir.
She smiled, Thérèse's eyes melted,
the dancer showed her loveliest charms.

They were three financiers, potbellied, blotchy-faced,
bald, blunt-fingered, with broad and bony feet;
they were considered to be worth several million,
and were treated in society as fine upstanding men.
But the society of a modern prophet

Qui se pique aux instincts d'assortir les métiers,
En eût fait des bouchers ou des palefreniers:
Ils en avaient vraiment l'encolure et la tête.
Pour la délicatesse ils ne dépassaient pas
Un garçon d'abattoir, un rustre d'écurie;
Ils ne comprenaient l'art que comme une industrie,
Et par eux chaque jour l'art descendait plus bas.
Ils doublaient tous les trois leur charge officielle,
L'un du Grand-Opéra s'était fait l'exploiteur,
Du journal de la cour l'autre était directeur,
Et le troisième avait la haute clientèle
D'un ministre, et par lui, dans un trafic d'enfer
Passaient les actions de nos chemins de fer.
Flatteurs des vanités et soudoyeurs des vices,
Ils étaient en amour l'idéal des actrices.
Aussi, royalement on les fêta ce soir.
Fleurs, parfums, vins et mets, tout était délectable,
On riait, on buvait, on se pâmait à table.
Mariette à l'écart, altière, alla s'asseoir.
Elle écoutait les voix des pauvres insensées
Par de faux sentiments faussement cadencées.
Le propos jaillissait impur, populacier,
De ces corps merveilleux qu'eût adorés la Grèce;
Comme un vase d'onyx rempli d'un vin grossier,
Leurs lèvres ne versaient qu'une écœurante
    ivresse.
Pâle, elle regardait cet hymen effronté
Que formaient la débauche et la rapacité;
Et l'or qui découlait de ces lâches caresses
Paraissait à ses yeux la pire des détresses.
De sa robe d'emprunt elle se dépouilla,
Et belle d'épouvante elle sortit de là.

Par une froide nuit elle errait dans la rue,
Emportant le fardeau de sa misère accrue.
Tout dormait, hors l'orgie, et sur les boulevards
Les masques avinés hurlaient de toutes parts.
Craintive, elle rasait les maisons comme une ombre,

who prides himself on fitting the trade to the character,
would have made them butchers or ostlers:
certainly they had the heads and bull-necks for it.
As for delicacy they did not surpass
a slaughterhouse lad or loutish stable-boy.
To them art was just another industry,
and each day they dragged it lower in the mud.
All three doubled their official appointments.
One became the exploiter of the Grand Opéra,
another the director of the Court circular
and the third had the high patronage
of a minister, through whom in an infernal trade
he dealt in railway shares.
Flatterers of vanity and bribers of vice,
they were the actresses' very ideal in love.
And so this evening they were being feasted like kings.
The flowers, perfumes, wines and dishes, all were exquisite;
and all at table laughed, drank and regaled themselves.
To one side haughty Mariette took her seat.
She listened to the voices of the poor fools,
in false cadences framing false sentiments;
in vulgar terms obscene remarks sprang forth
from these wonderful bodies which Greece would have
   worshipped;
like an onyx vase filled with rough wine,
their lips poured only nauseous drunkenness.
Pale, she gazed upon this shameless marriage
of debauchery and greed;
and the gold which followed these lascivious caresses
seemed in her eyes to be the greatest anguish.
In horror she threw off her borrowed gown,
and, lovely head held high, she left the scene.

Through a cold night she wandered the streets,
carrying the ever-weightier burden of her destitution.
All slept, except debauchery; on every side
the boulevards rang with shouts from wine-soaked maskers.
Fearful, she crept close to the houses like a shadow,

Et triste elle pensait: Que de femmes sans nombre
Dans un long désespoir voient leur cœur se fermer!
Oh! trompeuse est la voix de toute la nature
Qui nous parle d'amour! et chaque créature
Cherche en vain dans les pleurs l'être qui doit l'aimer.
Elle se souvenait de sa pure chimère
Qui riait sur les flots du grand Rhin écumant;
Aux bords du fleuve assise elle voyait sa mère,
Elle entendait Julien l'appeler tristement.
Ce n'est plus ton vieux Rhin, ce n'est plus ta jeunesse,
Ce fleuve, ces palais se déroulant au loin;
Ces marbres, ces jardins que la lune caresse,
C'est Paris endormi qui ne te connaît point!
Aux balustres d'un pont longtemps elle se penche;
Le ciel s'est éclairci, le fleuve est en repos,
Et sur les monuments reflétés dans les eaux
L'aube qui va renaître étend sa lueur blanche.
La ville semble alors un immense cercueil;
Ce calme, la fraîcheur qui monte de la Seine
Sur son front abattu passent comme une haleine;
Et dans ce grand silence elle apaise son deuil.
– 'Je n'ai rien ici-bas, que mon amour, dit-elle;
Eh bien! qu'il vive en moi, je n'en veux pas guérir;
Je veux toujours aimer, je veux toujours souffrir:
Des femmes sans amour la vie est trop cruelle!'

and sadly thought: What numberless women
whose hearts from long despair have closed at last!
Oh! How deceitful is the voice that speaks from all nature
telling us of love! And each creature
searches in vain, in tears, for the one to love her.
She recalled the pure imagined hope
that smiled to her from the great foaming Rhine;
she saw her mother sitting by the river,
she heard the sad voice of Julien calling her.
No more is it your dear old Rhine, no more your youth,
this river, these palaces unfurling to the distance;
these marble statues, gardens caressed by the moonlight,
'Tis Paris sleeping, where you are a stranger!
A long while she leans from a bridge's balustrade;
the sky has cleared, the river's now at rest;
and on the monuments reflected in the waters
the reawakening dawn spreads out its pale light.
The city now seems an immense coffin:
this calm, this freshness rising from the Seine
passes like a breath over her exhausted brow;
and in that great silence she soothes her sorrow.
'I have nothing here below but my love,' says she;
'Well! Let it live in me, I want no cure;
I want to love always, always to feel this pain;
for life is too cruel for women without love!'

Gustave Flaubert
from a letter to Louise Colet, 1854

You wrote all that [*La Servante*] with a personal passion which has interfered with your view on the fundamental conditions of all imagined art. Aesthetic is absent . . . This poem is weak and above all *boring*.

You have made art into an overflow of passions, a sort of chamberpot in which the overflow of I don't know what has collected. That does not smell good! That smells of hate!

Gustave Flaubert
from a letter to Louise Colet, 1853

It may be a perverse taste, but I love prostitution, for itself, independently of what is beneath. I've never been able to see one of those women in décolleté pass by under the gaslights, in the rain, without feeling palpitations, just as monks' robes with their knotted girdles arouse my spirit in some ascetic and deep corner. There is, in this idea of prostitution, a point of intersection so complex – lust, bitterness, the void of human relations, the frenzy of muscles and the sound of gold – that looking deeply into it makes you dizzy; and you learn so many things! And you are so sad! And you dream so well of love! Ah, writers of elegies, it is not on ruins that you should go to lean your elbow but on the breasts of these gay women!

Yes, something is lacking in a man who has never awoken in a nameless bed, who has not seen asleep on his pillow a head that he will not see again, and who, leaving at sunrise, has not passed bridges with the longing to throw himself in the water, since life seemed to be rising up in belches from the depths of his heart to his head. If it were only for the shameless dress, the temptation of the chimera, the unknown, the *caractère maudit*, the ancient poetry of corruption and venality! In the first years when I was in Paris, during the great evenings of summer heat, I would sit in front of Tortoni's [the famous café] and, while watching the sun go down, I would watch the whores pass. I consumed myself there with Biblical poetry. I would think of Isaiah, of 'fornication in high places', and I would walk up the Rue de la Harpe repeating to myself this final verse: 'And her throat is softer than oil.' I'll be damned if I was ever more chaste! I make only one reproach to prostitution: that it is a myth. The kept woman has invaded vice, just as the journalist has invaded poetry; we are drowning in halftones. The courtesan does not exist any more than the saint; there are *soupeuses* and *lorettes*, who are even more fetid that the *grisette*.

The Return from the Ball *by Tassaert, 1852*

Charles Baudelaire
Le Crépuscule du soir
from Les Fleurs du mal,
Tableaux parisiens XCVIII, 1861

Voici le soir charmant, ami du criminel;
Il vient comme un complice, à pas de loup; le ciel
Se ferme lentement comme une grande alcôve,
Et l'homme impatient se change en bête fauve.

O soir, aimable soir, désiré par celui
Dont les bras, sans mentir, peuvent dire: Aujourd'hui
Nous avons travaillé! – C'est le soir qui soulage
Les esprits que dévore une douleur sauvage,
Le savant obstiné dont le front s'alourdit,
Et l'ouvrier courbé qui regagne son lit.
Cependant des démons malsains dans l'atmosphère
S'éveillent lourdement, comme des gens d'affaire,
Et cognent en volant les volets et l'auvent.
A travers les lueurs que tourmente le vent
La Prostitution s'allume dans les rues;
Comme une fourmilière elle ouvre ses issues;
Partout elle se fraye un occulte chemin,
Ainsi que l'ennemi qui tente un coup de main;
Elle remue au sein de la cité de fange
Comme un ver qui dérobe à l'Homme ce qu'il mange.
On entend çà et là les cuisines siffler,
Les théâtres glapir, les orchestres ronfler;
Les tables d'hôte, dont le jeu fait les délices,
S'emplissent de catins et d'escrocs, leurs complices,
Et les voleurs, qui n'ont ni trêve ni merci,
Vont bientôt commencer leur travail, eux aussi,
Et forcer doucement les portes et les caisses
Pour vivre quelques jours et vêtir leurs maîtresses.

Recueille-toi, mon âme, en ce grave moment,
Et ferme ton oreille à ce rugissement.

Comes the Charming Evening
from The Flowers of Evil,
Parisian Scenes XCVIII, *1861*

Comes the charming evening, the criminal's friend,
Comes conspirator-like on soft wolf tread.
Like a large alcove the sky slowly closes,
And man approaches his bestial metamorphosis.

To arms that have laboured, evening is kind enough,
Easing the strain of sinews that have borne their rough
Share of the burden; it is evening that relents
To those whom an angry obsession daily haunts.
The solitary student now raises a burdened head
And the back that bent daylong sinks into its bed.
Meanwhile darkness dawns, filled with demon familiars
Who rouse, reluctant as businessmen, to their affairs,
Their ponderous flight rattling the shutters and blinds.
Against the lamplight, whose shivering is the wind's,
Prostitution spreads its light and life in the streets:
Like an anthill opening its issues it penetrates
Mysteriously everywhere by its own occult route;
Like an enemy mining the foundations of a fort,
Or a worm in an apple, eating what all should eat,
It circulates securely in the city's clogged heart.
The heat and hiss of kitchens can be felt here and there,
The panting of heavy bands, the theatres' clamour.
Cheap hotels, the haunts of dubious solaces,
Are filling with tarts, and crooks, their sleek accomplices,
And thieves, who have never heard of restraint or remorse,
Return now to their work as a matter of course,
Forcing safes behind carefully re-locked doors,
To get a few days' living and put clothes on their whores.

Collect yourself, my soul, this is a serious moment,
Pay no further attention to the noise and movement.

C'est l'heure où les douleurs des malades s'aigrissent!
La sombre Nuit les prend à la gorge; ils finissent
Leur destinée et vont vers le gouffre commun;
L'hôpital se remplit de leurs soupirs. – Plus d'un
Ne viendra plus chercher la soupe parfumée,
Au coin du feu, le soir, auprès d'une âme aimée.

Encore la plupart n'ont-ils jamais connu
La douceur du foyer et n'ont jamais vécu!

This is the hour when the pains of the sick sharpen,
Night touches them like a torturer, pushes them to the open
Trapdoor over the gulf that is all too common.
Their groans overflow the hospital. More than one
Will not come back to taste the soup's familiar flavour
In the evening, with some friendly soul, by his own fire.

Indeed, many a one has never even known
The hearth's warm charm. Pity such a one.

Charles Baudelaire
Épilogue
from Le Spleen de Paris, *1869*

Le cœur content, je suis monté sur la montagne
D'où l'on peut contempler la ville en son ampleur,
Hôpital, lupanar, purgatoire, enfer, bagne,

Où toute énormité fleurit comme une fleur.
Tu sais bien, ô Satan, patron de ma détresse,
Que je n'allais pas là pour répandre un vain pleur;

Mais comme un vieux paillard d'une vieille maîtresse,
Je voulais m'enivrer de l'énorme catin
Dont le charme infernal me rajeunit sans cesse.

Que tu dormes encore dans les draps du matin,
Lourde, obscure, enrhumée, ou que tu te pavanes
Dans les voiles du soir passementés d'or fin,

Je t'aime, ô capitale infâme! Courtisanes
Et bandits, tels souvent vous offrez des plaisirs
Que ne comprennent pas les vulgaires profanes.

Epilogue
from The Spleen of Paris, *1869*

With a happy heart, I climbed the mountain
from where the whole wide city can be seen
hospital, brothel, purgatory, hell, prison,

where every enormity blossoms like a flower.
You know well, O Satan, patron of my distress,
that I was not going there to shed a useless tear;

but like an old bawdy with an old mistress,
I wanted to get drunk on the great harlot
whose hellish charm keeps me eternally young.

Whether you still sleep in the sheets of morning,
heavy, dark, stuffed up with cold, or whether you dance
in the veils of evening, sprinkled finely with gold,

I love you, o capital most vile! Courtesans
and robbers, you often render pleasures
that profane common people do not understand.

Alexandre Dumas, *fils*
from À Propos the Lady of the Camellias, *1867*, *Preface to the second edition of the play*

Well, what about England, where the word 'censorship' scarcely exists?

Ah, yes, England! What a people! What freedom! Fifteen years ago, in France, a country blighted by censorship, it was possible to put on *La Dame aux camélias*, but I defy you to put that play on in London. For the entire period, it has been forbidden. By whom? We don't know. When censorship is not carried out by one person, it's done by everyone. 'Words, words, words', as it says in *Hamlet*, created as all masterpieces are, under a despotic government. Do you know what is difficult, whatever the government? It's not to put on a good play, it is to write one. Let's start from there. A masterpiece once written can wait ...

In this hidden commerce of venal love, the heart has completely disappeared. *La Dame aux camélias*, written fifteen years ago, could not be written today. Not only would it no longer be true; it wouldn't even be possible. One looks around in vain for a young woman who could justify the novel's progression from love, through repentance to sacrifice. It would be a paradox. The play survives on its former reputation, but it is already ancient history. Young people in their twenties who read it by chance or see it performed, will say to themselves: 'Were there ever girls like that?' And young women will exclaim: 'What a fool she was!' It is not a play, it's a legend; some would say a lament. I prefer legend ...

The excuses for prostitution are as follows: ignorance, an absent or corrupt family, bad example, lack of education, of religion, of principle, and *most important of all, an earlier mistake*, often committed with a relative, sometimes a brother or father (see the statistics at the prefecture of police), being sold by a mother; poverty, in short, and everything that goes with it ...

I assure you that I have no wish to destroy love, or adultery, or affairs, or even prostitution in our beautiful France, which gains from them its greatest fame. Nor would I deny the existence of irresistible and fatal passions outside the institution of marriage that no law can prevent, nor reason conquer; they carry the men and women under their influence not only beyond the world's codes of behaviour, but beyond the very edges of the earth. Such passions bring with them their own catastrophes, punishment, fame and pardon. They consume their victims' entire lives – people like Heloise and Abelard in real life, Romeo and Juliet in fiction. But the legends of love are few. All women want to be part of such love stories themselves; however they are well aware that they will find neither the hero of Verona nor the Paraclete's philosopher in their boudoir or in their drawing room over coffee or tea. But it is not to the Juliets or Heloises, if they still exist, that I address these comments. Such women are, and will continue to be, in the thrall of emotions against which my arguments, and any that philosophy could muster, would have no effect whatsoever. I admire them and am ready to sing their praises. Love at this level of intensity is almost on a par with virtue. I do not aim so high: I am only concerned with a more mundane kind of love. This love travels in carriages to plays and balls, laughs during and complains afterwards, again and again, and which, in its double formation – prostitution/adultery – without anyone noticing, gradually undermines the family, like rats undermining a house without its occupants' knowing. Furthermore, I must admit that I am tired of constantly hearing the same subtleties of argument, the same sophisms, on this old issue. And I wanted, before I die, to give myself the inestimable pleasure of publishing the truth of the matter, just as it is. Such an opportunity presented itself and I grabbed it. I would advise you to profit from it, Madam – if it is not already too late.

All women are born virgins. For the state of virginity to end, a man is required. If virginity is destroyed other than by marriage, dishonour begins and prostitution looms. Protect women from men, and men from women. Put the search for paternity into love and divorce into marriage.

'Oh! Oh! . . .'

You think this is impractical? Then find another way; I only care about the outcome; but hurry, because the house is already ablaze.

You don't want to? You think the status quo can continue; that, as long as we keep an eye on men – who make revolutions if you don't watch out – everything will be for the best in the best of all possible worlds? *Va bene*! Enjoy yourselves! Long live love! Leave women to get along on their own and, in fifty years at the most, our nephews (we won't any more have children of our own, only nephews) will see what remains of the family, of religion, of virtue, of morality and marriage in your beautiful France, where all the towns will have fine streets and all the public places will be squares in the middle of which people will have thought it wise to erect a statue to useless Truths.

Béatrice Perregaux
Madame Édouard de Perregaux, Countess

Béatrice Perregaux is a dramaturge, working in Geneva.

The source of the Lady of the Camellias was, of course, the historical figure of Alphonsine Plessis, born in Normandy in 1823, whose life and meteoric social rise are well known. Amongst the marks of this elevation was the title of duchess, granted by Louis-Philippe; a powerful friend in the King's entourage obtained for her a royal warrant giving her the right to use this title, so that she might attend royal weddings and court balls. This warrant was found among her papers after her death and included in the inventory of her belongings. It seems that it did not satisfy her. Did she thirst for the more legitimate and morally sounder position which the right marriage would bring with it? Whatever her reasons, Alphonsine Plessis signed a marriage contract on 21 February 1846, in London (District of Kensington, Paddington and Fulham, in the county of Middlesex) with the Comte Édouard de Perregaux.

Where did this convenient partner, this husband *in extremis*, come from? And are there descendants with anecdotes, no matter how vague, about this marriage?

Édouard's grandfather, Jean-Frédéric Perregaux, came from Neuchâtel in Switzerland, where he had a brilliant career as a banker. At Napoleon's instigation he founded the Bank of France in Paris. He died in 1808, and is buried among other great men in the Panthéon; he was created 'comte' posthumously. The beautiful portrait entitled 'Mme Perregaux' by Vigée-Lebrun in the Wallace Collection depicts his wife, formerly Adélaïde de Prael de Surville. Their grandson Édouard was a member of the exclusive Jockey Club but had not severed the strong family ties with his relations in Neuchâtel. In my family, two stories have been handed down.

Édouard brought Alphonsine to Switzerland – whether before or after their marriage is unclear – when he visited his family, who had been resident since 1825 in the Domaine de Fontaine André, a restored Cistercian abbey. But he kept Alphonsine out of sight and installed her for the duration of his stay in the nearby village of Saint-Blaise, at a hotel which still exists.

The second story comes from a relation by marriage, Madame Claudine de Perregaux. One day in 1915, when she was fifteen years old, her grandfather Frédéric de Perregaux came to her. A fire was burning in the fireplace of La Tertre, the family house. The old man was blind; he turned to his grand-daughter and gave her two packets of letters – one tied with a pink ribbon, the letters of Alphonsine – the other with blue ribbon, the letters of Édouard. He told her to burn them.

On Whit Sunday, 15 May 1989, Claudine herself repeated to me her grandfather's words from that distant occasion: 'These are the letters of a whore who brought dishonour upon our family.' She added, 'I shall hear these words and the voice that uttered them until the day I die.'

We must regret the destruction of these letters. If we were to condemn the morality in the name of which they were destroyed, we would be putting the moral code of a whole era on trial.

Martine Segalen
Myth or Reality?

Martine Segalen is a social historian and anthropologist, working at the Centre Nationale de la Recherche Scientifique in Paris.

Marguerite Gautier and Violetta Valéry are exceptions to the ordinary, and their destinies can be fulfilled only in fiction, whether novel, play or opera.

Where is the Norman peasant, brought up in poverty and beaten by her parents, illiterate until she was seventeen, who – within three years – could acquire the language, the social ease, the grace of deportment, the charm and the refinement of a girl brought up in the middle-classes? And, moreover, one whose education has succeeded so well that no trace of the painstaking learning process remains and all these qualities appear to be the gifts of nature? Any country girl less gifted than our heroine, arriving in Paris as a twelve-year-old orphan, would have been sheltered by some woman from her region. She would have become a seamstress or a laundress to earn a living, for such were the only trades open to a girl without education or qualifications. Daily contact with her customers would have taught her a few manners. Very quickly she would have become a grisette and, like Musset's Mimi Pinson, or Murger's Mimi and Françine – later conflated in the immortal character of Mimì in Puccini's *La bohème* – she would have taught students the ways of love; she would not have been looking for profit and luxury, yet gradually she would have learnt about another social world. Pregnancy might well have nipped this elevation in the bud. Seamstresses were often unemployed for half of the year, as work for them was very irregular; prostitution, at least occasionally, if not regularly, would have filled the gaps, and the traditional story of the grisette, which usually became more distressing as she advanced in years, would have been hers. The Alphonsines who died in the workhouse are legion.

Cleverly avoiding these pitfalls, Marguerite/Violetta, thanks to a strength of character, a quite exceptional intelligence of mind and heart, has graduated from being a lorette to become a 'courtisane', a 'demi-mondaine', one of those women who lived in the lap of showy luxury, kept by several lovers whom they often drove to rapid ruin.

Our heroine feels so much at ease in her new social garb that she shows the reactions of a city girl when she goes to the country, to a place very like the place she came from. When Marguerite goes to Auteuil/Bougival, she lingers for hours gazing in wonderment at the simple little flower with whom she shares her Christian name. At that time, the countryside around Paris was a place alive with the sort of activities in which she had participated as a child: wine-growing, market-gardening, working on vegetable allotments, and all manner of cottage industries and crafts.

Marguerite wishes to forget that she was a wretched country child and, after that stay in the country, where she sees nature adorned with all sorts of virtues associated with Rousseau, she is transformed: in her new persona she has forgotten the vices of the courtesan and allows herself to yield to the generosity of her heart and of her love.

The class gap between the real-life Marguerites and the woman of fiction is considerable; and therein lies the huge success of the novel, the play and the opera. Marguerite/Violetta has embodied for generations of wretched girls a living myth, a myth that was just what they needed to bring light and hope into their greasy lives, just as film stars do today.

Phyllis Luman Metal
Liberation – A Life's Work

Phyllis Luman Metal, grandmother and artist, now works as a crisis counsellor and fundraiser for the San Francisco Suicide Prevention group.

When I first became a prostitute in Paris, I felt that I had stepped across an invisible line. One side was where the rules were written out and on the other was unknown territory. A surge of energy poured through my body. Each time I stepped into a limousine I was a pioneer. The adventure of a new psyche challenged me. I found in this wide open territory the licence to explore past the brick wall of convention into the gyrating realms of impulses. It was a challenge to open doors and peek inside. And I felt so rich because not only did my pocketbook swell but I found nourishment in fulfilling hidden desires.

'How could you have any self-respect being a prostitute?' I have been asked. I am selling what I have the most right to sell. When a hundred dollar bill touches my palm, I know that I am worthwhile. The question has no meaning for me. It comes from such ignorance. The patriarch has brainwashed them. They think to be one man's property is respectable. I find that it is slavery. This occupation touches the core of life. Why should I dry up as a typist or a second-class worker in this man's world? As a prostitute I get men's best. I get their money and I get their secrets. It makes me rich. If men feel that I have escaped their control they are so right. They are angry because they have lost control and they try to negate their pleasure with me and condemn me. But it does not work any more. We women have joined together. We have knowledge. We have power. And we can take our lives in our own hands now. Mother goddesses are coming back in style. The castigating male gods are losing out. Lady of the Camellias ... if only you lived now, you would have strong sisters to help you. You would be more than a beautiful face that inspired wild passions. You could claim your soul. You could use your mind. You could write poetry. You could discuss politics. A diet of men's passions is thin gruel unless you can claim yourself. The sadness is not that you died of consumption but rather that you were not a person ... only a beautiful mirage, fragile as a flower ... but who were you?

I know who I am. And being a prostitute is only one hat I wear. After all, I was fifty-five when I first got in a limousine on the Avenue Foche, and prostitution gave me back my freedom from being a woman fitted neatly into a man's world. I grew up on my grandfather's ranches in Wyoming, down the Green River Valley and up on to the mesa. He was a Garrigue (a Huguenot family who fled to Holland and then to Martinique) and one of the pioneers of the West. I used to ride out for days on end and watch the antelope and hawks, and at night there was the diamond brilliance of the stars. But I was sent to a strict Episcopalian boarding school, where I was squeezed into a box of conventional behaviour. At nineteen I married a man with a sheepranch in South Wyoming, and we used to winter in a log cabin that had been Butch Cassidy's hideout. Every summer we would join my mother-in-law on a dude ranch for rich New Yorkers; she hated me, so to escape I joined a summer school at the University of Wyoming, where I met a young Jewish soldier from Brooklyn. He was a rebel against his middle-class family, in show business and the Communist Party. I had physical freedom on the ranch but Julian opened the doors to social freedom ... and the film world. We visited Gene Kelly regularly, and I realized that my husband was a closet gay; he also expected me to be a good Jewish wife and mother, and was outraged when I popped out with an idea. My third husband was a Norwegian, whose canning factory in Spain was confiscated by Franco; he enlisted in Franco's airforce but he was imprisoned for refusing to bomb Madrid; he returned to Norway during the German occupation and worked in the underground resistance; I met him when he was on merchant ships and I was his stewardess. But this wild and free Norwegian soldier of fortune expected me to be a traditional Norwegian wife. Then my Oaxa Indian husband taught me about Mexican culture, and my last husband and father of my three younger daughters helped me to become an artist. I am now a grandmother and a great-grandmother. Each of my husbands I had to leave because they abused me in one way or another. I was a prostitute for only one year when I was trying to help a jazz musician re-do his life, and later I was the mistress of a multimillionaire and member of the Bohemian Club. I have learned from all of my lovers, my husbands and my customers.

Lady of the Camellias, you seem to be so much alone for there was no intimacy for you with your lovers. You represented something. But where were you? Were you just a shadow in a romantic novel? Did you have opinions about who was ruling your country? Did you have a hobby? Or were you stuck in the stifling regimen of your time in history? You were extravagant because you were treated as an irresponsible child ... women of your time were not supposed to balance a chequebook and plan for their old age. Who were your role models? Did you just survive on the illusions men created about you? You were as much a victim of the system of male domination as were your sisters trapped in marriage. The old pretend game . . . to please. I am more fortunate than the Lady of the Camellias. I have lived to old age. I feel ripe. I have tried everything. In a long lifetime prostitution is just one more experience. I fit it in the package of my life along with marriages and children and going to art school.

For the last fifteen years I had a black lover who was a fine jazz musician. We found in each other the first-class acceptance which society denied us as second-class citizens . . . him as a black man, me as a woman. I could never accept being a Mrs Somebody . . . I wanted to be an equal somebody. And he wanted to walk tall as a man in America.

For years I have been a crisis counsellor at San Francisco Suicide Prevention doing the overnight shift (11pm to 9am) answering drug, suicide, mental health and geriatric lines. We were the official stress line for the entire Bay area after the earthquake of 1989. I have been a grief counsellor with a hospice, and an Aids and rape counsellor for a hospital. I have a BA in Social Welfare and am two-thirds of the way through my master's degree in Gerontology. I have worked three times for Mother Theresa in her programme with drunk Indians in Gallup, New Mexico. I have trained as an artist and a potter, and I love the Louvre, the Prado, and the Metropolitan. I am a Buddhist, and an Episcopalian, and I practise Yoga. I belong to 'Coyote', a prostitutes' rights organization in San Francisco; it stands for 'CAST OFF YOUR OLD TIRED ETHICS'.

Estela V. Welldon
Not Human Beings But Things

Dr Estela V. Welldon MD is a Fellow of the Royal College of Psychiatrists and Consultant Psychotherapist and Clinical Tutor at the Portman Clinic, London; she is the author of Mother, Madonna, Whore *(London 1988, USA 1992). That book deals with female perversion as a whole, and this is a compressed account of that discussion of the situations that lead to prostitution and of the nature of the prostitute–client relationship.*

In the novel *The Lady of the Camellias*, Marguerite and Armand have lost their mothers in childhood and are subjected to forceful, even brutish, fathers who apparently appreciate but actually exploit women. While Dumas modelled his protagonists to some extent on Marie Duplessis and himself, he invented another character, Armand's sister, to provide both the excuse in the plot for the father's intervention and the image of the virgin opposed to that of the whore. (He draws this contrast elsewhere: Marguerite's protector, the duke with whom she is supposed to have a platonic relationship, sees in her the living image of his dead, virginal daughter.) When Armand's father forces Marguerite to give up his son to avoid imperilling his daughter's 'proper' marriage, he says of her: 'She is young, beautiful and pure as an angel. She is in love, and she too has made love the dream of her life.' So she is obviously the one who deserves to be loved. Marguerite begs him: 'Kiss me as you would kiss your daughter.'

Dumas proposes that the relationship of Marguerite and Armand is not one of prostitute and client: it is a romance. Armand falls in love with her after learning that she is very ill. He is full of devotion and jealousy and is possessive of her. He does not pay for 'her favours'; on the contrary he 'unknowingly' benefits from her trade. She loves him and shares all her anxieties with him, including those of her profession, such as not being allowed to show her feelings, and being 'just a thing' to her clients. She tells him: 'You were the only person with whom from the first I could think and speak freely. Naturally we [courtesans] have no friends. We have egotistical lovers who spend their fortunes not on us, as they claim, but on their vanity ... For men like these, we have to be cheerful when they are happy, hale and hearty when they decide they want supper, and as cynical as they are. We are not allowed to have feelings for fear of being jeered at and losing our credibility. Our lives are no longer our own. We aren't human beings, but things.' Here Dumas has accurately grasped the prostitute's predicament. She feels prevented from sharing her intimate life with her clients, and not free, since it is the nature of the trade to offer cheerfulness and youth, not to reveal depression at the thought of ageing. A courtesan, though no stranger to her clients, suffers from the same predicament as the common street-walker because for the exercise of the profession they are both things rather than human beings.

David Coward remarks in his introduction to the novel (1986), 'Dumas's insistence that she [Marguerite] remains "virginal" in the midst of vice, like his wish to turn her into a saint and martyr, will nowadays strike some readers as a piece of special pleading', seem to me to be erroneous. I believe the opposite to be true. The key to this story/myth lies in the fact that the opposites of whore–madonna co-exist in the most delicate balance. Hence Dumas's beautiful description of Armand's vision of Marguerite: 'One could detect in this girl a virgin who has been turned into a courtesan by the merest accident of chance, and a courtesan whom the merest accident of chance could have turned into the most loving, the most pure of virgins.'

Marguerite defies most conventions attached to prostitution but the price Dumas makes her pay for this romantic defiance is to fall ill of consumption and die young ... 'God had been merciful to her since He had not suffered her to live long enough to undergo the usual punishment but had allowed her to die at the height of her wealth and beauty, long before the coming of old age, that first death of courtesans ... Her past appeared to her to become one of the major causes of her illness, and a kind of superstition led her to hope that God would allow her to keep her beauty and her health in exchange for her repentance and conversion.'

It is impossible to comprehend the phenomenon of prostitution by looking just at the prostitute, or just at the man who pursues her. A dynamic process is at work, an interaction between two people with their own histories, their present circumstances and their separate needs, which establishes an equilibrium through a contract. While outsiders may view prostitution as precarious, wrong or immoral, both prostitute and client see it as a way of fulfilling a need, and both hope for a successful (and complementary) outcome. This complicity provides both with some gratification and reassurance. Both share a split view of woman in the whore–madonna complex.

The client as well as the woman has problems that are not always obvious. Double standards are at work, which is not surprising since a contract based on money has been entered into, and the two parties are in some way accomplices, in other ways opponents. Prudence offers Armand words of wisdom when she says: 'Kept women always expect that there'll be men around who'll love them, but they never imagine that they themselves will fall in love. Otherwise, they'd put a bit on one side and, by the time they're thirty, they'd be able to afford the luxury of taking a lover who pays nothing.' She implies that the woman is so strongly convinced that she will always control the situation that she can imagine no change to it.

In prostitution both parties are seeking control – but control of what? To start with, there is a false understanding – that the encounter is only or primarily a sexual-genital one. Both are involved in a compromise whereby the sexual mother is taken over by the strict mother, provider of bodily ministrations. A process of projective identification takes place within both partners' minds in an attempt to resolve their primitive splitting. The prostitute now becomes in fantasy a mother with a young child – her client – submissive under her control; simultaneously she is a whore who is supposed to provide that 'youngster' with sexual gratification. This is made possible by a process of depersonalization, by a mutual and reciprocal process of splitting and by the denial of emotions that occur as a result. In prostitution the client at times becomes 'the dirty old man', with connotations of dirt associated with money, faeces corresponding to a pre-oedipal stage. At other times, he is the 'sugar daddy', easily associated with orality, sugar and milk; in other words, the client becomes, in symbolic terms, a mother who is able to feed the woman–baby–prostitute, to satisfy any whimsical needs she might have.

A pre-oedipal perverse dyadic process is at work, and the associated degree of risk demands a process of triangulation which is offered by a strict and punitive superego – the law – a symbolic father who is called upon to perform his duties. He is expected to extricate both parties from a perverse, unhealthy association and to create some sense of order. That is the role which Dumas creates for Armand's father; later the Duke, through his mourning, re-enacts it, casting Marguerite as his dead, virginal daughter.

Prostitute and client are acting out an 'ideal', illusory and collusive scenario in which the symbolic mother–baby unit tries to get away without the husband–father, while they are both challenging the law–husband/father to make a prosecution. But when it comes to the application of the law, the woman is charged, while the man and his emotional predicaments are dismissed.

The 'strange man' who pays for the prostitute's favours is the deteriorated and idealized image of her father. When pursuing prostitutes the man is looking for a mother he desires as a forbidden sexual object. Unable to obtain his sexual gratification he has to content himself with a denigrated maternal figure. She keeps alive the mother–madonna–whore split.

The woman leaves all emotions aside when she works as a prostitute, and is able, most of the time, to operate with skill and in complete detachment. Outside her work the same woman can feel much emotion, tenderness and care but will unfortunately tend to fall into sado-masochistic relationships, in which she is exploited by her partner.

Some prostitutes experience a caricature of intimate relationships involving revenge. This revenge, which appears to be directed against their socio-economic submission to a man's world, is actually against the mother. This urge for revenge involves a desire to be in charge, and gives a sense of elation while with her client. This conscious control fulfils an unconscious denigration of herself and her gender, because she afterwards feels debased. In this state she is too depressed to harbour vengeful fantasies against men (as is usually stated) but instead identifies with her male client in his contempt for her and her gender.

As prostitutes, women are unable to see themselves as individuals, let alone as sexual beings. Their self-esteem is very low, and in order to get out of this 'low' they start to solicit. When men are ready to pay for their services they feel enormously elated. Soliciting, then, is used as a 'regulator' of their self-esteem.

There are some circumstances in which women apparently seeking money in a client–prostitute relationship are at a deeper level actually seeking punishment. That is the case with women who engage in prostitution with such recklessness that they are easily caught. When such women appear in court on charges of soliciting they feel that the charge in itself will prejudice everyone against them and that nobody will bother to get to know about them, their upbringing, their emotional needs and personal circumstances. Such is their despondency that, expecting no real understanding, they usually make the law-enforcers collude with their inner persecutory needs and this leads to disproportionately heavy sentences. And, indeed, society feels so hostile, not only to prostitutes' actions but also, indeed, to their inability to defend themselves, that it is unable to separate their actions from their personalities. Thus sentencing can carry an unconscious recognition of their actions and of their need for punishment. This is articulated in the novel when Marguerite tells Armand of her meeting with his father: 'Your father believed implicitly in the conventional truths according to which every courtesan is a heartless creature, a kind of gold-grabbing machine always ready, like any other machine, to mangle the hand that feeds it and crush, pitilessly, blindly, the very person who gives it life and movement.' Yet she has accepted this demand and given up her lover.

The strong feeling of contempt which prostitutes show towards society ('I don't care a damn about them') covers up a massive projection of their own self-neglect. They are the ones who are ostracized, despised, isolated and eventually detained. They tend to view the world as something imposed on them because they are so much in need of a strong response from the outside. However negative or severe this response may be, it provides them in their daily lives with the narcissistic support which they are unable to obtain from within.

Most professions, regardless of how demanding they are of our time, emotional involvement and physical strength, leave us able to pursue separate public and private lives. In the intimacy of the latter we replenish our mental and physical resources. This is not possible for women who practise prostitution. This aspect of the predicament becomes obvious when they appear in court, where their private lives are exposed to the public. Since their profession involves them in offering and providing their clients with gratifications of a very intimate nature, their own private needs have to be ignored. Everything private becomes public, this being the nature of the conflict. Some women unconsciously hope that, once their problems are acknowledged and in the open, help will become available to them. Unfortunately it rarely happens.

Ruth Westheimer
Dr Ruth and Marguerite Gautier

Ruth Westheimer is the author of Dr Ruth's Guide to Good Sex *(London, 1986) and her weekly radio show* Sexually Speaking *is broadcast live by WYNY in New York; she has lectured at many universities in North America, and has written a book on the Impressionists. The following is Dr Ruth's response to an imagined call from Marguerite Gautier to her phone-in radio show.*

You know, Marguerite, you're very smart. You see that the people around you have been courtesans, and that they now depend on the money you earn. It's sad that you never know who your real friends are because, like in Hollywood today, you are surrounded by people who live off you. You feel very isolated. You can never make a good friend of a married woman because they see you as a threat, even if you don't have the least intention of attracting their husbands. But now you want a private life of your own, with children.

Society does recognize you as an exceptional woman. I like that you are calling me because you are showing other women that material wealth is not everything. Even though you have lots of debts, you are superb at your job; everyone who sees you drive in the Bois de Boulogne is a little bit jealous. In what you do you make men feel free, and at one with themselves. They can't ask the nice girls in their arranged marriages to do the sort of thing which they want. You're beautiful, and you're passionate. But if you really want a bourgeois life, there is nothing to stop you finding a man who would accept you.

So, you're calling me because you've fallen in love. What's the problem? Why can't you continue your life as you are doing? Doesn't he permit you to have the other relationships which pay for your services?

Why don't you try this idea? If you are with other men – and I understand that you are dependent on them for money – couldn't you fantasize that you are with him? Give it a try!

If your lover's father has asked you to give up his son for family reasons, I don't see that you should have to leave the place where your whole life is centred, and I can see that your lover would refuse to leave you. But maybe you should leave him for a little while, and go away with a friend . . . but you must take his father's money, even if you don't like it! Or suppose you ask the Duke – the one you sleep with who loves you because you remind him of his daughter – to lend you some money to start a business? Then wait until Armand is married and have the hottest love affair?

I know I keep talking to you about the future and you want him now. Maybe you should sell the rights to your story, and share the percentage in the musical rights.

You must remember how fortunate you are that here is a man you love, and who loves you. At least you have had a great love. Do not turn the experience into a negative one . . . Most people have never enjoyed love like this. It makes your heart beat faster, and gives you energy to walk with your head high.

As time passes, the pain of giving him up will get less. Spend some time each day with less fortunate people. Work in an orphanage. That satisfaction might be of help to you. Write a diary to tell me what you did to give pleasure to people . . . I don't mean sex. Or maybe you could teach me a few tricks, and your legacy to the world would be a sex manual which might even help the geishas . . .

What you need is a psychiatrist – but it's before Freud!

Barbara Cartland
A True Romance

Dame Barbara Cartland, DBE, Dame of Grace of St John of Jerusalem, is the author of over 550 books which have sold over 5 million copies world-wide.

During the Archer trial in 1986 a prostitute called Monica was asked: 'Have you ever read any of Jeffrey Archer's books?' She replied: 'No, but I'm mad about Barbara Cartland and I

*Doris Keane as Mme Cavallini (with Owen Nares as Tom) in
Romance, 1915: 'You are the fir-r-rst man I 'ave ever loved.'*

always believe that one day a wonderful man will sweep me off my feet, we will fall in love and live happily ever after.' I found that pathetic. Yet it confirmed my belief that every man and woman, whether they say so or not, is searching for real love which is both physical and spiritual. The search has existed all through history and men and women have suffered tortures, crucifixion and death for the love that was part of their faith.

La Dame aux camélias has always interested me because in 1924 I visited Madeira and found Doris Keane feeding the little green lizards. She was a legend to my generation. During the First World War she acted in a play called *Romance*, another stage version of *The Lady of the Camellias*, for over a thousand performances. She left her audience breathless and weeping bitterly at the end when she died from consumption, having given up the man whom she loved, because it was for his own good. Doris Keane played her part until she was ill, until she did not know where the world of illusion ended and that of reality began. She was fêted, acclaimed and adored. It was difficult to realize how compelling a personality she had been when I talked to a thin woman with dark shadows under her eyes from sleepless nights.

This is the essence of real love – that the person one loves is more important than one's self and no sacrifice is too great. Marguerite makes the great sacrifice and disappears, leaving a letter for the man she loves to tell him that she has another 'protector' and that all is finished between them. No woman could do more in the way of real love, and when she dies, lonely and miserable without him, it is impossible for anyone not to feel that she has paid the price for her sins. I believe, and I try to explain it in my books, that Real Love is so very different from the lust which is written about, filmed and accepted today.

For a man and a woman to love each other is, quite simply, the nearest thing we have to the Love of God, and in loving completely and absolutely with our bodies, our hearts and our souls, we touch the Divine. It is this love which makes *La Dame aux camélias* a classic love story which will continue being read until the end of time.

PART TWO

The Making of a Myth

Lucy Hughes-Hallett
The Beautiful Corpse

Lucy Hughes-Hallett is the author of Cleopatra: histories, dreams and distortions *(London, 1990).*

A turning point in Alexandre Dumas's novel, *La Dame aux camélias*: Armand Duval is about to narrate the circumstances of his first meeting with Marguerite Gautier. He pauses, keeping both the narrator (for this is a story within a story) and the reader in suspense while he retails a vignette from someone else's novel. A man catches sight of a woman so beautiful he falls instantly in love. He feels elated. There is nothing he would not do to win the right to kiss such a woman's hand. He walks after her, scarcely daring to look at the stockinged ankle revealed when she lifts her skirts clear of the dirty pavement. 'While he is dreaming of all that he would do to possess this woman, she stops at the street corner and asks whether he wants to go back to her place. He turns his head away, crosses the road and, deeply saddened, goes home.' Men are like that, says Armand. He feels the same way. When a friend offers to introduce him to Marguerite, remarking that it is not necessary to stand on ceremony with her, he feels a kind of terror. 'If someone had said to me: You can have this woman tonight and you will be killed tomorrow, I would have accepted. If someone had said: Pay ten louis and you will be her lover, I would have refused and cried like a child who had seen the castle of his dream vanish in the morning light.' The point has been made, twice, and so placed in the text as to stand as the epigraph, the moral, to the story of Armand's and Marguerite's relationship. The prostitute, in offering to gratify male desire, thwarts it. She translates erotic fantasies, which are essentially imaginative, into flesh. In doing so she destroys them and she must, in turn, be destroyed.

It is not because she accepts money from the Duke and presents from the Count, not even because she receives the Marquis at midnight wearing only her peignoir that Armand cannot forgive Marguerite. Nor is it on account of these transgressions against propriety that Dumas has to kill her. It is because she allows Armand himself to have sexual intercourse with her. Having done so (and because the story is told in the form of a flashback she is always in the state of 'having done so' even though the consummation of their affair does not occur until nearly half-way through the narrative) she becomes the personification of Armand's own sexuality, the sexuality which he would gladly see punished with a morning-after death.

Already, when Armand is introduced to her, Marguerite is ill. But long before the reader is given the account of that meeting we have been shown her dead and stinking, her eye sockets empty, her cheeks greenly putrescent. The heroine of this novel is a corpse. Alive she would be too dangerous. As an autonomous woman, who earns her own keep and uses her sexuality for her own profit or pleasure, she is an explosively disruptive figure. Armand's father believes her capable of blasting the marriage of people she has never met. Her money (just because it is hers) is an agent of corruption. Armand's future career, future happiness, would be blighted if he accepted it. Such a potently destabilizing force has to be neutralized. All the men who come into contact with Marguerite (with the exception of the easy-going Marquis) attempt to change her. They want to transform her into a girl fit to be a daughter – to desexualize her in other words. And they want her to die.

Throughout most of the period covered by the narrative she is financially dependent on a septuagenarian Duke who sees in her the likeness of his own dead child. When she is desperately ill he comes to visit her. Afterwards she remarks, 'It was doubtless the memory of his daughter's death which made him weep. He will have seen her die twice.' It was precisely this that he always wanted from Marguerite. Her death sustains, rejuvenates him. 'One might even say that he rejoiced secretly to see how the disease has ravaged me. He was proud to be still on his feet while I, young as I am, was prostrated by suffering.' The Duke's morbid obsession echoes in miniature the novel's main plot. In *La traviata* Verdi has a group of carnival revellers sing a chorus in praise of the sacrificial ox outside the courtesan's window on the day of her death. Her life must be sacrificed in honour of fathers' love for their virgin daughters.

Even Armand repeatedly confesses to taking pleasure in the contemplation of Marguerite's mortality. He recalls the first time he heard she was seriously ill. 'The heart is strange; I was almost glad of this malady.' Later he admits that the pain he felt on hearing of her death was nothing by comparison with what he felt when he saw the Count go into her apartment at midnight. When she comes to him for the last time she is all but dead already, chilled and helpless. 'I undressed her without her making a single movement and I carried her, frozen as she was, into my bed.' In that state he 'loved her so much that in the midst of the transports of her feverish passion I wondered whether I shouldn't kill her to ensure that she would never be another's'. Her illness pre-empts him. The last section of the novel is a long-drawn-out account of her painful end. Armand is not the only sadist. For Dumas, for the host of readers who have been moved by this book, the spectacle of an unchaste woman's death is intensely exciting.

Marguerite's death is not only the beginning and the end of the novel. It is the reason for the very existence of the narrative. The narrator has seen a placard advertising the sale of her property. Idly curious, he goes along. The public has invaded her apartment as her clients once invaded her body, peering and fingering, bidding for objects (hairbrushes, cosmetic-pots) infused with the titillating glamour of accessories to sex. The narrator describes the apartment as a 'gorgeous sewer', an oxymoronic space where fascination and revulsion are in perfect balance. He cannot keep away. He encounters Armand, loses contact with him and in an attempt to find him again hunts out Marguerite's burial-place. The sexton tells him that Armand pays for her grave to be covered perpetually with fresh camellias (the flowers that in her lifetime had advertised the cycle of her menstrual periods). Standing beside it the narrator finds himself wishing to sound its depth 'to see what the earth had done to the beautiful creature that had been thrown to it'. That is precisely what Armand wants too. Shortly afterwards, in the ghastly scene which is both the novel's prelude and its climax, he has the body exhumed. Only once he has seen its decomposition will he be free of its spell.

The disease that kills Marguerite is, officially, tuberculosis but the terms in which it is described suggest that a truer description of it would be sexual arousal. The malady, says the narrator, 'continued to give her those feverish desires which are the nearly inevitable result of chest complaints'. To the more impressionable Armand her 'ardent nature' seems to spread an atmosphere of voluptuousness around her, just as a delicious fragrance seeps from a phial of perfume. 'From time to time, perhaps as a consequence of her state of illness, there flickered in this woman's eyes flashes of desire of which the expression would be a revelation of heaven to him whom she might love.' This malady is infectious. Armand is obsessed by her for two years before becoming her lover. Each time he sees her, 'I became pale and my heart beat violently.' This febrile state, part disease, part rapture, is inseparable from Marguerite's life as a courtesan, and from Armand's fascination with her. It is when he sees her coughing blood that he finds the courage to declare himself. Once she has promised to accept him she presses his hand to her chest, allowing him to feel 'the violent palpitations'. Disease makes their relationship hectic. It also guarantees Armand's safety. Despite his determination to deny the fact, it is evident that no entanglement with Marguerite can hold him long.

So much is commonplace. The portrayal of sexual passion as a demonic frenzy with fatal consequences has a long tradition. What gives Dumas's story its subtlety is the fact that he opposes, not sex and chastity, but sexual excitement and sexual satisfaction. One of the most remarkable aspects of Marguerite's life as a prostitute is how seldom she actually fucks. True, Armand has to wait (furious with jealousy and humiliation) while she receives the Marquis but their assignation is undescribed and it leaves the bed unrumpled (Armand checks). The Duke, her main client/lover, treats her as a daughter. She rejects the Count. It is only in the country, once she has abandoned her life of depravity, that she and Armand keep the curtains drawn and spend whole days in bed.

Their idyll is interrupted as though the prostitute, the purveyor of sex, has no right to sexual fulfilment. Indeed, in presuming to seek it, she has made a literally fatal mistake. 'If I took care of myself I would die,' she told Armand when he first implored her to live a quieter, healthier life. 'This feverish life I lead is all that keeps me going.' She may mean simply that she has to work in order to earn. Dumas insists at every point that the reality underlying the romantic and erotic story is economic. Money is the crux. But Marguerite may also be hinting at the fact that as an outcast from the institution of the family she cannot risk succumbing to the myth that validates that institution, the myth of romantic love.

In *La traviata* Violetta understands quite clearly that love will be her crucifixion as well as her delight. While frenetically pursuing pleasure she can maintain her equilibrium, but she cannot afford to be thoughtful or cautious, just as a tightrope walker cannot afford to pause and look down. In admitting tenderness she is making herself vulnerable. Consenting to love Alfredo, she takes a flower from her corsage and gives it to him, telling him to return when it is withered. The emblem of their affair is a memento mori. She is conniving at her own death.

Dumas defines the courtesan as 'a woman who is neither mother, nor sister, nor daughter, nor wife'. He remarks that such women die as they are born, 'sans éclat'. They come from nowhere, they have no place, no role, in a society made up of families. They must not attempt to trespass on to territory reserved for insider women. When Marguerite and Armand attempt to set up house together, to share their bed and their property like man and wife, they bring down society's retribution on their own heads. Armand consults the family lawyer and prepares to hand over family property. It is the beginning of the end.

The courtesan disrupts economic systems as well as sociological ones. *La Dame aux camélias* describes the clash of two incompatible economies. The male characters have money, and they acquire pleasure and power by giving it away. The women earn money by selling pleasure and they obtain power (or fail to do so) by saving what they earn. Hence the striking difference between the rhetoric employed by the two groups. The men (pampered recipients of unearned income) can talk about love and betrayal, but Marguerite, Prudence and Olympe, paid workers for whom love is an expensive self-indulgence, talk about debts and about fees paid for services rendered.

The courtesan ruins men. In doing so she exposes the instability of money, the artificiality of its value. Marguerite's lovers give fortunes to support her. Something compels them to do so – against all reason – just as something compels her to squander huge sums. This is a part of the courtesan's allure. The financial profligacy for which she is the occasion is metaphor for a Dionysiac release from responsibility. Unlike the common street prostitute she poses a risk, not only to a man's health, but to his wealth, the outward and visible sign of his social identity. Squandering their money, her clients act out a fantasy of self-dissolution, jeopardizing their social status, even risking their identity as men. The ruin from which Armand is rescued is signalled by his gambling and by his willingness to allow Marguerite to spend her money on him. By accepting her money he puts himself in the position of her dependent – a position both he and his father find abominable. It makes a pimp of him. Worse (though this is not voiced in the text) it makes him the equivalent of a prostitute (or any woman), someone who is given money by a sexual partner.

His inability to support his mistress scrambles social and sexual hierarchies: his gambling is a conventional metaphor for economic chaos. The gambler's winnings, neither inherited nor earned, are insubstantial fairy gold. The courtesan offers her clients/lovers access to a dizzyingly free space, outside economic reality and the stratifications of class and gender. The prospect of 'ruin' is the most potent of her fascinations. It is also the reason why she cannot be allowed to live.

Armand, like the reader, always knows that Marguerite is dying. Her death is terrible to him. But it is also what he has been waiting for. Gazing into her grave he has got her at last – she will never be another's now. More importantly, he knows that she cannot get him. In *La traviata* Verdi makes the central relationship of the story that between Violetta and the elder M. Germont. The courtesan and the father are each more worldly-wise than the young man for whose love they contend. Eventually they join forces to conspire against him for what they agree to be his own good. And just as Alfredo is a helpless bone of contention in their hands, so Marguerite is in the hands of the novel's narrator and other characters, of Dumas, and of the reader. She never means any harm, but her lovers (those described within the text and those who read it) cast her as a bringer of ruin. They make their own image of her, worship it, lay gifts before it, give their all for it and then kill it. Her person symbolizes the illusion that eroticism can create its own space outside society. That illusion promises anarchy: the person who stands for it has to be destroyed. And once Marguerite is dead those who have survived the threat she posed can weep for her with complacent pity. Dead as she always-already is, she becomes the ideal erotic fantasy-figure, one who offers ruin without finality, love without commitment, frenzy without self-loss. Her beautiful body, the body that so dazzled Armand that he neglected duty and familial love, must be seen to rot. Its corruption guarantees that Armand's life is safe.

From Fact to Fiction

Although Dumas's eleven-month affair with Marie ended in 1845, he told friends that he remained obsessed with her memory. He was returning from Spain when he heard of her death, and he hurried back to Paris. It is not certain that he assisted her husband at the exhumation of her body and its interment in the Montmartre cemetery. He did buy back, at the auction of her property, his first present to her, a chain of gold and pearls, and the letter with which he had broken off their liaison. This note, elegantly drafted and written, appears almost word for word in the novel:

'My dear Marie. I am not rich enough to love you as I would wish, nor poor enough to be loved as you would wish. Let us forget each other then: you a name to which you must be more or less indifferent, I a happiness which has become impossible for me. It is useless to tell you how sad I am, since you know already how much I love you. Goodbye then, you . . . have too great a heart not to understand the cause of my letter, and too much intelligence not to forgive me for it. A thousand memories. A.D. August 30, midnight.'

Much later he gave it to Sarah Bernhardt, in token of her sensational performances of the role of Marguerite Gautier.

Marie Duplessis
letter to Agénor de Guiche

Agénor de Guiche, one of the richest and most handsome men of Paris in the 1840s, and only five years older than Marie, introduced her into high society. Once, when he was away from Paris, she wrote him this distraught letter:

I would also like to ask your advice whether I should or should not go away with Mme Weller, I am very embarrassed for I hardly understand this woman who is so excessively good towards me and suddenly changes her manner, so I am awaiting your reply and a friend's advice ... Write me quickly a nice long letter, tell me all you are thinking about, what you are doing, tell me also that you love me I need to believe it, it would be a consolation in your absence, my good angel, I am very sad, I love you more tenderly than ever. I kiss you a thousand times on your mouth and everywhere. Farewell my darling angel, do not forget me too much, think sometimes of the one who loves you much.

The jewel box of Marie Duplessis (collection Mary Jane Phillips-Matz; photo Tom McGovern)

Marie Duplessis
letters to Édouard de Perregaux

Édouard de Perregaux was twenty-seven when he met Marie in 1842. He married her on 21 February 1846, in London. They parted company almost immediately afterwards.

Dear child, I am a little unwell . . . I will go to bed early this evening, and won't see you . . .

How cross I am, my dear Édouard, not to have received your letter earlier. Zélia wrote to me to ask if I could pass the evening with her; I accepted, having nothing better to do. If you like, we will dine together tomorrow . . . Waiting for your reply, my little brother, I kiss your blue eyes a thousand times, and am all yours.

*

My dear Édouard, be so good as to give the porter the papers I need the most. You would oblige me by asking M. Breton not to make me wait too long for my jewels; for you know I desire to leave as soon as possible, and I cannot go without them, since they are necessary to conclude my affairs . . . As you are not coming with me to Italy, I do not know why you have said to many people that you would come later to find me there. Do you really want to harm me? You have always known that that could prejudice my future, which you wish to be absolutely sad and miserable. I freely forgive you for that, but I beg you not to forget the subject of my letter. Marie.

*

My dear Édouard. In everything you write me, I see only one thing to which you wish me to reply: you wish me to put in writing that you are free to do whatever seems good to you. I told you this myself yesterday, I say it again and I sign: Marie Duplessis.

Forgive me, my dear Édouard, I beg you on my knees –

If you love me enough for that, nothing but two words, my pardon and your friendship, write to me *poste restante* at Ems, duchy of Nassau. I am alone here and very ill. So, dear Édouard, quickly forgive me. Farewell. Marie Duplessis.

Alexandre Dumas *fils*
Élégie *from* Péchés de jeunesse, *1847*

For many years this Elegy *was forgotten, since Dumas remembered recalling all of the edition of one hundred copies, apart from the fourteen that had been sold, and using the pages as wrapping paper.*

M.D.
Nous nous étions brouillés; et pourquoi? Je l'ignore:
Pour rien! Pour le soupçon d'un amour inconnu
Et moi qui vous ai fuie, aujourd'hui je déplore
De vous avoir quittée et d'être revenu

Je vous avais écrit que je viendrai, Madame,
Pour chercher mon pardon, vous voir à mon retour
Car je croyais devoir, et du fond de mon âme
Ma première visite à ce dernier amour

Et quand mon âme accourt, depuis longtemps absente
Votre fenêtre est close et votre seuil fermé
Et voilà qu'on me dit qu'une tombe récente
Couvre à jamais le front que j'avais tant aimé

On me dit froidement qu'après une agonie
Qui dura quatre mois le mal fut le plus fort
Et la fatalité jette avec ironie
À mon espoir trop prompt le mot de votre mort

J'ai revu, me courbant sous mes lourdes pensées
L'escalier bien connu, le seuil foulé souvent
Et les murs qui, témoins des choses effacées
Pour lui parler du mort arrêtent le vivant

Je montai. Je rouvris, en pleurant cette porte
Que nous avions ouverte en riant tous les deux
Et dans mes souvenirs j'évoquais chère morte
Le fantôme voilé de tous nos jours heureux

Elegy
from Sins of Youth, *1847*

M.D.
We quarrelled; and why? I don't know:
over nothing! The suspicion of an unknown lover
and I, who abandoned you, today I weep
that I left you and moved on

I wrote to you that I would come, Madame,
to seek forgiveness and see you on my return,
for I believed from the depths of my soul
I should pay my first visit to this last love

And my soul hastened, after so long an absence,
to see your window closed and your door fastened shut
and someone told me that a new grave
hides for ever the face I so much loved

I was coldly informed that after four months
your dying throes reached a peak
and then ironic fate cast the news of your death
on my too eager hope

I saw once again, weighed down by heavy thoughts,
the familiar staircase, the often crowded doorway,
and the walls – witnesses of things forgotten –
which stop the living to speak to them of death

I went up. Weeping, I opened the door which,
laughing, we opened together
and in my memory I conjured up, my dead beloved,
the veiled phantom of all our happy days

Je m'assis à la table où, l'un près de l'autre
Nous revenions souper aux beaux soirs de printemps
Et de l'amour joyeux qui fut jadis le nôtre,
J'entendais chaque objet parler en même temps

Je vis le piano dont mon oreille avide
Vous écouta souvent éveiller le concert
Votre mort a laissé l'instrument froid et vide
Comme en partant l'été laisse l'arbre désert

J'entrai dans le boudoir, cette oasis divine
Égayant vos regards de ses mille couleurs
Je revis vos tableaux, vos grands vases de Chine
Où se mouraient encore quelques bouquets de fleurs

J'ai trouvé votre chambre à la fois douce et sombre
Sanctuaire d'amour par la mort consacré
Le soleil éclairait le lit dormant dans l'ombre
Mais vous ne dormiez plus dans le lit éclairé

Je m'assis à côté de la couche déserte
Triste à voir comme un nid, l'hiver au fond des bois
Les yeux longtemps fixés sur cette porte ouverte
Que vous aviez franchie une dernière fois

La chambre s'emplissait de l'haleine odorante
Des souvenirs joyeux, tandis que j'écoutais
Le tic-tac alterné de l'horloge ignorante
Qui sonnait autrefois l'heure que j'attendais

Or c'est là qu'autrefois, ô ma chère envolée,
Nous restions tous les deux lorsque venait minuit
Et depuis ce moment jusqu'à l'aube éveillés
Nous écoutions passer les heures de la nuit

J'ai rouvert les rideaux qui, faits de satin rose
Et voilant au matin le sommeil à demi,
Permettaient seulement ce rayon qui dépose
Le réveil hésitant sur le front endormi

I sat at the table where, one beside the other,
we used to sup in those sweet spring evenings
and I heard every object speak as one
of that happy love which once was ours

I saw the piano to which I would be an eager listener
while you called up the music
your death has left the instrument cold and empty
as when summer passes and leaves the trees bare

I went into the boudoir, that heavenly oasis
brightening your glances with a thousand hues;
I saw again your pictures, your great Chinese vases
where still flowers stood dying

I found your chamber both sweet and sombre,
love's sanctuary consecrated by death;
the sun shone upon the bed that slept in the shadow
but you lay sleeping no longer in that sunlit bed

I sat beside the empty couch,
sad as a nest in the deep winter woods;
my eyes long fixed on the open door
that you had passed through for the very last time

The bedroom filled with the fragrant breath
of happy memories, while I listened
to the rhythmic ticking of the unknowing clock
which in days now gone chimed the hour I awaited

For it is there, in the past, O my dear departed,
that we lay together when midnight came
and, awake from then till dawn,
we listened to the night hours pass

I opened the pink satin curtains
which half-veiled your rest from morning
and allowed in the single ray which would gently set
its waking light upon your sleeping brow

Mais vous toutes les nuits éclairée à sa flamme
Vous regardiez le feu dans le foyer courir
Car le sommeil suivait de vos yeux, et votre âme
Souffrait déjà du mal qui vous a fait mourir

Ainsi qu'un ver rongeant une fleur qui se fane
L'incessante insomnie étiolait vos jours
Et c'est ce qui faisait de vous la courtisane
Prompte à tous les plaisirs, prête à tous les amours

Vous souvient-il des nuits où, brûlante amoureuse
Tordant sous les baisers votre corps éperdu
Vous trouviez, consumée à cette ardeur fièvreuse
Dans vos sens fatigués le sommeil attendu?

Vous souvient-il encore dans le monde où vous êtes
Des choses de ce monde et, sur les froids tombeaux
Entendez-vous passer ce cortège de fêtes
Où vous vous épuisiez pour trouver le repos?

Maintenant vous avez parmi les fleurs, Marie,
Sans crainte du réveil le repos désiré
Le Seigneur a soufflé sur votre âme flétrie
Et payé d'un seul coup le sommeil arriéré

Pauvre fille! On m'a dit qu'à votre heure dernière
Une main mercenaire avait fermé vos yeux
Et que sur le chemin qui mène au cimetière
Vos amis d'autrefois étaient réduits à deux

Eh bien! Soyez bénis, vous deux qui, tête nue,
Bravant l'opinion de ce monde insolent
Avez jusques au bout, de la femme connue
En vous touchant la main mené le convoi blanc

Vous qui l'avez aimée et qui l'avez suivie
Qui n'êtes pas de ceux qui, ducs, marquis ou lord
S'étant fait un orgueil d'entretenir sa vie
N'ont pas compris l'orgueil d'accompagner sa mort.

A.D.

But every night, illumined by its flames,
you used to watch the fire blazing in the hearth;
for sleep fled from your eyes, and your heart
already suffered from the illness which killed you

As a worm eats a flower which fades,
incessant sleeplessness consumed your days,
and that is what made you the courtesan
ready for every pleasure, always ready for love

Do you remember nights when, burning with love,
your frantic body writhing beneath kisses,
you found the sleep you longed for, consumed
in the burning fever of your wearied breasts?

Do you still remember, in the world where you are,
the things of this world, and above the cold tombs
can you hear this procession of revelries
where you sought exhaustion in order to find rest?

Now among the flowers, Marie,
you have found the rest you desired, without fear of waking,
the Lord has breathed upon your withered soul
and paid your arrears of sleep once and for all

Poor girl! I was told that a hand whose care was bought
closed your eyes in your last hour
and that on the way to the cemetery
your friends of the past were no more than two

Well! Be blest, you two with heads uncovered
braving the judgement of this arrogant world
and accompanying the white hearse of the woman
you knew from the touch of a hand

You who loved her and who followed her
are not those dukes, marquesses or lords
who deemed themselves proud to maintain her life
but understood not the pride of accompanying her death.
A.D.

Alexandre Dumas *fils*
from Act II of The Lady of the Camellias, *1852*

ARMAND: Marguerite, you're mad! I love you. But I don't mean that you're beautiful and that you will please me only for three or four months. You are all my hope, all my thoughts, all my life; I love you! What more can I say?

MARGUERITE: Then you are right: it would be better if we stopped seeing each other from now on.

ARMAND: Of course, because you don't love me!

MARGUERITE: Because . . . You don't know what you're saying!

ARMAND: Then, why?

Marguerite Gautier, illustration by Gavarni for
The Lady of the Camellias, *1856*

MARGUERITE: Why? Do you want to know? Because I spend hours dreaming this dream from beginning to end; because there are days when I am tired of the life I lead and I catch a glimpse of another; because in the midst of our turbulent existence, our heads, our pride, our senses are alive, but our hearts swell, can find no kindred spirit and suffocate us. We seem happy and are envied. In fact, we have lovers who ruin themselves, not for us as they claim, but out of vanity; we come first in their amour-propre, last in their esteem. We have friends, like Prudence [the madam], whose friendship goes as far as servitude, but never disinterest. It hardly matters to them what we do, provided that they can be seen in our boxes, or that they can drive in our carriages. All around us are ruin, shame and lies. So sometimes I dream, without daring to tell anyone, of meeting a man who would be sufficiently noble to ask me to account for nothing, and to wish to be the lover of my

Olympe, illustration by Gavarni for
The Lady of the Camellias, *1856*

dreams. I found such a man in the Duke; but old age is neither a protection nor a consolation, and my soul has other needs. Then I met you – young, ardent, happy; the tears that you shed for me, the interest you took in my health, your mysterious visits during my illness, your openness, your enthusiasm, led me to see in you everything I have desired from the depth of my loneliness. In an instant, like a madwoman, I built a whole future life on your love; I dreamed of the country, of purity. I recalled my childhood – we all had a childhood, whatever we may have become – I was wishing for the impossible; one word from you proved that . . . You wanted to know everything. Now you do.

ARMAND: Do you think that after such a speech I could leave you? Do we run away when fortune comes to greet us? No, Marguerite, no; your dream will be fulfilled I swear. Don't ask for reasons, we are young, we love each other, let us go forward following our love.

MARGUERITE: Do not deceive me, Armand; remember that a violent emotion could kill me; remember who I am, and what I am.

ARMAND: You are an angel, and I love you!

Alexandre Dumas *fils*
from Act III *of* The Lady of the Camellias, *1852*

MARGUERITE: My God, yes. I'm listening.

DUVAL: You are ready to sacrifice everything for my son. But if he accepts yours, what equivalent sacrifice could he offer in return? He will take the best years of your life and when he has had enough – as he will – what then? Either he will behave like most men do: he will throw your past in your face and leave you, saying that he's just doing what others would do; or he'll do the decent thing and marry you, or at least keep you with him. This liaison, or this marriage with neither chastity as a foundation nor religion as a support, nor a family as a result, may be excusable in a young man – but in a man of mature years? What ambitions can he cherish? What career will be open to him? What consolation will my son be to me, after spending twenty years trying to make him happy? Your relationship is not the fruit of two spirits, nor the union of two innocent natures; it is a passion of the most earthly and human kind, born of the caprice of one of you and the fantasy of the other. What will be left when you both grow old? Who can say that the first wrinkle on your brow will not tear the veil from his eyes, and that his dream will not fade with your youth?

MARGUERITE: Oh! Reality!

DUVAL: Can you imagine your old age together, doubly deserted, doubly isolated, doubly useless? What will be remembered about you? What good will you have done? You and my son must follow

Marguerite's sister, illustration by Gavarni for
The Lady of the Camellias, *1856*

two completely different paths: chance brought you together for a moment, but reason must part you forever. In the life you have chosen, you cannot see what will happen. You have been happy for three months, but this happiness cannot last; lock the memory away in your heart; it will give you strength – and that is all that you have the right to ask of it. One day, you will be proud of what you have done and all your life you will keep your self-esteem. It is as a man of the world that I address you, as a father that I beg you. Come, Marguerite! Prove to me that you truly love my son – and be brave!

MARGUERITE: (*to herself*) Whatever she may do, a fallen woman can never redeem herself! Perhaps God will pardon her, but the world never will. And, in all fairness, by what right do you think you can take the place in the heart of a family which virtue alone may occupy? You are in love – so what? That's no reason.

Armand's sister, illustration by Gavarni for
The Lady of the Camellias, *1856*

However much you might prove your love, no one will ever believe you, and fair enough. Who are you to talk of love or the future? What kind of new words are these? Just look at the mire of your past! What man would want to call you his wife? What child would want to call you his mother?

(*To* M. DUVAL) Everything you say to me is true, Sir; I've said it all to myself, in fear, many times. But because I was the only one to say it, I didn't hear myself through. You say the same thing to me, so I have to believe it; I must obey. You speak to me in the name of your son, in the name of your daughter – and it is only right that you should invoke their names. Well, Sir, one day will you tell this beautiful and pure young woman – because it is for her that I wish to sacrifice my happiness – that somewhere there is a woman who had only one hope, one thought, one dream in this world, and that at the mention of her name, this woman gave it all up, broke her own heart and died as a result ... for I shall die, Sir, and then, perhaps, God will pardon me.

Alexandre Dumas *fils*
from The Lady of the Camellias, *1848*

Armand stopped just short of the grave to wipe his face which was streaming with large drops of perspiration. I took advantage of the halt to catch my breath, for I myself felt as though my heart was being squeezed in a vice.

Why is it that we should find a mixture of pain and pleasure in sights of this kind? By the time we reached the grave, the gardener had taken the pots of flowers away, the iron railings had been removed and two men were digging with picks.

Armand leaned against a tree and watched.

The whole of his life seemed to be concentrated in those eyes of his.

Suddenly, one of the picks grated on a stone.

At the sound, Armand recoiled as though from an electric shock, and he grasped my hand with such strength that he hurt me.

One gravedigger took a wide shovel and little by little emptied the grave; when there remained only the stones which are always used to cover the coffin, he threw them out one by one.

I kept an eye on Armand, for I was afraid that his sensations, which he was visibly repressing, might get the better of him at any moment; but he went on watching, his eyes fixed and staring like a madman's, and a slight twitching of the cheeks and lips was the only indication of a violent nervous crisis.

For my own part, I can say only one thing: that I regretted having come.

When the coffin was completely exposed, the superintendent said to the gravediggers:

'Open it up.'

The men obeyed, as though it were the most ordinary thing in the world.

The coffin was made of oak, and they set about unscrewing the upper panel which served as a lid. The dampness of the earth had rusted the screws, and it was not without considerable effort that the coffin was opened. A foul odour emerged, despite the aromatic herbs with which it had been strewn.

'Dear God! Dear God!' Armand murmured, and he grew paler than ever.

The gravediggers themselves stepped back a pace.

A large white winding-sheet covered the corpse and partly outlined its misshapen contours. This shroud had been completely eaten away at one end, and allowed one of the dead woman's feet to protrude.

I was very near to feeling sick, and even now as I write these lines, the memory of this scene comes back to me in all its solemn reality.

'Let's get on with it,' said the superintendent.

At this, one of the men reached out his hand, began unstitching the shroud and, seizing it by one end, suddenly uncovered Marguerite's face.

It was terrible to behold and it is horrible to relate.

The eyes were simply two holes, the lips had gone, and the white teeth were clenched. The long, dry, black hair was stuck over the temples and partly veiled the green hollows of the cheeks, and yet in this face I recognized the pink and white, vivacious face which I had seen so often.

Armand, helpless to avert his eyes from her countenance, had put his handkerchief to his mouth and was biting on it.

As for me, I felt as though my head was being constricted by an iron band: a mist settled over my eyes, my ears were filled with buzzing noises, and it was as much as I could manage to open a small bottle I had brought with me just in case, and take deep breaths of the salts which it contained.

At the height of my dizziness, I heard the superintendent say to Monsieur Duval:

'Do you identify the body?'

'Yes,' the young man answered dully.

'All right, close it up and take it away,' the superintendent said.

The gravediggers pulled the shroud back over the dead woman's face, closed up the coffin, took one end each and headed for the spot which had been pointed out to them.

Armand did not move. His eyes were riveted on the empty grave: he was as pale as the corpse which we had just seen . . . He might have been turned to stone.

I saw what would happen when, away from this scene, his grief subsided and would consequently be no longer able to sustain him.

I went up to the superintendent.

'Is the presence of this gentleman', I said, gesturing towards Armand, 'required for anything else?'

'No,' he said, 'and I would strongly advise you to take him away, for he seems to be unwell.'

'Come,' I said to Armand, taking him by the arm.

'What?' he said, looking at me as though he did not recognize me.

'It's over,' I added, 'you must come away, my friend. You look pale, you're cold, you'll kill yourself with such emotions.'

So I took him by the arm and dragged him away.

He allowed himself to be led off like a little child, merely muttering from time to time:

'Did you see the eyes?'

And he turned round as though the sight of them had called him back.

But his stride became jerky; he no longer seemed capable of walking without staggering; his teeth chattered, his hands were cold, violent nervous convulsions took possession of his entire body.

I spoke to him; he did not reply.

It was as much as he could do to allow himself to be led.

At the gate, we found a cab. And none too soon.

He had scarcely sat down inside, when the trembling grew stronger, and he had a severe nervous seizure. Through it, his fears of alarming me made him murmur as he pressed my hand:

'It's nothing, nothing, I simply want to weep.'

And I heard him take deep breaths, and the blood rushed to his eyes, but the tears would not come.

I made him inhale from the smelling bottle which had helped me and, by the time we reached his apartment, only the trembling was still in evidence.

I put him to bed with the help of his servant, ordered a large fire to be lit in his bedroom, and hurried off to fetch my own doctor to whom I explained what had just happened.

He came at once.

Armand was blue in the face. He was raving and stammering disconnected words through which only the name of Marguerite could be distinctly heard.

'How is he?' I asked the doctor when he had examined the patient.

'Well now, he has brain fever, no more and no less, and it's as well for him. For I do believe that otherwise, God forgive me, he would have gone mad. Fortunately, his physical sickness will drive out his mental sickness, and most likely in a month he will be out of danger from both of them.'

The letter which Alexandre Dumas wrote to Marie Duplessis breaking off their affair.

Théophile Gautier
Camélia et Pâquerette
from Émaux et Camées, *1852*

On admire les fleurs de serre
Qui loin de leur soleil natal,
Comme des joyaux mis sous verre,
Brillent sous un ciel de cristal.

Sans que les brises les effleurent
De leurs baisers mystérieux,
Elles naissent, vivent et meurent
Devant le regard curieux.

A l'abri de murs diaphanes,
De leur sein ouvrant le trésor,
Comme de belles courtisanes,
Elles se vendent à prix d'or.

La porcelaine de la Chine
Les reçoit par groupes coquets,
Ou quelque main gantée et fine
Au bal les balance en bouquets.

Mais souvent parmi l'herbe verte,
Fuyant les yeux, fuyant les doigts,
De silence et d'ombre couverte,
Une fleur vit au fond des bois.

Un papillon blanc qui voltige,
Un coup d'œil au hasard jeté,
Vous fait surprendre sur sa tige
La fleur dans sa simplicité.

Belle de sa parure agreste
S'épanouissant au ciel bleu,
Et versant son parfum modeste
Pour la solitude et pour Dieu.

Sans toucher à son pur calice
Qu'agite un frisson de pudeur,
Vous respirez avec délice
Son âme dans sa fraîche odeur.

Et tulipes au port superbe,
Camélias si cher payés,
Pour la petite fleur sous l'herbe,
En un instant, sont oubliés!

The Camellia and the Daisy, *1852*

We admire the hothouse flowers which, far from their native sun, like jewels set under glass, shine beneath a crystal sky.

No breezes lightly touch them with their mysterious kiss; they are born, they live and die before the gaze of curious eyes.

Sheltered by diaphanous walls displaying the treasure held within, they sell themselves for riches, like lovely courtesans.

Charming clusters stand arrayed in Chinese porcelain, or from some gloved and dainty hand a ballroom posy swings.

But oft amid the grass so green, withdrawn from sight and fingers' touch, deep in the woods there lurks a flower, hid in silence and in shadow.

A fluttering white butterfly, an idle skimming glance, and you'll discover all at once the flower's stemmed simplicity.

Beautiful in its rustic finery, it opens to the azure sky, shedding its modest fragrance for God and solitude.

Though your hand comes not near the calix so pure, which modesty causes to tremble, with delight you will drink in the soul that is lodged in its scented freshness.

And tulips of mien superb, camellias dearly bought, are forgotten in a moment, for the little flower in the grass!

George Sand
from the Preface to the second edition of Indiana, *1842*

George Sand (1804–76) was the pen-name of Aurore Dupin, descended on her father's side from the Maréchale de Saxe, and brought up by her mother and paternal grandmother. Married at eighteen to Casimir Dudevant, she had many lovers including Alfred de Musset and an eight-year affair with Frédéric Chopin. In her first novel, Indiana *(1831), she frequently intervenes in the narrative, and her preface to the second edition indicates her belief in politically* engagé *literature, referring to the 'prostitution jurée'*

Indiana by Charpentier, engraved by Robinson

of marriage without divorce. Her reworking of Manon Lescaut *in which the man is the amoral protagonist is* Léone Léoni (1842). *A passionate republican, she took an active part in politics in 1848, and continued during the Second Empire to be the most influential French woman writer of her time, with 60 novels, 25 plays produced in Paris, 26 short stories, a long autobiography and some 16,000 letters. She shared this taste for the moral and social purpose of writing with Alexandre Dumas* fils *but it was with Flaubert that she had her most revealing correspondence, discussing questions of gender and sexual stereotypes, and the status of women as artists and scholars.*

Thus I repeat, I wrote *Indiana*, and I had to write it; I yielded to a powerful, God-given instinct of grievance and reproach – God who creates nothing without purpose, not even the meanest of beings, and who intervenes in the smallest of matters as well as the greatest. But what's that? Was what I was defending so small? It is that of one half of the human race, it is that of the entire human race; for woman's unhappiness leads to that of man, as that of the slave leads to that of the master, and I tried to show this in *Indiana*. I was told that it was an individual cause that I was pleading; as if, supposing that I was moved by personal feelings, I had been the only being to suffer in a radiant and peaceful society! Enough cries of grief and sympathy replied to mine for me to think now that I do know where the supreme happiness of others lies.

I do not believe that I have ever written anything under the influence of an egotistical passion: I have never dreamt of even protesting against such a thing. Those who have read my work without prejudice will understand that I wrote *Indiana* with an albeit hastily thought-out, but deep and legitimate, sense of the injustice and barbarity of the laws which still govern the existence of women in marriage, in the family and in society. It was not my intention to draw up a treatise on jurisprudence, but to campaign against opinion; for that is what holds back or promotes improvements in society. The war will be long and hard; but I am neither the first, nor the only, nor the last champion of such a fine cause, and I will defend it so long as there is a breath of life in me.

Thus I have thought through and developed the feeling which drove me at the start, in response to the blame and attacks I have received for it. The unjust or malicious criticisms taught me a deal more than the calm of impunity could reveal to me. For this, I am grateful to the blundering judges who enlightened me. The motives for their attacks have shone a bright light on my own thinking and left me feeling sound in my judgement. A true intelligence profits from everything, and what would discourage vanity redoubles the ardour of dedication.

These reproaches, addressed by me to the greater part of the journalists of my day, from the bottom of a heart now calm and sure, should not be seen in any way as a protest against the freedom of the French press invested in it by public morals. It is obvious to everyone that the press often badly fulfils and still misunderstands its mission in modern society; but no one can deny that the mission in itself is providential and sacred, at least unless they do not believe in progress, unless they are the enemy of truth, the blasphemer of the future, and an unworthy child of France. Freedom to think, freedom to write and to speak – revered accomplishment of the human spirit! What are the petty sufferings and ephemeral cares caused by your errors and abuses when weighed against the infinite benefits which you promote for the world?

George Sand
from the Preface to The Devil's Pond, *1846*

We believe that the mission of art is a mission of feeling and love, that today's novel should replace the parable and the apologia of more naive times, and that the artist has a wider and more poetic task than to offer a measure of prudence and conciliation to soften the horror which his paintings inspire. His aim should be to make objects lovable by his care for them, and I would not reproach him if he finds it necessary to embellish them a little. Art is not a study of positive reality; it is a search for an ideal truth, and *The Vicar of Wakefield* was a more useful and healthier book for the soul than *Le Paysan perverti* or *Les Liaisons dangereuses*.

Marceline Desbordes-Valmore
Amour, 1843

Marceline Desbordes-Valmore (1786–1859) was born into a working-class family in Douai. She had no formal schooling. When her father went bankrupt in 1797, her mother took her as an actress around France and to Guadeloupe, where her mother died. For the next twenty years she toured with her actor husband as an actress and singer. In 1823 she became a full-time writer, and eventually wrote three novels, fifty stories and much poetry. She won many admirers, including Hugo, Lamartine, Baudelaire and Sainte-Beuve. Verlaine included her on his list of 'poètes maudits'.

This poem was first published in Bouquets et Prières *in 1843, and the author dedicated a copy to Alexandre Dumas. He replied in these terms: 'My dear and good sister, I received your letter at 4 p.m. By 5 p.m., my son and I had read it. You have never written anything more attractive. You are the only woman who writes poetry like angels should when God tells them to smile and pray in turn.'*

Marceline Desbordes-Valmore

Que sais-tu, cher ingrat, quand tu ris de mes larmes,
Quand tu les fais couler sous tes mordantes armes,
Que sais-tu qui des deux joue au fort entre nous,
Toi superbe et railleur, moi pliée à genoux?
Que sais-tu, pauvre enfant, lorsque tu me méprises,
Si ce n'est pas un peu de ton cœur que tu brises,
Et, si tu n'iras pas quelque jour réclamer
Cette part à ma cendre, étonné de m'aimer?
Car, tu ne t'en vas pas enfin quand je t'en prie:
Que veux-tu? que sais-tu, fier de ta moquerie,
Si tu n'outrages pas ton Dieu pleurant en moi
Triste dans sa grandeur d'être raillé par toi?

Oh! n'as-tu donc jamais sur ma frêle figure,
Vu passer entre nous un lumineux augure,
Quand je creuse mon âme à chercher, inhumain,
Le fil mystérieux qui suspend dans ta main
Cette âme, pauvre oiseau dont tu serres les ailes,
Et qui les voit tomber sans descendre après elles,
Comme heureuse, après tout, de perdre le pouvoir
D'échapper à son sort : Aimer, pleurer; te voir!

Dis toi-même: où va-t-on, devancée et suivie
D'une image, une seule attachée à sa vie?
Où fuir, alors que, cher et fatal à la fois,
Un seul mot d'une voix couvre toutes les voix!

On s'est connu si jeune! on s'est dit tant de choses!
On a vu se lever tant de jours, tant de roses,
Tant de soleils sereins se promener aux cieux,
Vous regardant ensemble et les yeux sur les yeux!
Tu n'y songes donc pas: ces tendres habitudes,
Ces soucis partagés, ces rêveuses études,
Ces printemps tout chargés d'éclairs, de fleurs, de miel,
A toi c'était la vie à moi, c'était le ciel!

Hélas, avant la mort d'où vient que je te pleure?
De nos doux rendez-vous qui donc a manqué l'heure?
Le temps va comme il veut; l'amour s'est arrêté;
Ne me reviendras-tu que dans l'éternité!

Love

How do you know, ungrateful beloved, when you laugh at my tears, when you make them flow with your sharp-edged words, how do you know which of us fights most fiercely, you proud and mocking, I on my knees? How do you know, poor child, when you spurn me, that it isn't a part of your own heart you are breaking, and that one day you may reclaim that part from my ashes, astonished to find you love me?

For after all, you do not leave me when I beg you to: what is it you want? How do you know, proud mocker, that you do not outrage your God weeping within me, sad in His greatness to be jeered at by you?

Oh! Are you so inhuman that you have never seen a shining warning cross my weary face as I plough my soul to seek the mysterious thread by which this soul hangs from your hand? It is a poor bird, whose wings you hold fast and who watches them fall without following them, content, after all, to lose the power to escape its fate: to love, to weep; to see you!

Tell me yourself: where does a person go whose life is bound to one vision alone, going before her and pursuing her? Where should she flee when a single voice, at once beloved and fatal, obliterates all voices?

We were so young when we met! And we said so many things! We saw so many dawns together, so many roses, so many suns in cloudless skies, gazing at each other, our eyes on each other! So you do not dream of them – those tender ways, those shared thoughts, that dream-like contemplation, those springtimes of lightning-flashes, of flowers and of honey: for you it was life, for me it was heaven!

Alas, why should I weep for you before you die? Which of us neglects our sweet rendezvous? Time passes as it will; love has ceased; will you only come back to me in eternity!

Je pleure . . . allons, va-t-en. Du haut de ma fenêtre,
Je vais te voir passer: je vais te reconnaître
De ce beau temps d'alors; et puis, comme autrefois,
Crier à Dieu: Mon Dieu! vivre est beau: je le vois!

Ne ris pas. Va courir à ton ombre, la gloire;
Va repeupler ton coeur qui n'a pas de mémoire;
Va, mais pour t'excuser ne jette rien sur moi:
Je suis à ce détour plus savante que toi.

Avant de te blesser je me tuerais moi-même;
Je trouve des raisons; j'en invente: je t'aime!
C'est le sort et le cœur qui t'a mal arrêté,
S'immole pour t'absoudre et saigne à ton côté.

L'amour vrai, tiens, c'est Dieu remontant au calvaire.
J'ai lu dans un beau livre, humble, grand et sévère,
Dont l'esprit devant toi me relève aujourd'hui:
'L'Eternel mit la femme entre le monde et lui.'

Moi, je suis une femme aussi comme ta mère!
Elle me défendrait de ton insulte amère:
Plus grand que son amour, mon amour se donna!
Une femme aima trop, et Dieu lui pardonna.

Crois donc que pour aimer il faut un grand courage;
Que rester immobile au pied d'un tel orage,
Ce n'est point lâcheté, comme tu dis toujours:
C'est attendre la mort sans disputer ses jours;
C'est accomplir un vœu, fait au bord de l'enfance,
De ne rendre jamais l'offense pour l'offense;
C'est acheter longtemps, par pleurs et par pitié,
Une âme, qu'on voulut pour soeur et pour moitié,
Une chère âme, au monde et donnée et perdue,
Et qui par une autre âme, au ciel sera rendue!

Ainsi, crois à l'amour. Il est plus fort que toi:
S'il vit seul, s'il attend, s'il pardonne, c'est moi.

Alors comme toujours, elle parlait en rêve;
Toujours le rêve étrange et pur et triste: un jour,
On l'entendit trembler comme un chant qui s'achève;
Puis il ne chanta plus. Moi je l'écris: AMOUR!

I'm weeping . . . so leave me. From my high window I will see you pass: I will recognize you from those happy days gone by; and then, as before, cry to God: 'My God! to live is beautiful, I can see him!'

Don't laugh. Go, run after your shadow, after glory! Go, find new cares for that heart whose memory fails it; go, but when you seek excuses, don't blame me: I am more expert in that than you.

I would kill myself before hurting you; I would find reasons; invent them: I love you! That is fate, and the heart which has caused you pain absolves you by its own self-destruction and bleeds by your side.

True love, let us say it, is God ascending once more to the cross. I read in a beautiful book, humble, great and severe, whose ideas raise me up today before you: 'The Eternal places woman between the world and Himself.'

I, I am a woman just as your mother is! She would protect me from your bitter insults: greater than her love, my love gave itself! A woman loved too much, and God forgave her.

So believe that it needs great courage to love; that to stay unmoving in such a storm is not cowardly, as you always say; it is to wait for death without arguing when it should come; it is to fulfil a vow made when still a child, never to render hurt for hurt; it is to buy a soul with tears and with pity, over days and years, a soul desired as a sister and as the half of oneself, a dear soul, both given and lost to the world, and which will be sent back to heaven by another soul!

So, have faith in love. It is stronger than you: if it lives alone, if it waits, if it pardons, it is I.

So, as always, she spoke in a dream; always the same strange dream, both pure and sad: one day it was heard with a tremor like that of a song rising to its end; then it was heard no more. But I write its name: LOVE!

George Sand
from a letter to her son Maurice, 1850

Marriage without love, that is life imprisonment ... I understood you to say not long ago that you did not think yourself capable of loving for ever, and that you could not answer for yourself ever being faithful in marriage. Do not get married in that frame of mind, for you will be cuckolded and you will have deserved it. You will have at your side a brutalized victim, or else a jealous fury, or a fool you will despise. When we are in love, we are convinced that we will be faithful. We can easily be mistaken but we believe it, we make vows in good faith, and we are happy as long as we persist with it. If exclusive love is impossible for life (which has not been proved to me) at least let there be some beautiful years when we think it possible ... The day when I see you sure of yourself, I will be content ...

George Sand by Charpentier, engraved by Robinson

Jules Michelet
Love, *1858*

She does nothing as we do. She thinks, speaks, acts differently. Her tastes differ from our tastes. Her blood has not the same rate as ours, at moments it rushes, like a storm shower. She does not breathe as we do. Anticipating pregnancy and the future ascent of the lower organs, nature has caused her to breathe mainly by the four upper ribs. From this necessity results woman's greatest beauty, the gentle undulation of the breast, which expresses all her sentiments in a mute eloquence.

She does not eat as we do, or as much, or the same dishes. Why? Chiefly because she does not digest as we do. Her digestion is troubled at every moment by one thing: she loves, from the very depth of her bowels. The deep cup of love (which we call the pelvis) is a sea of variable emotions which counter the regularity of the nutritive functions.

These internal differences are produced externally by yet another, more striking one: woman has a language of her own. Insects and fish remain mute. The bird sings. It seeks to articulate. Man has a distinct language, an exact and luminous speech, the clarity of the word. But woman, above man's word and the song of the bird, has an entirely magical language with which she interrupts that word or that song: the sigh, her impassioned breath.

Incalculable power. No sooner is it felt than our heart is stirred. Her breast rises, sinks, rises again: she cannot speak, and we are convinced in advance, won over to all she wishes. What argument of a man's will act so powerfully as a woman's silence?

... And if there must be a chambermaid for other delicate attentions, I shall offer you one who eagerly aspires to the position, who has a hundred times more enthusiasm than Mademoiselle Julie, than Mademoiselle Lisette and all the celebrated examples of the type, and one who furthermore is not sly, who will never gossip about you to the neighbours, who will not grimace behind your back when you are speaking, etc.

— But where is this treasure to be found? I shall hire her, she is what I need . . .

— Where is she? At your side.

Here is your subject, O queen, who petitions to enter into your service; he believes he has been promoted if you raise him to the dignity of *valet de chambre*, to the feudal position of Chamberlain, Chief Domestic, Grand Master of your house, or indeed, Physician-in-ordinary (at least with regard to hygiene), for his zeal knows no limits. All these court duties he will accomplish *gratis*, and in addition, along with the functions of men, he will execute those of women, proud and honoured, madame, if Your Majesty will accept his very humble services.

Charles Baudelaire
from Intimate Diaries: My Heart Laid Bare, *1862–4, LV*

In love, as in almost all human affairs, harmony is the result of a misunderstanding. This misunderstanding concerns pleasure. The man shouts: 'O my angel!' The woman coos: 'Maman! Maman!' And these two fools feel that they think as one. – The unbridgeable gulf, from whence derives the incommunicable, remains unbridged.

Louise Colet
Him, *1869*

I will not therefore define love but I have experienced it very completely in my heart, in my mind and my senses and I assure you that it scarcely resembles the descriptions penned and the hypocritical avowals made by many women; very few dare to be forthright on this subject; they fear to seem shameless and I believe, pardon my pride, it is only the most honest who tell the truth on this matter: love is not a misery, love is not a matter of remorse or mourning; it can provoke all that through the agony of a rupture, but at the moment when it is felt and shared, one's whole being opens up and the heart is filled with joy and courage.

Hilary Spurling
A Nice Reflection

Hilary Spurling is a writer and critic.

Reading *La Dame aux camélias* for the first time, nearly one and a half centuries after it was written, is a disconcerting experience. The story was, as its narrator insists, closely based on a true one. The young Dickens and the young Dumas both thought of writing it up at the time. In Dumas's version (begun four months after his heroine died in fact), the fiction becomes a flattering glass designed to reflect society in the softest and most forgiving light. Practically everyone in it behaves impeccably, especially Marguerite herself, Armand, and Armand's noble, kindly and upright old father (a far cry from the real Dumas *père*).

On the face of it, the story might not seem particularly edifying today. Twentieth-century readers have been schooled to feel less optimistic about the original case history which disclosed a neglected, abused and sexually exploited child, probably already at the age of twelve being offered to other men by her own father, selling herself to the highest bidder in Paris by the time she was sixteen, and dying almost before she was into her twenty-third year of a disease fatally connected with her promiscuous lifestyle. Dumas's readers are invited to feel pretty comfortable about their own intrinsic superiority to women like Marguerite. She represents, after all, a section of society that can safely be written off as both morally and physically sick: 'souls that bleed from wounds oozing with the evil of their past, like infected blood from a sick body . . . '

Images like this one sound horribly familiar today. What is disconcerting is the story's upbeat tone. It is not only the readers who are to be congratulated. So are Armand and his father for having each, in his different way, ruthlessly exploited Marguerite. She herself claims to count her life well lost for the privilege of being wept over by Duval *père* ('On my forehead I felt two tears ... which were ... the waters of baptism which washed away my former sins'). All parties prove in the end a credit to themselves, including Armand's respectably married sister – 'young, beautiful and as pure as an angel' – for whose sake Marguerite agrees to sacrifice herself, and whose life would be irretrievably smirched if she ever so much as heard Marguerite's name mentioned.

It comes as no surprise to learn that Dumas himself was an insecure, illegitimate child, and had been made to suffer cruelly for it when young. At bottom his myth of a fallen woman is obscured by the equally alluring, equally artificial dream of respectability, solidity and spotless bourgeois virtue embodied in the Duval family. They live in the country, which is where Marguerite and Armand enact their brief improbable idyll during which she skips about the garden chasing butterflies like a ten-year-old, and sits for hours on end enraptured by a daisy on the lawn. Slugs have no place in this garden, any more than on the florist's flowers from which she takes her name. Marguerite is, like her own camellias, expensive, exquisite, immaculately groomed, on sale nightly, and always dewy fresh again next morning.

There is, admittedly, a worm in her bud, or rather a whole can of worms, but it is a can Dumas has no intention whatsoever of opening up. On the contrary, the whole point of this story is to leave its readers reassured and strengthened, like the inquisitive Parisians on the day of Marguerite's death sale, who come crowding into her apartment to go through her things, finger her toiletries, have a good poke about in her bedroom, and go home feeling all the better for their ordeal.

Nicole Ward Jouve
The Purloined Necklace
How the necklace of the Lady of the Camellias ended around the neck of a woman of duty, or how what looks like a story about women is a story about men but ends up being a story about women after all.

Nicole Ward Jouve, novelist and literary critic, teaches in the Department of English and Related Literature in the University of York, and divides her time between France and the UK.

The first gift of Dumas *fils* to Marie Duplessis: a necklace. A modest gift, such as the young man could afford: the gold links of a man's watch-chain, and pearls to make them fit for a

Jeannine Dumas, aged forty, wearing the necklace of the Lady of the Camellias

woman. After Marie's death, when all her possessions were being auctioned by her creditors, the young man went to the sale. He bought the necklace. Years later, he was to give it to his second daughter, Jeannine. A photograph, reproduced in Maurice d'Hartoy's *Dumas fils inconnu ou le collier de la Dame aux camélias* (Paris, 1964), shows her wearing it. She was a very respectable young woman, and became more so as she went along. She married a Monsieur de Hauterive and took his name, she was a heroic nurse during the First World War, she received the Legion of Honour. She died and was buried in 1943. Her biographer, the editor of her letters from her father, adds that an unknown hand placed the necklace of the Lady of the Camellias on her grave.

What was that for?

To signify that what most graced Jeannine was her fidelity to her father, her father's story, the story of the Lady of the Camellias?

Or that the only interest of Jeannine, as indeed of Dumas *fils*, arose from that one moment of grace, Dumas's love for Marie Duplessis? That Marie was what made them significant, that the only noteworthy thing about Dumas *fils* had been that he immortalized her?

Or that the Lady of the Camellias, though she died childless, at twenty-three, had after all had a daughter – a posthumous daughter – and that the necklace had passed on through the women, as is fitting. Jeannine acknowledged her inheritance by wearing the necklace, and became the living emblem of vanished Marie: the necklace belonged to her tomb.

Or yet again, that Jeannine had become the embodiment of the aborted dreams of both Marie and Dumas. Of Dumas, because she reached the respectable, the solid, the upper classes that the ageing playwright, now enamoured of middle-class virtues, championed, writing against prostitution, against immorality, praising domesticity. Of Marie also: for Marie had been upwardly mobile. She had changed her plebeian name of Alphonsine Plessis. She had been self-taught, rising in a few years from the virtually illiterate fifteen-year-old who had been pandered by a debauched father, to be the elegant, witty, tasteful young woman with a fine turn of phrase who was fit company for dukes, whom a Comte had married. But that had been in England; it had never been quite legal. Jeannine de Hauterive, with her thoroughly official marriage, reached not to the demi-monde, but to the upper class: and what a name, 'of High Bank', for a girl who had been born just within marriage! Her elder sister was illegitimate, since Dumas *fils* married her mother, Princess Naryshkine, only after her husband's death. He himself had been illegitimate, his father never having married his mother Catherine Labay, a grisette like Alphonsine Plessis must have been. The name 'Dumas' derived from the first illegitimate birth, the first Alexandre, the grandfather, later to become one of Napoleon's generals and the father of Alexandre Dumas *père*. Dumas was the surname of his mother, Marie Dumas, a black slave woman. One Marie, already . . . Four generations and a century later, a daughter at last made it to a proper particle, a genuine 'de', de Hauterive after all these aborted 'du': Dumas, Duplessis . . .

They say that the pearls of the necklace faded when Marie died. She was so young, she had been terrified of death, had clung to the hand of her faithful maid – in a last convulsion of youth, at the point of death, she had stood up, and screamed. Was it then that the pearls faded? All the brilliance of the story comes from her. The shimmer vanishes as you move away from her, from the diamonds and flowers and loves of the demi-monde towards what after all can only be called 'le monde' . . . It is her grave on which people continue to heap flowers, white flowers, not on that of Dumas *fils*, his lying-in statue bizarrely arrayed in a monk's robe less than two hundred yards from hers . . .

Yet, if you look at him, through whose words she is remembered, you find a story that seems to have more to do with men than with women.

Take his daughter for instance.

He wished she had been a son.

'If you ever have a son,' Dumas *père* wrote to him, 'don't bring him up as I brought you up.' Was it because he wished he could do for a son what his father had never done for him that Dumas *fils* so wished to have a son? His father was a gorgeous man: genial, splendid, expansive, generous, immensely successful. Self-centred, bent on success, ambitious, a womanizer. A 'prodigal father', he aptly called him, one whom you cannot help but forgive because he is so lovable, so wonderful . . . Yet you can never make up for bad fathering. If anyone ever did, surely Dumas *père*, with his beaming encouragement and munificence, did. But he could not heal the scars of the rough treatment of the irate young father he had been, who wanted to write in a garret and was disturbed by his baby's cries, who abandoned the young mother and married a capricious and unloving mistress in her place, who forcibly removed the boy from his mother's custody and unthinkingly put him in an eccentric boarding-school where he was bullied. Biographers tell of a dream Dumas *fils* had, many years on, long after his father had removed him from that evil school, looked after him, given him bountiful allowance, made him his boon companion and confidant: staying in the same room as his father, Dumas *fils* dreamt he was murdering him. And so strong was the urge to do so when he woke up that he had to get up and leave.

Dumas *père* was dissolute, if a charmer. He had a string of mistresses. It is said he shared some with his son when his son first began to live with him. He boasted he had had a kiss from Marie Duplessis.

Mystery number one: why would the son, who knew him, who half-loved half-hated him, make him into the benign yet stern patriarchal father of *The Lady of the Camellias*, the embodiment of Duty who, in the name of a pure and virginal daughter, appeals to Marguerite Gautier to let go of his son? It is well known that Dumas *fils* left Marie Duplessis because he could not keep up with the pace of expenditure that she set. Why invent the fatherly intervention in a story that spurted all at once, written over less than three weeks in the emotional wake of Marie's death, in the forest of Saint-Germain, where they had been happy? A story that is, by his own admission, profoundly autobiographical?

Mystery number two: why should he invent that he was at his beloved's bedside as she lay dying, instead of miles away in Marseilles? This is not so hard to unravel: it was an emotional and dramatic requirement.

But why invent a virtuous father? Was it to protect his father from identification through disguise? One laughs at the very hypothesis. Dumas *père* revelled in publicity. Was it because a fatherly intervention helped set up the drama? There is more truth in that. Indeed the father's intervention which is only discovered at the end of the novel, posthumously revealing Marguerite's nobility through her diary, becomes the crux of the play and the centrepiece of the opera: it turns a happy romance into a tragedy. It stops the story from becoming a kind of *Adolphe*, where love leads to weariness, where the lover wastes his life-chances on a mistress who has alienated him from respectable society, and who goes on desperately loving him after his love has faded. You could also say, following that line of thought, that the father becomes the Commendatore in *Don Giovanni* intoning the Law of the city, of respectable society against he or she who dares defy it. This is the great battle between Mme de Staël's Corinne and Lord Neville's father. The Will of the Father will have its way. None can stand against it. Add to this Marguerite's self-sacrifice, when she pretends to become a *traviata* again: in fact she has become a genuine Marie, who readily answers the messenger's call, conceives her own death so that a Son shall be saved, gives up her beloved for the salvation if not of mankind at least of the Family. The Madonna and the Magdalen are effectively merged, pitted against/loving the Father whose fatherly kiss-on-the-forehead is quite unlike the kiss with which Marie Duplessis surprised Dumas *père*. A pretty good dramatic concoction. Yes, the invention of the virtuous father, you could argue, is a piece of dramatic genius.

Yet I think that it came for other reasons too. The father's intervention ennobled the affair. It meant that the lovers did not separate because of money (as they had), or because Marie was not sufficiently in love with Dumas *fils* (some biographers say that she was much more in love with Liszt, later, than she had ever been with young Dumas). Deeply moved by her death, by that ghastly reburial he had attended, when he had seen Marie already decomposed, young Dumas could dream up an absolute love thanks to an imagined interfering father. He needed the father for that. He also needed him because he had always needed him. Because he had spent his boyhood dreaming of the possibility of such a father. Inventing him, he fulfilled his dream as, reinventing Marie through Marguerite, he fulfilled his dream of her love. He also fulfilled his hate. For it was the father's fault if Armand Duval lost Marguerite Gautier. As once the father had thrown the screaming baby violently on to a bed, as the father had forcibly separated the young boy from his loving mother, so Duval *père*, later Germont, treacherously becomes the undoer of both Armand and Marguerite. And the swine does it again: he so embodies duty, speaking for the Pure Daughter and making kindly noises to the spurned Marguerite, that you cannot even hate him for all the harm he does. Just as Dumas *fils* could not hate his swine of a father for all the harm he had done him, because he could also be so wonderful and such fun.

If Dumas *fils* had had a son he would have known how to bring him up.

He had two daughters instead.

And so he decided to treat the second one, Jeannine, as if she had been a boy.

That way everything would be made good.

That way, he reveals how what truly mattered to him was fathers and sons not men and women. (The autobiography of Edmund Gosse, who translated Dumas's novel, is titled *Father and Son*.)

Little Jeannine was barely eight when Dumas *fils* changed her into Janot, Johnnie. He warned her against her nerves. Woe to her if she were ever to turn into a 'demoiselle'. 'What sorrow for me who am so happy to have a boy. It's all very well for that madcap of a Colette' (the elder sister), he added 'to be a woman. As for you, beware of becoming one.' Colette was weak in spirit, had to be encouraged and reasoned with. Janot was to give her sister a manly kiss on her father's behalf: Colette, being who she was, would enjoy being kissed by a man. Dumas congratulated Janot on her 'philosophical bent', and for showing the world 'a soul that is a match, and more than a match, for circumstances and even natural injustice'. He encouraged her to write verse, sent her rhyming models, urged her to study Boileau. Dumas *petit-fils* might be in the making . . . The father was overjoyed when finally, at eleven, Jeannine signed her letters to him 'your son'. She had fulfilled his dearest wish of her own accord. 'Be a man, it is the happiest thing that can befall a woman . . . The more you grow up, the more my son you will be, for I see that you are becoming sensible and serious.' After the birth of Colette, he explains, seeing what a madcap she was, he had asked God for a son. He got a daughter instead, but God told him, 'Take one more daughter, and I promise you she will be as gentle, good and tender as a woman can be and as sensible, brave and hard-working as a man. You will then have a son and a daughter all at once.'

But now the son had prevailed. She could shake hands with Dumas *fils* 'as men do' whilst she kisses his wife and other daughter, who were merely 'weak women'. He asked her/him to put all her/his trust in him, who knew a great deal about life, and to make up for all the bad housekeeping for which her/his mother was responsible: Dumas *fils* was estranged from his wife, he used Janot as a go-between, delegating to her as the other man in the family the duty of looking after the increasingly neglected wife and daughter. He guarded Janot against religion, the Catholic education normally given to her sex and forbade her to sing in church (she had a beautiful voice). Instead he fortified Janot with moral maxims, as a Roman father might have done. He was happy that her 'great good sense' should have enabled her to emerge from that 'inferior sex' in which her sister had remained. He wrote: 'Woman is a circumscribed being, passive, an instrument, always available, in a perpetual state of expectancy. She is the only unfinished work that God allowed Man to take and to complete. She is a castaway angel' (*un ange de rebut* – almost 'a refuse angel').

Those who debate femininity, nature and nurture, might be piqued by this: for Dumas *fils* makes out that women's inferiority is natural, God-given. Man has to finish Woman, to make her complete. And yet, since he can, through education, instil the manly virtues into one daughter, indeed, since God has created her woman-man, a son and a daughter rolled into one, doesn't nature produce its own freaks? Is Dumas *fils* complaining against what women are, or what culture makes them into?

That Jeannine should have accepted to become Janot is not surprising. The bribe was irresistible – she became her father's favourite child. In the game they played, both father and daughter agreed that manhood, or maleness, must be seen as the superior estate. They then both tried to rise up to it. When as a young girl Jeannine eventually fell in love and was disappointed, her father said he was relieved, she was too good, she had to show frailty somewhere: her frailty had been womanly. He reassured her that he loved her, and looked forward to her turning back into a male: 'I kiss you tenderly, my dear Janot, even more so than in the days you were a boy. Become a boy once more as soon as you can, and let me be the first to know.'

What is surprising about this higher evaluation of maleness is that all the evidence in Dumas's own life pointed to the contrary. His mother had had the virtues of order, self-control, domesticity, fortitude, fidelity, that his giant of a father so lacked. His daughter developed all these qualities, while he himself, in his own life, fell short of them, even when he was most extolling them. He, the admirer of mastery over the passions, the apostle of the sanctity of the family, began an affair with, and three months after his wife's death married, Henriette Régnier, forty years younger than himself. Jeannine then said how she regretted not having been the elder child so she could have more 'influence' over her father, adding: 'It is the punishment of those who have loved women too much that they go on loving them for ever.' Both the reaction and the aphorism savour of Dumas *fils*'s own paternal attitude to Dumas *père*: 'My father, this child I had when I was very little' . . . Since it is the woman who shows the self-control, since Dumas *fils* had portrayed a Marguerite ready to make the ultimate sacrifice for her lover, since he had, after all, made his reputation and fortune thanks to his affair with the *Lady of the Camellias*, it is a little surprising that he should come out with statements about 'anges de rebut'.

At any rate, in later life, he needed, and got, his daughter's complicity in fashioning an ideal male model. A fatherly model. This is a story of fathers and sons, continuing over the next generation. That Jeannine should call herself 'your son' meant that he could at last become the father he wished he had had.

The father who had separated him from the Lady of the Camellias?

In the course of that game of pretending to be the wise, the beloved son, the little guardian of mother and sister, the distributor of 'manly' kisses, Jeannine was of course the gainer. She learnt self-control, and was proud of it, she had independence and none of the religious or medical pressures to which girls were subjected. She was allowed neither to be hysterical nor pious. Ironically, she later became a devout Catholic.

Was Dumas *fils*, as he invited her to renounce her sex, asking her for the ultimate sacrifice, rather as Duval *père* asks from Marguerite? Give up your love; give up your sex, and with it perhaps the possibility of love . . . A good thing Jeannine turned out to be so truly sensible, after all: and escaped with her Monsieur de Hauterive . . .

Was it because she had become the son, Dumas *petit-fils* indeed, that Jeannine learnt to cherish the Lady of the Camellias? Her biographer says she wore the necklace 'like a sacred object': it looked like a man's watch-chain . . . Her whole life through she had flowers brought to Marie's grave. Had she become the (male) lover by proxy, the heir to a holy trust?

Or did she – I return to my earlier question – did she wear the necklace as a daughter's heirloom? Was Marie her imaginary mother? And was that the one piece of femininity in a woman who tried so hard to be as full of fortitude and sense as an ideal man?

For it is, when all is said and done, the figure of Marie Duplessis that emerges from this strange crossing of gender: emerges as inescapably and doggedly female.

What a thing to say! And what do I mean? Because of the gear? The camellias? Camellias were the most expensive flower, a sign of wealth, not gender. A Monsieur Latour-Mézeray who always wore one in his button-hole and who, over the years must have spent 50,000 francs on his button-holes alone, was called 'l'homme aux camélias'? The phrase was first used for a man . . .

Do I say, female, because she wore flowers and diamonds and sumptuous frills and necklaces (*Le Collier de la reine, The Queen's Necklace*, of Dumas *père* who also wrote *The Three Musketeers*) because she was bought by men? Is that how you define femaleness?

Well . . . one kind of femaleness, yes. Largely cultural. Not to be advocated, though I own to the fascination, for me, of the glamour and desperation and style. Marie Duplessis was, made herself into, a typically nineteenth-century trope. The courtesan/actress. The one who, as Verlaine put it, 'n'est chaque fois ni tout à fait la même / Ni tout à fait une autre . . . ' – Neither quite the same nor quite another. The one who circulates, between men, between images, identities, names, yet never ceases to be powerfully herself. Alphonsine Marie Marguerite Violetta, in Gosse's translation becomes Camille (on account of the camellias?), and in the meantime Eugénie Doche on stage, and then Rose Chéri and Desclée and Talandiera and Sarah Bernhardt and Eleonora Duse and Edwige Feuillère and Callas and . . . The actresses, the singers get a splendid part from her, give her splendid form. She is youth she is beauty she is seduction she is pleasure she is love she is death. As with Carmen, the speed of the trajectory from youth and passion to death is of the essence of the appeal. But unlike Carmen or Tosca, the living woman, the real Marie, the one whose actual necklace passes on, whose actual body is seen by her ex-lover to be rotting in the earth, whose actual grave is still covered with flowers by crowds of anonymous admirers, survives.

Does she survive thanks to a novel, a play – the opera is already more distantly removed from her – or do the novel, the play, if not the opera, survive because of her? Because she was such a spirited and remarkable and vital person that her magic endures? It is the *truth* of Marie Duplessis's existence, Jules Janin claims in his *Memoir of Marie Duplessis*, that has ensured the survival of a 'futile novel', 'brought out carelessly', 'hardly destined to live a day'. At the end of this story of fathers and sons, would-be fathers and would-be sons, it is Marie – imperial like Tamburlaine the Great with his white, red and black pennants – Marie with her flowers that were white except for five menstruating days in the month when they were red – Marie with all that black at the end – who finally endures. Stage Marie, sitting in her box at the opera – then on stage again – grave swathed in flowers like a Diva – back in her box watching and watched. Life-and-death Marie.

Toril Moi
'I Desire the Law'
La traviata *or the Misguided Daughter*

Toril Moi teaches in the Literature Program of Duke University, North Carolina, and is the author of the Julia Kristeva Reader *(London, 1986).*

In Italian *traviare* means to be misled, or to lead astray, or in other words, to lead off the right road. As it happens, this is the meaning of the English *seduce* and the German *verführen* as well. In Latin *ducere* means to lead, and so does the German *führen*. *Traviamento*, *seduction*, *Verführung*: these words proclaim the

significant link between the question of sexuality and the question
of guidance. But effective guidance is impossible without what
Freud would call positive transference: the pupil must believe that
the teacher possesses the knowledge required for the task. Or, in
other words: she must believe that her teacher is indeed the 'subject supposed to know', the instance that possesses true insight and
wisdom. This, Jacques Lacan argues, is the position of Socrates in
relation to his disciples. Transference is what makes the disciples
love their master: love is indeed the precondition for the process
that leads to wisdom. No wonder that Socrates proclaims that
Eros is just another word for philosophy.

Transference, then, has to do with trust and love, but also with a
rather exaggerated belief in the teacher's capacity for correct
guidance. For if transference is necessary to start the process of
guidance, it is established only to be undone. The aim of the
teacher, after all, is not to produce eternal students, but eventually
to make herself superfluous. Unlike teaching, seduction seeks not
to undo the illusion of knowledge, but to store it up by every available means. To seduce is deliberately to substitute illusion for reality; it is not to teach, but to mislead. In order efficiently to seduce,
one must encourage trust and love, so as to set oneself up as the
subject supposed to know in the eyes of the unsuspecting victim.
The crime of seduction is not only sexual, it is epistemological as
well: Valmont's seduction of Cécile – whom he fondly describes as
his 'pupil' – remains the quintessential example of the genre.

Etymologically speaking, then, *La traviata* is a woman who has
been seduced, led astray, induced to take a wrong turn. If such a
woman is 'fallen', the implication is, it is due to the lack of proper
guidance more than to any intrinsic flaw in her character. Guilty of
gullibility rather than of corruption, Violetta serves as a warning
to fathers and daughters alike. At first glance, however, it may be
hard to square this interpretation with Verdi's opera, where
Violetta appears to be a fallen woman from the start. Yet if
Alfredo wins Violetta's heart it is because he promises not only to
love but to protect her, that is to say, to act like a good father
should. In this sense, he is above all a substitute for his own father:
loving Alfredo, Violetta finds the path to her final filial encounter
with Germont.

In the opera, much more than in Dumas's novel, the father is the incarnation of the Law, the incarnation of reason, compassion and love in their socially acceptable forms. Such an authority figure cannot be mistaken: however stern Germont may be, we – the audience as well as Violetta and Alfredo – know that he is *right*. In this sense, we are all led to believe that Germont is indeed the subject supposed to know: in *La traviata* the victim of seduction is not so much Violetta – after all, her seduction by Alfredo eventually leads to redemption – as we ourselves. Or, to put it differently: the ideological trick of the libretto, powerfully backed up by the music, is to seduce us into accepting its eloquent praise of the power and prestige of the father in nineteenth-century bourgeois ideology.

But *noblesse oblige*: if prostitution flourishes, the opera implies, it is because too many men fail to shoulder their responsibilities towards the pure, but defenceless, women surrounding them. Failing to come across as credible teachers and reliable guides, such men contribute to the corruption of innocent young women. The problem with men, in other words, is that they fail to impose the fiction of their own infallibility on guideless and gullible women. By restricting their attempts at seduction to the crudely sexual, in other words, they fail to carry off the greater, epistemological imposture successfully attempted by Germont. For if Violetta suffers and dies, the libretto suggests, it is because she did not have a father like Germont in the first place. Thanks to his unstinting efforts on her behalf his own daughter can remain angelically pure, unlike Violetta, her unfortunate double.

Violetta's true desire, like that of so many seemingly wayward daughters, is to please the father. By sacrificing herself to his wishes, she masochistically expiates the guilt she feels for having broken his law in the first place. While her sin may be caused by male fallibility, her body is forced to succumb to the burden of the weakness of men. In Verdi's opera, as in nineteenth-century bourgeois ideology in general, female masochism is not only encouraged but rewarded with redemption: in the end, Germont returns to claim Violetta as his daughter. Luckily for him, his generosity has no real effect, since Violetta conveniently dies before he has to introduce her to the rest of the family. On her deathbed Violetta envisages Alfredo's marriage to yet another young and unsullied daughter-figure, to be blessed from on high by Violetta, her predecessor and true sister.

The unspoken contradiction in the text, marvellously masked by the emotional investments constructed for us by the music and the plot, is the fact that Germont objectively encourages Violetta to take up her old profession again, thus saving one daughter by prostituting the other. If everything in this opera conspires to make us believe that, unlike his son, Germont would never avail himself of the services of a prostitute, nothing in fact proves that he wouldn't. Verdi's ambiguities are those of his time: *La traviata* explores – and enacts – the limitations of a society torn between its moral repudiation of prostitution and its own structural promotion of the very same profession through exploitative economic practices and double moral standards.

Christine Brückner
'We're Quits, Messieurs!'
A Monologue in which a Parisian courtesan, known as 'The Lady of the Camellias', takes stock of her life.

Christine Brückner is the author of twenty-five books, notably stories for children, and of Desdemona – if you had only spoken!, *'uncensored speeches of eleven incensed women', translated by Eleanor Bron (London, 1992).*

Marguerite Gautier is discovered sitting in front of her dressmaker's dummy. She is wearing very little, but by no means too little. The dummy is dressed in the clothes which she herself will later wear. As she talks to the dummy, she removes its clothes and puts them on herself, at the same time applying make-up with the help of a hand-held mirror. Later she places a man's hat on the undressed dummy, which she then addresses as her lover Armand Duval and as the latter's father.

In the course of the monologue we hear someone knocking repeatedly at the door and on each occasion the Lady of the Camellias calls out: 'No, Nadine!' or 'I'm not receiving visitors, Nadine!'

MARGUERITE: I'm not your poor Marguerite Gautier! I don't want to be treated like some pitiful creature. I've lived life in the fast lane, I'll die quickly. People who live slowly die slowly. In my village they would say she has a weak chest and that she couldn't last much longer.

Consumption! I'm wasting away. Sickness makes me even more delicate, even more beautiful. It just takes longer to recover.

I've got until evening to get myself ready. Not even Nadine's allowed to see me in this state.

God is merciful in letting me die while I'm still young, while I'm still beautiful and desirable. I'm like a candle that gutters and then goes out. My friend Prudence says, candles flare up briefly before they go out. She likes to talk posh, though she's not in the least bit posh herself.

They'll bury me in the cemetery at Montmartre, between famous men, some of whom will have been my lovers. I've not kept a diary. When I came to Paris, I could hardly write my own name. I'm discreet. I want my coffin covered with white camellias. I'll seduce the gravedigger into decorating my grave.

(*There is a knock at the door.*) No, Nadine! No one!

I dance till I'm out of breath, I drink champagne till my head begins to spin. Towards morning I'll doze a little, then Prudence will come, have a good look round to see what she may inherit and tell me all the latest gossip. They'll have to get rid of all this junk to pay my debts. Nadine will stay on for a while to look after me but as soon as she starts to feel frightened she'll be off. I'll be alone in the end, completely alone, just like my mother.

It's from her that I inherited this consumption, it's the only thing she ever had. You don't have to cough, you can cough gently, you can wipe the drops of blood from your lips without anyone noticing. My cheeks are red with fever, I don't need rouge any longer. My eyes are even darker than before, they glint with fever.

Oh, Marguerite! You need to be entertained, you're getting sentimental. You need champagne, candied grapes, fresh camellias. I'll go to the theatre. It doesn't matter what's on. When I enter my box, every opera-glass will turn to me, not to the stage. I excite the audience more than the play. Who will sit next to the Lady of the Camellias? Who will get into her carriage and spend the night with her? I go to the theatre to be seen, not to see others. The real scenes don't take place on stage. The audience doesn't care who's playing Lady Macbeth, but the Lady of the Camellias is always the Lady of the Camellias. You don't need a programme to know that. What will she be wearing this evening? The dress the colour of mignonette trimmed with priceless chinchilla? Or the lilac one with Brussels lace? A red camellia? Or a white one?

As long as there's life still in me, I plan to live! You didn't understand a thing, Armand! I don't want to take things easy and put off the moment of dying. What's the point of that? You were no more successful than all the others in trying to catch me. 'Look after yourself, Marguerite! Drink lots of milk! You should rest now, Marguerite!'

It would never have suited me. A courtesan mustn't fall in love. My time's running out, I can't waste what's left sitting in a summer house in the country, waiting to see how long I can last. I warned you, Armand! It was your 'fate' to love Marguerite Gautier! You wanted me to be the centre of your life, but I'm not the centre of anyone's life. The Lady of the Camellias is an extra, Armand! We were happy together for a few weeks, that's enough. It has to be enough. When we moved to the country, I wanted to escape from my illness but it followed me. I'd have been bored to death there. I prefer walking in the Champs-Elysées. Not through fields. People expect me to be tender with them, not passionate. I'd never fallen in love before, Armand. I only ever loved my little dog, I'd have died for him. Everything we love dies. You behave as though you're an Othello but you're not an Othello, or you'd have killed me out of jealousy. I'd have thanked you for it. Fidelity – that's a word that women like me shouldn't know exists. I earn my keep through infidelity. It's more lucrative.

(*There is a knock at the door.*) No, Nadine, I have to rest.

Why didn't you want to be my lover? I could have afforded to keep you, the others should have paid for it. Why be so proud? Everything I own I've worked for. An apartment in the Rue Laffitte. Chinese vases. A carriage, a maid. And you? You get your yearly allowance by doing nothing. Because your mother was well-off and you inherited her money. *My* mother used to beat me, that's all I ever got from her. She died when I was twelve and so I moved to Paris. Paris! I made something of it. You were never interested in my background, Armand. Those who know poverty as a child have more experience of life than a rich person can ever acquire.

(*The Lady of the Camellias has now removed the clothes from the dummy and put them on herself. She places the man's hat on the dummy's head.*)

That's how it is, Monsieur! I mean Monsieur Duval Senior, the worthy Monsieur Duval, the father of my lover. I didn't want any trouble. It's your son's hat, Monsieur! He forgot it. He ran away. In tears. Poor Armand! He looks like you, Monsieur. Be patient with him, he'll be as upright as you yourself ever were. Go on and live your respectable life, reach a ripe old age and, above all else, stay comfortably off, that's the most important thing of all! Make sure that the worthy Duval family leads a respectable life. You told your son not to live in sin with a woman of easy virtue. But there wasn't much that was sinful about those summer weeks in the country. I'd say it was more of an idyll. How should a tart know whether respectability gives people pleasure? It certainly makes them bored, otherwise those respectable gentlemen wouldn't come to me in the Rue Laffitte. I'm a kept woman, Monsieur Duval. You wanted to save your son from me. Or did you also want to save me and set me on the right course? Are married women not kept by their husbands? For the whole of their lives, until their dying day? And what if they, too, take a lover? They do so in secret. Women are secretive. A man shows off with his beautiful, elegant mistresses, the more beautiful and elegant they are, the more it flatters his vanity. And their wives are happy to be left in peace. I know what I'm talking about, Monsieur! Ah, Monsieur! I respect your respectability, but it's no great money-spinner as far as I'm concerned. I can choose my lovers. Where's the wife who can do that? I go to bed with a man for pleasure, not out of marital obligation.

You don't talk about that in the circles from which you come? You ought to. Should I have scrubbed steps when I came to Paris? Should I have taken in washing, carrying it up the back staircase? I could have been a model at the Académie, but I'm a bit on the thin side, it comes from being hungry. And from being beaten as a child, Monsieur. Is this the time to spend my savings on opening a little shop – now that I'm sick and growing old?

Should I work as a milliner? I prefer buying hats to making them. Do I look like someone who should be pitied? I can see the envy in wives' eyes, although they insist, of course, that they despise a woman like me. I eat the best Paris can offer, I drink champagne. I spend a few pleasant hours with the man of my choice, and when he tires me I send him away. Nadine likes working for me. We're like sisters, as thick as thieves, we laugh and make fun of the gentlemen who come here. I give her presents. I don't suppose your own staff find life as amusing and as varied as Nadine. People slip her banknotes when she blurts out that I like candied grapes, that camellias are my favourite flower, when I go to the theatre, when I leave the house, and where I go!

(*There is a knock at the door.*) Just a moment, Nadine!

Monsieur Duval! Before you, you see an independent woman! When a lover starts to bore me, I send him away. I don't have to fit in with the demands and whims of any husband. (*She looks at herself critically in the mirror.*) I've lost weight, all that's left are flounces and pleats. Most men are common, Monsieur Duval, they like dirty jokes. They need to be able to go somewhere to recover from family respectability, to be with someone who has no memory. I'm not educated. Why should I be? I talk. Most men like chatter. I wanted to surround myself with beautiful things. Dresden china. Velvet. Lace. Why shouldn't these beautiful things be intended for me as well? They were presents. I showed how grateful I was for them.

Isn't it a wonderful feeling to squander? Flowers. Presents. Oneself? Should I have squandered my youth and beauty on a single man? Wasn't I too good for your son?

Didn't that thought ever occur to you?

(*She looks in the mirror again. To herself.*) Grey hairs, crowsfeet round my eyes, do you want to wait till then, Marguerite? You've had everything. Even a great love. What else can life offer you?

(*Again to the dressmaker's dummy with Duval's hat.*) You, too, could have become my lover, Papa Duval! I like you, in your way. My lovers mustn't be too impetuous any longer. For the sake of your son, in order to frighten him away!

I help the gentlemen to unwind. I tinkle away at the piano. Should I have had lessons? Practised regularly? No one expects me to play the piano for them. But I play them the first few bars of a little song to put them in the right frame of mind, breaking off at just the right moment out of the kindness of my heart. I can't sleep before two in the morning. I like to have someone sitting here in the big armchair and talking to me. I have a meal brought up from the restaurant, the champagne is just the right temperature. Sometimes there's a bit of kissing and cuddling, but not always. A courtesan can't afford moods and bad tempers. Migraines are for married women. Plenty of men have ruined themselves because of me. And I've ruined my health. We're quits.

It all works out nicely. The Lady of the Camellias wasn't available to all and sundry. I could choose who I wanted. I can still choose, at least for a while. Does a woman have to watch how she spends the money that a man has thrown away with barely a moment's thought? Who says so? Be off with you, Monsieur Duval, be off with you! I don't like seeing old, respectable men, they make me feel old, too.

Armand! Poor Armand! You're gambling now, gambling away your money, hoping to win so that you can afford a lover who belongs to you alone. Do you want to lock me up in a cage like a bird and put me on display in the Tuileries? And you alone would have the key, so that you can let the bird flutter freely for a while when it suits you. And on the label are the words: 'Proprietor: Armand Duval.' Property is theft, Proudhon says.

I've got ears and eyes. I've learned to close them, it's part of the job. Did you really think that all my gentlemen left their ideas hanging on the hatstand together with their hats? Your life in the country! You've been reading too much Rousseau. 'Retour à la nature!' Bonapartists, legitimists, republicans. The Bonapartists were always the most generous, that's why I went to Napoleon's funeral.

Where are your wits, Armand? Do you expect me to sit in your cage, surrounded by camellia bushes? Do you expect me to pick the petals off the flowers? 'Armand loves me, Armand loves me not, he loves me more than anything, he can't help it . . . ' Don't spoilt little boys in Paris play that game? Or is it only for silly little country girls?

I demanded blind obedience from you, it was supposed to frighten you away. My illness should have frightened you off. But a 'no' attracts men like a magnet. You say you feel pity for me, but pity and prostitution don't go together. There's never been a market value for the Lady of the Camellias. For one man a bunch of flowers is enough, for another not even his entire fortune would do.

You can spare me your reproaches, Messieurs!

(*Calling out*.) Nadine, get the carriage ready. I'm going to the theatre.

Everett Quinton
'*Tootaloo Marguerite!*'

Everett Quinton is an actor with The Ridiculous Theatre Company of New York, founded by Charles Ludlam.

If you haven't heard Everett Quinton as Marguerite Gautier you haven't lived. So why not live? Garbo was beyond belief. Everett Quinton is something else.   *The New York Post*

Charles Ludlam wrote *Camille* for himself to play the title role from a gay man's point of view in the early 1970s, at the height of gay liberation. All his plays have the politics of oppression as a major theme. In *Big Hotel* this surfaces in different forms of self-oppression, both internal and political. The reason his company has survived – apart from the fact that we're marvellous – is that people want to know what we have to say, and we give them honest theatre. But why did he choose *Camille*?

Part of the reason is that his company is steeped in theatrical tradition – we are all very aware of the stars, and grand plays lend themselves to being reworked whatever the date and place, *Medea*, for instance. With *Conquest of the Universe*, Charles took the structure of Marlowe's *Tamburlaine* and set it in Outer Space. In its compactness, Charles's *Camille* is closer to the libretto of the opera than Dumas's play. But the play is well made; it is witty and amusing, and our *Camille* would be impossible without the character of Nichette, in the same way that Medea needs the nurse. Nichette is, so to speak, the flip side of the coin. She is also a transgressant, until she gets married and makes herself into an honest woman; according to the morality of their society she is still, so to speak, on the black list. This brings us back to why *Camille* is relevant today – anyone who has felt oppressed will relate to the reality in the play.

The notion of self-oppression is in Marguerite Gautier. It's embedded in the novel, in the way the characters are forced into accepting the moral code of the time. We can't even say that, for the whores, it was an honest way of life: life for them was grim, for even whores with a heart of gold were – and are – forced to work and work.

A lawyer friend, discussing the difference between legalizing and decriminalizing prostitution, favours decriminalizing it. This takes the strain off the docket, and gives prostitutes the freedom to work. Legalizing them turns them into slaves, bound to whatever the law prescribes for them.

Modern audiences may find it difficult to accept that a 21-year-old prostitute is very experienced, and she was not at the top of her profession without being very good at it. And she was not nice – the famous line about 'lying to keep my teeth white' – is a quotation from Marie Duplessis. She was illiterate when she was thirteen but she had a quick wit, and she knew what it was to pull herself up. Dumas makes it clear that she was not a conventional beauty but that she had an inner radiance. She was, according to the time, too tall and too skinny – gangly even – but her way of presenting herself was her charm.

The laughter in our play is vital because it is part of the mockery, of mocking the oppressor. Even the last line ('Much will be forgiven you because you have loved too much') sometimes gets a laugh because the audience is anticipating Nichette's final 'Tootaloo, Marguerite'. The laughter shows up the bullshit of oppression. As a gay man, I am aware that heterosexual society has held exclusive rights to the way the world is supposed to be organized, and to the interpretation of the Bible. When I realized this I was able to go back to being a Christian. How could I leave my salvation to the interpretation of heterosexuals sitting in judgement? It was up to me to interpret it – not exclusively, of course, but so that I could deny what they say and reinterpret it from a homosexual point of view, and to interpret it without homosexuality being a sin. This realization made me happy. A straight friend of mine, a Baptist minister and a psychotherapist, told me that she always takes communion when she is in a Catholic church as a protest. That's right! People with the wrong ideas cannot deny me my salvation, my own self-respect, from the living Christ.

But not so for poor Marguerite who finally accepts from Armand's father that she has no right to love as herself and she does not (as I was choosing to do) reject both society and religion. Moral arguments sound right because they have been formulated over thousands of years to fit the ears of the uneducated. Once you begin to hear through the ears of Marguerite Gautier, you are losing the fight. In the rules of debate, the person who raises his voice will lose the argument and the moralist wins easily because his opponents start to cry. As soon as emotional language is used, the old self-oppressor comes into play. There is no difference between Marguerite Gautier and the queers in a 1950s movie who ended up hanging in the closet because they believed they were vile and damned.

How often do I have to convince myself as a gay man that I am the equal of anyone in the world? And that no one can make me less equal? But it's not a mystery to me why so much homosexual behaviour is clandestine sneaking around – it's due to centuries of the idea of 'the love that dare not speak its name'. Yet self-expression is as real as the moon in the sky.

Marguerite Gautier, alone of all the characters, speaks the truth: she knows she is going to die, and accepts the fact that she will be condemned by society. She is a universal character and it is a mistake interpreting her through the eyes of a man or a woman. Marguerite Gautier's problem is not gender specific. Maybe it was a hundred years ago but I doubt it. To play the role, you have to rise above the particular to the universal. That a woman sacrifices herself for a man is only one aspect of the role. I like being able to include Marguerite Gautier in my repertory, and to play Bluebeard the next night.

Lavinia Byrne
A Nun's Tale
A response to the religious metaphors that surround the personality of Marie Duplessis in her fictional afterlife

Lavinia Byrne is a nun and psychiatrist.

That Mr Dumas insulted porters. Said they were all called Joseph. Just because he couldn't be fussed to learn people's names. Never bothered to find out about the missing characters in his stories either you know. And Mr Verdi's librettist was no better. Certainly didn't mention me. My name's Genevieve by the way; well Sister Genevieve since I joined the Order. I'm Annina's sister. Our mother was Violetta's wet nurse. That's why I'm reproaching myself now. My mother helped bring her into the world and I should have helped see her out.

Only she wouldn't have gone out if I'd had my way. Shocking waste really the way that poor child suffered. Annina tells me she had a good look back into the room that last sad day after Violetta got her out of the way with some story about a letter. Saw her look into a mirror and sing ever so tragical. Heard her lament her fading looks and speak about her tormented weary soul, her bleeding conscience. The priest had been mind, had given her comfort. I mean even Mr Dumas remembered that. But it wasn't much help. There's no comfort really for what had gone wrong with her. It was all those mirrors see. That's the secret of the thing.

I had the sisters pray for her when I heard about it and came up from the country just as soon as I could. The sisters understood mind. Well, most of them. There's always some as gets a bit edgy when you talk about, well, you know, loose living. That's where the Church gets its bad name. You see, it goes on about women. Whore, angel, all of that. Then it works people up something rotten by talking more about the anger of God than any kind of news. Folk who don't know themselves well enough to make their own way in life. They're the ones like Violetta, the ones who can't see straight.

That was Violetta's problem you see; she couldn't never see herself as she was. All her images of herself came to her from other people. There were men to tell her how lovely she was, men to spoil her and men to swoon all over those flowers she carried around with her. The crowd she mixed with didn't help her much either. Only when that lovely Mr Alfredo took her off to the country were the mirrors taken away. Between ourselves I thought he was ever such a lovely gentleman. He helped her begin to see herself straight. It didn't last mind. That father of his came along stirring things up with all his talk about best of times. Many's the poor woman I've seen brought to her knees – and worse – by men talking about sacrifice. She thought she could trade her own bad reputation for some young woman's good one. Had no sense. You can't ever be sure how things are going to work out for other people. Even Our Blessed Lord didn't imagine his sacrifice would buy a perfect world.

That was the difficulty though. Even as a child she kept using words like passion and desire. She heard them in church and used them in bed. No wonder she got a bit confused. No wonder it was confusing for the rest of us when she thought she could make heaven on earth without realizing how fragile she was. Splintered really in the end, just like all that glass she kept looking into.

Mieke Kolk
La Belle Dame sans Merci

Mieke Kolk is a lecturer in Theatre Studies at the University of Amsterdam.

'Yea, I am found the woman in all tales
The face caught always in the story's face.' Swinburne

Poor Marie Duplessis! Beautiful and wan, bejewelled and wasting away. Dead before she was twenty-five. Girls in her time had to hurry if they were to make anything of their lives. In the world in which Marie practised her disreputable and disorderly career, the doors of marriage opened only for sixteen-year-old virgins with handsome dowries nestling in their chaste little laps. Marie could be admitted to a family circle only when her posthumous lovers, an author and a composer, interred her for ever with the ghosts in their own family closets. Dead, and thus safely transformed into a relic.

Modern critics tend to regard the theme as old-fashioned. They are wrong. Men's fear of an independent woman finds an outlet in an aggression which has merely changed its face when it was discovered that she had a mind of her own. The symbiosis of power and sexuality is too deeply rooted to be washed away by common sense and an abortion clinic. The early nineteenth-century patent on marriage cemented by love is still too profitable to be laid to rest.

Poor Marguerite Gautier. Poor Violetta. If only they had called you Magdelena we, as good Christians, would have to hold out our hands in forgiveness; but as it is you are forced to join the ghostly, weaving ranks of real or fictional wicked women, dancing through the literature of your time. And to the sickly smell of decay is added the stench of the dead flowers that barely dissipates the scents of the long night of passion. The fascination for your tainted body verges on a form of necrophilia; the beads of death-sweat on your mask of voluptuousness roll down like pearls of a glossy male impotence.

He must have been a nice enough young man, Dumas *fils*. Perhaps rather silly like the young lover in the book, play and opera with his mock histrionics at Flora's party. The eternal son of the eternal father. And daddy always knows best. In their hands, you were promoted to a pure white blossom, a coloratura cherub, who in perfect self-sacrifice rid the family of your own indecorous presence. In search of love, for love, in the name of a love which was bartered to support the patriarchal status quo. A culture that needs such heroines is damned.

One last thing. That miniature which in a maternal gesture you passed on for future generations. Was it an artistic prop, or did you really bestow it upon your author–lover? I hope so. To die beautifully is one thing, to lose your life without leaving a memento is another.

Michelene Wandor
The Song of Armand Duval's Maid

*Michelene Wandor, author and playwright, co-authored a
dramatized version of* The Wandering Jew *by Eugène Sue for the
National Theatre, London, in 1987.*

There is nothing special about me. I am not beautiful, I am not
glamorous, I am not rich, I am not decadent. I am ordinary
and anonymous. When I go out in the street no one notices me.
When I go out in the street I notice a particular, beautiful woman;
every day she is with another man. Every day she wears new, beautiful clothes; a bright plume in her hat, long gloves that slide up to
her delicate elbows, her hair curled, her eyes laughing, adored by
the man sitting opposite her, adored and envied by all who pass.

You would think she and I had nothing in common. Me, with
my drab brown hair, my hunched shoulders, me with no time to
spend admiring the view and being admired by others. But we
have. She, it is said, is passionately in love for real. The courtesan
who spends money, the woman with many lovers, has finally
allowed her heart to be touched by a man without any money at
all. This is what we have in common. My heart too now belongs to
a man without money. But it is not the lack of money that is
important. It is the fact that I do not know whether he loves me.
This is where my courtesan and I part company. She and her true
love have had their idyll; but she cannot abandon her way of life
and he cannot keep her in the style to which she is accustomed.
And so now she has a new lover, and to spite her, and to conceal
his own hurt, he has taken a new mistress whom he flaunts before
the world.

And meanwhile, in my drab brown way I dream my own true
love. I invent conversations I shall have with him, in which I shall
so catch his attention that he will look deep into my eyes, and he
will not see drabness but warmth and excitement and sparkle.
The night will wear on as we are engrossed in one another until
it will be too late for him to make his way across town, and he will

touch me lightly on the hand, and our loving will be as beautiful and passionate as that of any courtesan and her follower.

The next day he will hold my face in his hands, my loose hair cascading down over his arms, and he will vow eternal devotion, and he will take me away from this town that teems with the poor and we will live in a house far from here, where the sea will lull us to sleep and the mountains will cool our heated bodies, and we shall have children and love and love.

Sometimes my dream makes me smile because it means that I still live with hope. Sometimes my dream makes me sob deep, hard sobs, because I cannot believe that he will ever notice me. Even when my reason tells me that my dream is impossible, even when I listen briefly to my reason and tell myself to get on with my life, I can still be taken unawares by a glimpse of his face, of the way his hair curls over his shoulder, by the way his eyes pass over me, and then my impossible future passes again before my eyes.

I live with my dream. I do not understand the way it arrived I do not know whether it will ever go. And meanwhile I watch him languish for love of her, I see him pass the time with a woman whom he does not love in order to spite her whom he does. I polish his shoes and I wash his linen and I smile to myself at the fact that at the very least I can serve him and be near him, and yet remain invisible to him. It is invisibility that makes my dream safe and protected.

She will die soon. I have no feelings about her. I have never even been jealous of her. I am sorry that she will die, as I would be to see any other young woman of my own age die. Sometimes I think that when she dies, his eyes will light on me and I will console him, even if only for a night. And then I smile to myself. If his love for her is as permanent as mine is for him, it does not matter whether she lives or dies. And so our dance continues, and no one knows who has written the music.

Simone Benmussa
'Il traviato' or The Funeral of a Marguerite

Simone Benmussa, for many years dramaturge and general
assistant to Jean-Louis Barrault, has written many plays,
including The Singular Life of Albert Nobbs *and* Appearances.

I was strolling around the San Moisé district of Venice, two steps away from Teatro la Fenice, when I saw people coming down the steps of a small palazzo. Without thinking I walked through the crowd and up the steps. The concierge was already closing the door but told me, when I asked him what was going on, that an auction sale had just taken place. The lady of the house, the Contessa Duplessis, had died. Widowed some years before, she had been relatively poor and the sale of her possessions was going to provide funds to send her five children to some distant relations in France.

I entered a room which had perhaps been the drawing-room. Nothing remained, bar the marks left by the furniture on the floors, and those left by the pictures on the walls. Over there I could imagine the mirror because of a dark oval shape, and indeed within it I saw the shadow of her face. 'It is over, Sir, there is nothing left to see.' The concierge, in the doorway, was talking to me, a little puzzled I suppose by the stranger staring quietly at that empty wall. I turned around. 'There is nothing left to buy. I arranged to send what could not be sold to the Giudecca women's prison . . . It could all come in handy there.' All the time he was talking to me, he was crumpling in his hand a piece of paper which he dropped when he left. I followed, and picked it up absent-mindedly. It was a letter.

LETTER TO THE FLIGHTY FRENCHMAN, LETTER TO ARMAND.
Venice, 6 March 1853

I am writing from Venice. From the family house where they brought me back, the Prodigal Wife, as a prisoner after a brief escape. Husband and children hold me here, just as the bridges

of my city lock me in, far from you, the fickle creature who for a
short time took me from them. I do not know how to write to
you, I cannot express so much misery, except in broken cries. I
need a new language; it would not sing the song of today's sad
Violetta, it would not tell the tale of your French Marguerite,
it would bespeak betrayal and despair. I know you will not
answer this letter, my Reprobate. Shall I send it? Can you
remember? Every new day brought you new men, new women,
my Traviato, whilst I died for the thousandth time . . . And then
one day She came, the one you were to choose from all the
others. My husband, I know, came to ask you to give me up.
You laughed: 'But I do not love her! I love another!' You sent
him away: 'Keep what goods are yours! She will forget soon
enough' . . . But what am I?

Am I . . . goods? Or good? . . . Or bad? Bad for whom? . . .
Good for whom? . . . Good for what? I will forget? . . . Nothing
will be erased. I imprint deep in my memory what is past and
what I now dream of, that it may haunt and slowly destroy you.
And so, Frenchman, listen and I will pour deep inside you, into
your heart of hearts, into your very soul, into the very fibre of
your being, I will pour, mingled as our saliva used to be, the
story of your shame and the story of my grief, as you whored
and I silently lost my hold over your life and over mine: now
that I barely exist at all. Somebody else took you from me,
somebody more 'useful' you said. From that I conclude that I
am useless. Remember how you protested: 'No, I do not love
her, I do not love the Other . . . I could no more split myself
from you than split myself in two . . . But please understand, I
must not write to her, I have to talk to her, she has to hear my
living voice . . . she knows I have never stopped loving you . . . '
You were smiling, Counterfeiter. Your living voice indeed! . . .
But what about the life of my voice? I was a songstress and you
killed my song. Now I can only write. Her voice unfaltering, she
had all the answers. She was clever, she made you sing a different tune. Now I hear your voice no longer: you send me words.
Do you fear the sound of your voice? . . . I tore up your last
letter but snatches keep coming back to me; my world is
exploded but in that enormous eruption, fragments of what you
have written still haunt me; scattered words, broken words,

syllables . . . which say . . . what? Feverishly I pick up the pieces
. . . Clumsily I put back together words which tell of parting,
sentences which signify . . . the end. And when I fell, the earth in
an enormous surge rose and then collapsed on to itself, engulfing me. Buried in that gigantic tomb, mine was no ordinary
burial. Do not look for me in San Michele but remember that
wherever you take a step, I shall be underneath. Wherever you
go you will have to keep dancing if you want to escape me,
ceaselessly you will have to lift your feet from this earth, and
they will be leaden. May your feathers be tarred and clipped,
beautiful Angel. You will live on your knees, my Cripple, my
Claudius, dragging your useless wings. As for her, who watches
and keeps watch, a ridiculous bird hopping on short legs,
graceless creature that she is, let her be present at your
transformation. You will shake and tremble: try as you may, try
as you will, no more dancing, no more jumping, not one single
step. Your body will stumble and falter, my silver-tongued
Libertine, and seize up, thereafter immobile, petrified.

Your,
Marguerite, Violetta, Camellia

'La traviata' means the one who has gone astray.
The world première of *La traviata* was on 6 March 1853 at La Fenice.
San Michele is the cemetery of Venice.

Naomi Segal
Our Lady of the Flowers

*Naomi Segal is a Fellow of St John's College, Cambridge, where
she teaches French and comparative literature. She is the author of
five books, including* Narcissus and Echo: women in the French
récit *(1988) and* The Adulteress's Child: authorship and desire in
the nineteenth-century novel *(1992).*

The original of the Lady of Camellias, Alphonsine Plessis, did
not, it seems, particularly like camellias. Nor did she adopt,

when she chose a pseudonym, a name at all associated with flowers. Alexandre Dumas, on the contrary, borrowed something of the Catholic flavour of the name she did choose – Marie – and, going less far than Genet's brilliantly perverse *Notre Dame des Fleurs*, dropped the pronoun and specified the bloom. Further avatars of the Lady have since displaced the image of the flowers into further versions of womanhood. Just as Genet chose the Madonna as the perfect name of homosexual masculinity, Proust before him (and for much the same reason) similarly identified the aberrant desire – for which he wrote a passionately disguised apologia – with flowers, fertilization, the bee's eye for blossoms.

Dumas changed Alphonsine/Marie into Marguerite (a daisy), English translations took up her emblem by naming her Camille, Verdi created the longest-lasting legend by renaming her Violetta. By stages, the most banal of flowers, chosen with a certain cruelty perhaps to flatter the 'common' courtesan, becomes transformed in scent and significance into a name that carries the ambiguity of the two extreme images of the female body: the modest violet and its homonym violate/*violer*/*violée*. The blushing flower blushes because her body displays the no-sex that makes her violable.

What readers remember about Marguerite Gautier's use of her flower is that she displays it to flaunt her openness or unavailability, wearing a white bloom for twenty-five days of the month, a red one for the other five. The naive narrator, claiming that 'no one ever knew the reason for this variation in colour', signifies his failure to accede to her sex (in either sense). Marguerite chooses to bar entrance to herself precisely by showing them that the body they want is no more than female and that the flower-imagery is nothing other than a changing colour and an *odor di femmina*. Pre-empting the conventional symbol, she says it with flowers, so that after all she guards her meaning: the violet knows what it is to blush.

The text is all about her body. The frame-narrator and Armand both recognize her fetish-possessions (lusted after by males and females alike) as an extension of herself that is at once metonym and metaphor. She is both art object and commodity. Armand cannot decide if her being anybody's makes her less or more his. The scene in the opening frame in which, anxious to see her dead, he has her corpse exhumed and, by fixing on eyes that are now sightless, no longer magnetic holes, becomes able both to catch and to survive her illness, sets up a morality according to which, in order for Marguerite Gautier to be an angel, she must live her body as diseased. It is not surprising that Armand attaches himself to the sickness in the woman who, healthy, has no time for his pity, nor that he 'can't bear to see her bright and cheerful'.

Dumas's novel of 1848 fits into a sub-genre of romantic prose in French, the confessional *récit*. Among this genre, three examples – this one, Prévost's *Manon Lescaut* (1731) and Mérimée's *Carmen* (1845) – have become more famous in musical adaptations, and it cannot be a coincidence that these are the examples that present the misloved heroine as a *femme fatale*. In almost all *récits*, the woman dies and the man tells the tale. She is usually older than he (though this trait is less insisted upon in the *femme fatale* versions) and always treats him maternally. The hero has generally lost his mother in childbirth, has a worldly, powerful father, and tells his story to a sympathetic older man. He adores the woman but contrives to murder her, more or less literally, closing the account of anger and guilt that began with the childbed death.

Marguerite Gautier has much in common with the frequently cited Manon Lescaut, and also with the more glitzy eponym of Carmen, published just three years earlier. As dark, thin, ravishing as Carmen she, like her, devours sweets, yet she is too potent to be childish. Like Manon she is clever, witty, practical, anything but uncanny – except in so far as a clever woman is always seen by her narrator as threatening and uncontrolled. Manon implicitly, Carmen directly, stand for the dark-lady demon that is the obverse of the infibulated Madonna – yet both are so healthy that they must be more or less murdered if they are to die. Our Lady of the Camellias, alone amongst the fatal women, fades away out of sheer selflessness.

The most impressive and disturbing facet of Marguerite is not in her body but her way of living it; by an irony of which she is entirely conscious she keeps herself alive by the over-indulgence that is killing her. Through this expedient, the opera, the sweets, the sex, dancing, dining till dawn, she sublimates her body by controlling its time: night becomes her day, she chooses when to die. Thus the indirect conspiracy of father and son to condemn her in the name of a spotless womanhood (a sister who can never be her sister) is almost in vain. Armand's desire and all his talk of love does not, in this sense, reach her. It is so far an interlude that we can perhaps understand his need to see her body hollowed, stenching but fixed, as a promise that now at last he can speak for her.

Marguerite's downfall is that she cannot withstand the temptation of sanctity. To be able to control that perfect sister by giving her at once a chaste brother, a virtuous father and the three families acquired on a respectable marriage is too much for the fatal woman to resist. She herself has no place in a familial chain, 'neither mother nor sister nor daughter nor wife'. The problem she poses is that she has no function in the structure that bases and outlaws desire. Repeatedly men offer her foster-places: the dead daughter, the relative, mother, 'wife or sister', but none of these positions fits her, and Armand is instead put back among his kin – a sainted mother, an irrationally respected father, the sister conserved in a virginal stupidity that excludes her from knowledge in an exact balance on her side to the frame-narrator on his. There is no position for Marguerite in the four-cornered symmetry of nuclear desire. Even the likes of her have a childhood, she points out, but she expects this hardly to be believed; she has no roots. In the play, she addresses herself with bitter clarity: 'By what right do you think you can take the place in the heart of a family which virtue alone may occupy? You are in love – so what? That's no reason. However much you might prove your love, no one will ever believe you, and fair enough. Who are you to talk of love or the future? What kind of new words are these? Just look at the mire of your past! What man would want to call you his wife? What child would want to call you his mother?'

Marguerite is no one's daughter – her dog is dearer than her mother, who beat her, and Armand replaces her dog. But if she is no man's wife or mother, she is irrevocably the sister of that underclass of woman with whom she is everywhere identified. A camellia on the corsage, she is the badge of this body of women, as surely in her difference as in her similarity. Nothing she can do exempts her from being the exception that proves the rule. Yet while in the play we see her fast-talking among male and female friends, in the heavier mediation of the novel she is as isolated as Manon or Carmen. Cast always as 'one of them' (even in her own utterances) she has no way of forming a first-person plural sentence. The frame-narrator's closing words merely reiterate his failure of view: 'Marguerite's history is an exception ... Had it been a commonplace, it would not have been worth writing down.'

If the woman's body has no place in the incest that sanctifies, it is indeed a 'bag of excrement', an inside with no outside, nothing but entrance. Access to it is castration, loss, pollution. Faced with the father's offer of the devil's bargain, Marguerite recognizes herself as filth. But this is the dirt that breeds flowers. The *fleurs du mal* are not only heaped on graves, they also grow there.

Valeria Moretti
Violettas, Marguerites and Camellias

Valeria Moretti is an Italian author and playwright, who has written a dramatic study of the Brontë sisters.

One is Violetta, like a flower. And like a flower also, the other is called Marguerite.

Like flowers, these women bloom and die in the enchantment of the evergreen garden which is love. Camellias flower in that garden. White as the snow, ethereal as the soul. But are the souls of women truly white? Apart from colour, how many attributes do they have? Was Arthur Schnitzler right to count only thirteen aspects in a young woman?

Let's make a pact: we'll meet again when the camellia has faded. But do camellias really fade? Or do they last for ever like the garden where Nature exhausts herself so as to flower again?

Is not passion just the dizzying whirl of a dance which an unexpected fit of coughing may end?

Violetta, like Salome, displays her beauty in the steps of a dance. But it is she, the seductress, who will be seduced because, in spite of appearances, it is the one who is enchanted who creates the enchantment. These Violettas and Marguerites know how to dance with a grace that is all their own, and they would never stop dancing if it were not for a bouquet of camellias to remind them that they will waste away and die of love.

A drop of blood intrudes to stain the white glare of happiness. Tuberculosis, the romantic and literary illness of the century! The heart which Violetta has sacrificed beats out the time of its own destruction with bouts of coughing. The past will never return. 'Addio, del passato bei sogni ridenti . . . ' ('Goodbye, sweet laughing dreams of the past . . . ') Violetta, the fallen woman, sacrifices herself in the name of the 'good', not knowing that goodness is far weaker than evil, more vulnerable in its spirit and closer to heaven than this earth.

The Sinner of Giovanni Verga's novel is another flower: Narcisa. She takes a lethal dose of opium because he does not love her as he once did. She dies in his arms, like Violetta. Or Giacinta, Luigi Capuana's adulteress and suicide. She will not admit love can end. Madame Bovary's ghost hovers in the background.

The camellias keep fading under the overwhelming influence of that disease called love. For 'les belles dames sans merci', life is the kiss of cyanide.

It is not chance that a dustman's daughter become a star gave the definitive face to Marguerite, the daughter of a peasant become a prostitute. That most tragic of actresses, Greta Garbo, was a solitary priestess who spared nothing in the 'ceremony of farewells'. She vacated her own present so that her image might shine more purely as legend. 'She was . . . ': the imperfect was the only tense she aspired to – like the ageing Countess Castiglione who covered all her mirrors with black veils. Divine sleepwalkers, ready to forfeit their own lives so as not to be forgotten.

Greta Garbo: a ghost, a vision . . . and yet in the history of cinema no actress has portrayed passion with such intensity. Strangely, the voluptuous abandon of the characters she played reflects the emotional checkmate of so many Violettas who give more than they would ever have taken.

Greta, a dustman's daughter. Marguerite, the daughter of a peasant. *Femmes fatales*, yes. (Their gaze, like that of Barbey d'Aurevilly's heroine Altachiara, can unflinchingly withstand the glare of a panther.) Damned, no. The devil does not claim their souls as in some black folk-tales because, like certain 'nice girls' who draw out the vampire's kiss till dawn comes to annihilate him, their hearts are pure.

The young Werther meets a madman gathering flowers for

Charlotte in mid-winter. Flowers once again in our path. Werther would like to be mad as well but he isn't. To be so, he must die – by his own hand.

Is it not perhaps the sweetest of madnesses to die of love? In the garden of love, love lasts for ever because it is never fulfilled. If it reaches fulfilment, it is already over.

The heroine, Juliette, of George Sand's novel Léone Léoni *(1842), a 'fallen woman' who displays unbreakable devotion to her cruel and unfaithful lover. Painting by Fabre, engraved by Robinson.*

PART THREE

Love and Art for Sale

Philip Hook
The Fallen Woman in French Nineteenth-Century Painting

Philip Hook is a director of the St James's Art Group, London, and was for ten years a director of Christie's. He is the co-author of Popular Nineteenth-Century Painting *(London, 1986).*

Augustus Egg, Past and Present *no. 3, 1858: 'August the 4th. Have just heard that B– has been dead more than a fortnight, so his poor children have now lost both parents. I hear she was seen on Friday last near the Strand, evidently without a place to lay her head. What a fall hers has been!'*

The most famous English nineteenth-century picture of a fallen woman, *Past and Present* by Augustus Leopold Egg (1858), shows as the climax of the sequence the destitute young mother huddled miserably under the arch of a bridge. On the wall behind her is a significant poster. It advertises 'Pleasure Trips to Paris'. Paris was perceived to be the ultimate in wickedness, the capital city of fallen women. Paris was where, in the words of the contemporary *London Art Journal*, artists had perfected a reprehensible technique for handling such matters: 'Cleverness of innuendo, a certain semblance of decorum preserved in the midst of sentiment dubious, such is the cunning subterfuge which has made French novelists, dramatists and painters notorious.'

It is certainly true that French painters produced a wide range of images of fallen women. But, as the *Art Journal* points out, their 'cunning subterfuge' was to do so within the framework of established genres and subjects. What were these genres? It is worth taking a look at the subjects which a visitor to the Paris Salon, organized by the committee of the École des Beaux Arts as the showcase of contemporary French painting, could expect to see in the middle years of the century.

He would have been confronted with a large number of pictures painted in the academic tradition, a tradition that harked back to the neo-classicism of David and continued to flourish most conspicuously in the work of Ingres. Ingres was an exceptional painter; his many followers generally were not. They painted grand themes from the past in melodramatic fashion. Their efforts became known derisively as 'Art Pompier'. This was an allusion to the helmets, closely resembling those worn by Parisian firemen of the period, which often feature in the pictures whose subjects were drawn from Antiquity. As far as the authorities were concerned, Antiquity was still the touchstone of eternal merit. The Prix de Rome, for which the best young artists competed annually, set subjects almost exclusively drawn from classical history and myth right up till its demise in 1881.

Our visitor would also have been diverted by a variety of pictures ostensibly portraying life in the Middle East. From the 1830s onwards French artists began to travel to North Africa and Asia Minor in search of colourful and exotic subject matter. Orientalism was an exciting discovery. In the hands of painters like Delacroix and Chasseriau it became a significant part of the romantic vocabulary but in the hands of their many lesser followers it deteriorated into a vehicle for cheap sensationalism.

There would have been the usual quota of portraits of the rich, the famous, and the fashionable. And then there would have been the small but increasingly controversial group of pictures painted by men who called themselves 'Realists', artists who aimed to paint contemporary life in the raw. This group included young rebels like Courbet and Manet. Their work was viewed with suspicion. They walked through a minefield of potential disgrace, risking official banishment the moment they were judged to have gone too far. Such pictures of theirs as did get past the committee were the subject of considerable attention and not a little hypocritical outrage.

A perceptive visitor might have detected a trend in French painting, a mood that was increasingly setting it apart from the painting of fifty years before. This was the influence of the new patronage for pictures, the self-made urban bourgeoisie, men whose priorities were different from the old aristocratic picture buyer. What was this influence? It tended towards trivialization and towards sensationalism; it was at times a vision of the most maudlin sentimentality, and at others prurient and voyeuristic. Thus, while subject matter did not change, its treatment did. Ways were found of heightening the impact. In the process, the depiction of women changed: there was an increasing pictorial exploitation of women for the edification of a largely male clientele, a growing emphasis on women as objects.

The Academics continued to paint nudes, but nudes with an excitingly heightened sense of realism. Comparing a nude painted by David with one by Cabanel of fifty years later gives an idea of the difference. Rigorous neo-classicism gives way to accessibility. A classical setting was excellent cover for the presentation of a luscious, ultra-naturalistic naked girl. Prudes might raise their hands in horror, but the protection of Antiquity was an effective defence against their outrage, while voyeurs might relish the image secure in the knowledge that they were looking at Art. Classical mythology, history and the Bible were all raided for subjects to lend the veneer of propriety. Artists came up with a whole range of Venuses, Psyches, Nymphs and Sirens. There was the Judgement of Paris, The Rape of the Sabines, Gyges and Candaules, Phryné, and Olympia; there was the Bath of Bathsheba, Potiphar's Wife, and Susannah and the Elders. There was Lady Godiva; not to mention all the allegorical themes, such as Truth, Hope, the Four Seasons, the Three Graces, which might be used as an excuse for painting more naked women. They are women who have taken their clothes off for the delectation of the spectator. Generally the spectator is the person looking at the picture. But in some pictures there are also spectators built into the composition itself, as in especially voyeuristic themes like Susannah and the Elders, Gyges and Candaules, or Phryné.

Phryné was painted most famously by Jean-Léon Gérôme in 1860. When exhibited at the Salon that year the picture created a storm of interest. Phryné was the famous Athenian courtesan, the model of Praxiteles and Apelles, who was tried before the Elders for impiety. Her lawyer Hyperides decided on the sensational ploy of getting her to strip in front of her judges, arguing that no one so beautiful in her natural state could be guilty of such an accusation. One can sense Gérôme himself thereby building into his subject

Phryné before the Judges *by Gérôme, 1860 (1861 Salon)*

(the moment when she stands revealed) its own defence against accusations of pornography. Everyone comes out happily from the exercise. The moralists are appeased: the ostensible message is that Beauty cannot harbour Impurity. The voyeurs are amply satisfied. Phryné, the fallen woman, is raised again by her own beauty. And the Elders, who came along expecting a day's routine legal work, get an unexpected bonus.

Two years later, in 1863, Alexandre Cabanel exhibited at the Salon his *Birth of Venus*. This flagrantly titillating nude was given a stamp of the highest approval when it was bought by the Emperor Napoleon III. A voluptuous naked woman stretches herself across the crest of a wave, indolently coquettish. There is no implicit purity in this lady's beauty, unlike that claimed for Phryné. This Venus is wantonly alluring. Her classical trappings are incidental. Jean-François Millet, the high-minded painter of peasants toiling honestly in the fields, saw through it all when he wrote of this sort of Salon nude: 'I have never seen anything which seemed to me a more frank and direct appeal to the passions of bankers and stockbrokers.' Cabanel's Venus is a woman offered for the stimulation of tired financiers.

There may be some sort of socio-geometric law to be formulated

The Birth of Venus *by Cabanel, 1863*

arising out of the pose of Cabanel's Venus: any woman in a French nineteenth-century painting depicted horizontally becomes both literally and metaphorically a fallen woman. It might seem decent to make an exception to this rule for corpses, but even here there is sometimes an ambiguity. Dead women exerted a not altogether healthy fascination for some artists, whose sensual exploitation of themes like Ophelia and female martyrdoms hints at ideas which were developed more fully by decadent fin-de-siècle painters. An underlying misogyny is already detectable by the middle of the century, a misogyny that surfaced later in symbolist preoccupations with woman as demon, 'la belle dame sans merci', woman as harbinger of death, and woman as mystery. Some of Henry Lehmann's portraits of women from the 1840s, such as the Princess Belgiojoso or Madame Alphonse Karr, also strike this note of heightened spirituality, of mystery, even of menace.

In addition to classicism a second even more alluring setting to legitimize pictorial nudity and the display of fallen women was developed at the Salon. This was the Middle East. Artists focused

Mme Alphonse Karr *by Lehmann, 1845*

special attention on the harem, the slave market, and the women's bath houses. It was a popular mixture. The public, who had learned from Maxime du Camp's account of the Cairo slave markets that 'people go there to purchase a slave as they go here to the market to buy a turbot', might outwardly affect horror but it didn't stop them speculating excitedly the next time they passed the fishmonger. Harems and slaves answered western man's most enduring private fantasy, the idea of a variety of captive women being kept solely for their master's pleasure, as objects *par excellence*. The official line was that nudity in the seraglio was regrettable, but it was a fit subject for the walls of the Salon because (a) the participants in these scenes of the heathen orient knew no better and (b) they were far distant from the experience of the European spectator. The flagrant depiction of the interior of a Parisian brothel would have been unacceptable, although this is what the spectator is being shown in thin disguise.

The disguise grew increasingly thin because a number of factors blurred the dividing line between east and west. Despite their eastern trappings, the girls depicted so realistically did not look very different from French women. This was because very often they were French women. Muslim females were forbidden by their faith to sit for artists, so home-grown models were employed, conveniently heightening the impact of familiarity for the French spectator. Indeed many harem pictures were painted by artists who had never left their Parisian studios, far less visited the Arab world. To experienced eyes, the women therefore looked exactly what they were: French coquettes in fancy costume. Here is Flaubert describing a Parisian courtesan lighting a hookah: 'She suddenly grew languid and lay motionless on the divan, with a cushion under her armpit, her body slightly twisted, one knee bent and the other outstretched. The long snake of red morocco formed loops on the floor and coiled round her arm. She pressed the amber mouthpiece to her lips and gazed with half-closed eyes through the spirals that enveloped her.' He could just as well be describing a Salon harem picture.

Baudelaire on the other hand draws attention to the reverse process, the way western women might actually find themselves sold into the slave trade. This is his description of a picture of an Arab slave market exhibited at the Salon in 1846 by Octave

The Bathers *by Tassaert, 1837, a painting from the collection of Dumas* fils

Tassaert (the favourite artist of Dumas *fils*): 'These are true women, civilized women, whose feet have felt the rubbing of shoes; they are a little common, a little too pink perhaps, but a silly sensual Turk is going to buy them as superfine beauties. The one who is seen from behind and whose buttocks are enveloped in a transparent gauze still wears upon her head a milliner's hat, a hat bought in Rue Vivienne or at the Temple. The poor girl has doubtless been carried off by pirates.' Baudelaire has identified here once more the most thrilling element of appeal to the contemporary public of harem and slave-market pictures: the women, for one reason or another, were often clearly western.

It is extraordinary what artists could get away with provided they played to the rules and confined their fallen women to

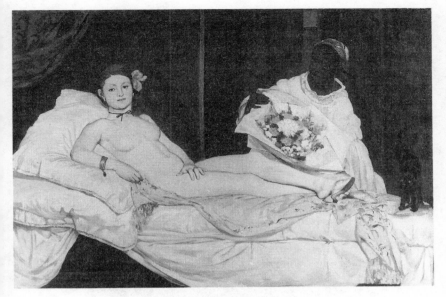

Olympia *by Manet, 1863*

approved settings like Antiquity or the Middle East. The moment
the setting became unequivocally contemporary, however, and the
women undeniably of the demi-monde, then the trouble began.
There was a fundamental resistance to modern life in pictures. It
was considered irredeemably ugly, and its costume laughably inel-
egant. The problems Manet encountered with pictures like
Déjeuner sur l'herbe (1862–3) and *Olympia* (1863) illustrate the
hypocritical reaction of the establishment to the portrayal of
authentic fallen women. The uncompromising way in which
Olympia stares straight out of the picture at the spectator was too
brazen for comfort. The 'high-mindedness' of Gérôme's Phryné,
the coyness of Cabanel's Venus are both missing. Manet's nude is
a picture of a successful professional prostitute who makes no
bones about her calling. The stark contrast of clothed males and
unclothed females in *Déjeuner sur l'herbe* was also too explicit
and challenging for the prejudices of the conventional majority. 'A
commonplace woman of the demi-monde,' wrote one contemporary critic, 'as naked as can be, shamelessly lolling between two
dandies dressed to the teeth.'

Courbet's realism was equally unacceptable. Here was a painter whose avowed intent was 'épater [to shock] les bourgeois'. In the 1850s and 1860s he painted a series of nudes, often 'baigneuses', in which technique and subject matter combine to produce an effect of overwhelming, almost aggressive, intimacy. The same Napoleon III who was happy to acquire Cabanel's *Venus* is reported to have struck out with a riding whip at Courbet's *Baigneuses* in the Salon of 1853. It was the violent reaction of a man who for a moment sees his fantasies stripped away and feels himself exposed by the truth which confronts him.

As the century progressed, even conventional painters became more daring in treating fallen women in contemporary settings.

The Bathers *by Courbet, 1853*

Their motives were generally sensationalist and voyeuristic. Henri Gervex's *Rolla* was rejected by the Salon of 1878 but created enormous interest when exhibited in a private gallery in Paris. It showed a woman spread naked across a bed after a night of passion. Her lover Rolla, the hero of Musset's poem, is broke and has paid for his pleasure by selling his last pistol. Now he is seen leaving the girl's bedroom to commit suicide. What apparently tipped the judgement of the authorities against this picture was the depiction of the girl's abandoned corset and dress next to the bed. As Degas is reported to have told Gervex afterwards: 'Tu vois, on a compris que c'est une femme qui se déshabille' ('You see, people understood that she's the kind of girl who takes her clothes off'). The distinction is an important one. The 'femme nue' is ideal. The 'femme qui se déshabille' is a fallen women. The invasion of the territory of the former by the latter is a significant feature of mid-nineteenth-century French painting.

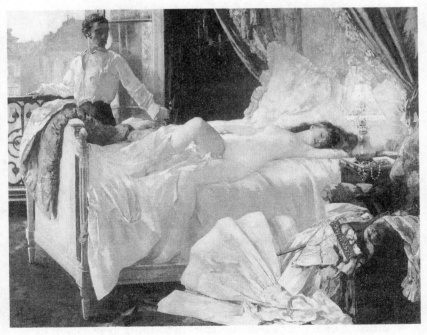

Rolla *by Gervex, 1878, on the subject of Musset's poem of 1833*

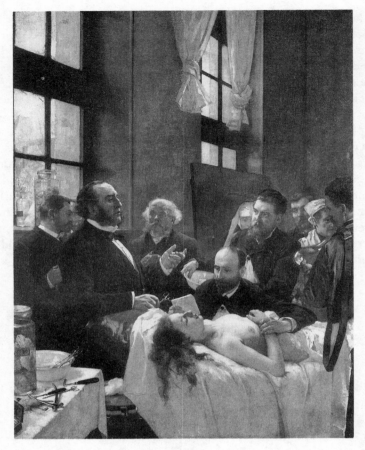

Before the Operation of Dr Péan *by Gervex, 1887*

In the period 1830–70 there was a parallel change of mood in French painters' perception of women. It is evident in the way women are presented in portraiture. There is a growing concentration on materialism at the expense of spiritual qualities, a tendency to emphasize exterior show rather than interior depth. Castagnary pinpointed this development when he wrote in 1872:

In former times ladies had themselves painted for their husbands, for their children. Artists in painting them sought to express the sweetness of their souls, the elevation of their spirits, or the nobility of their feelings. Whereas before, a reserved and discreet demeanour was prized, now only the loudest colours are employed – never before has the human creature, its physiognomy, its soul, been sacrificed so savagely to its garb. Heads are nothing – all the space is taken up by material! And what material! The most showy and sparkling satins! The painter doesn't just drape his models, he overwhelms them. The woman is like a prize cow, to be dressed up and covered in ornaments. What vulgarity of taste, what flashiness of effect!

This, of course, is a divergent strand from symbolist misogyny, the germ of which was noted earlier. But it underlines the tendency, evident in much of the painting already considered, to present women as objects. French painters gave their public a variety of these images; women as indolent coquette (Cabanel's *Birth of Venus*); woman as male-dominated plaything (in the harem); woman as object of beauty who must expose herself to justify herself (*Phryné*). Now Castagnary identifies one more, woman as prize cow, a mindless being fulfilled only when dressed up and prettified. The descent from the human to animal has been accomplished. Women fell constantly in Paris in the nineteenth century, as Augustus Leopold Egg points out. And French artists were not above giving them a gentle push.

James Pradier
Phryné, *1845*

Phryné *was one of the most talked-about exhibits in the 1845 Salon. Whether Pradier originally conceived this elegant marble statue as the celebrated Greek courtesan, or a woman with a vase, or a nymph bathing, is obscure: Baudelaire, for instance, analysed the work in detail but made no allusion at all either to its subject matter or to its title. It is typical of many nineteenth-century sculptors to find a pleasing pose in a studio model, or in a figure in nature, which suggested an historical event or a fictional character; once the composition was chosen, they would expand upon it and refine it with historical references.*

Phryné by James Pradier, bronze, 1845

Pradier's Phryné *does not illustrate any of the key episodes in the life of the Greek courtesan who has fascinated writers and artists through the ages. Referring to Quintilian, Diderot praised Baudouin's drawing of 1763 ('Phryné accused of impiety before the Areopagites'), where 'unveiled Beauty triumphs over morality': 'You, who sit like the offended gods' avengers, look at this woman it has pleased them to create and, if you dare, destroy their beautiful work.' This scene was frequently chosen for literary treatments in Pradier's youth; it appeared from time to time as a subject in painting, but not as a large-scale statue. Although the fashion for life-size sculptures of antique courtesans preceded Pradier's* Phryné, *it seems that his was the first monumental representation of this theme.*

In the climate of the 1840s, the sculpture is evidence of a cult of pagan beauty but, curiously, there is no sign in Pradier's work of any pronounced erotic titillation. His Phryné *is proud but*

*restrained and even modest: some thought she was too little the
courtesan. Phryné was the mistress of Praxiteles and of Apelles,
who saw her let her clothes fall before the assembled Greeks, and
sketched her likeness as a 'Venus Anadyomena' – a subject dear to
the Neoclassicists, because it combined into a single model the
ideal beauty of each part of the female body. Pradier celebrates the
beauty of the female form and ignores the historical accounts that
she was the prudent dispenser of the wealth which her beauty had
conferred upon her. (She offered to provide the funds to rebuild
the walls of Thebes which Alexander had destroyed.) Pradier
offers neither an image of Phryné's moral profligacy, nor a defence
of her as a friend of culture and the arts.*

*The figure seems self-absorbed, curiously detached from the
spectator, and involved in an ambiguous gesture that confused the
critics – is she pulling her drapery back on, or is she letting it fall?
She belongs in a tradition, stretching from Antiquity, of representations of women bathing or at their toilette, who are observed,
often by their own choice, and who thereby become objects of a
voyeuristic gaze of varying degrees of erotic titillation. Pradier
often returned to this theme in the 1840s in statues both large and
small. The Nyssia of 1848 is another instance. He gave Phryné an
unusual expression but there are no surprises in the composition
of the figure; like others, Baudelaire saw in it 'a prodigious blend
of concealments'. Several sources for the pose come to mind,
notably Ingres's 'Venus Anadyomena', although Pradier's work is
notably more slender. He used the polychromy with discretion.*

*Thoré, a contemporary critic, praised the sculpture because it
was Greek in its conception and perfect in execution: 'That kind of
beauty is as fine as the austere beauty of the Middle Ages, or the
tormented beauty of the Renaissance . . . It is a purely plastic
beauty, like that of Antiquity, concerned not with a woman's soul
but with the shape of a line and the perfection of the outline. If this
woman were destined to be a mother, she would need a fuller
figure, and more tenderness in the curvature of the waist . . .'*

*The work was sent to the Great Exhibition in London in 1851
where it won the Council of Presidents' medal, the highest award
given to a French sculpture.*

Vincenzo Vela
The Contessa d'Adda, *1849*

O ne is far more aware of bedclothes, canopy and embroidered coverlets – discreet indications of the departed's social status – than of the significance of the overwhelmed little human object that threatens to disappear among their richly material profusion. Apart from the crucifix in her hand, there is nothing to hint that the Contessa is doing more than taking a peaceful nap amid tastefully luxurious surroundings.   Linda Nochlin, *Realism*, 1971

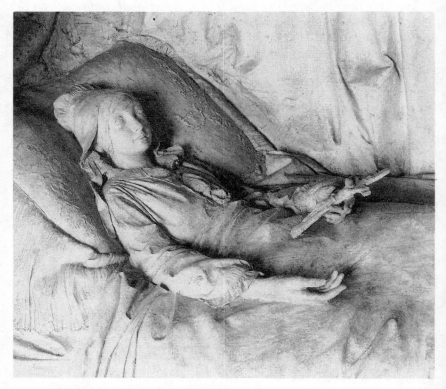

The Contessa d'Adda *by Vincenzo Vela, plaster model for the tomb at Arcore, 1849*

Salvatore Grita
The Vow against Nature, *c. 1860–70*

This is the only work of Salvatore Grita (1828–1912), a Sicilian working in Florence, that has survived. His titles were always related to newspaper headlines of a social or tragic nature. Camillo Boito, a contemporary critic, mentioned this habit disapprovingly, but continued: 'The expression of moral decay that is hinted at in the midst of physical suffering is subtly indicated ... the whole figure is so convincingly rendered that the

The Vow against Nature *by Salvatore Grita, c. 1860–70.*
Inscribed on the base are the words: 'To the protectors and supporters of the vow against nature Grita dedicates this work.'

smile dies on one's lips ... there in the midst of every virtue is the germ of sin.' The dedication of this sculpture refers to the polemic against monastic vows current in much romantic art, for example The Nun of Monza *or the lines of Aleardi:*

Così la Vergine – d'amor privata
Compie da vittima – la sua giornata
Oh voi riditelo – erme dimore
Di meste suore!

So the Virgin – deprived of love
Ends her days – as a victim
Oh, you laugh at it – solitary home
Of melancholy Sisters!

Émile Hébert
And For Ever!! And Never¡¡

This plaster sculpture by Émile Hébert caught Baudelaire's eye at the 1859 Salon, but he could not identify the source of the sculpture's title, with its curious punctuation. The art historian Jeanne Stump (The Register of The Spencer Museum of Art, *University of Kansas) has suggested that the title may recall Paul de Kock's novel* Ni toujours ni jamais, *which appeared in 1835, about which the* Grand dictionnaire universel du 19e siècle *(1874) declared:* 'The moral of this book is that in love *never means nothing,* always *not much, and in short that in getting married the man and woman promise more than they can carry out.' Many poems treat the themes of the* danse macabre *and of Death and the Maiden, and the sculpture offers a poignant link between romantics and symbolists.*

A charming piece of sculpture (chamber-sculpture, shall we call it? although it is doubtful if the ladies and gentlemen of the bourgeoisie would want it to decorate their boudoirs) – a kind of vignette in sculpture, but one which nevertheless might make an excellent funeral decoration in a cemetery or a chapel, if executed on a larger scale. A young girl, generous and supple of form, is being lifted and swung up with a harmonious lightness; and her body, convulsed in ecstasy or in agony, is resignedly submitting to the kiss of an immense skeleton.   Charles Baudelaire, *Salon*, 1859

And For Ever!! And Never¡¡ *by Émile Hébert, 1859*

Alphonse de Lamartine
Chant d'Amour, *1822*

Et quand la mort viendra, d'un autre amour suivie
Eteindre en souriant de notre double vie
L'un et l'autre flambeau,
Qu'elle étende ma couche à côté de la tienne,
Et que ta main fidèle embrasse encor la mienne
Dans le lit du tombeau.

Elisa Mercoeur
Élegie, *1825*

La mort couvre mes yeux de ses voiles funèbres,
Son froid glace mon coeur;
Ma voix s'éteint, je cède, je succombe:
Je suis heureuse de mourir,
Puisqu'aujourd'hui la même tombe
Va pour jamais nous réunir.

Victor Hugo
Fantômes, *1828*

La mort aux froides mains la prit toute parée,
Pour endormir dans le cercueil.
Pour danser d'autres bals elle était encore prête,
Tant la mort fut pressée à prendre un corps si beau!
Et ces roses d'un jour qui couronnaient sa tête,
Qui s'épanouissaient la veille en une fête,
Se fanèrent dans un tombeau.

Love Song

And when, followed by another love, death,
Smiling, will come to put out both torches
Of our shared life,
May he put my couch next to thine,
And may thy faithful hand still embrace mine
In the bed of the tomb.

Elegy

Death covers my eyes with his funereal veils,
His cold chills my heart;
My voice is extinguished, I give up, I succumb:
I am happy to die,
Since today the same tomb
Will reunite us for ever.

Ghosts

Death with cold hands seized her all adorned,
To put her to sleep in the coffin.
She was still ready to dance at other balls,
Death was so hurried to take a body so beautiful!
And these day-roses which wreathed her head,
Which blossomed the night before in celebration,
Withered in a tomb.

Jean Béraud
Mary Magdalen in the House of the Pharisee, *1891*

Béraud's Mary Magdalen in the House of the Pharisee *was acclaimed by the public when it was shown in 1891, although the critics disliked it. Contemporaries recognized the duc de Quercy, a poet, as the model for Christ, Ernest Renan as Simon the Pharisee and Alexandre Dumas* fils *standing at Christ's left hand. Only recently has the Magdalen been identified as the courtesan Liane de Pougy, who became Mme Armand Pourpre and then Princess Georges Ghika, and ended her days as Sister Anne-Marie, a tertiary lay sister of the Order of Saint Dominic; she died in 1950.*

The Laglenne sisters are urging me to take communion. I want this communion, I am seeking Jesus. One thing's for sure, at my first communion I was not seeking anything at all, in those

Mary Magdalen in the House of the Pharisee *by Jean Béraud, 1891*

days I was a heedless, greedy little beast, a hot-blooded young animal chafing at the bit, laughing at Hell, pausing at neither the
Passion nor the Cross, glimpsing death only to cock a snook at it
... Now that I have been through every kind of suffering, have
measured the infamy of human beings and the cruelty of fate, the
insecurity of every living thing, God has become necessary to me. I
want Him, I need Him, I seek Him, I call on Him, I pray to Him.
Perhaps holy communion will speed my efforts towards success?
Liane de Pougy, *My Blue Notebooks*, 14 April 1922

The Trials of *Madame Bovary* and *Les Fleurs du mal*

*Two famous cases concerning public morality took place in Paris
in 1857: Flaubert's novel* Madame Bovary *was acquitted, while six
months later Baudelaire was convicted for his anthology* Les Fleurs
du mal, *and it was published with six poems omitted. The ban was
not lifted until 1949. The Prosecution was led by Ernest Pinard in
both cases. This is an extract from the trial of* Madame Bovary.

COUNSEL FOR THE PROSECUTION, M. PINARD: Adultery is
stigmatized, condemned by name, not because it is unwise enough
to expose disillusion and regret, but because it is a crime against
the family. Suicide is stigmatized and condemned, not because it is
an act of cowardice – it sometimes demands a measure of physical
courage – but because it shows contempt for duty in this life and is
a cry of disbelief at the next.

Such morality gives realist literature a bad name, not because it
paints the passions. Hate, vengeance, love – the world is made of
little else, and art must paint them; but realist literature does so
without restraint, with no sense of proportion. Art without rules
ceases to be art; it is like a woman taking off all her clothes.
Imposing the one rule of public decency upon art is not to enslave
it, but to do it honour. There is no greatness without rules. These
then, Gentlemen, are the principles that we profess, this the
doctrine that we conscientiously uphold.

COUNSEL FOR THE DEFENCE, M. SÉNARD: Let me turn now to
the other details of the crime of outrage against religion. This is
what the public ministry tells me: 'It isn't just religion: you have
outraged eternal morality; you have insulted death!' How has
death been insulted? Because at the moment when this woman is
dying, a man passes by in the street, a man whom she had met
more than once, begging for alms, by the carriage in which she
used to return from her adulterous encounters. It was the Blind
Man that she was used to seeing, the Blind Man who sang his song
while the carriage slowly climbed the hill, the man to whom she
would toss a coin, and whose appearance made her shiver. This
man passes by in the street: and at the precise moment that divine
mercy pardons, or promises to pardon, the unhappy creature
expiating the errors of her life by her terrible death, human mockery appears to her in the form of a song heard under her window.
My God! You find that an outrage? M. Flaubert is only doing
what Shakespeare and Goethe did: they made sure that, when
death was imminent, some song, whether of lamentation or mockery, would be heard to remind the person about to go on to the life
everlasting of some pleasure lost forever, or of some sin to be expi-
ated. Let us read:

> And indeed, she was looking slowly about her, like one waking
> from a dream. In a clearly audible voice she asked for her
> mirror, and lay for a moment or two with her face bent above it,
> until two large tears trickled from her eyes. Then she threw back
> her head with a sigh, and collapsed on to the pillow.
>
> At once her breath began to come in pants. Her tongue
> protruded from her mouth to its full length. Her eyes rolled
> wildly and grew pale like two lamp globes which have just been
> extinguished. She might have been thought already dead, had it
> not been that her ribs were agitated by a terrifying spasm of
> quick breathing, as though her soul were struggling for freedom.
> Félicité knelt before the crucifix, and even the chemist was a
> little unsteady on his legs, while Monsieur Canivet gazed with
> unseeing eyes into the square.
>
> Monsieur Bournisien had returned once more to his prayers,
> his forehead resting on the edge of the bed, his long black
> soutane trailing behind him on the floor. Charles, kneeling at

the opposite side, stretched out his arms to Emma. He had taken her hands and was pressing them, trembling at each beat of her heart, as at the thundering fall of stones from a doomed ruin. As the death-rattle became more marked, the churchman hastened his prayers. They mingled with Bovary's stifled sobs and at times all other sounds seemed to vanish in the low murmur of the Latin syllables which rang out like a passing-bell.

Suddenly there was a noise of heavy clogs from the street, and the tap-tapping of a stick. A voice rose high and distinct, a hoarse voice, singing:

> Souvent la chaleur d'un beau jour
> Fait rêver fillette à l'amour.

Emma raised herself like a galvanized corpse, her hair in disorder, her eyes fixed and staring.

> Pour amasser diligemment
> Les épis que la faux moissonne,
> Ma Nanette va s'inclinant
> Vers le sillon qui nous les donne.

'The blind man!' she cried.

And she started to laugh in a fit of horrible, wild, despairing mirth. She thought she saw the hideous face of the beggar standing out from the eternal darkness like a symbol of terror.

> Il souffla bien fort ce jour là
> Et le jupon court s'envola!

She fell back on the mattress in a convulsion. All in the room drew close. She was no more.

Note, Gentlemen, how at the supreme moment, there is the recollection of error, regrets and a tremendous poignancy and sense of horror. This is not just the whim of an artist making a contrast which has neither utility nor morality. It is the blind man that she hears in the street singing his terrible song, the song he would sing when she used to return sweating and ugly from her adulterous trysts; it is the blind man that she sees on each of these occasions; it is the blind man who pursues her with his song, with his importuning; it is he who, at the moment of divine mercy, comes to personify the human rage that rails against her, even to the point of death! And that is called an outrage against public morality! I would say, rather, that it is a homage to public morality, that you couldn't have anything more moral. I would argue that in this book education's weaknesses come alive, that it is based on the real, on the living flesh of our society, and at every point, the author asks this: 'Have you done what you should for the education of your daughters? Is the religion you have given them sufficient to sustain them through life's storms, or is it nothing but a heap of carnal superstitions which leaves them helpless while the storm rages? Have you taught them that life is nothing to do with making dreams come true, that it is something prosaic to which they must accommodate themselves? Have you taught them that? Have you done what you should for their happiness? Have you said to them: "Poor chil-

Flaubert dissecting Emma Bovary, *a caricature by Lemot in* La Parodie, *September 1869*

dren, beyond the path that I show you, in the pleasures that you pursue, all that awaits you is disgust, leaving home, trouble, disorder, collapse, convulsions, seizures" . . . ' And you look to see if something in the picture is missing; the bailiff is there, there too the Jew who has been selling to satisfy this woman's caprices, the furniture has been seized, the sale will go ahead; and the husband still knows nothing. The only thing left for the unhappy woman is to die!

But, says the public ministry, her death is voluntary. This woman dies when she chooses. Could she have gone on living? Was she not damned? Had she not drunk the last drop of shame and degradation?

Yes, on the stage, there are women who have deviated from the straight and narrow, gracious, smiling, happy, and I do not want to say what they have done. *Questum corpore fecerunt.* I shall say no more. When we are shown them happy, charming, draped in muslin, extending a graceful hand to count, marquis or duke, and often answering to the name of marchioness or duchess themselves, that's what is called respecting public morality. And it is the man who shows you an adulterous woman dying in shame who is committing an outrage against public morality!

Judgement was given in Flaubert's favour on 8 February 1857. His reaction was this: 'I would have you know that people rank me with young Alex. My Bovary is now a Lady of the Camellias! Boum!'

The case against Baudelaire for Les Fleurs du mal *was heard on 20 August 1857. 'Nothing', said the verdict, 'could dissipate the harmful effect of the images he presents to the reader, and which, in the incriminated poems, inevitably lead to the arousal of the senses by crude and indecent realism.' The reaction of Baudelaire's great contemporaries was very different: Flaubert wrote to him, 'You've found a way to inject new life into Romanticism . . . You're as resistant as marble and as penetrating as fog', while Victor Hugo commented, 'Your "flowers of evil" are as radiant and as dazzling as stars . . . You have just received one of the few decorations the present regime can bestow. What it refers to as its justice has condemned you in the name of what it likes to call its morality.'*

Charles Baudelaire
from a review of Madame Bovary, *1857*

As for the deep inner focus of the fable, it is indisputably the adulterous woman; she alone, the dishonoured victim, possesses all the hero's graces. I said just now that she was almost male, and that the author had ornamented her (perhaps unconsciously) with all the virile qualities.

Let us examine them attentively:

1 Imagination, that supreme and tyrannical faculty, has been substituted for the heart, or for what we call the heart, from where reasoning is normally excluded, and which usually dominates a woman as it does an animal;

2 The intense energy for action, quick decisions and a mystical fusion of reasoning and passion, which characterizes men made for action;

3 Immoderate appetite for seduction, for domination and even of all the vulgar means of seduction, down to dressing up with costumes, perfumes and cosmetics, – the whole may be summarized in brief: dandyism, the exclusive love of domination.

And yet Madame Bovary gives herself; carried away by the sophistry of her imagination, she gives herself magnificently, generously, in a wholly masculine manner, to fools who are not her equals, exactly like poets give themselves to foolish women ...

4 Even in her convent education, I find proof of Madame Bovary's equivocal temperament. The good sisters noticed an astonishing aptitude for life in the girl, for profiting from life and guessing its delights; – here is the man of action!

Philip Ward-Jackson
Love and Art for Sale in the July Monarchy

Philip Ward-Jackson is Deputy Conway Librarian at the Courtauld Institute of Art, London.

After the death of the real-life *dame aux camélias*, Marie Duplessis, respectable people flocked to the auction of her personal effects. Dramatically inverting the chronology of events, Alexandre Dumas *fils*, in his fictional account of the famous courtesan's last fling, used the auction as his opening scene. The prime pickings, as described in the novel, are an array of gold and silver items by Aucoc and Odiot, Boulle furniture, Dresden figurines and Sèvres china. Smart possessions indeed, and for the historian of taste not entirely without interest, in that they indicate an accommodation with pre-revolutionary styles paralleling the identification of the courtesan herself with the abbé Prévost's fictional courtesan Manon Lescaut.

A rather more complete description of the apartment of Marie Duplessis herself is provided for us by Jules Janin in his preface to the 1852 edition of *La Dame aux camélias*. Its contents suggested to this writer the 'admirable choice of a discriminating and wealthy antiquary'. They seemed to indicate above all a nostalgia for the delicacies of the eighteenth century, for that 'little art of coquetry, grace and elegance, in which even vice has its wit, where innocence has its nudities'. Contemporary art was represented there only by two works of Vidal, including his portrait of the courtesan herself, and by the paintings of Diaz, who, Janin tells us, 'she had been amongst the first to adopt'.

Elsewhere, we read of bedroom furnishings which are more eloquent of robust debauchery: a Boulle bed with caryatid feet, columns at its corners, carved with vines and cupids, and supporting vases. This had been replaced during Marie's last illness by a simple rosewood couch bed, so that the effect of delicacy and refinement was unimpaired in the eyes of the visitors at the auction. As described by Janin and Dumas, the interior has nothing of the 'mauvais lieu' or of artistic pretentiousness. Janin is even at pains to create a wistful and valetudinarian effect by omitting all harsh notes. Was not Marie herself, like her knick-knacks, a fragile decorative thing 'smashed by the first shock'?

About the collectables enumerated by Dumas there is also a calculated opacity. Their aristocratic or 'haut bourgeois' refinement implies a rejection of the rich profusion of allusive artefacts available to the Parisian shopper of the 1840s. Dumas *fils* was perfectly aware of the amount of 'cultural construction' and of stage setting behind that curious phenomenon known as 'modern love'. He preferred to disregard it, no doubt in order to preserve the effect of purity and inevitability in his heroine's destiny. His story was

Paris fashions in the Illustrated London News, *November 1848*

already immediate enough, and his object was to make an event of yesterday into a lasting fable, a classic tale in a modern setting.

The apparent indifference of the fictional Marguerite Gautier to the allurements of décor is not shared by the high-living prostitutes in the novels of Flaubert and Balzac. Writing retrospectively of the life of the period in *L'Éducation sentimentale*, Flaubert, with typical understatement, describes the effect on Frédéric Moreau of Rosanette Bron's bedroom. It was really, he says, 'an environment designed to please', though he goes on to add, in an authorial aside which is the reverse of typical, that 'these elegances would today be deemed wretched for the likes of Rosanette'. It must be remembered that *L'Éducation sentimentale* was written only in the later days of the Second Empire, at which time the immensely wealthy courtesan, Thérèse Lachmann, the Marquise de Païva, was using a team of architect, sculptors and painters, to upstage all love nests within living memory. How could Rosanette's painted cupids, swan's-down and pink silk compete with the Palace of Art known as the Hôtel de la Païva?

On the other hand, Balzac's Josefa in *Cousine Bette* shows us that La Païva may well have had serious rivals in the days of the Bourgeois Monarchy. Josefa is not content with the sort of reproductive sculptures which, thanks to refinements in the sand-casting process, were then flooding the Parisian market. She is surrounded by 'those admirable productions to which the great unknown artists who are creating the Paris of today . . . had all contributed'. These artefacts, by their uniqueness, conferred on the courtesan an air of unique desirability. 'The models having been broken, the decorative forms, figurines and more monumental sculptures were all originals. This is the last word in luxury today. To possess things which have not been vulgarized by two thousand opulent bourgeois . . . '

The vision shared by these authors is one of love and art commodified, each providing the other with mutual support and advertisement. This is one of the main themes of *L'Éducation sentimentale*, in which Rosanette oils the works for the con-man Jacques Arnoux. Some of the objects adorning the captious apartment to which we have already referred are recognized as the erstwhile furnishings of Arnoux's offensively named shop, 'L'Art Industriel'. At the centre of the web of dubious transactions,

The grand salon *of the Hôtel de la Païva (now the Travellers' Club) at 25, Avenue des Champs Élysées*

Arnoux's apparently faithful wife is herself unwittingly prostituted by her husband, who conscious of Frédéric's infatuation with her, duns him continually for loans and other assistance. The aside in which Flaubert so uncharacteristically tells us that Rosanette's furnishings would be outdone draws attention to the ineluctable nature of this collaboration between art and commercial sex. It was a development that the republican caesura of 1848 would not bring to an end. What during the July Monarchy may have looked like a charming charade would develop in the Second Empire into a full-blown industry of degradation.

For Flaubert the collaboration did nothing to improve either art or prostitution. Vulgar romanticism had eroded what he saw as the barbaric splendour of prostitution as it was practised in civilizations less tainted by commercialism, and artists had debased themselves by creating a backdrop for life as a carnival in which the number of transactions could be multiplied through the confusion of identities. One channel through which this was visibly achieved was the vastly expanded popular press and the increased circulation of newspapers and periodicals, providing new opportunities for the manipulation of public attitudes.

Amongst visual artists exploiting this situation, one man, Gavarni, seemed to acquire in the 1840s unique prestige as illustrator, and, by implication, inventor of urban life. His imagery and captions are saturated with somewhat self-congratulatory 'boulevardier' cynicism. He was at once caricaturist and flatterer. In the same way that journalists and designers in our time have seized upon and consolidated images of a social type – the Sloane Ranger or the Punk – Gavarni was credited with having encapsulated the 'lorettes' and 'Débardeurs' of his time. The lorette seems in Gavarni's construction of her to be a particularly harmless, even charming sort of scrounger, an informal sexual trader who might attach herself to a student or a bourgeois, according to the advantage she saw in it, but who supposedly did not ration her favours too strictly in terms of time and companionship. She was a kind of Robin Hood of sex, recycling her gains from the more affluent as fun and affection for her harder-up but probably better-looking lovers. This image was imbued with some of the glamour which Gavarni had retained from his days as a fashion illustrator, and it remained highly selective, frozen in time, to the extent that the after-life of the lorette either as the dying Mimì, or in her more fortunate reincarnation as 'poule de luxe' was not envisaged. Astonishingly, as Baudelaire pointed out, the creator of these potent role-models had probably never, himself, set foot in a 'bastringue', one of those dance halls frequented by the type of people most likely to identify with his creations.

By the time we meet her, transformed by Dumas *fils* into Marguerite Gautier, Marie Duplessis had no need of these low sentimental patterns. She had become 'one of nature's aristocrats'. However, within her own consumer bracket, she shares with the lorette and the earlier grisette a preference for the pretty but inconspicuous over the flashy, only the discreet twinkle of the diamonds at her ears hinting, for the curious 'flâneur', at the power of her purse. None the less, the circumstance in which Armand Duval, in the novel, first encounters Marguerite is a coded reference to that aphrodisiac, 'prostituted' art which, in its more select manifestations, provided the setting for Balzac's Josefa. It also brings momentarily to view an earlier episode in the love-life of Alexandre Dumas *fils*, some aspects of which he must have wished buried for ever.

Armand sees Marguerite Gautier for the first time as she enters the shop of Susse in the Place de la Bourse. As Susse was originally, and remained, a stationer, it is possible that she was there only to purchase expensive notepaper. All the same she would have found it hard not to notice the mythological and modern statuettes, and other works of art, into which Susse had quite recently diversified. Part of Susse's stock-in-trade since 1840 had been an assortment of pieces by the Prix de Rome sculptor James Pradier, whose wife, Louise, had seduced the young Dumas in 1843, the year before he met Maris Duplessis.

In any consideration of the cultural construction of the courtesan, the case of Mme Pradier (née d'Arcet), must be of outstanding interest. Dumas himself later mythologized her in his novel *L'Affaire Clemenceau*, and she was certainly one of Flaubert's models for the character of Madame Bovary. Her marriage to Pradier at the age of nineteen was already her second, her first husband, an architect, having succumbed to cholera shortly after their wedding. Pradier had also enjoyed a previous liaison with Juliette Drouet, who later became Victor Hugo's faithful mistress. By the time of his marriage to Louise, Pradier was a middle-aged, well-established sculptor, known to his friends as Phidias because of his taste for classical and mythological themes. Not being a pedant, and happy to make a little extra money on non-official work, Pradier increasingly experimented in the statuette form. A number of these statuettes were erotic by the standards of the times, so much so that the *Journal des Artistes* accused the sculptor of courting celebrity 'by selling obscenities for the temptation, fascination and demoralization of youth'.

There has always been speculation about who were the models of particular works by Pradier. When it came to his wife, he

Woman putting on her stockings *by Pradier, bronze, 1840–45*

appears, understandably, to have avoided gossip by exhibiting her features only in harmless religious and allegorical subjects. Yet, by all accounts, her presence in the studio was a definite attraction. Her husband was an ebullient, party-loving character, who delighted to be seen by the public in shirt-sleeves hewing the marble, an unusual activity as it happens amongst the grander sculptors of the day, most of whom had little idea how to carve. Louise was only too happy to entertain, especially the more famous visitors. This, according to Maxime Ducamp, was how she saw her role. 'I saw myself', he quotes her as saying, 'drawing into my home the established members of the Institute, discovering, protecting the younger artists, inviting poets and composers, knowing how to keep the interest of men of the world, becoming, in a word, the point of interaction between two societies which exist side by side without mingling. I had dreamed that I would be a sort of Medici, whose Salon would be a neutral territory, an élite territory, in which the distinguished in art, intelligence and aristocracy would come together and fraternize.' Unfortunately the celebrities, and others, looked for and were granted less intellectual favours by Mme Pradier. Not far into the marriage, she began a series of liaisons with other men, feeling herself in the end carried away by a force beyond her control. According to a confessional document amongst the Flaubert papers, only one of the three children she bore during her marriage could claim the sculptor as its father.

When Dumas *fils* came to write his thinly veiled account of the Pradier ménage in *L'Affaire Clemenceau*, he attributed to the sculptor himself some of the blame for his wife's infidelities. The narrative implies that Pradier had been far less reticent about his wife's peculiar attractions than appears to have been the case, and Mme Iza, the *femme fatale* of the novel, gloats over images of herself by her husband, displayed in shop windows. Towards the end, a friend reproaches the sculptor for these indiscretions: 'After passing from hand to hand, in the species of marble and bronze, she decided to reveal herself before believer and unbeliever alike. A venal Galatea, she sprang to life for the first comer, and not content with offerings of flowers, love, tears and blood, she demanded also diamonds and gold.' This was a reference to Ovid's tale of the metamorphosis of Pygmalion's statue into his love object. Feminists may not find it surprising that, after the event, Dumas's sympathies were all for the sculptor, whereas the woman in the case became, in his imagination, evil incarnate.

Pradier, it seems, was less disturbed by his wife's infidelities than by the fact that she was making free with his money. It was this which persuaded him to seek a divorce. Amongst the various accusations which he levelled against her in his legal deposition, the sculptor claimed that 'She had, at no. 7 Rue Bourdaloue, an apartment which she had had grandly furnished as a place to receive the younger Dumas, whose debts, it is said, she paid off.' Dumas adamantly denied this, and Pradier eventually withdrew it, but claiming he was under pressure from Dumas to do so, pressure which ill-health disinclined him to resist. These *revendications* followed upon Mme Pradier's discovery *in flagrante* and the legal dissolution of the marriage. When it was all over, Mme Pradier proceeded to live openly as a kept woman with a variety of lovers.

The *Journal des Artistes* was not the only voice claiming that Pradier had prostituted his art. This reputation caused him to lose the major commission for the tomb of the Duke of Orleans, oldest son of Louis-Philippe, and heir to the French throne. The King himself was predisposed to favour him with the commission but the earnest and pious painter, Ary Scheffer, protested Pradier's debasement of his art as a disqualifying factor. Scheffer's 'spirited colloquy' with the King is recorded in a posthumous memoir of the painter's life:

> 'Pardon, Sire, but Pradier is not equal to the task.'
> 'And pray why not?'
> 'Because, Your Majesty, Pradier has made too many things to sell, of late years, or "shop articles".'
> 'Ah, well, that is no matter; Pradier shall do it all the same.'
> 'Pardon, Sire, but I say Pradier will not do it.'
> 'How not do it! And what if I order him?'
> 'That will make no difference. The wishes of the artist will carry more weight with him than any command, even that of a monarch.'

In other words, supposing this conversation to have been accurately reported, which one may reasonably doubt, this interdict was supposed to have been one that the artist's own conscience would reinforce.

It is ironical, given the disaster of his own family life, that Pradier should have been the artist chosen to sculpt a group representing The Marriage of the Virgin for the Church of La Madeleine, Marie Duplessis's parish church and the scene of the memorial service held for her after her death. Constituting part of a programme devised by civil servants to illustrate the social applications of biblical morality, Pradier's group faces, across the nave, a pendent Baptism of Christ by François Rude, the two groups confronting the visitor on entering the church with the types of these two familial sacraments. To get this far, the visitor has already had to pass through monumental bronze doors, whose panels are adorned with reliefs using episodes from the Old Testament to illustrate the Ten Commandments. At the far end of the interior of the church, and as if acknowledging prostitution as the chief target of this moral rearmament, a marble figure of Saint Mary Magdalen is borne heavenward by three powerful angels.

The high altar, with its group of the apotheosis of the Saint, was commissioned from the Italian-born sculptor Carlo Marochetti by

'Honour thy father and thy mother' *by de Triqueti;*
detail of the bronze doors of La Madeleine, 1838

the Ministry of the Interior, which was obliged to defend it, once executed, against the attacks of the independent 'Conseil de Fabrique' for the church. The Conseil observed, quite rightly, that it failed to conform to any known traditional iconography and protested that it was far too prominent. To which the Secretary for the Fine Arts replied that its unconventional character would inevitably excite criticism but he was impressed with it and felt that it was perfectly in accord with the character of the building.

One aspect of the church's character had been determined by the expiatory function assigned to it when it was returned to the Catholic religion after the fall of Napoleon. In that context, the Magdalen symbolized Catholic France bewailing her revolution-

'Thou shalt not covet thy neighbour's wife' *by de Triqueti;
detail of the bronze doors of La Madeleine, 1838*

ary transgressions. After the Revolution of 1830 that function was
removed but the Magadalen was retained in view of the church's
dedication to her, and ended up as the centrepiece in a programme
designed to promote Catholic family values. In this context, her
meaning was clear enough, though never apparently alluded to in
official documents, and that she was repentant there had to be no
doubt.

La Dame aux camélias brings together, as does Verdi's opera to
an even greater extent, the currents of worldliness and religiosity
which in the visual arts were generally segregated, although
amongst the paintings and lithographs of the period there are
examples of what can only be called 'Hogarth with angels'. The

The Magdalen Born Aloft by Angels *by Marochetti;*
the High Altar of La Madeleine, 1843

painter who stirred this particular equivocal mixture with the
greatest skill, Octave Tassaert, proves, unsurprisingly, to have been
the visual artist most cherished by Alexandre Dumas *fils*. After
Tassaert's death, Dumas, in a preface to a short monograph on the
artist, boasted of the possession of fifty of Tassaert's paintings.

Significantly in our context, one criticism of Tassaert which
Dumas felt obliged to refute was the claim that the artist had 'trop
battue monnaie', that he had been a commercially minded artist.
He argued that the artist had died in poverty and that, apart from
drink, his needs in life had been few. He insisted besides that he
had met Tassaert but once, implying that there had been no
occasion for salesmanly blandishments. These would scarcely have

'You'll pay for this!' *by Tassaert, 1832*

been necessary in view of the deep affinity between author and painter. Like Dumas, Tassaert came from an artistic background. His grandfather had been a sculptor with an international reputation, and it was probably a matter of pride to him that his grandmother's portrait by J.-B. Greuze had been exhibited at the Salon of 1765. Assessors of his contribution to the development of nineteenth-century painting have rightly credited him with a major role in the revival of a sentimental/erotic pictorial content redolent of the previous century. In coloration too, he evolves for certain subjects a palette whose mauvy greyish harmonies and morbid transparent flesh tones derive directly from Greuze.

Tassaert's first ambition was to be history painter, a far from dependable vocation. To supplement his income, he cultivated a sideline in erotic subjects, designed for circulation in the newly popular printing technique, lithography. Whilst they use the romantic conventions of lighting and costume, Tassaert's erotic prints are brash, verging on the caricatural. It was probably the discovery of the comparative viability of this subject matter which prompted him, during the 1840s, to introduce the sensual element into oil paintings of modest and easily affordable dimensions, whose stylistic refinement is in distinct contrast to the crudity of the prints.

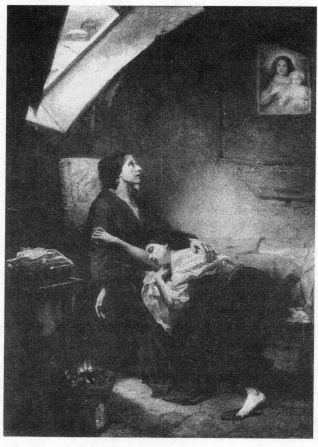

An Unfortunate Family, or The Suicide *by Tassaert, 1852. This painting was commissioned by the state in 1849 in response to the artist's plea for financial assistance and was widely praised.*

Charles Baudelaire would have liked to see Tassaert become the ultimate painter of physical love but it was finally as the painter of misery and of suicide that he was to make his mark. The concluding irony was that the artist, partially blind and totally alcohol dependent, ended his life by the same means as the despairing subjects in a number of his own paintings, asphyxiating himself with the fumes from a coal fire. In the paintings, the motif of the brazier, a blatant anecdotal expedient, indicates that his subjects have no future and prompts thoughts about their past lives and loves. For Dumas *fils* the alternations of rococo gallantry with its shadow side in the work of Tassaert were fuel for what, in the writer's case, would finally develop into an impassioned diatribe aimed at loose living and neglect of domestic responsibilities.

Though the various factitious worlds I hope to have described here are hinted at in *La Dame aux camélias*, they are for the moment purposefully understressed. The heroine herself displays in front of her friends, even before the start of her affair with Armand Duval, a total indifference to the expensive artefacts by which she is surrounded. On the level of fictional invention, Dumas opts for the apparently natural and inevitable. His heroine's sickness stands in for the self-inflicted expiations of Tassaert's Magdalens ancient and modern. For contemporary readers, aware of the artifice pervading the world of 'modern love', the narrative must have gained a force from its exclusion of a potential welter of description. This was a literary renunciation equivalent to the moral sacrifice made by Marguerite herself, and, as Baudelaire observed, 'Relative to pure dream, to the unanalysed impression, the art of definite forms, positive art is a blasphemy.'

PART FOUR

Reincarnations

Reincarnations

While the book took Dumas a month to complete, and was his first, and greatest, success, friends urged him to adapt it into a play and, after initial hesitation, he wrote the five acts in eight days. Inevitably the censor objected to its immorality, as his father had foreseen, and the ban lasted for three years – until the coup d'état of Napoleon III in December *1851* put the high-living duc de Morny in the Ministry of the Interior. On 2 February *1852*, Morny with the cream of fashionable Paris attended the Vaudeville for the triumphant first night. Two favourites of the Parisian stage took the principal roles: a beautiful blonde Irish actress, Eugénie Doche, played Marguerite; Armand was taken by Charles Fechter, son of an English mother and German father. Dumas absented himself from the celebration dinner afterwards saying he was to have supper with a woman – his mother, long separated from his philandering father.

Verdi claimed his opera was a fiasco when it opened at La Fenice on 6 March *1853* and that it was the same but better cast when successfully revived at the rival Teatro Gallo di San Benedetto on 6 May *1854*. It now appears that his revisions between the two sets of performances were more substantial than he admitted. In the following year the aristocratic Maria Piccolomini created the role of Violetta in Turin, and thereafter in Paris and London.

It has remained a cornerstone of the repertory. The book is still read and, even if the play has lost favour, there has been no shortage of film treatments, notably with Garbo (George Cukor, *1937*, Camille) and Huppert (Mario Bolognini, *1981*, Vera storia della Donna delle camellie). Almost every year sees some new interpretation. Frederick Ashton created Marguerite and Armand for Margot Fonteyn and Rudolf Nureyev (*1963*); John Neumeier choreographed another version for Marcia Haydée in *1967*.

Mary Jane Phillips-Matz
Art and Reality:
the Traviata of Verdi's Private Life

Mary Jane Phillips-Matz is the author of a biography of Verdi to be published by Oxford University Press, and for this article she also gratefully credits Drs Alberto and Gabriella Carrara-Verdi, and The Metropolitan Opera Guild, Inc. (Opera News).

Paris, in the autumn of 1846, was journey's end for two women whose names were later connected because of the odd circumstances of their lives. Marie Duplessis, the *Lady of the Camellias*, and Giuseppina Strepponi, an Italian soprano, would surely never have been mentioned in the same sentence had Giuseppe Verdi not written *La traviata*. He, then, is the catalyst both for Duplessis, who is now remembered chiefly as the heroine of his opera, and for Strepponi, who was his mistress and later his wife. In 1846, Duplessis came home to Paris to die, came home from London, married at last, after years of brittle celebrity as a courtesan. Battling consumption, she was only twenty-two; but her days as a hot-house flower were over. Strepponi arrived in Paris in October that year. At thirty-one, she moved from Milan to seek a new life and second career as a singing teacher, having been forced into disastrous early retirement by a series of unwanted pregnancies and the ruin of her voice.

With her hopes of success in Italy shattered, Strepponi had turned her back on the shambles of her life, leaving behind her illegitimate children; her mother, sisters, and brothers; several former lovers; and a covey of theatrical agents and impresarios who had paid dearly – as she had – for what she later called her 'sins'. In spite of all her problems, she had many assets left; her intelligence, her musicianship and her experience in the theatre were among them. Far more precious in 1846 was her relationship with Verdi, whose support – backed by his fame – put the seal of promise on her new venture. She left Italy armed with a letter of recommendation from Verdi to his French publishers, whom he ordered to help 'la mia raccomandata', 'the woman I entrust to your care'. They counselled her on where to live, helping her to find an apartment and studio in the same building in the Rue de la Victoire where the French diva Rosine Stolz lived. They placed her advertisement in theatrical papers, promoting her voice lessons and her salon concerts, where Verdi's music was featured as she waited for his arrival, scheduled for the spring of 1847. Because opera was her world, Strepponi may have been in the audience at the Opéra in December 1846, when Marie Duplessis went to the theatre for the last time. A few weeks later, Duplessis was dead; and soon Dumas *fils* was at work on his novel, *La Dame aux camélias*, the story that later fired Verdi's imagination and became the source of *La traviata*, the 'Love and Death' of 'The Woman Who Went Astray'.

Dumas's affair with Duplessis, his 'traviata', ended as Verdi's life with Strepponi began. The composer and the soprano had met in Milan in 1839, during early rehearsals for his first opera, *Oberto, conte di San Bonifacio,* which was planned for a cast that included her as the prima donna. A delay prevented her from singing in the première; but Strepponi got the leading female role in Verdi's *Nabucco* in 1842, the year, as he himself said, that launched him on his next sixty-eight years as absolute ruler of Italian opera; his name became a veritable synonym for opera itself.

In all those years, Verdi depended heavily on Strepponi for the kind of advice that she – the daughter of one composer and niece and protegée of another – was uniquely prepared to give him. But if she brought him the precious baggage of her knowledge and experience, she also brought the burden of her past. In its hardships and its triumphs, Strepponi's story is almost without parallel in the history of music. She was a seventeen-year-old voice student when her father died in 1832, leaving behind his wretched widow and the five young children she had borne in quick succession as he struggled to make his reputation as a maestro di capella, organist and opera composer. The family was so poor that they even sold his clothes after he died; one of Strepponi's sisters was put in the city's foundling home in Lodi when no one could be found to care for her. The Strepponis' entire future depended on Giuseppina – called Peppina – graduating from Milan Conservatory and getting engagements to sing. This she did, winning honours on her graduation in 1834 and beginning her professional career later that year. She had just turned nineteen when she began to ride a roller-coaster of studying, coaching, rehearsing, travelling and singing in almost every major theatre in Italy and in Vienna as well. As the sole provider for her mother and siblings, she lifted her 'large family', as she called them, from the dregs of misery. Her earnings covered a respectable apartment in fashionable Via della Guastalla in Milan and the university studies her brother needed to become a doctor.

In the theatre, however, success came with a price-tag attached: the help of a patron, manager or impresario often had to be paid for in coin that involved long and illicit relationships with those in power. Peppina Strepponi became the mistress of a kind, decent, simple man, her agent Camillo Cirelli, who was about thirty years older than she, with a wife and daughter living in Milan. During the first three years of her career, with non-stop professional engagements, she came to look like the brightest young star of the Italian stage. She secured a contract with Alessandro Lanari of Florence, who was known as the 'Napoleon of Impresarios', and was marching quick-step from one triumph to another when she discovered that she was pregnant. Camillino, her son by Cirelli, was born in January 1838 as she, defaulting on contracts, waited out her pregnancy and recovery in Turin. Less than two months after the birth, she returned to the stage and to Lanari's territory – Rome and Tuscany. By the middle of June 1839 Strepponi was pregnant again, and even she was not sure who the father of her child might be. Cirelli finally accepted paternity of the daughter, Giuseppa Faustina, a.k.a. Sinforosa, who was born in Florence at the beginning of February 1839 and abandoned in a foundling hospital there as Strepponi got out of her childbed to rush to Venice and fulfil her contract with Lanari at the Gran Teatro la Fenice. By April 1839, although she was ill, she was back in Milan, where she made her debut at La Scala and met Verdi for the first time.

The proposed production of Verdi's first operas at La Scala was the opportunity he, his wife, their families and his ambitious sponsors in his home town had been dreaming of for years. Loaded with debt, Verdi was married to his patron's favourite daughter, Margherita Barezzi, who had had two children by him in three years. She, an ambitious, strong-minded red-head whose uncle described her as having 'a good voice and heart', and her family had helped him escape from a dead-end job as Busseto's town music master and move to Milan, where he could sell his compositions to publishers and impresarios. And he did, in fact, meet with some success, having some of his songs published and being reviewed in important newspapers when he conducted at amateur music societies' concerts; but it took him years to convince any theatre to take the risk of producing his first opera. When the chance came in 1839, the impresario of La Scala agreed to stage *Oberto, conte di San Bonifacio*, which had a modest success – 'just enough', as Verdi said, to show how much promise he had. Although Strepponi had been scheduled to be his first prima donna, she was not free when the work finally reached the stage; yet her acquaintance with Verdi dated from the early rehearsals.

With his career launched, Verdi remained in Milan, where Margherita, his wife, and his only surviving child both died. By 1840 he was a widower. Strepponi went back to her hectic round of engagements but just as she began to get her career back on track she found she was again pregnant. Having had children in 1838 and 1839, and having been ill for several months in 1840, she had provoked to fury the impresarios and managers who had to change their programmes to accommodate her recoveries. Thus she found herself with little support in this new crisis: facing financial ruin, she sang 'to the end', as she said, dragging herself from one performance to the next and thanking God when her voice held up for three consecutive days. One of her lovers, Count Filippo Camerata dei Passionei, the son-in-law of Princess Elisa Bonaparte, had failed her at the last, coming to Trieste to reproach her for a supposed affair with the tenor Lorenzo Salvi and leaving without giving her money. He returned to Ancona and to his temperamental wife, Napoleone Bonaparte Baciocchi, abandoning Strepponi in her despair. A daughter, Adelina Rosa Strepponi, was born to the soprano in November 1841 in Trieste and left with the wife of a tavern keeper and poultry-dealer there as Strepponi boarded a steamer for Venice, on her way to Milan and the meeting with Verdi that changed the course of their lives.

During Christmas week of 1841 Verdi took his new score, *Nabucco*, to Strepponi's apartment to let her look at her part and ask for her support. This she willingly gave. She would sing the leading role; she persuaded the star baritone Giorgio Ronconi to sing the title role; and Ronconi and she persuaded the impresario of La Scala to produce it that season. As she later said, she 'saw the new star rising' in the operatic sky; her advocacy of Verdi was so passionate that it pushed Donizetti into writing of '*her* Verdi' when he described the *Nabucco* rehearsals to a friend. So it was that Strepponi, with her voice a mere shadow of what it had been three years before, sang Abigaille in Verdi's *Nabucco*, a landmark première that stunned the world of opera when it appeared in March 1842 at La Scala.

After the première, Strepponi struggled to salvage something from the shipwreck of her career but it was too late. A few scattered engagements, some humiliating moments when her voice failed her utterly on stage, long periods of rest that did no good. 'If she would only give up all the buggering, stupid love affairs that are ruining her, if she would only think of what will happen, if she would think of her future', then she might be saved, wrote her loyal, old protector to Lanari in 1843. The relentless schedules and the pregnancies, however, had taken their toll: her career was over.

It was Verdi, her 'redeemer', as she later called him, who gave her new life and let her become 'the new woman' she saw in her future. As his mistress after 1843, she was often with him in Italy, but Paris was the setting for their first truly shared life. Verdi joined her there in the summer of 1847, living first in the Rue Neuve St Georges, just around the corner from her house, then living with her in Passy and Paris – openly. In Paris, he said, no one bothered him; no one pointed to him on the street or invaded his much-prized privacy. Had they stayed there, Verdi and Strepponi might have grown old in peace, as Rossini and Olympe Pélissier had. But when the Revolution of 1848, a cholera epidemic and Verdi's lust to own land all came together to force their decision to return to Italy, they descended into a veritable hell of family arguments, gossip, debt, insult and even hatred, as the whole town of Busseto turned against them.

In September 1849, Strepponi arrived in town as the mistress of Verdi and of the fine palazzo he had bought three years earlier. Had he been content with it, they might have had no problems;

but in May 1848 he had taken on a killing burden of debts and mortgages to buy a group of three small farms at Sant'Agata, a hamlet in the nearby Duchy of Piacenza. To run them, he depended on his parents, Carlo and Luigia Verdi, whom he settled in the farmhouse even as he began to borrow from his father, who sold two properties of his own and turned all the money from the sale over to Verdi. Even this was not enough; Verdi fell behind and in December 1849 failed to meet one of the very large payments he had pledged to make. From the end of 1849 until well into 1853, his parents, Strepponi, the Barezzis and the Bussetani moved from one crisis to another, in an atmosphere of turmoil that covered the years of composition and production of *Luisa Miller*, *Stiffelio*, *Rigoletto*, *Il trovatore* and *La traviata*. All were hammered out against the backdrop of debt payment deadlines and a steadily worsening family situation. To this deadly mix may have been added the problems resulting from the births of two illegitimate children to someone associated with Verdi's household. Over time, it all came down to the struggle between Verdi's will and Busseto's desire to control him.

They 'had made him', the Bussetani said, even to his face, with their huge investments of money, time and energy. Without them, he would be selling wine and groceries in a country tavern-store, as indeed most of his cousins were at that time.

They would not have Strepponi in the town, scandalized as they were that she 'had taken the place' of Busseto's much-loved, spirited Margherita Barezzi, who had fought so hard for Verdi and his cause. The Bussetani suspected (correctly) that Verdi was not married to Strepponi, whom they saw as a 34-year-old theatrical whore whose pregnancies had been there for all to see, in full view, on the stage. And who knew where her hapless children were, while she was ordering the maids around in Verdi's palazzo on the main street of the town? Giovanni Barezzi, Verdi's brother-in-law, told his heirs that he had accused the composer of bringing a prostitute into town. Giovannino, who had lived with Verdi in Milan before and during the production of *Nabucco* and attended all the rehearsals, would have met Strepponi then, if not indeed in 1839, for he, like Verdi, had been educated there. Like all the Barezzis, he followed his father in rejecting Verdi's mistress. Later Strepponi recalled the fury and the insults that were shouted up from the street. Stones were thrown through the windows of the palazzo. Verdi was accused of being an atheist, even as his father kept going to church twice a day and the parish priest (one of the old enemies from his youth) tried to bring his household into line. Did they eat meat on fast-days? Who went to Mass and who to Confession? And over it all hung the debts to the creditors and to Carlo Verdi, whom his son had still not repaid.

Under fire day and night, Verdi decided to break completely with his parents, to whom he stopped speaking early in 1851, while he was composing *Rigoletto*. He ordered them to leave the farmhouse at Sant'Agata so he and Strepponi could move there themselves – a move, incidentally, that must have reduced their running expenses considerably, given the very modest condition of 'my hut' (as he called the farmhouse at Sant'Agata) at that time. Forcing on his parents an insulting and even degrading legal agreement, he also agreed to settle his debts with his father, to whom he owed more than 2,300 lire on 28 April 1851. Carlo and Luigia Verdi moved into a simple tenant house in a village near Sant'Agata, using a loan from their son to pay the first year's rent. He agreed to pay them a monthly allowance and give them a horse. This left him poor but not ruined.

On 1 May 1851, Verdi and Strepponi moved from Palazzo Cavalli-Orlandi in Busseto to the riverside hamlet of Sant'Agata, where he took over the management of the farms himself and launched his fifty-year career as a gentleman farmer of the Piacentino. Yet even at Santa'Agata they were not to have peace. By December 1851, they had decided to close the house for the winter and go back to Paris, perhaps telling no one of their plans. Verdi's mother had died in June; his father and aunt were housekeeping together, sometimes in the country, sometimes in the Palazzo Cavalli-Orlandi. A major breach between Verdi and his Barezzi in-laws had not been healed, in part because of Strepponi's hatred for the young Barezzis, in part because of the ambivalence felt by Antonio Barezzi (Verdi's father-in-law and patron) towards her. The elder Barezzi had met, respected and liked Strepponi so long as she was in Milan or Paris. But having her in Busseto was quite another matter. And it is entirely possible that the Barezzis' criticism of Verdi's way of life drove Strepponi and Verdi to leave Sant'Agata only a few months after they had moved there. Money was very short; the mortgages still remained to be paid; other debts loomed. So Verdi sent Strepponi to Milan to borrow 10,000 francs (500 gold Napoleons) from his publisher, Casa Ricordi. As soon as the money was delivered to him in Piacenza, Verdi paid the entire amount to the Levi family, moneylenders in nearby Soragna. He and Strepponi then left for Paris.

They had been there only a few weeks when Verdi got a 'cold' and 'stinging' letter from Antonio Barezzi. This circumstance, and Verdi's famous reply, sowed the seeds of the idea that Verdi had lived through a 'real' *La traviata* in his personal life and that Barezzi was the 'real' Father Germont of the story. When Verdi answered, on 21 January 1852, he defended his right to privacy and accused the Bussetani of setting Barezzi against him.

> Here I have revealed to you my views, my actions, my wishes, my public life – I might say. And since we are now revealing things, I have no difficulty whatever in raising the curtain that hides the mysteries shut behind my four walls, and telling you about my private life. I have nothing to hide. In my house there lives a free, independent lady, a lover (as I am) of the solitary life, who has means that cover her every need. Neither she nor I owes any explanation for our actions to anyone at all; but on the other hand, who knows what relationship exists between us? What business connections? What ties? What rights I have over her, and she over me? Who knows whether she is or is not my wife? And if she were, who knows what particular motives, what reasons we have for not making that public? Who knows whether it is good or bad? And if it were bad, who has the right to hurl curses at us? But I will say that in my house she must command equal or even greater respect than I myself, and that no one is allowed to fall short in that for any reason whatsoever; that she really has every right [to that respect] because of her conduct, her spirit, and because of the special concern that she never fails to show for others.

The letter and his passionate self-defence convinced Barezzi, who was reconciled to Strepponi at last, perhaps because Verdi threatened to leave Busseto for ever if the town did not end its hate-campaign against him.

It was against this backdrop of wrenching family conflict that

Verdi and Strepponi saw Dumas *fils*'s play *La Dame aux camélias*, which opened at the Théâtre du Vaudeville in Paris on 2 February 1852. Verdi had written to Barezzi just two weeks before, in reponse to his 'stinging letter'. It is a family tradition among the Verdi heirs that Verdi himself told his foster daughter (and heir) Maria Filomena that he began to write the music for what later became *La traviata* as soon as he left the theatre that night, without ever having seen either the novel or the printed drama. She in turn passed on this information to her son, who repeated it to his children, the present heirs. Verdi had a copy of *La Dame aux camélias* sent to him some time in the late summer or early autumn of 1852 and thanked his Parisian publisher for sending it. By that time, he apparently had much of the opera 'sketched out' in his head and some of it on paper. The original musical sketches, still at Sant'Agata, have not been published, although two pages, showing 'dinner at the house of Margherita [Gautier]', were reproduced in Gatti's *Verdi nelle immagini*. They show, according to Gatti, the passion and fire of inspiration as Verdi wrote, furiously, racing to get his ideas on paper.

His decisions to compose *La traviata* for the Gran Teatro la Fenice in Venice may well have grown out of his experience between September 1849 and the end of 1852. By March 1853 the opera was ready. It had its première on 6 March; and although it was certainly not the 'fiasco' Verdi described, and although it was positively *not* shipwrecked by an overweight and aged prima donna (she was the only singer who got any applause at all), it did not satisfy its perfectionist, demanding creator. One year later, on 6 May, it was 'redeemed' in a fine production at the Teatro Gallo di San Benedetto in Venice, after having closed the previous season with a decent box office at La Fenice.

It would be a great mistake to equate any of the characters in *La Dame aux camélias* directly with Verdi, Strepponi, Barezzi or Carlo Verdi but the general tone and feeling of the opera, its intensely personal and compassionate atmosphere, its setting as a family drama, is not unlike the very situation Verdi lived through just before he wrote it.

Life bettered art in this case. No one in the play or the opera matches the stature of the real 'characters' involved: Verdi; his pious, self-righteous father; his adored father-in-law; his mistress-

later-wife in her dignity and pain. Verdi and Strepponi later helped
Carlo Verdi through the illnesses of old age and cared for Barezzi
until his death, closing his eyes and hearing him murmur Verdi's
name at the last. And out of their hour of strife came *La traviata*,
which is perhaps Verdi's finest tribute to the human condition.

Giuseppe Verdi
letter to Giuseppina Appiani, 1847

I look forward to going to Paris, which has no particular seduction for me, but which I am sure to like because there I shall be
able to live as I please. It's a great pleaure to be able to do as one
likes!! When I think that I shall be in Paris for several weeks, without being involved in musical affairs, without hearing a word
about music (because I shall show the door to all publishers and
impresarios), I almost swoon with relief.

Giuseppe Verdi
letter to Luigi Toccagni, 1847

What do you want me to say about myself? That I am always
the same, always discontented with everything? When fortune favours me I want it against me; when it is against me I want
it to favour me; when I am at Milan I would like to be in Paris;
now that I am in Paris I would like to be – where? – I don't know –
on the moon. For the rest I enjoy here complete personal freedom,
such as I have always desired without ever being able to obtain it. I
don't visit anybody, I don't receive anybody, nobody knows me
and I don't have the annoyance of seeing myself pointed at, as in
Italian cities. I enjoy good health; I write a lot; my affairs go well;
everything goes well except my head, which I always hope will
change, and which never does change. Farewell.

Franz Liszt
letter to Marie d'Agoult, Lemberg, 1847

And poor Mariette Duplessis has died ... She was the first woman I ever loved, and now she is in some unknown cemetery, abandoned to the worms of the tomb! Fifteen months ago she told me this: 'I will not live; I am an odd girl and I will not be able to hold on to this life which I have no idea how to lead, and which I can't stand any more. Take me, lead me wherever you like; I will be no trouble to you. I sleep all day, go to the theatre in the evening and at night you may do what you will with me!'

I never told you what a singular attachment I felt for this charming creature during my last stay in Paris. I had told her that I would take her to Constantinople, because it was the only journey which I could reasonably have made her undertake. And now she is dead ... I know not what strange chord of an ancient elegy vibrates in my heart at her memory! ...

Unfortunately Marie d'Agoult's side of the correspondence has been lost but she evidently replied with more information concerning Marie Duplessis and Lola Montez, the notorious 'Spanish' dancer who had become the mistress of Max I of Bavaria.

Franz Liszt
letter to Marie d'Agoult, Iassy, 1847

I was very pleased with the two paragraphs on Lola and the poor Mariette, for to be perfectly frank, I was beginning to reproach myself for having written to you about her in my last letter from Czernowitz, fearing that you might find these two subject-objects rather risqué. If by chance I had been in Paris while la Duplessis was ill, I would have done my Des Grieux act for fifteen minutes and would have tried to save her at any price, for hers was truly an exquisite nature, and what is generally described (perhaps accurately) as corruption, never touched her heart.

Believe me that I felt for her a sombre and elegiac attachment, which, without her knowing it, put me in the vein of poetry and music. It was the last and only shock I have felt in years. It is useless to try to find an explanation for these contradictions, or the human heart; all the more so because 'The world, dear Agnes' is a strange thing!

Liszt by Lehmann, 1840

Giuseppina Strepponi
letter to Pietro Romani, Paris, 1848

You envy me because I am out of Italy? You are wrong, for here the artists are as badly off as in Italy, and what with political agitations one is never sure of a quiet night's rest. So much for your guidance! You ask about my voice? How I am amusing myself? My voice has suffered and is as it was at the end of my time with Lanari. I am not amusing myself at all, because what is amusement to so many others is boredom to me. Winter is the brilliant season in Paris – society, balls, festivities, dinners, etc. Well, when I am obliged to sing at some house or other, I stay just as long as is necessary, and then run home. I don't like dancing, I don't like dinners, and if I had enough to live on without working I should perhaps stay in Paris for the freedom one enjoys here, but they would not see me any more, anywhere.

Giuseppina Strepponi
letter to Verdi, Leghorn, 1853

We adore the country, and in the country one lives cheaply – and enjoys oneself so much. When I think that there are, at Sant'Agata, those dear *culatelli* [horses] Solfarin and Menaffiss, who pull your modest carriage with such gusto and cost so little ... when I think that I have my Poli-Poli, Pretin, Matt, Prevost, etc., etc. [caged birds], which look at me with eyes full of affection and *greediness*, which cost so little and amuse me so much ... when I think of our flowers and few feet of garden, which gives us as much pleaure as if it were the Eden of the Earthly Paradise – I ask whether city life has ever given us such pleasures and whether, in consequence, two or three months a year of this cursed *city* are not more than enough to put us in a fever of desire to return to the country?

La traviata in London
from the Illustrated London News, 31 May 1856

The great musical event of the past week – the greatest event we may add since the first appearance of Jenny Lind at Her Majesty's Theatre nine years ago – has been the début, within the same walls, of Signora Piccolomini – a name, we believe, destined to be joined to those of the Catalani, Malibrans, and Grisi, who, in our time, have shed lustre on the Italian stage. This event too was accompanied by another – the first performance in England of a new opera by the most popular Italian composer of the age. But Mdlle Piccolomini's connection with this incident is the only circumstance which gives it interest. A new production from the prolific pen of Maestro Verdi is a thing to which we are pretty well accustomed; and it happens that the new production in question, La traviata, is the weakest, as it is the last, of his numerous progeny. It has pretty tunes, for every Italian has, more or less, the gift of melody; but even the tunes are trite and common, bespeaking an exhausted invention, while there are no vestiges of the constructive skill – none of the masterly pieces of concerted music which we find in the Trovatore or Rigoletto. Even in Italy the 'traviata' has owed its whole success to the young and charming primadonna; and it was Piccolomini, not Verdi, who was the object of the splendid ovation of last Saturday night.

La traviata is an Italian version of the younger Dumas's drama, La Dame aux camélias, which has made so great a sensation at the Théâtre du Vaudeville. Even the Parisians, lax as are their ideas of stage morality, were somewhat startled by its subject, though for months and months they have flocked in crowds to see it. An attempt to bring it on the English stage was prevented, some time ago, we understand, by the Lord Chamberlain's refusal of licence. In the Italian opera the groundwork of the story and the principal incidents remain the same; but the details are softened down, and the piece, as it stands, is scarcely more objectionable than others (the Favorita, for instance) which pass current on the Opera stage. It is, moreover, irresistibly pathetic; and he must be a stern moral-

Act I   VIOLETTA: Sarò l'Ebe che versa.

Act II, scene 1   GERMONT: Sia pure – ma volubile sovente è l'uom.
VIOLETTA: Gran Dio!

Illustrations of the first London performances of La traviata

Act II, scene 2 ALFRED: Partirò, ma giura innante che dovunque seguirai i miei passi. VIOLETTA: Ah no, giammai.

Act III VIOLETTA: Grenvil, vedete? Tra le braccia io spiro di quanti ho cari al mondo.

ist indeed who can witness unmoved the sorrows of the erring but most interesting heroine.

Violetta (represented by Mdlle Piccolomini) is a youthful beauty belonging to a class indicated by the term *La traviata*, which may be translated 'the outcast', or (as in the libretto) 'the lost one'. . .

Such is the part in which the young actress first appeared before the English public; and nothing could be more charming than her whole performance of it. It embraces the most brilliant gaiety and the deepest pathos; and it is difficult to decide in which phase of the character she was most successful. Signora Piccolomini is not above one or two and twenty, and looks still younger. She is small and slight, but exquisitely formed, and full of grace. Her features are instinct with intelligence and feeling. In the first scene, where she appears as the sprightly hostess of a gay party, nothing could be more attractive than her exuberant but perfectly elegant vivacity. In this scene there is a little Anacreontic song, sung by her with Calzolari (in the part of the lover), and accompanied by the chorus. This air, so pretty that it raised expectations as to the general quality of music which were disappointed, was sung so delightfully with such fire and *abandon* that it threw the audience into a transport of enthusiasm which did not subside during the whole performance. In the great scene of the second act, between Violetta and Alfred's father, where the girl, after a fearful struggle, resolves to sacrifice herself for her lover's welfare, Mdlle Piccolomini showed still higher powers. The tumult of contending passions, ending in a noble and dignified resolution, was painted with a truth and beauty not to be surpassed. As to the closing scene of the whole, we cannot attempt to describe it, made up as it is of a thousand minute traits of nature and feeling which went at once to the heart of every one, suffusing many bright eyes with tears, and moving even the most 'unused to the melting mood'. Rachel's dying scene in *Adrienne Lecouvreur* is the only thing to which we can compare it.

Mdlle Piccolomini, young though she be, is already an actress of the highest class. We cannot as yet say the same thing of her as a singer; though we have no doubt that in this respect, too, she will reach the summit of her art. With the most precious endowments of nature she is profusely gifted. She has a lovely voice, a pure soprano, of a sympathetic quality, and great power and compass.

The beauty of its tones, too, is heightened by the sensibility they express; and she sings with great refinement and delicacy. One thing only she has yet to learn – that finished execution which is the result of consummate art, and of which the finest specimen is to be found in the singing of Alboni. But this is a defect which time and study will be sure to remove; and it is but a slight spot amid the blaze of so many beauties . . .

Nature waives ceremony with certain beings. Great musicians are recognized in the first tones, and noble minds declare themselves by an impulse. This was the case with Maria Piccolomini, who made her first appearance at Her Majesty's Theatre on Saturday last. Descended from one of the most ancient and most illustrious patrician families of Rome, this gifted girl, urged on by an invincible impulse – with that confidence of success which is so often the companion of real genius – cast aside all the prerogatives of her high station, and, despite the tears and the entreaties of her noble relations of the house of the Piccolomini and the Amalfi, she made her début at Rome to earn the laurels and the fame of Corinne.

Rank, position, fortune, family tradition, even the grim portraits of her mail-clad ancestory, were of no avail against the mighty tide of song that surged within the gentle breast of this girl of seventeen summers.

She made her début at Rome in 1852, at the Argentine Theatre, in Donizetti's opera of *Poliuto*. It is only those who have witnessed an Italian audience on a 'first night' – whether the début of a new singer or of the production of a new opera – that can know the ordeal which has to be gone through. Debarred from taking any part in politics, unaddicted to the manly sports of more northern nations, the voluptuous yet intelligent Italian courts the Muses; the pit of the Opera House is his arena, it is the touchstone upon which the true gold of a prima donna is tried beyond appeal. The scene at the Café Martini at Milan, half an hour before the Opera on a first night, is a scene as unique as it is curious. The glories, alas! of the Scala, have passed away. The 3rd November, 1852, was such a night in Rome.

We cannot do better than quote this passage from a letter written under the impression of the scene:

A new prima donna has appeared at the Argentine Theatre . . .
Her voice is exquisitely sweet – full of liquid birdlike notes – and
is, moreover, of considerable power and compass. She is little
more than seventeen years of age, and of considerable personal
attractions. With such advantages as these, the success of any
prima donna would be tolerably certain. But what has raised the
enthusiasm of the Roman public to an unusual height is the fact
that the young débutante is niece to one of the Cardinals, and a
member of the historical family of the Piccolomini. So great is
her enthusiasm of the music, and so strong is her passion for the
exciting triumphs of the theatre, that her venerable relative,
fearing the young girl's health might suffer in case of a refusal,
at length yielded his consent to her appearance before the
public. It is said that the Grand Duchess of Tuscany, with whom
Mdll. Piccolomini is a particular favourite, used her influence in
bringing about this result . . . It is only under the sky of Italy that
one sees the passion for art so strong as to induce a young girl,
rich and beautiful, and a member of an illustrious family, to
appear upon the stage and it is among the Italians that such an
act has more than the colouring of romance . . .

*Act Two scene 2 at Her Majesty's Theatre in May 1856; an illustration
from the* Illustrated London News

Remarks on The Morality of Dramatic Compositions with particular reference to *La traviata*, etc.
Anonymous pamphlet published by John Chapman, London, 1856

Some dramatic compositions, lately represented, have called forth considerable animadversion in the newspapers on the ground of immorality. To ascertain the character of a work in this respect, it is necessary to ascertain what Morality and Immorality are. *Morality consists in that voluntary conduct which tends to the happiness, welfare, and good of mankind. Immorality is that voluntary conduct which has an opposite tendency.* Unfortunately, however, many of our customs, usages, laws, institutions, are founded upon *false morality* ...

There is a system of rank abomination in the world against which all noble, elevated, sensitive, refined, and generous natures, secretly perhaps, but not the less intensely on that account, are everywhere in a state of determined revolt. This monstrous system may be described as *Compulsory Association, enforced companionship; the keeping indissolubly bound together by law two persons whose society is uncongenial to each other.* This is the most intolerable and humiliating of all slaveries, – of all degradations the most foul and abominable. The end and object of marriage, as of every other institution, should be the happiness, welfare, and good of mankind; and therefore, as mutual attachment and the happiness derived from each other's society is the only basis of marriage, when these are at an end, the parties should be at perfect liberty to separate, and form, if they choose, more congenial alliances, as if the former had never existed.

Adultery and seduction are the consequences of erroneous and vicious institutions ...

What is Love? ... Love resolves itself into deriving pleasure from the society of its object ... Now is it reasonable – is it just – that because we entertain that passion for another, we should reduce them to a state of galling intolerable slavery and subjection, and even murder them on suspicion of not submitting to it; and kill *ourselves* afterwards, in madness and despair? Yet in a dramatic composition, popular in this summer of 1856, the heroine – a lady, a princess – is made to say, that if she were jealous she would transform herself into a wild beast, and revel in tearing her victim limb from limb. And the long and loathsome tirade in which these demoniacal, supernaturally atrocious sentiments – so dangerous and corrupting in their influence and tendency – are expressed, was approvingly quoted by admiring critics. And while

'*The Great Social Evil' by Leech*, Punch *12 September 1857.
Time: Midnight. A Sketch not a Hundred Miles from the Haymarket.*

BELLA: '*Ah! Fanny! How long have you been Gay!'*

the Tartuffes and Pharisees strain at such gnats as *La traviata*, they can bolt such camels as *Medea*, harness and all.

In passing up the Haymarket about midnight, in the summer time, may be witnessed a most harrowing spectacle. Multitudes of young girls – little creatures with almost infantile forms – whose childlike undeveloped faces, and forced unnatural gaiety, inflamed by the excitement of deleterious stimulants – (many of them perhaps have not tasted food for twelve hours), struggling with internal anguish and despair, wreathed into ghastly smiles, are seen wandering about. And it is to these unhappy young creatures that pity is denied, – it is against them that a putrescent Conventionalism is to bar the gates of mercy; and they are never to be named except to be denounced; as if society by ignoring their wrongs could blot them out of existence, and erase from the ominous page of its *debits* the very names of the victims and the monsters it has made. Shame! shame! shame! It would not be difficult to show that *good* may conduct to their frightful situation. Innocence, a loving and affectionate disposition, and personal beauty, may attract the seducer and enable him to succeed in ruining their possessor, while the ill-tempered, the ill-natured and the ugly escape.

The gratitude and the admiration of the wise and good will ever be due to those who unostentatiously, at the prompting of a genuine benevolence and in spite of pharisaical sneers, leave all the blandishments of patrician life – the attractions of home – the luxuries of a refined civilization – to watch by the bedside and smooth the pillow of agony and sickness in the foetid hospitals of a remote and desolate region, amidst all the horrors of war. But may there not be found even a yet nobler work for such noble spirits without travelling so far? When charity does not begin at home, at all events it should end there. Let them, then, attempt something for the *salvation* of their unhappy fellow-beings, and prove it to be *untrue* that

> — every woe a tear may claim,
> Except an erring sister's shame.

La traviata at the Royal Italian Opera
from the authorized programme, 1857

The first act commences with a gay party in the house of Violetta (the heroine), a young and beautiful creature, thrown by circumstances and the loss of her parents in childhood into a course of voluptuous living. She is surrounded by a circle of gay and thoughtless beings like herself, who devote their lives to pleasure. Amongst the throng who crowd to her shrine is Alfred Germont, a young man, who becomes seriously enamoured with Violetta. Touched by the sincerity of his passion, she yields to its influence, a new and pure love springs up in her heart, and for the first time she becomes conscious of the misery of her position and the hollowness of the pleasures in which she has basked. In the second act, we find her living in seclusion with her lover, in a country-house near Paris, three months after the events narrated in the preceding act. Alfred accidentally discovers that Violetta has been secretly selling her houses and property in Paris, in order to maintain this establishment; and, revolting at the idea of being a dependant on her bounty, he leaves hurriedly from Paris, to redeem his honour from this disgrace. During his absence, his father, who has discovered his retreat, arrives, and, representing to Violetta that his son's connection with her is not only lowering him in the opinion of the world, but will be ruinous to his family, inasmuch as his sister was betrothed to a wealthy noble, who had however declared his intention of renouncing her, unless Alfred would give up Violetta, the generous girl resolves to sacrifice her affection and happiness for her lover's sake, and returns alone to Paris, whither Alfred, overwhelmed with despair when he discovers her flight, follows her. We are then transported to a saloon in the hotel of Flora, one of Violetta's former friends, during a festival given by the fair mistress of the mansion. There Alfred again meets Violetta, now under the protection of the Baron Douphol, and being unaware of the generous motive which made her desert him, he overwhelms her with reproaches, and flings the miniature she had given him at her feet, in the presence of the company. Degraded and heartbroken the unfortunate Violetta returns home

to die; and in the last act we find the sad romance of her life drawing to its close. Alfred, too late, learns the truth, and discovers the
sacrifice she has made to secure his happiness. Penetrated with
grief and shame, he hastens, with his father, to comfort and console her, and to offer her his hand and name in reparation of the
wrong he has done her; – but too late. The fragile flower, broken
on its stem, can never more raise its beauteous head. One gleam of
happiness, the purest and brightest she had known, arising from
her lover's assurance of his truth, and his desire to restore her reputation, gilds the closing moments of her life, as with a gentle sigh
her soul parts from its fragile tenement of clay.

DRAMATIS PERSONAE

VIOLETTA VALERY, the Lost One
FLORA BERVOIX, her friend
ANNINA, confidential servant of Violetta
ALFRED GERMONT, lover of Violetta
Signor GEORGE GERMONT, his father
BARON DOUPHOL
GASTONE VISCOUNT DE LETORIÈRES, friend of Alfred
MARQUIS D'OBIGNY
DOCTOR GRENVIL
JOSEPH, servant of Violetta
A messenger

Chorus of gentlemen and ladies, friends of Violetta and Flora;
matadores, picadores, gipsies, servants of Violetta and Flora.

Scene Paris and its environs.
Time the commencement of the eighteenth century. The first
act is supposed to take place in the month of August, the second
in January, and the third in February.

Joseph Bennett
from the obituary of Maria Piccolomini,
28 December 1899

The world is apt to forget, and perhaps it is well. There might otherwise be too many unpleasant things in its memory. But things that are agreeable and charming also pass to oblivion. Who, for example, has once called to mind, during many years past, the name and claims upon remembrance of Maria Piccolomini? Yet, forty years ago, there was no better known or more popular person in England than the young Italian prima donna, the niece of a Cardinal, a member of two historic Roman houses, and – which is even more important – a fascinating girl, and a delightful actress.

Maria Piccolomini in 1857

In 1860 the favourite retired from the stage, became the Marchesa Gaetani, and, save for a few appearances three years later, on behalf of her sometime manager, Lumley, disappeared from public ken. Her death has just been announced to a world which did not know that she still lived.

The musical critics of the day did not like Verdi. He was blatant; he was, in short, bad all round. So, good men, they came forward in the interest of public morality to protest against the libretto which the composer had set to music. Their damnatory phrases read funnily now. 'It is opposed to all the highest moral interests,' said the *Saturday Review*, 'to excite our sympathies on behalf of such a character as Violetta . . . Vice is vice, in what light soever it may appear, and we are sinning against right when we make it seem more fascinating than virtue.' There was a grand press chorus to this effect, the only important exception being the journal then exercising the greatest influence in musical matters. Said *The Times*: 'If any of the incidents employed . . . offend the delicacy of audiences like those which assemble in Her Majesty's Theatre, all we shall say on the matter is that those audiences have less familiarity with the various phases of life actually and daily occurring around and amidst them than we have hitherto given them credit for. To do them justice, however, the audience last Saturday seemed to accept the story in a very contented frame of mind, and it is the musical critics alone who, in their tender care for public morals, have protested.' This cold water douche did not quench the fires of moral fervour burning in the bosoms of the censors, who went on protesting till they found that *La traviata* was accepted as no worse than *La favorita*, against which they themselves had flung no stones.

Referring to the death scene the *Morning Herald* declared that her efforts were 'worthy of all panegyric as an exemplification of histrionic art'. 'The acting of this wonderful girl beggars description,' cried the *Morning Post*. The *Daily News* likened her to 'the goddess fair and free, In Heav'n yclept Euphrosyne'. The *Times* held that a more accomplished actress had seldom trod the lyric stage. The *Examiner* asserted: 'Out of impurity she produces something exquisitely pure, and out of absurdity a pathos irresistible . . . A great vocalist the young Italian never was. She held no rank in the firework school . . . '

The obituary recalled an incident which perfectly illustrated Piccolomini's character. She received a letter proposing marriage, and wrote this reply in French in a beautiful Italian hand:

> Sir – I cannot sufficiently express my surprise on receiving your letter through Mr Smith, and, at the same time, my gratitude for your honourable and amiable intentions regarding myself. The request you have made is so serious that you will acknowledge it right for me to point out that when one is asked to confide to another one's destiny and happiness for life it is at least necessary to have the advantage of intimately knowing him, and that, unhappily, is not my case. It is for you to remove all difficulties on the point. That which troubles me is the dissatisfaction of your father, though my birth, conduct, and education should remove every obstacle. I am happy to say that my family are of independent means, and the only thing they would insist upon is that I shall not live too far from them. It is now for you, Sir, to give me your views; it being understood that should fate crown your wishes there will be other matters to arrange with my family. – Accept, Sir, the sentiments of my high consideration.
>
> Maria Piccolomini

The letter is dated Liverpool, 9 August, 1859, and now forty years later, the curtain has been rung down on the life-drama to which it belongs.

Mercedes Viale Ferrero
Staging a Tragedy of the Day

Mercedes Viale Ferrero is a historian of theatre and costume, and a contributor to the Storia dell'opera italiana *(Turin, 1990).*

On 1 January 1853, Verdi wrote to his Neapolitan friend De Sanctis: 'I am doing the *Dame aux camélias* in Venice . . . A subject of the time. Someone else would perhaps not have done it because of the costumes, because of the period and because of a thousand other silly scruples.' So Verdi foresaw that the costumes would present a problem and yet he was quite sure about wanting them to be contemporary ('of our day'). On 6 January, the impresario Lasina wrote to the Presidenza of the Teatro alla Fenice: 'Maestro Verdi desires, requests and begs that the costumes of his opera *La traviata* should be modern, as they are, and that the period should not be changed, as the Poet Piave has done, to the time of Riscelux [Richelieu].'

When Verdi spoke of 'silly scruples', he was obviously thinking of the censorship. The censors must indeed have intervened since Piave informed the Presidenza on 5 February 1853, that Verdi 'agreed with very bad grace that the period should be put back, but he would not allow wigs'.

It is generally assumed that moral considerations lay behind the censors' objection to modern costumes: not only did *Traviata* offer an undesirable and vicious picture of contemporary reality, but in the event the 'sinner' was morally superior to the characters who were supposed to be 'respectable'. While this is certainly true, the case can be approached from another angle.

So-called 'comic' operas could (and often were) played in contemporary settings but *La traviata* was a tragedy, and in a different category. With this subject Verdi was breaking at least two theatrical conventions: the first was this distinction between theatrical genres; the second was that the opportunity for spectacle, the 'merveilleux', which was a particular feature of tragic opera, would be lost in a contemporary setting. Verdi did not normally break with stage traditions simply for the sake of doing so. He usually maintained the traditional sequence of external and internal scenes, for instance, alternating scenes that did and did not use the full stage; and he shared the prevailing taste for historical designs.

In this case, however, transposing the action to a distant and different period would have altered the meaning of the drama: and this he would not tolerate, or at any rate only 'with bad grace' and in the certainty that it was merely a temporary compromise. And yet in a few countries, for instance in England, Piave's proposed alternative setting at the time of Richelieu was observed.

Even in Paris, at the Théâtre-Italien in 1857, the performers appeared dressed in the fashions of the seventeenth century, so much so that *L'Illustration* carried a series of vignettes which caricatured the 'genre Louis XIII' of the costumes.

But not all the performers. The Parisian illustrations of 1857 or those from Siena and Turin in the previous year show that the prima donna, Maria Piccolomini, wore dresses that were contemporary, or almost. The only difference between Siena and Turin was an elaborate overgown, reminiscent of the previous century but back in fashion under the Second Empire, as we can see from Winterhalter's portraits of the aristocracy and the widely disseminated fashion plates in the *Courrier des dames*. Moreover Maria slightly reduced the size of the lace *volant* which in Turin covered her arm down to the elbow: in Siena it fluttered around her *décolleté* while in Paris it could scarcely be glimpsed in the centre of her corsage. In London the *volant* had disappeared altogether and her costume was a contemporary ballgown. It looks as though Maria Piccolomini had her own costume, which suited her (very elegant) figure, and that she varied it with accessories. Certainly it was much more attractive than the 'period' costumes and it contributed to the myth of this singer put about in France: she was a 'young woman of great fortune, related to all that is most elevated in her country', whose 'dramatic genius' irresistibly impelled her 'to make the public tremble and weep'.

Daniela Goldin
From Marguerite to Violetta

Daniela Goldin lectures in medieval and humanistic philology at the University of Padua, and is the author of La vera fenice *(Turin, 1985), a study of librettos and librettists in the eighteenth and nineteenth centuries.*

Always on the look-out for new subjects, Verdi encountered *The Lady of the Camellias* in 1852. It was a 'subject of the time', he wrote, locating the originality and the generally controversial nature of his future opera in the topicality of its events and characters. Challenge and provocation were, of course, essential elements of his theatrical vision. For him, composing an opera involved breaking rules, at the risk of upsetting what the public expected, whether by flouting musical and even stage traditions, or by confronting contemporary morality and social conventions.

In Verdi's work and thought, Violetta may be related to Rigoletto. Condemned by conventional morality, she is isolated in one sense on the edge of society while enjoying a positive quality generated by her unconventionality and her profound generosity. The subject of *The Lady of the Camellias* would never have stimulated Verdi's creative imagination if Dumas had left it as a novel – a sort of documentary fiction – and not adapted it for the stage. The play compressed the novel so as to throw three themes into relief for Verdi: a pleasure-loving society, the demi-monde, depicted in conversation scenes for many characters which offered rich theatrical opportunities; the love and the sacrifice of a protagonist who, in spite of everything, is not integrated into that society; and the confrontation and clash of two characters (Marguerite and Georges Duval, father of Armand-Alfredo) which by itself constituted a drama within a drama. These three themes function reciprocally. Verdi's synthesis sacrifices important characters from the play and inserts other characters and sequences impossible to eliminate from opera (for instance, love duets) but he does not let them interfere in the crucial interaction of the three *topoi*. The role of Alfredo, a musical support for Violetta with no distinct dramaturgical profile, is operatically obligatory but it is not drawn with comparable psychological subtlety.

Verdi fixed upon the conversation scenes so typical of French theatre to highlight Violetta's solitude in the 'teeming desert of a city they call Paris' (*La Traviata*, Act I, scene v – a phrase that he had himself used, in correspondence, to describe it). He transformed them into celebrations and choruses whose dramatic function is more than merely decorative: they demonstrate the protagonist's sensibilities and anxieties and, for instance in the second act, provide a contrast which prepares the personal tragedy.

As for the interview between Germont and Violetta, it defines more completely the protagonist who in Act I was presented as 'franca e ingenua' ('a frank and simple girl'), safe in her youthful thoughtless vitality and sensible to the affecting and conscious novelty of her emotions, her 'commedia'. If in that act Verdi's Violetta is a literal translation of Dumas's Marguerite (whom he described as 'gay with a gaiety sadder than remorse'), in Act II the character assumes a different weight through the confrontation with Germont, and this increased cultural significance is attributable to the historical distance of the French prototype. Dumas's Marguerite resigns herself to renouncing Armand when she realizes that her love is incompatible with the virtue (*vertù*) of a 'daughter . . . as pure as an angel', that is Armand's sister, who alone could merit 'justice' and aspire to a 'future'. She comes to an irreversible realization of her own social *status* and of her role as lover ('I have lived for love, and I die for it'), rather than a submission to the wish of her interlocutor-antagonist. Verdi's Violetta, however, has to settle her account with 'the voice of honour', a conventional sentiment which Germont represents on stage and which seems to be the basis of a society irretrievably hostile to the 'poor sinner'. Death alone can reconcile Violetta to the world of the Germonts. Such a radical solution confirms the final victory of the dominant productive class, which claims to respect a strict moral code, over the generous, free and anticonformist individual whom Verdi had wished to exalt with his music.

Lynda Nead
'Traviata-ism' and the Great Social Evil

Lynda Nead is a lecturer in the history of art at Birkbeck College, London, and the author of Myths of Sexuality: Representations of Women in Victorian Britain *(London, 1988).*

The daughters of Dives, knowing all about the plot of the *traviata*, visit the opera to witness the apotheosis of a consumptive prostitute, and arrive home through the Gehenna fair nightly held in the Haymarket; – yet we are expected to credit that they lay their heads on their pillows without considering what it all means. *The Lancet*, quoted in William Acton, *Prostitution*, London, 1857

Ruined women throng the neighbourhood of the opera-house, and that is their natural place of gathering, since they know that within it such pieces as *La traviata*, of which a harlot is the heroine, are glorifying their trade, by representing harlots as fit companions to young noblemen, amidst the applause of fashionable crowds.
Baptist Noel, *The Fallen and their Associates*, London, 1860

When *La traviata* opened at Her Majesty's Theatre in 1856 it tapped into a contemporary obsession with the subject of the fallen woman. Prostitution in the mid-nineteenth century was described as 'the great social evil'; it was seen to have consequences that went far beyond the realm of morality and that bore serious implications for the political, social and economic stability of Britain. If, as Samuel Smiles claimed, 'the nation comes from the nursery' (*Self-Help*, London, 1859) then the prostitute not only threatened this crucial domestic heart of society but also the general advancement of the nation and empire.

Prostitution was regarded as an urban vice and the city that excelled all others both in terms of its civilization and its immorality was London. And it was in the crowded West End of London – amidst the theatres, night-houses and dancing-rooms – that prostitution was believed to be most concentrated. The name of the Haymarket became synonymous with prostitution; an imaginary, hellish street where prostitutes urinated, swore and jostled passers-by.

But how did this nightmarish image of street prostitution relate to the fictional fallen woman represented on the stage at Her Majesty's Theatre? Anxiety and anger about *La traviata* focused on two main issues, both of which involved a blurring of the dramas being played out on the stage and in the street. Firstly, there was the terrifying possibility of respectable young women being contaminated simply by the knowledge of immorality. Not only were they subjected to the spectacle of street prostitution on their way to the theatre, but they were then also allowed to witness the deification of a courtesan when apparently safe inside the theatre. A little knowledge was clearly a dangerous thing, but the fear that innocent women might be corrupted by the mere awareness of vice suggests how precarious and uncertain Victorian morality really was.

The second problem was that the opera appeared to glamorize the prostitute. By turning the lowest form of life into the highest form of art, the opera made the prostitute temporarily acceptable, even respectable. The opera and other forms of high culture such as the art exhibition were acceptable forms of public entertainment where the middle and upper classes could reinforce their social and cultural identity. *La traviata* interfered with this activity; it crossed the boundaries of propriety and threatened to seduce its audience into an acceptance of immorality. Here, it seemed, was entertainment without education, sensual pleasure without moral edification.

And, above all, there is the sense of moral panic; of the wealthy and respectable classes barricaded in the theatre from the dangerous hordes outside on the streets, only to find that sin has seeped in and is being brazenly impersonated across the footlights. *La traviata* is more than an opera about a consumptive prostitute; it belongs to and is part of a whole set of cultural and social histories. When first performed, its subject could not be distanced as a romantic, even sentimental costume-piece; instead it spoke to contemporary fears and anxieties. By turning the fallen woman into entertainment, it fuelled the debates about the effects of prostitution on respectable society and, worst of all, seemed to dissolve the boundaries between the pure and the fallen. In *La traviata* the street enters the stage and corruption, it seemed, could spread across the footlights.

Isabelle Emerson
What If?

*Isabelle Emerson is Associate Professor of Music History at the
University of Nevada, Las Vegas.*

It is a tempting to ask at the end of *La traviata*: what if Violetta
had not died? What if she had not succumbed to the obligatory
disease for wayward women in the nineteenth century but had
recovered? Wouldn't she have married the remorseful Alfredo
(perhaps even with the blessing of Papa Germont)? Might they not
have produced little Violettas and little Alfredos – living witnesses
to the high moral *married* character of the parents? If so, what
would those little Violettas and Alfredos – but especially the
Violettas – be like?

In fact, Violetta's daughters have continued to populate the
operatic stage – their sad stories tugging pleasantly at our heart-
strings even as their tragic ends satisfy the demands of morality.
From Auber's *Manon* of 1856 to Pizzetti's *La figlia di Jorio* of
1954, we have approvingly observed the careers of coquettes,
grisettes, courtesans, prostitutes, who must finally pay in a more
or less uncomfortable manner for their way of life (the finding of
'true love' is the usual catalyst for punishment).

Chronologically, Violetta's oldest daughter would be Auber's
Manon, a sweet, light-hearted child who scarcely understands the
lecherous demands of the rich Marquess. Her naivety is in keeping
with the nobility of the Marquess *in the end* and with the jolly
'Happy Slave' chorus that introduces us to life in Louisiana. None
the less, the price for her immoral life is death, and she pays it in
the Louisiana wilderness(!), as an off-stage chorus tells us that
'Love is ending in a sweet dream.'

Puccini's Manon Lescaut (1893) is more hardened (having no
doubt learned from the fates of her sisters, Auber's Manon and the
Manon Lescaut of Massenet's 1884 opera). She is quite ready to
go off immediately with her true love, Des Grieux, perhaps
because she has guessed that her cousin intends to act as pander
and sell her to the first good bidder. Later she is also happy, if

bored, to enjoy the riches of the lover procured by her cousin. It is her fatal desire for worldly goods that does her in – she cannot leave behind the jewels of her wealthy patron, and thus she and Des Grieux are caught by the police. He, of course, is released, but she, denounced as an 'immoral woman', is deported. In a desperate effort to save his Manon, des Grieux goes with her to America: a happy end seems possible. But inexplicably we find them once again in the Louisiana wilderness where Manon expires effectively.

Sympathy for this Manon is in short supply. She is selfish, materialistic, and perhaps not very bright, since she ruins not only Des Grieux but herself as well. The coquette has become the destroyer. This Manon is a near relation to Zola's Nana but without Nana's good-natured generosity – and, to be fair, without the depth of portrayal given Nana. In Manon's two-dimensional way, however, she is as dangerous, as much the corruptor as Nana, and therefore she cannot enjoy the happy end that *seems* to be in store at the Act III curtain.

A decade later (1904) Puccini turned to the Orient to find a courtesan who could win our hearts and sympathies. But why is Cio-Cio-San so appealing? She isn't ill. And she commits the crime in occidental eyes of killing herself at the end. Is it because she is so helpless? Is it because she is so much the victim, even believing herself to be married according to American law when in fact she has entered into only the flimsiest of marriages of convenience? Is it because Lieutenant Pinkerton emerges as so craven? He betrays her; she does *not* betray him. Or is Cio-Cio-San so appealing because she poses no threat to society, to order, to men? Her response to Pinkerton's duplicity is not to challenge the dictum of society – why doesn't she say, 'Look here, he married me first!' – but to destroy the disturbing element – herself.

Even Magda in the same composer's *La rondine* (1917), for all her independence and her often remarked 'differentness' refuses to threaten the existing order. She is Violetta without a cough. She gives up her wealthy lover and the accompanying worldly goods to fly with Ruggero (= Alfredo) to the country where they enjoy bliss marred only by unpaid bills. Ruggero, modern man to the core, writes home for permission to marry – and *gets* it in a letter from his mother filled with touching references to 'motherhood that makes love holy'. The letter read, surely, to the accompaniment of Magda's gentle sobs concludes: 'The honest old home of your old parents is brightened with joy to welcome the chosen girl. Give her my kiss!' This brings Magda to her senses. She immediately declares, 'I came to you contaminated; I cannot enter your home', to which Ruggero protests fairly vigorously (this is after all 1917) but to no avail. Magda quickly transforms herself into his mother and tells him that when he is cured of his passion he is to remember her: 'You return to your serene home, I assume my flight and my suffering . . . Say nothing more, let this grief be mine.' And off she goes, returning to her wealthy lover and her demi-monde life. She, like Cio-Cio-San, very much like Violetta, will not challenge the society that denies her – the fallen woman – entry into respectability. (Let us hope, however, that she will invest her unlawful gains wisely and die – if not surrounded by loving children – at least in comfort, as does a retired courtesan much admired by Nana.)

But do none of Violetta's daughters rebel against the society that coldheartedly condemns them, that offers them only posthumous redemption, that will not permit them to slip off quietly to the country and regain physical and moral health? (Even nature – refuge, source of health, of strength, of virtue for 'good' people – takes offence at the presence of the fallen woman: it is the wilderness that kills Manon in both Auber's and Puccini's operas.) What about Carmen? Or Lulu? Surely these powerful figures can overcome the strictures of society.

Carmen *is* a rebel; she is an outlaw – in her work life and in her love life. She does as she wishes – smuggles goods, defies the police, loves whom and where she will. But she is defeated in the end by the good bourgeois, José. José embodies all the attributes of the middle class: he is a promising young soldier, he has a doting mother, and he will surely soon marry the admiring, sweet, pure, virginal Micaëla. Carmen destroys his army career, lures him into a criminal life, and then abandons him for a bullfighter (isn't this sex role reversal?). Still, all José wants is to settle down with her to a life of happy domestic criminal activity. When she refuses, the good bourgeois kills her. Carmen cannot be permitted to live; she is far too dangerous, and part of that danger is that she acts like a man. She is ruthless, remorseless, and exudes power. She destroys carelessly, not for personal gain, but indifferently. Her sexuality is overt and overwhelming; she uses it not to make a living but for her pleasure. Is this perhaps why the opera was a fiasco in the Paris of 1875?

This is the same Paris that, according to Zola, was dominated by the demi-mondaine: his sybaritic Nana moves at all levels of society, corrupts and ruins at all levels of society, and is herself untouched by the decadence surrounding her. At the height of her triumph she cashes in her winnings and retires. She is thoughtless, good-natured, often generous, seldom mean, and destroys everything she touches. Nana is, like her sisters, destroyed finally by the one thing she cares about: unlike her sisters that one thing is not a man but a child. Her urgent maternal love – usually the greatest of virtues – compels her to nurse her son during his fatal bout of smallpox. Alas, she is infected and dies horribly, her body, especially her face, reflecting the foul corruption in which she had blithely flowered. No wonder Nana never became an operatic heroine!

Is Berg's Lulu wicked or helpless? Does she corrupt or is she corrupted? We are specifically told in the Prologue that she was 'created to work evil, to entice, to lead astray, to poison, to murder – all without the victim's awareness'. But *who* created her? Berg, via Wedekind – both of them carriers of the nineteenth-century *femme fatale* bacillus. The events of the opera descend into progressively greater viciousness and depravity – but in each case, isn't it Lulu who is acted *upon*? Forced to react to the desires of her companions? Certainly the end (planned but not completed by Berg) suggests this interpretation, for to support her male and female lovers Lulu turns to street prostitution – the most dangerous form of the profession. Her punishment is swift and grisly: on the evening of Christmas Day she is murdered by Jack the Ripper. The moral community has been served by this most dreadful executioner of prostitutes.

The Mila of the 1904 D'Annunzio tragedy upon which Pizzetti based his 1954 opera, *La figlia di Jorio*, is reputed to be a prostitute. This reputation leads two fieldworkers to try to rape her; she is rescued by Aligi who, immediately smitten, goes off to her cave to enjoy with her a pure love. Aligi's father comes to retrieve him, turns his attention to raping Mila (who was, by her reputation, asking for it after all), and is killed by his son. Aligi is to be executed for this crime, but Mila using her magical skills convinces everybody, including Aligi, that she killed the father. She goes to be burned at the stake 'serenely' because she knows she has saved Aligi. One wonders what attracted this mid-twentieth-century composer to a theme so redolent of nineteenth-century woman-as-victim theme. Is this machismo or verismo?

By now it seems clear that Violetta's daughters haven't departed very much from the model established by their noble ancestor. Where, oh where, is opera's Miss Sadie Thompson? One more figure appears, however. A very rich, very old lady, Claire Zachanassian, visits her poverty-stricken home town in Dürrenmatt's 1956 play, *Der Besuch der alten Dame*, set to music in 1971 by Gottfried von Einem. She has come back for vengeance. In return for the life of Alfred Ill who, years earlier, seduced then abandoned her, forcing her to enter a brothel to support his child whom he refused to acknowledge, she will make the town rich. Greed wins the day. The ex-prostitute departs with Ill's body as part of her luggage, leaving behind a great deal of money and ... shame? After all the heroines who have achieved immortality through suffering for their immorality, we finally have a victim who refuses to play out the role. Instead she revenges herself not only on the individual who wronged her but on the entire community that passively supported or overlooked his action.

'What if ... ?' Finally, what if Verdi had turned to Zola, Maugham, or Dürrenmatt for his libretto about the consumptive consumer? What if Violetta, instead of submitting to Giorgio Germont's unending demands, had reacted in the spirit of the profession he wished her to return to? Perhaps the meeting of Violetta and Papa Germont might have concluded on a different note. Something like the following:

Germont announces that he has come to reclaim his son from the clutches of the woman who has bewitched him and lured him away from home and family. Violetta replies, as in 1853, 'Sir, I am a lady and in my own house.' Germont, struck by her noble stance and *form*, finds himself drawn to her; the attraction is strengthened by the subsequent news that she has given over to Alfredo all her worldly goods. The good father points out that love seldom lasts and, pressing home his point, reminds her that beauty fades, that hers is now in full bloom (said with admiring looks), and that she should in short sell the merchandise while it's in good condition. Violetta, gripped suddenly by anger that has fermented for a century, perceives at last the hypocrisy and injustice of his demands. Why should Alfredo's angelic young sister have a greater claim to love, to marital bliss, than she who has beauty, intelligence, wit, and knowledge gained through a career of honest, straightforward dealings with the world? She resolves to avail herself of her professional expertise.

She therefore turns her beautiful face to Germont and with contrition in her voice tells him she concedes to his demands. 'O Father,' she says, as she did in 1853, 'embrace me to strengthen me in this ordeal.' Germont takes her gently in his arms, then murmuring to himself 'So beautiful, so noble, so . . . fine', aims a kiss at her forehead. But he misses or she moves. Their lips meet. He embraces her more passionately, and they sink to the floor. At this instant Alfredo enters, crying out eagerly, 'My Violetta!' He takes in the scene with horror: 'My father!' Rising, Violetta replies, as Nana might have done in a similar situation, 'What does it matter after all?' and Alfredo runs out screaming, leaving Violetta stretching her arms out in a gesture of wonder which slowly turns to triumph as she regards the trembling body of Germont at her feet.

Yes, 'what if . . . ?' indeed.

Maggie Hemingway
Look Behind You ...

Maggie Hemingway wrote four novels (most recently Eyes*) and two works for the composer David Matthews:* Cantiga, *a dramatic scena, and* From Coastal Stations, *a song-cycle.*

'Imponente ... ' whispers Violetta. 'Command me ... ' And we know it is all over.

It is the one unbelievable moment in both the novel and the opera – the one moment we want to refuse to believe. We have watched in horror, scenting tragedy, as first Alfredo is withdrawn from the scene, then Violetta's manservant and then her maid, until finally she is alone in the drawing room of the small house in the country and we know that in the shadows outside Alfredo's father waits, judging his moment. The tension of the situation is so cleverly managed that this noble paterfamilias who has only his son's welfare and his daughter's good name at heart has been metamorphosed into an incarnation of evil out to destroy love, while the self-assured Violetta has been transformed into an unprotected damsel in white muslin. We almost long to leap from our chairs like children at a pantomime and call out to her, 'Look behind you!'

But what is this fear? Violetta has no need of us. We have seen Violetta. She is the most beautiful woman in Paris, charming and gay and perfectly self-contained. We have heard about her. She is bold enough to advertise her availability each evening at the opera by carrying white camellias or red, yet she makes brazenness look like modesty. She is at the very pinnacle of her career, maintained like a duchess by princes. But Violetta has not merely acquired the graces of society. She is now in love and love has given her even greater strength. In love she has found her true self and a new life. For love she has, before our eyes, renounced all her wealth and glittering success. She seems breathtakingly invincible. Alfredo's father steps out of the shadows – and the drama is shattered.

It is unbelievable. But it is necessary. It is necessary that the contemporary nineteenth-century code of values be upheld, for the greater security of the nineteenth-century reader and audience.

The moral order must be seen to prevail. Alfredo's father wins. And Violetta's heart is broken. Perhaps it is also necessary so that the dream of love can be preserved intact. Suppose Violetta had triumphed and she and Alfredo had gone to live in poverty in Paris. How long would their love have lasted? How long before Alfredo got bored, kicking his heels in a *petit bourgeois* life to which both of them would probably remain outsiders? How long before the stories would begin to circulate in their *quartier* about her and her past existence? If love died, stifled slowly, or strangled by resentment, what would they have left in their lives together? One thinks of the two lovers in Tolstoy's *Anna Karenina*; of the courage of Anna and the surprising steadfastness of Vronsky. They began, those two, with much higher credentials than Violetta and Alfredo, but even they were unable to sustain their love against the prevailing moral order. Love destroyed in such a way is far worse than love cut down in full bloom, for love has been seen to die, leaving former lovers only despair or cynicism. But love thwarted in the full strength of its passion still in a way lives on. The memory of it remains vivid. It is thought of with longing, in its arrested perfection, for what it might have been. It is this vision of love that sustains Violetta in the tragedy of her death. It is for this dream of what love might be that we long for Violetta to triumph. We watch her on stage turn to Alfredo's father . . . And it is in this very moment before she hangs her head and whispers 'Imponente' that we are sure she will.

Rhian Samuel
Violetta and Germont

Rhian Samuel, composer, teaches composition at Reading University.

*L*a *traviata* is undoubtedly a testament to nineteenth-century sexual double standards; but when Violetta capitulates to hypocritical social mores, women everywhere find themselves acquiescing with her. How can this be?

La traviata is a woman's opera; Verdi reserves the greatest music for his heroine. He paints her with a full range of colour, most notably in the aria 'A fors'è lui' which, as it shifts from mood to mood, trades one memorable melody for another. But resistance to the dominant order is offered neither by Violetta nor ultimately by Alfredo, her lover, who follows in the dishonourable tradition of Purcell's Aeneas, perhaps the most famous operatic wimp. *His* first main aria, 'Un dì felice', with its own memorable melodies, is soon interrupted by Violetta and later she even appropriates his tune 'Di quell'amor'. The dominant order itself is represented by Germont *père*, Alfredo's father. Differences between the treatment of this character in novel and opera may at first seem slight but actually show the decisive role of music in reconciling the audience – even a modern feminist one – to the fate of the heroine.

In novel and opera the father is at first stiff and self-righteous, the personification of contemporary hypocrisy (indeed, the character somewhat resembles Dumas *père* – who was not averse to dallying with courtesans). But (male) opera directors have often presented Germont as a kindly parent-figure, laying down the law in spite of himself. This apparent contradiction is possible because during his brief meeting with Violetta not only does his view of her shift radically but, more importantly, he himself undergoes a transformation.

In the novel Marguerite describes this meeting in a deathbed letter to Armand. Duval opens by insulting her but relents when she proves her financial independence, though he still questions both her resolve to relinquish former habits and the lasting strength of the relationship. Finally, he invokes his daughter's name. In her letter, Marguerite insists that, despite his powerful arguments, Duval was only a catalyst in her decision to relinquish Armand. His observations 'had already occurred (to me) many times before'; after listening to him, *she told herself* 'all the things (he) dared not say ... ' When she admits, 'I was, when all was said and done, nothing but a kept woman', Duval is left strangely neutral and we, the readers, are left frustrated, protesting against an unseen enemy.

In Act II of *La traviata*, the meeting begins similarly. Germont insults Violetta and she responds with dignity, 'Donna son io ... '

(I am a lady sir, and in my own house ...) His gratuitous aside 'Quai modi!' (What bearing!) does little to endear him to us. As in the novel, Violetta now offers proof of her financial independence. Here, however, the order of events is subtly altered. Abashed but hardly daunted, Germont launches into his petition with an aria about his daughter: 'Pura siccome un angelo' which proves to be only his overture. When Violetta, gradually appreciating his intentions, shows her agitation ('Non sapete'), Germont responds with a cunning descent from the high moral ground to play on woman's greatest weakness – her fear of ageing. Violetta falters at his insinuating remark ' ... ma volubile sovente è l'uom' (but men are often inconstant), and Germont, seizing his chance, amplifies his theme in the aria, 'Un dì, quando le veneri' (One day when time has banished all those charms). In *La traviata*, despite his perfunctory conversion, Germont has remained the antagonist.

This aria ends with a surprising change of sentiment: 'Siate di mia famiglia l'angiol consolatore' (Become the guardian angel of my family), but the musical setting – simply a continuation of the melody – denies a change of heart. Thus the plea can either be (charitably) interpreted as an off-hand, almost thoughtless, utterance or viewed as Germont's cynical attempt to press home his advantage. His persuasion succeeds: a sudden key change signals the beginning of Violetta's capitulation in music which faintly recalls 'Di quell'amor': 'Così alla misera' (Thus hope is now dead). Beneath her lament, Germont repeats his new-found suggestion like a submerged refrain; the music to which it is set becomes gradually more tortuous and agitated until at last the words seem endowed with a sincerity so patently lacking at their first utterance.

Violetta completes her submission with a pathetic, simple aria in E♭ major, 'Ah, dite alla giovine' (Oh, say to the young girl). Instead of gloating, Germont responds with some of the most heart-rending music of the opera, the upward-sighing 'Piangi, piangi, o misera ... ' (Weep, weep, oh unhappy one ... and now I feel in my soul all the suffering that is yours). This music erases any remaining sense of hypocrisy; Germont's ruthlessness has given way to compassion. At 'Piangi', the music modulates darkly to a distant key (C♭ major; see Ex. 1) before returning to E♭ major for Violetta's second verse. This time, Verdi adds a subsidiary line

Ex. 1

for Germont; again the dark modulations of 'Piangi' appear. Now the oboes and cellos, playing Germont's line with him, move through it and upward to Violetta's, joining the melodies and making them one (see Ex. 2). The most distant key of C♭ major by sleight of hand (the addition of one single note, A♭, at *x* in Ex. 2) becomes the very means of returning to the simple purity of the original key, E♭ major.

Ex. 2

Through darkness we come to light; the couple end together, Germont singing 'Corragio, e il nobile cor vincerà' (Courage and your noble heart will triumph) while Violetta repeats 'e che morrà' (and [she] will die). The words, 'vincerà' and 'morrà' are fused along with the music.

Julian Budden, the noted Verdi expert, has pointed out (in *The Operas of Verdi*, vol. 2, London, 1978) that Verdi altered the vital passage between Germont's 'Un dì' and Violetta's 'Ah, dite alla giovine' (her lament, 'così alla misera') between the first and second versions of the opera, lowering the key by a semitone and adding a part for Germont. Although Budden asserts that the key was probably changed for pragmatic reasons, he passes no comment on the addition of Germont's line. How significant is it? The source of the repeated text ('Siate, siate l'angiol consolator') is the previous aria where Germont was portrayed at his most calculating; on the other hand, the increasingly chromatic line culminates in a twice-heard melodic motif (B♭-C♭-F-B♭-E♭) which reappears in the passionate 'Piangi' (see Ex. 3). Thus the addition, even if a composer's afterthought, provides a crucial link. Through it we witness Germont's transformation from one extreme to another, and are drawn with him to his ultimate reconciliation with Violetta.

Ex.3

What then of Violetta's female audience? How does Verdi reconcile them (us) to her fate? Through the power of music, he diverts our attention from the abstract concept of hypocritical social mores towards a fundamental human issue: the sublimation of conflicting emotions. Thus does this 'testament to nineteenth-century sexual double standards' transcend its origins.

Sophie Fuller
The Silence of Violetta

Sophie Fuller is currently researching a book on British women composers.

In 1983 I went to see Zeffirelli's film of *La traviata*. Such glorious camp – all those mirrors and chandeliers, all that passion and drama. The music was so powerful and seductive. I bought the records and wandered round the house singing 'Di quell'amor' for days ... But the story was so ridiculous. Why on earth didn't Violetta simply ignore the self-righteous Germont? And having sacrificed love and happiness, why did she have to die as well?

Years later I sit and think about the ladies of the camellias – Marie Duplessis, Marguerite Gautier and Violetta Valéry. Novel, play, opera, film ... One of the most pervasive myths of romantic love and woman's sacrifice ever created by man. And they are all men – Dumas, Piave, Verdi, Zeffirelli ...

Of course it started with a real woman, Alphonsine Plessis, who recreated herself as Marie Duplessis, a beautiful and successful courtesan in mid-nineteenth-century Paris. Marie Duplessis was in control – she knew what she wanted and how to get it. But the culture and ideology of the age had created an image of woman as passive and preferably sickly, a creature incapable of creation or any action other than sacrifice. And how many heroines of the nineteenth century live to see the end of their opera, novel or play? One of Marie Duplessis's lovers, Alexandre Dumas, set the legend in motion by recreating her as Marguerite Gautier, a woman doomed to sacrifice and death.

As the myth of the lady of the camellias moves from novel to play to opera the themes of sickness, sacrifice and death become stronger. The facts of Marie Duplessis's life and the power of a celebrated courtesan retreat further and further into the distance. In turning his novel into a play Dumas had to dispense with many descriptions and explanations. Marguerite loses much of her command over her life and her situation. We miss many of those vulgar little details about sex and money that almost make the

Marguerite of the novel believable. Any remnants of Marguerite's power disappeared when Piave turned the play into an opera libretto. Everything in the opera happens so fast. One moment (the end of Act I) Violetta has decided it would be folly to love Alfredo and the next (the opening of Act II) Alfredo is telling us that they are living together in the country, gloriously in love. Gone is the gradual firing of Marguerite's love, gone is Armand's jealousy, gone are almost all the sordid financial details.

But we must remember that this is an opera. There is now an added dimension – the music. And it was the music that initially pulled me into Violetta's story. Opera and opera singers demand certain conventions that may detract from or change the story. So there are dancing gypsies and matadors at Flora's party in Act II. And there are two male singers who need enough music to tempt them into the roles. Is this why Germont keeps turning up everywhere? At Flora's party? At Violetta's deathbed? With *two* numbers when Violetta has left Alfredo? Or are Piave and Verdi hammering home the voice of bourgeois respectability? And was it the need for another important tenor number that explains why Alfredo opens the second act?

I can see another reason why it is Alfredo rather than Violetta who opens this act, who first tells us that they are in love, that she has changed her mind and moved away from her friends and lovers in Paris to the country to be with him. The story of the Lady of the Camellias is one told by men. In the novel Marguerite's story is distanced by not one but two narrators. The only time that we hear Marguerite's voice directly is when we are given the diary that she kept as she was dying. If only Marie Duplessis had kept a diary that could be found in a dusty old attic somewhere . . .

Violetta does not open Act II because, in spite of all this beautiful music, Violetta's voice is strangely muffled. This is not her story but the story of the men that surround her. She sings . . . but what does she sing? What music does Verdi give her? How does he use music to tell us her story?

The central theme of love in the opera is 'Di quell'amor'. If any one tune can represent an opera, this is it for *La traviata*. This is the tune I sang as I did the washing-up. This is the bit that runs through our heads as we leave the opera house. But it is Alfredo's tune. It is he who sings it first, as he declares his love to Violetta in

Act I. When she sings of love in this act all she can do is repeat Alfredo's music. Her own music is the coloratura which Verdi uses to paint the flightiness, the whoredom that Piave had to leave out of the libretto. So Alfredo gets 'Di quell'amor'. He also starts the famous *brindisi* 'Libiamo'. Violetta again echoes him even though dramatically it makes little sense for Alfredo to be singing the praise of drinking and high living when a few moments later he will be urging Violetta to give up such a life. Alfredo is also the first to sing 'Parigi, o cara', when in the last act they briefly dream of a future together before Violetta dies.

So what is Violetta's memorable music? The most moving part of her momentous duet with Germont is probably 'Dite alla giovine'. But this is when I am most annoyed with her, when she has given in, given up. A number moving in its simplicity maybe, but it is Germont who gets the heart-rending semitones on 'piange, piange . . . ' Then there is her passionate outburst to Alfredo just before she leaves him – 'Amami Alfredo'. We have heard this before in the opening orchestral prelude. But doesn't it also remind us of 'Di quell'amor'? The same opening three notes, the same falling pattern . . . Violetta has no music of her own to express her love for Alfredo. All her passion and drama come as she gives up her love or as she is dying. Violetta has no voice to express joy or happiness, only sacrifice and tragedy.

Verdi's most obvious distancing of Violetta comes not in anything she sings but in the way he uses the orchestra to tell us about her. As she writes the fateful letter to Alfredo it is the clarinet melody rather than her vocal line that depicts her anguish and sorrow. Those high unearthly strings in the prelude that are heard again at the opening of the last act give us a clear idea of how Verdi sees her – frail, pathetic, pitiable. But could we really expect anything else? Why should Verdi have any greater insight than Dumas or Piave? For these men it was impossible to give a woman, let alone a prostitute, a voice to express happiness or power. The most they could give her was their pity and forgiveness, in itself too radical for many of their contemporaries. A Violetta created by Piave and Verdi could do no more than yield to the self-righteous Germont and sacrifice everything, even her life. Like so many women, the Lady of the Camellias has been silenced.

Riikka Hakola
in conversation with Jussi Törnvall
A Finnish Violetta

The Finnish soprano Riikka Hakola made her debut as Violetta in November 1992, and in 1993 it was in this role that she gave the first performance in the new opera house of Finnish National Opera in Helsinki. She talks here with the dramaturge of Finnish National Opera, Jussi Törnvall.

Riikka Hakola as Violetta with Peter Lindroos as Alfredo, Finnish National Opera, 1992 (photo Kari Hakli)

RH: What kind of man did the 'real' Violetta try to find, why did she let men exploit her and why did she have to use men herself?

JT: The 'real' Violetta, Marie Duplessis, was fourteen when she left home. Her father was a drunken ne'er-do-well, the son of a Normandy whore. He had two daughters, Delphine and Rose Alphonsine, which was Marie's real name. He had no means to educate them and he gave them as servants to a seventy-year-old farmer who seduced Marie, and she escaped to Paris.

RH: Where she had to find a way to live. She wanted to be independent – although psychologically shattered, her spirit was strong. As a courtesan, selling sexual favours, she still had something admirable about her that those 'proper' people lacked. Maybe it was this strength of will, this determination to enjoy the pleasures that money can buy, that these frustrated high-society people didn't have. Parties lit up when she was present, and she brought something different to this society to which she did not belong but in which she moved as an ornament. What was she looking for in men after all her negative experiences?

JT: Marie was degraded by her father; her image of men had been distorted from childhood. She wanted revenge, to humiliate men; she was perfectly aware of her charm and exploited it.

RH: But in the opera Violetta has a quality of soul which is appreciated only when she is dying, when all the 'respectable' people genuflect before it. Verdi suggests that her feverish desire to enjoy life is due to her awareness that death is not far away, and perhaps this also makes her appreciate honesty and the finer feelings of humanity. Verdi does not make her part of the society in which she moves; she is always an outsider. Her pale complexion proclaims this – her beauty is admirable, exceptional by the standards of the time. It is also, for her, a fatal premonition: 'Oh qual pallor!' is the cry of one who has seen death itself in the mirror.

JT: The prelude gives us two important atmospheres: the opening is full of sorrow, and the end associated with enjoying life. The beginning in B minor moves into the main key of E major: death and resurrection. Then it changes into brittle A major for the party music. The prelude is thus a portrait of Violetta.

RH: This prelude has a magical meaning for me. Crying, despairing, longing, a rose fading and withering ... a death of something beautiful which at the same time cannot die.

JT: The moment when she first sees Alfredo is very important. She has seen hundreds of society men but now she experiences something altogether more powerful. As she turns to the audience, she must have a totally different radiance, and we must know that something quite decisive has happened – we must recognize it even before she does ...

RH: She acts at first towards Alfredo as though he could not affect her, and behaves with practised sophistication towards him as she does to other men. It is his sincerity that compels her to abandon this assumed nonchalance.

She has to confront the new feeling within her. This relationship offers her an emotional world that she has forgotten ... she hears that Alfredo has been to see her when she was ill, not caring what she looked like. Nothing like that happened to her as a child. Alfredo offers her respect. Violetta imagines what it is to 'love and to be loved, a joy she never knew'.

'Sempre libera' is full of despair and confusion; it overflows with forced gaiety. What is harder in life than to find the truth? Violetta goes through despair to find her truth and to be brave enough to live with it.

JT: 'Sempre libera' repeats the struggle we first heard in the prelude. For Violetta this is the turning point; she is singing through tears and 'running at such high revs' that we can hear her desperation, and the love she cannot declare.

She's 'running at such high revs' that you can hear her desperation, and the love she cannot declare. Through her confusion we catch a first glimpse of her nobility ... How very different are Gaston and Flora from Alfredo and Violetta! Although both women are courtesans, Verdi gives an infinitely deeper portrait of Violetta: it is unimaginable that Alfredo could love Flora because they exist on different emotional, spiritual planes.

He also handles her relationship with Germont very delicately. Act II shows how she melts the ice between them by agreeing to make her sacrifice. She yields in a duet which, in length and complexity, resembles the father–daughter duet in Act III of *Rigoletto*. Here Violetta imagines that she sees her own father in Germont ('Qual figlia m'abbracciate'), and he is astonished to discover nobility in her.

RH: After all, she could have said she wasn't interested or asked for a lot of money. Short broken phrases indicate Germont's embarrassment when he recognizes her pure intentions.

JT: Every phrase in the next duet for Alfredo and Violetta speaks volumes. It is a bitter paradox that she must lie to her beloved because she wishes to honour her agreement with Germont. The phrase 'Amami Alfredo' at the very end begins on the notes and in the key of the love theme 'Ah, quell'amor'.

RH: It is also ironic that their deep love is sanctified by denial and expiation through death. Pure and successful love is not interesting on stage – it is dramatically more interesting to show love that cannot be fulfilled.

JT: Verdi's choice of keys gives the opera a particular coherence and colour. Mostly he uses flat keys which are rounder, darker in colour than the sharp keys. For the Act I party A major creates a light, flirtatious, 'champagne' atmosphere. At the *brindisi* it changes to B♭ major. In the waltz with Alfredo ('Un dì felice') the key moves into E♭ major, which has a certain warmth. 'Ah, fors'è lui' starts in F minor but changes into A♭ major in the course of the aria. At the end of the opera Verdi adds one further flat to arrive at D♭ major. For the bacchanal chorus Verdi adds A minor Verdi over D major. As a consequence it sounds grotesque, like something out of hell.

RH: There is a constant battle between major and minor keys in Violetta's music, and this tension reflects the two personalities within her. Behind the woman devoted to pleasure there is another full of profound sorrow. Violetta tried to fill her life with pleasure but her life, as a whole phrase, is a tragedy. When she appears at Flora's party we can feel the menace, as though everyone is waiting for a storm to burst, and Violetta's vocal line is in effect the line of tragic fate. The F minor of the card-playing music suggests that curtains of sorrow will descend over the room of partying guests.

JT: This conjunction of F minor and A♭ major also occurs in her first act aria but here the A♭ major sounds like a minor key –

RH: Just as in her life she tried to play in the major key and ended in the minor. In the last scene, her voice is thinner and has lost the strength of the second-act lyricism and purity, and the first act's coloratura and bravura. When she reads the letter from Germont we sense the loss of happiness, beauty, love and life itself. The aria that follows could not be more different in tone from that in the first act.

JT: It is the only time Verdi uses A minor in the whole opera. Very thin, transparent. Breaking orchestral phrases. When talking about their love Verdi uses A major.

RH: The figure in her phrase also changes into A major when she remembers Alfredo. The memory gives her strength. Her sickness is also shown in her breaking lines. She is trying so hard to be brave. 'I am too young to die' . . . there is some new energy within her, and Alfredo's very arrival prolongs her life . . . but it is too late for him to offer her the possibility of happiness, and their last duet is a fantasy.

Gemma Bellincioni
The Stage and I

Gemma Bellincioni (1864–1950) was a great star of the verismo *Italian opera. She created the role of Santuzza in Mascagni's* Cavalleria Rusticana *(1890) and the title role of Giordano's* Fedora *(1899). Verdi praised her interpretation of Violetta, and in her autobiography (1920) she remembered the first time she sang the part.*

After Lucia I sang *Traviata* and it was a triumph! I remember how, the first evening, in that great scene with the money, I just missed breaking my neck from the terrible fall I had when Alfredo, with a dramatic gesture, flung the money in my face . . .

I had warned that idiot who played the Doctor to be ready to catch me as soon as he saw me sway. But he forgot to do so, and since I took on the part so whole-heartedly as to forget everything else as soon as I found myself on stage, I fell backwards like a log in such a realistic manner that the public burst into unrestrained applause! ... For several days, however, I felt that fall, and that applause, in my bones ... but in recompense, it helped me understand the powerful effect that conviction can have on the soul of an audience! ... After that triumphant evening, the manager had my name printed on the poster in large letters! ... What joy I felt! ... I went out with my mother with the express purpose of seeing that big poster with those large red letters that seemed to smile at me when I passed them!

Irmgard Arnold
Felsenstein's Violetta

Irmgard Arnold, soprano, born in Lippe and brought up in Munich, joined Felsenstein's ensemble at the Komische Oper, Berlin, in 1950, where she played over twenty roles, notably – apart from Violetta – Aminta in Die schweigsame Frau, Gabrielle *in* La Vie parisienne, *the Vixen in* The Cunning Little Vixen *and Golde in* Fiddler on the Roof. *She was created Kammersängerin in 1954. She sang Violetta at the Komische Oper, East Berlin, in a production by Walter Felsenstein in 1960. Here she remembers the letter she received from him on the first night, and reminisces about his production.*

This discourse was collated by Detlef Sölter. A singer and director, he has worked at the Staatsoper and Volksoper in Vienna, and with Harry Kupfer in Berlin.

Irmgard Arnold as Violetta at the Komische Oper, Berlin, 1960

Dear Mrs Arnold,

In spite of your exertions in these last days you accepted my criticism of the dress rehearsal with so much attention and concentration that my usual detailed 'first night letter' is superfluous.

I have no doubt that when you receive this, you will be concentrating only on the party which you are throwing tonight, which – because of your absence from Paris for a whole year – will decide your position in society and, therefore, your entire existence. Of course everything will depend upon the first impression you give your guests. Just to please them is not enough for you. You demand to be thought healthier and more beautiful than ever. And no compliment – no matter who makes it – can satisfy you; your appetite for success is insatiable. In this fever you are not just the mistress of your own salon but the prima donna of the demi-monde, and you work yourself up to such a pitch of self-confidence, to a state of unimaginable and superb radiance, that you launch recklessly into the *brindisi*, which becomes – for you – an exercise in hypnosis. Only in such a frenzy could you, supreme in all the arts of love, succumb without noticing it to a man, and to a new emotion.

I am sure that you would come to your senses after the ball and the splendid night were it not for the unexpectedness of Alfredo's assault upon your heart. You have no defences against his ardour because you are suddenly so worried about your health. When you realize that your recovery was an illusion, you feel such a greed for life and craving for happiness that you cannot help yourself yielding to his declaration of love.

You ask: 'Why does he tell me all that again?' Because I want to remind you that no one can act unconsciousness or surprise: to be believable, you must bring yourself to forget yourself, and in this state the slightest hesitation, the slightest lack of concentration will drop you fatally back to earth. This is why I must always feel the quaver rhythm in this scene, which Verdi marked 'allegro brillantissimo e molto vivace'. I don't know any character in literature whose life and fate are portrayed so continuously, and with so little transition, as Violetta. If you manage this effect in the first act, there remain, of course, superhuman demands in the rest of the drama, but there are no more problems in establishing the character.

Tonight I wish you as a reward for your admirable determination in this particularly hard (because too short) rehearsal period, all the courage and self-confidence which you need for this terrifying battle.

Yours

Walter Felsenstein

A 'terrifying battle'! We had only seven weeks' rehearsal. As far as I know this was the shortest time Felsenstein ever fixed for production rehearsals – at least at the Komische Oper. Normally he would rehearse three or four months; this time we had to manage almost the same amount of work in half the time ... which meant three 3-hour rehearsals a day in order to work on as many details as ever. And that does not include what we called 'table-rehearsals'. Felsenstein began directing several weeks before the first production rehearsal. He attended music calls to stop singers learning to sing mechanically, like the senseless unspooling of a tape recorder, or to produce merely beautiful notes as in a concert. Even at this early stage he participated in the interpretation and we worked together on the nuances of expression which we thought that the score contained. Very, very often, for example, we worked through the *brindisi* and my big aria in the first act: these were the numbers on which Felsenstein especially set his heart.

His conception of a production always included the time before the first note of the overture and after the final chord. For him every character had a past and a future, which lay beyond the written text, and which had to be worked into the performance.

In *La traviata* the first thing he did was to transfer the action to the year 1868 – the time of the Second Empire. He explained it this way: 'Under the benevolent sun of Napoleon III a financially powerful upper class had developed, whose members enjoyed their new lifestyle to the fullest extent. For this demi-monde the day began at nightfall and finished at dawn. Violetta the courtesan was extremely desirable to such wealthy men . . . ' This was precisely the kind of society which he thought Verdi described.

Because of her beauty, her guile and her charm, Violetta has risen to be the queen of this world. At the moment she is, so to speak, Baron Douphol's personal property: he wants the leading courtesan in Paris as a status symbol. But for a year, her house has been shut up because her tuberculosis has forced her into a sanatorium. As is clear from his letter, this was very important for Felsenstein: I had to show in the first scene how she felt on her reappearance in society – this night would decide whether she would ever again be the queen of the demi-monde, and not only her reputation but her financial survival would depend on her success.

Both physically and mentally she has prepared herself for hours for this appearance. She is excessively nervous, unsure whether she can match up to public expectation. Furthermore she must hold her own against her rival, Flora, who has profited from her absence to further her own 'career'. In order to work myself in to this sense of extreme agitation, Felsenstein told me to stand backstage in front of a huge mirror for fifteen minutes before the performance began. I was absolutely not allowed to confuse this condition with my own stage-fright!

Violetta does not immediately fall in love with Alfredo. Felsenstein wanted me to show that Violetta is at first only interested in knowing whether she can have the same impact upon a good-looking country boy as on other men. But then – having called upon him to sing the *brindisi* simply to taunt Douphol – something unexpected happens which she cannot explain: she has the crazy idea to hypnotize Alfredo. It is she who in fact sings the *brindisi*; Alfredo is merely her medium. Felsenstein felt that it was inconceivable that this anaemic provincial lad could create such a song; he can do so only at Violetta's inspiration. This demonstrates her extreme excitement: she wants to prove her strength by forcing her own emotional state upon Alfredo through words and the melody.

Felsenstein wanted the relationship between Alfredo and Violetta to be unpredictable. Alfredo is literally transfixed and Violetta does not notice that in the pleasure of bewitching him she is bewitching herself. She is overcome by an emotion which she has never known. I sang my verse of the *brindisi* to the guests and not to Alfredo, in order to goad him. The verse we sang together was like a fever. The guests watch us intently, as if they expect physical intercourse between us at any moment. The effect of these strong emotions upon Violetta is a coronary. But so iron strong is her will to maintain the appearance of health that she still manages to deceive her guests.

Her disease is not beautiful. Felsenstein did not think that Verdi intended to write an opera about the illness and suffering of a consumptive woman. He perceived Violetta's illness as the result of her way of life, which was indeed determined by her society. It was, however, only one element in the tragedy that she associates love with an ambition to be accepted in bourgeois society. For a former courtesan there could be no greater joy than to marry with a white veil and a father's blessing, to live married to Alfredo, and to have children. Felsenstein observed that, 'Through her love and the ambition to build an existence for them both she could change Alfredo – fundamentally an insignificant character – into a "useful" human being. But she does nothing of the kind. Violetta's real tragedy is that she fails to condemn bourgeois society and its phoney moral code.'

Violetta's Act I aria reveals the extreme pressure she suffers. It is the great scream of a tortured, uprooted creature, fighting a terrible battle with herself. For her – the 'Queen of Love' – a new perspective has opened: to be loved and to love. According to Felsenstein: 'She does not want to sing an aria here – but she simply does not know what she should do! She blurts out the music breathlessly, involuntarily expressing her utter confusion.' In the opening section ('Ah, fors'è lui'), Violetta hardly dares to open her mouth, for fear of banishing the vision. So strongly does she experience the scene once again that she borrows the melody of Alfredo's love.

The *allegro* ('Follie!') is a cry: 'What has become of me?' She makes one last attempt to escape enslavement to the intolerable and exquisite sensation which overwhelms her. Felsenstein observed that here Verdi gave her music that does not really correspond to her personality: the refined courtesan is trying to persuade herself that she could survive by offering cheap pleasures in a vulgar brothel. Alfredo's voice, which of course exists only in her imagination, interrupts this self-imposed humiliation, and sings the truth.

The final coloratura ('sempre libera') must not be sung as a brilliant display of fireworks; they are Violetta's rebellion, her desire to destroy the voice within herself. At that moment I groped around me, to find support. As I fell, I caught a table-cloth, pulling the cloth, the china, cutlery and glasses with me. The curtain fell on Violetta's total collapse; she had been defeated by an emotion of which she had no knowledge.

Violetta longs for the blessing of Alfredo's father, the highest accolade of bourgeois society. In Act II comes the moment which she has been expecting and dreading for so long. Since Germont comes of his own free will, she presumes that he has come to fulfil her desire. As a result, his attack hurts her the more deeply. One way which Felsenstein showed Germont's heartlessness: when I collapsed at the end of the duet Germont at once tried to stand me up again, as though I were puppet, so that he would not be seen with an unconscious woman.

The final act of this great music theatre piece must never be sentimental – that would be banal! We wanted to show the degree of schizophrenia in which Violetta lives during the whole opera and which here comes to a crisis: it is the schizophrenia of an extreme vitality and a presentiment of death. Felsenstein's Violetta has retired into a shabby attic. Her illness has got worse and her only hope is to see Alfredo again. She takes new strength from reading his letter again and again. In those moments she is calm, and seems to be healthy. But gradually her agony increases, exacerbated by memories of her former life. Felsenstein wanted to show how she is torn between these two extremes and how this torture destroys her.

When Alfredo arrives she finds the strength to accuse God. From Him she demands life: 'With Alfredo You gave me my true life, everything else was a lie. Now You must let me live at his side! I must not die now!' She cries out against this injustice. Felsenstein loathed any form of sentimentality. When she believes she is quite healthy, she speaks with great resolution. Felsenstein told me on no account to play the scene 'like some disembodied angelic spirit'!

Margot Fonteyn
Marguerite and Armand, *March 1963*

Frederick Ashton had earlier been drawn to the idea of a ballet on the subject of Marguerite Gautier, the heroine of Alexandre Dumas's novel. He studied the story of Marie Duplessis, on whose life the novel was based, and he almost mounted the ballet to music written by Jean Français for a version presented at the Paris Opéra. At the last minute he decided to shelve that production, and another two years passed until he heard a piece of music by Liszt that brought the story rushing back to his imagination, all the elements fitting together. In the meantime, Rudolf had burst headlong into our world.

Fred liked the coincidence that Liszt actually had an affair with Marie Duplessis, and he quoted her words beseeching Liszt to take her to Italy with him: 'I will be no trouble to you. I sleep all day, go to the theatre in the evening and at night you may do what you will with me.' The words were particularly touching − I don't know why. I think they contain something of that vulnerability of the feminine woman, like Marilyn Monroe. I fell in love with the character of Marguerite.

Fred cast Michael Somes as the father of Armand, and choreographed our renunciation scene alone. When it was finished, Rudolf joined the rehearsal. As Michael and I played the scene over, an electrical storm of emotion built up in the studio. We came to the end, and Rudolf tore into his entrance and the following pas de deux with a passion more real than life itself, generating one of those fantastic moments when a rehearsal becomes a burning performance.

Margot Fonteyn and Rudolf Nureyev in Marguerite and Armand, *Covent Garden, 1963 (photo Cecil Beaton; courtesy of Sotheby's, London)*

There were more photographs taken during the rehearsals of this ballet than for any other I can remember. Cecil Beaton took his own inimitable pictures; no one has equalled his airy style of photography, evoking mood, period and personality in so masterly and subtle a fashion. The costume fittings did not go at all smoothly – they seldom do. Beaton designed matchless costumes for me, but I had a slight wrangle about the red camellias which, for reasons of modesty connected with the novel, I was embarrassed to wear. Without liking to explain, I insisted on wearing white flowers. Meanwhile, Rudolf was vehemently refusing to wear the long coat-tails of the original design, saying he didn't want to look like a waiter. It was no use my pointing out that Bobby had looked elegant and poetic in *Apparitions*. Rudolf chopped the coat-tails to a length that satisfied his keen sensibility to his own proportions, regardless of what might suit anyone else or what the designer thought. He had discarded wigs altogether with the first *Giselle* dress rehearsal, and rapidly developed a strong personal style, with an instinct for forthcoming fashions in his street clothes that anticipated long hair and Nehru collars.

There was a high degree of expectation before *Marguerite and Armand*, generated by Ashton's choreography and Beaton's designs – and by now a web of romantic attachment that had very publicly been spun about Rudolf and myself. Hardly anyone knew where truth ended and fantasy began. But what a plum of a ballet it was for me, and what a success for all of us.

On the day of the first performance Rudolf brought me a little white camellia tree, which seemed to symbolize the basic simplicity of our relationship in the midst of so much furore. It was only for a year that we had been dancing together. As we were taking innumerable curtain calls, with flowers raining down from the gallery slips, I said, 'Well, now do you think you will stay another year, even though you are so unhappy with us?' He replied, 'Margot, you know I will never be happy anywhere.' For he was still defensive and dreadfully critical. It was as if he had expected England to be a veritable paradise and all who dwelt there brilliant creatures of great beauty. Naturally we were a bit of a disappointment. On the other hand, when I apologized for us being so ugly he replied, 'I did not say I not like. Ugly can be charming.'

Peter Brook
The Writing on the Wall
from the Observer, *17 March 1963*

Between 1947 and 1950, Peter Brook was Director of
Productions at the Royal Opera House, Covent Garden, and his
stagings included Salome *with designs by Salvador Dali. After*
directing Eugene Onegin *at the Met in 1957, he gave up producing*
opera altogether until he formed his own company in Paris at the
Bouffes du Nord. In 1963 he was invited by the Observer *to*
review the Royal Gala performance of Marguerite and Armand.

It was a journey into the past. More than fifteen years ago I had
written about the ballet for the *Observer*, and in those days my
own work as a director was what was called 'balletic'. Covent
Garden was the centre of my life, the ballet a thing of great meaning: I was in love with qualities which I knew had once existed and
which the wartime world so completely lacked.

Bérard was my idol – Europe seemed the treasure-house of the
world – poetry meant refinements: it was elegance and finesse that
lifted life from the humdrum; the suggestion seemed stronger than
the whole, the fashionable and the witty seemed more living than
the clumsy: the theatre was the opposite of the outside world.

Today I feel a long way from all this and my excursion to the
Gala Performance was a chance to confront one set of values with
another. Is it true, I wondered, that the great red curtain no longer
holds any promise of magic? Is a bare stage really more exciting
than tiers of gilt? How subjective is this? Am I just bored with the
romantic past or has it really been corroded by time?

Time is a vital factor in the theatre. Daily as our optic vision
varies, so the surface changes and the manner of our statements
must adapt. No two audiences are the same and the art of production is in an endless state of flux and evolution. (This was the
theme of my running fight in opera in the same Covent Garden, for
musicians can never grasp why the composer's stage directions are
not *right* for eternity.)

Obviously, superficial things date the quickest. None the less everything in the theatre is subject to the clock – even the expression of deep feelings can turn hollow; even the feelings themselves can become lifeless – because nothing in the theatre is real, everything is form, and so even deep emotion observed is only an imitation of itself – and so liable to decay.

Marguerite and Armand is consciously a romantic ballet. Its ingredients are drawn from the past, its creators belong to the present. How living can the result be? Unlike my friend Kenneth Tynan, I am very susceptible to *Giselle*. Am I open to a new *Giselle* in the same way?

I understand the ballet as a form through which certain notions can be expressed in finer shades than in words: strands of feeling can be caught with marvellous subtlety, even moral values such as generosity or nobility can be given concrete shape. The classical dance is the greatest of all alienation devices: when the dancer has mastered all the incredible technical difficulties, then these difficulties become the screen on which, as he transcends effort, a line of feeling can be presented almost in objectivity.

Such a gesture is certainly not topical. It can be as abstract as geometry, it can trace patterns that relate to music as one instrument does to another. It can explore relationships between body and space, body object and movement. Also it can sing. Ashton's work is like the spontaneous act of song.

In *Marguerite and Armand* over the music Ashton improvises freely, composing a flowing line of melody all his own, closely related to Liszt's score, yet utterly independent and in this respect the work is simple, beautiful and most satisfying. Its transparency is such that Ashton can even permit himself the audacity of stillness – the breath is caught, the gesture suspended in pauses which, like the silences of Marguerite Duras, are as lyrical as any steps.

In this ballet Nureyev and Fonteyn play as actors: extraordinary actors who bring to each moment and each movement that quality of depth which makes the most artificial of forms suddenly seem human and simple. All great art eventually is realistic: the art of these two dancers leads them continually to moments of truth.

When Fonteyn curtsied before a stamping and cheering house, pale, frail and removed, it could have been Duse: when she and Nureyev stood together tired and tender a truly moving quality was expressed: they manifested to that audience a relationship graver, paler and less fleshbound than those of everyday life.

It was certainly a great occasion and yet it was incomplete. *La Dame aux camélias* as a ballet is under the same laws as the famous old play. We know the play best through Edwige Feuillère and our admiration here is centred only on the actress. The story is flimsy stuff and it is only as a vehicle that it has endured. The ballet in turn is a vehicle for two star artists and this is both its strength and its limitation.

Consider the tradition of the English theatre up to most recent times – this most honourable tradition was related not to matter but manner, it was the genius of our actors, whether du Maurier or Gielgud, that could turn indifferent material into gold. Despite its joys this theatre has withered away.

Let me refer to Kenneth Tynan again. He was the prophet of the great changes in the legitimate theatre and his sceptical reaction to his evening at *Giselle* must not be dismissed. On the contrary, I believe that the ballet must look out, for the writing is on the wall.

Indeed, I treasure the miraculous green-and-white memory of *Symphonic Variations*. I love Balanchine and Graham: I believe form is its own reality: dancing is its own reality: yet *Marguerite and Armand* cannot be judged on movement alone. It takes a subject and the subject cannot be ignored. The silhouette of the ballet is part of its meaning: it is a relationship: the same two dancers, the same gestures, would have a different weight and a meaning in another context. Were they in practice costume in limbo it would be different. Were they in modern clothes in another story it would be different. The necessity to consider the content is even more plainly indicated here, where the centre of gravity of the ballet is not in acrobatic movement, but in acting, in emotion through character and eventually through the evocativeness of plot. The ballet implies that a pure exchange of personal emotion can exist like a pure movement. The choice of the legend of *Camille* for a ballet assumes that twilight and melting images, candlelight and swirling skirts, still correspond with our yearnings. I doubt it. Romance seems to me an empty husk.

It is clear that Ashton and Beaton considered this problem and felt that the language they use must relate to the present day. Beaton turned from gauzes and Victoriana towards a more modern style that hints at contemporary sculpture and Coventry

Cathedral. Ashton has stated that he is influenced by *Last Year in Marienbad*. On to the cyclorama in a Brechtian way they project a giant photograph of Nureyev. This has been much criticized but to me it is a fascinating clue to their intentions. The problem of the projection is not that it was an experiment that failed, because it added nothing. These two artists were clearly after something and it could also be that they did not go far enough.

Why did they avoid the conventional form of a story ballet? Why did they avoid the completely romantic set that Cecil Beaton could so easily have provided? Why those projections? To me, it was a clue that in their hearts the two creators were not quite sure either that romance holds water today. Perhaps somewhere there was a wish to add a new element, another dimension to this old story. *Marguerite and Armand* looks back, and yet we feel its creators are standing on the threshold of a country which they half acknowledge and refuse to enter.

In tribute to *Marienbad*, I am sorry that Ashton did not ask Robbe-Grillet for a subject instead of using Dumas. As he thinks of projections I hope he will now continue to explore their alienating functions. Our obsession with private emotion and with individual agonies has worn thin: our need for understanding the relation between the private and the public gesture is acute. We are ripe in ballet for a *Hiroshima Mon Amour*. The film linked the intimate rapport of two lovers with the outside world through a structure so formal and poetic that it drew close to a path the ballet could follow.

Josephine Barstow
in conversation with Rebecca Meitlis
The Adjusted Woman

*Josephine Barstow's assumption of the role of Violetta in 1973
was one of the great performances to establish English National
Opera at the London Coliseum. Since then this celebrated British
singer has performed much of the Verdi repertory both in English
at the Coliseum and in Italian around the world, especially
Leonora in* La forza del destino, *Elisabeth in* Don Carlos, *Amelia
in* Un ballo in maschera *and Lady Macbeth in* Macbeth. *Among
her many other dramatic soprano roles are Beethoven's Leonore,
Richard Strauss's Salome, Puccini's Tosca, Janáček's Elena
Makropulos and Shostakovich's Lady Macbeth of Mtsensk. She
created the role of Benigna in Penderecki's* Die schwarze Maske
*in 1986. She talks about her attitude to performance with
Rebecca Meitlis, co-director of the ENO Baylis Programme.*

JB: I have developed a very great affection for Violetta as a person
and an enormous admiration for her. She's just a lady that I know,
and that I like. She's part of my life.

RM: What is it that inspires your affection?

JB: Her incredible generosity of spirit; it makes me feel humble.
I've never felt that the way she earned her living was anything
other than a profession that she was extremely good at! She
brought grace and charm to the lives of many men, and auto-
matically attracted those who craved beauty and distinction. She
belonged to a world that was flourishing in Paris at the time, the
world of the courtesan, but she elevated all aspects of her life, and
she made art of her life; she was an artist. She made an art of being
a courtesan. She didn't do it consciously, of course – she was a
woman of natural grace. She would have brought this quality to
whatever she did, whether she was a milkmaid, or a business
woman.

But there is much more to her than that. She had, like most of
Verdi's soprano heroines, what I can only define as a spiritual

quality which enabled her to make her sacrifice. She was convinced that by renouncing Alfredo she would free him and enrich his life. In doing this she terminated her own life – she consciously terminated her own spiritual life because she knew that she needed Alfredo's love. She didn't just die of consumption, she died of no longer being able to live without him.

RM: This sacrifice makes me angry. It incenses me that she succumbed to what Germont was putting to her – this story about the pure sister who couldn't marry if Alfredo was with his whore.

Josephine Barstow as Violetta and John Brecknock as Alfredo, English National Opera, London Coliseum, 1973 (photo Donald Southern)

JB: Well. She was a realist. That's what's so sympathetic about her. Whatever we think about Germont's arguments, she recognized that in that world, at that time, he was – although in a very heartless way – telling the truth. And while she might not really affect the future of the pure little sister, she would certainly affect Alfredo's because she wasn't a woman that he could make his wife.

RM: Yet she says that she is making the sacrifice because of the sister, doesn't she? And she says that Alfredo would not believe her if she were to say that she didn't love him any more . . .

JB: But he *does* believe it. Alfredo's reaction proves him to be unworthy of her . . . He could have said, 'That's nonsense, who's just been here? What's caused you to say this?', if his love had been as great as hers . . . but he is a product of a small-minded bourgeois world, and he is always aware – however great he professes his passion to be – that she is not good enough to marry. If this was not so, why did he immediately believe the worst, and then even go further and humiliate her publicly? Knowing what kind of delicate creature she was, how could he do that? He may have acted out of enormous passion and hurt, but if he had been as great a human being as she was, I don't think he would have behaved in that way. That's why I care about her so much.

RM: How, then, do you respond to Germont? When he interviews Violetta and persuades her to make the sacrifice, it is notoriously difficult to stop this turning into a love scene.

JB: It is one of several scenes in Verdi operas between an older baritone and a young soprano, and the father–daughter relationship seems to have been very important to him. *Boccanegra* and *Rigoletto*, for instance, are built around this tension. Verdi has a very personal intuition about the duet between Germont and Violetta. At first Germont is unprepared to recognize what kind of a woman he has to deal with. He has a line, 'Qual modi, pure . . . ' when she receives him. Very soon a sensitivity grows between them. He comes to realize her qualities – it is he, not Alfredo, who writes to her, and we feel his infinite regret at the consequence of what he had done to her.

RM: Although he comes from a class with quite different values than Violetta's, don't you feel he has had, or might have had, a relationship with a courtesan, or at any rate a mistress?

JB: If he has, he would never have lived openly with her. The fact that she is keeping his son, rather than the other way about, is not his central anxiety. A good bourgeois would have kept her in a different department of his life, and have another department to show to the world – which is hypocritical, but it's how a lot of society operates still.

RM: What about Violetta as a sick woman? When you were preparing this role, how did you imagine that sickness?

JB: She is brave and she has come to terms with her sickness. Although consumption is fatal, there are many remissions, and during this sickness you look very beautiful – it gives your skin an almost transparent look. She has learnt to disguise the coughing, and to live, as was then more common than now, with the prospect of an early death. It is cruelly ironic that the relaxed life in the country in Act II is medically speaking just what she needs. The chance of a longer life is taken from her.

RM: But is this healthy life 'taken from her?' When she gives up Alfredo, she does not have to go back to her former world. She could have gone into a nunnery, which would have been a sacrifice. But she deliberately placed herself in a position where Alfredo would be jealous of her.

JB: She goes back to the world she knows. We see her at the beginning of the opera not as a happy woman but as an adjusted woman – her first reaction to Alfredo is shock that perhaps here, at her own party, is someone who will really love her for herself. I'm sure she never considers any alternative to the one that Germont puts before her: it is he, the voice of bourgeois morality, who tells her to go back to the world where she belongs. There's no need for Alfredo to follow her – he could have gone back to the country to his sister's wedding. Or *he* could have gone into a monastery, for God's sake!

RM: Do you see her as a victim?

JB: Yes, in the same sense that she has a capacity for self-sacrifice – and that's what I admire. Many Verdi sopranos are prepared to die for an ideal, usually love, but it might equally be – in our age – some political ideal. The important thing is that they can see beyond themselves.

RM: What always rankles in me is that male composers and writers create women who are such gleaming ideals – who love, and are talented and beautiful – and who are then destroyed. It seems inevitable that Violetta and Tosca have to die.

JB: Tosca is absolutely different!

RM: But she still has to die!

JB: Tosca has nothing of the spiritual quality of Violetta. She's a passionate woman who finds herself in an impossible position, and kills to get out of it, and then kills herself. It's a much more sordid level of life and much more mundane than *Traviata*.

RM: Yet in 'Vissi d'arte' she sings of her art, just as you were saying about Violetta.

JB: Well, in my opinion, Tosca may have been a good singer, but she would not have the detachment to be a great creative artist . . . her passionate animal quality on stage would no doubt have excited audiences . . . If Violetta had been an opera singer, she would have been a great creative artist.

RM: Let me take an extreme example of something that must happen quite a lot. When we were rehearsing *Lady Macbeth of Mtsensk* at the Coliseum I remember that you found it difficult to create the role of Katerina, that is, the title role of an opera by one man – Shostakovich – in a production of another – David Pountney. In the case of Violetta, the text is by Dumas, adapted by Piave, with music by Verdi, and there is generally a male conductor and director. How does this affect you?

JB: I do not see myself as a woman fighting a feminine cause in a man's world. One consolation of a theatrical career is the fact that one's femininity is indispensable! In *Lady Macbeth of Mtsensk*, Shostakovich himself has clouded the issue. He portrays a black world and treats all the characters except Katerina harshly and satirically. Only Katerina's music is romantic. But that for me is where the problem lay. I could see no justification whatever for the three murders which she commits. Shostakovich justifies her. He made a socio-political comment when he argued that she was forced into these crimes by the world in which she lived, and his music romanticizes her – but I found it impossible to play her like that. For me the key to the role is 'the enormous black lake' which she says is deep inside her. I 'played' that black lake and the audience gave me their sympathy. I didn't ask for it. I used to stand there at the end and think, 'I don't give a damn for any of you, for anything.' The irony is that if you do not demand the sympathy of an audience, they give it to you – they too are capable of experiencing the character from the character's point of view.

As a performer you have to get inside the characters you represent. And when you understand them, you start to see their situation from their point of view, you start to like them and eventually to love them: it follows that you try to gain the audience's sympathy for them. This is a trap – the spiel which I have just given you about Violetta is totally from her point of view because I see her from inside her. To a certain extent I have idealized her as a person, in the same way that Verdi idealized her with his music.

RM: How personally involved do you get in the character you are interpreting?

JB: The rehearsal period is the time for discovering as much as possible about the character. You need to get inside her skin, and find out what it is like to live her life. On stage that is not my task: I don't somehow become Violetta or Katerina – when I play the character I am portraying it. In performance I must not be involved; I must be in control, laying bare different aspects of the character so that the audience is involved and they, not I, experience a catharsis.

One of the rarest aspects of Violetta – that is very rare among operatic characters – is that from the beginning to the end you know what she's thinking! In some operas there are great blank passages when the character is just being – Tosca, for instance, is a sensual creature: she doesn't think, she only reacts to stimuli. Violetta is continually working her way towards something.

RM: When you were working on the role, did you make any personal discoveries about the character? Did you find something in yourself in common with her?

JB: With her? I don't think we've got very much in common – I've got more in common with Katerina Ismailova! Violetta has a wonderful tenderness and poise, which I don't think I've got. Think of her opening scene – she's perfectly in control of the party, she knows precisely where everyone is going to and coming from. I admire her most for her natural grace. One of the enjoyable things about being a performer is that you don't have to possess the characteristics yourself to be able to perform them!

RM: What models did you choose for Violetta?

JB: I was very much influenced by Greta Garbo. Her Camille always makes me sob – not so much the story itself as the fact that this jewel of a performance by such a great artist is surrounded by plastic – the rest of the film is so shoddy. That breaks my heart every time.

RM: But that's actually the reality of Violetta in the nineteenth century!

JB: Absolutely. There is a great deal in common between these two women. Garbo has a wonderful laugh. When she throws her head back and gives a dry chuckle, and I used to try to find moments to play that! But never very successfully!!

RM: There is something magical about Garbo . . . You feel that she has filled you . . .

JB: Cleansed you, and that's what all great performances should do. Of course, I arrived at my conception of the character of Violetta almost entirely through the music.

RM: Isn't it a problem when such beautiful music is dealing with something as sordid and mundane as Germont's proposition?

JB: She rises above the situation. It is not her fault that the sacrifice which is asked of her is unworthy: it is how she responds which is the core of the piece. And her response is a great response.

RM: While you're speaking in these religious terms of sacrifice, I can't help thinking of the men who created the society which made this demand of her. So few women have been able to be true to themselves. Has Violetta actually been true to herself? When she is on her deathbed, she is still longing for love – the sacrifice is still causing her pain.

JB: That's what sacrifice is about. She takes on the burden *because* she thinks it is worthwhile to spend the rest of her short life in desperate pain. She believes in the value of what she is doing, and she has a woman's strength to bear things – that's a very Russian, and old-fashioned, point of view, but most women do have more stamina and doggedness than heroism . . .

RM: Maybe all this talk of suffering and sacrifice is unnecessary: Phyllis Luman Metal envisages her life as generous, and fun, and life-enhancing.

JB: Phyllis is not unusual in being able to manipulate men; many women fulfil themselves through men. Phyllis's life seems heroic because she has freed herself of the social attitude to her profession that it is humiliating to sleep with men for money . . . It's the money which we find humiliating . . . However, a lot of women pay men – the gigolo syndrome is still strong.

RM: Although Violetta doesn't feel ashamed of her profession, Germont makes her feel it's wrong. How would Phyllis Luman Metal have reacted in this situation?

JB: Phyllis hasn't been asked to face such a situation. She lives in a world which is much more liberal than nineteenth-century Paris. She says she's been married five times and she has never had to renounce the man she wanted.

RM: Do you know anyone who has made such a sacrifice?

JB: Most female opera singers have at some time to sacrifice their private lives to their career, whether it is a matter of never living in one place, or even not having a family. But I do not have any personal knowledge of a decision of the order of Violetta's . . . And yet, modern audiences are still fascinated by characters who make sacrifices which they themselves have never had to consider; it has to do with artistic endeavours. An artist seeks to ennoble himself and the rest of the world through his achievements. The audience watching Violetta sacrifice herself for her ideals, and transcend herself, is ennobled by it.

Sian Edwards
in conversation with Nicholas John
Conducting Traviata

Sian Edwards is Music Director of English National Opera.

SE: *La traviata* was the first Verdi opera I got to know well, and I love it. I worked as Bernard Haitink's assistant on Peter Hall's Glyndebourne production in 1987. Before I had read the book or the score I was worried about the nineteenth-century idea of heroines as victims of society or *femmes fatales*, the idea that women were created by men for their appreciation and destruction. But I found I could identify with Violetta because, like so many of Verdi's women characters, she is immensely strong. Think of Elisabeth in *Don Carlos*, who sacrifices her love and her life for the sake of the country and her people, and suffers an appalling marriage but never loses her dignity. All around her the characters pale into weakness; though sad, she never loses her ideals. In her inner strength, Violetta is very much akin: when she dies, the opera ends – the men are left utterly helpless and stupid.

Verdi's sympathy for her is comparable to Shostakovich's for Katerina in *Lady Macbeth of Mtsensk*. Shostakovich shows how she could be driven to murder because her life was hell. Like Verdi, he does not make a moral judgement.

NJ: How do you approach the opera and what do you look for in a soprano for this role?

SE: I'm an instinctive sort of performer and very often I don't feel any dramatic necessity in modern works. One of the great experiences of working on *Traviata* is its extraordinary dramatic drive, so that when you reach Act III you feel completely different from the start. For the soprano this almost means that each act requires a different voice: the first act sets up the drama, and it is crucial that she should be able to sing it really well, but then she must allow herself to develop with the dramatic line.

Violetta must have a sparkle in the eye; although she is a tragic character she has an exceptional *joie de vivre*; she leads Alfredo on before she falls in love with him. It needs what I might call an Italian 'ping'. The singer has to have the technique to let herself go with emotion, and to throw off the notes evenly and lightly, with agility and without apparent effort. If this music is very virtuosic and exciting, the second act begins with an intimacy and relaxed domesticity which is the very reverse. Against this background Verdi creates a massively dramatic outpouring in the duet with Germont, where all the strength and pathos of the character are displayed. This culminates in the agony of the lines 'Amami Alfredo' when she cannot tell the truth of what has happened. The third act requires a still heavier voice with intense pathos, and Verdi even asks the singer not to sing but to speak as she reads Germont's letter; the effect is as though the music has dried up within her.

Looking at Verdi's previous opera, *Rigoletto*, it is with Rigoletto himself, rather than with Gilda, that we can see a useful comparison. He also is the professional entertainer of a corrupt society, the outsider whose consuming love and passion for vengeance (in that case) wreck his own life. Violetta forces herself to return to the world she knows will kill her so that she may uphold her ideals. In *Trovatore* (written immediately afterwards) the tragedy is on more heroic lines. And yet Violetta's character has the nobility of a princess, although she is a whore . . .

NJ: And how do you respond to the men?

SE: Alfredo seems to be totally wrapped up in his own experience. Life is empty, he says in Act II, when she is not there: it's a picture of a young lover – of either sex!

It is possible to present Germont in a sympathetic light and to invest him with a charisma that is very persuasive. For me this apparent benevolence, this benign music, only makes him the more cruel, since he uses it as he forces Violetta to give up the one thing which she values. Verdi admires Violetta because he understands that for her it is a choice of love before wealth, and he divorces the reality of her prostitution from the image he creates of a woman who is free to choose. Yet he paints a vivid picture of her awareness of the benefits of luxuries – the horses she was so proud and fond of – and this contrasts with Alfredo who doesn't even notice how the bills are being paid. For Verdi her physical beauty allows her to transcend the sordid past. Germont, however, treats Violetta as expendable and the last scene, in which we witness him recognize that she was truthful, is not sufficiently impressive to efface the memory of his cruelty, and to make us believe that he too has come upon an emotional journey.

He twists the knife when he tells her that her love for Alfredo can never be blessed by Heaven: 'Per voi non avran balsamo/I più soavi affetti!/ Poichè dal ciel non furono/ Tai nodi benedetti.' These rather obscure verses imply more than that she could never hope to marry his son by suggesting that they could never sanctify the marriage with children, without which no union is complete. And she understands this implication, knowing that she cannot live long enough to bring up a family. As soon as he senses that he is winning, he offers her the alternative of saving the proper family of his real daughter. He invites her to be the angel of consolation for the Germonts ('Siate di mia famiglia/ L'angiol consolatore . . . ') and, when she accepts, he is able to place her upon a pedestal. She requests an embrace meaning to be acknowledged as a daughter; but Germont uses that embrace to negate her womanhood, and to place her where she can no longer engage with himself or his son as a woman. From the moment she admits that she can never be a mother, she concedes his victory and becomes a martyr.

What appeals to me about Violetta is that she is in control when she makes this sacrifice, or rather that she has such a realistic appraisal of her position. The word *traviata* does not make it clear whether she left the path of virtue because she was led off it, or whether she went of her own accord. My guess is the latter! In the first act we see her cynicism, the girl who has seen the world in six years. In the second, we see her acknowledge the truth of what she knows of society.

NJ: Does the fact that she capitulates to Germont and what he stands for annoy you?

SE: A great deal of literature and art has been created by men for men. It is up to us now – both men and women – to see that women have their own voice. We can see ourselves not just through men's eyes but through our own eyes; and we can also see men through our eyes . . . Which is not to say that immense influence was not held by women in the last century but that today

women do not have to be on the margins of society to do something of their own. Even though Violetta has made her career in a
degrading way, Verdi respects her personal qualities of courage,
passion, daring. Dumas, on the other hand, makes it quite clear
that although *she* died what mattered was *his* loss.

Of course I respond to this text as a woman: we've spoken
about Germont's cruelty and the ending shows that, although we
can say society destroyed her, she also made certain choices in her
life and takes the responsibility for them. I see no evidence that she
ever regrets being a courtesan, or that she is bitter; Verdi never
writes a number where she expresses remorse. He points up the
hypocrisy of Germont wanting to protect the family, since
Germont is part of that society which created a dichotomy of
angels and whores, and he shows its debauchery.

I love the way Verdi uses brashness: after the sad music of the
prelude, very much associated with Violetta's tragedy, the opera
opens with incredibly rude and brilliant party music: it is energized
and trivial. Another example is the interruption of carnival music
in the last act. It would be interesting if someone would write an
opera now mixing lots of banal tunes with something stronger for
the real moments . . .

The chorus represent a world which is greedy for sensation, and
their fast entrances and exits are symptomatic of a wild and wonderful whirlwind of entertainment. They rush to sympathize and
to condemn with the shallowest of instant judgements. Compared
with this rapacious, uncaring world, Violetta's inner strength and
stability are wholly admirable.

Her vulnerability is an intrinsic part of her appeal: it's still the
case that people, especially women, try to emulate that by becoming anorexic – not on purpose but it's a way that they can be more
attractive, or be loved, because they exude a need for it. There's a
paradox with Violetta that, despite her strength, she has this
terrible disease. Her return to health is associated with the country
idyll and we get the impression that neither can last.

NJ: But how beautiful is the death which Verdi gives her? Are we
to interpret TB as a polite way of referring to the wages of sin, or
at least as a punishment for her past?

SE: Her ending is triumphant. She has held on to what she

believes, for all that Germont tries to wheedle her away from her ideal, and in this way she is heroic. The men are left with a vision of death: their last words – 'O mio dolor!' [Oh, my sadness!] – are quite selfish. It is as if she has slipped through their fingers. Germont's role is ambiguous: at the moment when he has accepted her, she has gone.

The music and drama of this opera are so absorbing, and the character of Violetta so fascinating, that I find that I am always willing her to recover – hoping that this one time she'll leap off the bed and say, 'Hey, I'm all right! Let's go shopping!!' Of course for the conductor that really would be a shock.

Helen Field as Violetta, a photograph for the 1988 English National Opera production. (photo: Pascal Delcey)

Helen Field
in conversation with Nicholas John
The Challenge of Violetta

Helen Field, soprano, comes from North Wales, and has sung a
wide repertory with Welsh National Opera and the other British
companies, and has also made important appearances in
Amsterdam, Berlin and North America.

NJ: It was your performance of the role of Violetta in the 1988
English National Opera *Traviata* that was the starting point for
this book. That production by David Pountney, conducted by
Mark Elder and designed by Stefanos Lazaridis, received mixed
reviews but you are no stranger to unusual productions, or to
strenuous rehearsal periods, having worked with directors from
widely different traditions. Previously you had worked with David
Pountney on the title roles in Janáček's *Jenůfa* and *Cunning Little
Vixen*, and following your performance in his production of
Tippett's *Midsummer Marriage* at ENO, you created the role of Jo
Ann in Peter Hall's production of Tippett's latest opera, *New
Year*. A number of your personal successes have been achieved
with German directors – you worked with Joachim Herz and Götz
Friedrich on *Madama Butterfly*, Harry Kupfer on Marzelline in
Fidelio, Peter Stein on Desdemona in *Otello* and Michael Hampe
on the Governess in *The Turn of the Screw*. For ENO you made
history with another Verdi role: on our 1984 American tour when,
at the last minute, you were invited to sing Gilda at the Met in
performances of Jonathan Miller's 'Little Italy' *Rigoletto*.

HF: The roles of Violetta and Gilda are similar in that their main
arias require a high coloratura soprano, while the rest of the parts
demand a full lyrical quality. It is hard for a heavy dramatic soprano to achieve the different qualities of *La traviata*, especially the
lightness, dexterity and brilliance of Act I. On the other hand, the
intensity of a range of emotions in Act II demands a strength in the
middle part of the voice which is difficult for a light young lyric
soprano to achieve. In Act III, as Violetta becomes increasingly ill,

the actress must predominate over the singer to portray – vocally as well as physically – disease, despair and ultimately death. From the technical point of view the role is so demanding that no one soprano possesses all these qualities – and yet it is one that many can tackle with success in certain areas, if not all of them. I like this challenge.

In many ways for me the first act is the most difficult of the three. Violetta immediately has to be shown to be the life and soul of the party, a person with magnetic appeal and not just a drunken prostitute. As soon as she meets and falls in love with Alfredo, she has to negotiate her way through a tricky aria. Through the superficial brilliance one has to convey a depth of character and swiftly changing emotions. The time passes so quickly: this aria shows her confusion – is this true love? Is it for me? How she resolves this is taken for granted, and in the second act you settle down to the core of the role, the scene with Germont. *La traviata* is not essentially about her relationship with Alfredo.

NJ: Do you like to research the cultural background of a role?

HF: I prepare the music but not the interpretation . . . I don't think about that very much until rehearsals begin. If singers arrive at rehearsals with fixed preconceptions, it's difficult for them to adapt to directors' wishes. It's our duty to do what we are asked to do, or at least to try to. My previous experience of this role was in François Rochaix's totally different – very conventional – production for Opera North, and the experience was useful because I sang the role in Italian. But I tried to come to David Pountney's rehearsals with an open mind.

For me the key thing is to be faithful to the music, and to sing it as the composer intended. I am a spontaneous performer, and leave the actual performance very much to instinct. In rehearsal I think a lot about the production but it's boring if it appears to be premeditated on stage. You have to launch yourself into a performance and hope for the best. Then something else takes over. The producer can give you 95 per cent of role but you have to add the vital 5 per cent of electricity.

NJ: I'm interested in what you want out of producers and out of your public because this role is about performance: Violetta performs in public, and she does what is expected of her by society. Yet *you* are at your most affecting when you appear to be most private and vulnerable, wearing just a shift . . .

HF: I admit I don't like wearing heavy frocks and restricting costumes. I like freedom to move and breathe. My favourite roles are the ones where I have had that freedom, for instance Janáček's Vixen, Strauss's Daphne, Marguerite in Gounod's *Faust* and Butterfly. One can say such a lot through body language, and a tight corset restricts the breathing.

As for producers, I like ones who inspire you to think for yourself. I try hard to do what I am asked to do but I feel singers sometimes don't offer producers enough of their own approach. It can help a producer enormously if he sees that contribution: for instance Peter Stein in *Otello* worked a scene around us after he had seen how we responded to the dramatic situation. The total opposite would be Joachim Herz, who very much dictated in *Butterfly* the way he wanted me to interpret the role. These very different ways of working both enabled me to give some of my best performances. In the end, of course, a producer can only give you so much, and you have to help him and your colleagues because team work is the most important element in achieving a good operatic performance.

NJ: In this opera do you find yourself arguing not only with the producer but disagreeing with the character? You instinctively perceive that the heart of the score is Violetta's sacrifice.

HF: Yes – that's the trouble with the role. She wouldn't actually have done that – at least *I* wouldn't have done that! You find yourself asking who would. Even if she knew she was going to die she would surely have hung on to her happiness until the last minute. To throw it away for someone she hasn't even met . . . It's pure romance. I suppose that she sought religious consolation through self-denial because she knew she had not long to live. Verdi's music is so persuasive that we accept the hypocrisy and double standards of Germont's arguments, and believe the reasons for Violetta's self-sacrifice.

NJ: How do you concentrate on your performance and still keep an eye on the audience?

HF: It's surprising how much you can notice from the stage, and I detest seeing someone yawning! Performers are very responsive to an audience – it's a two-way thing. The audience senses an electric atmosphere and artists feed off their 'awareness'.

NJ: Do you mind when an audience interrupts you with applause?

HF: All applause is gratefully received! It's nice to feel people are enjoying it, although it can break concentration in the middle of a scene. We are talking about performance, not about real life: *La traviata* is a legend, a myth. Once you understand that distinction, you can see there could be a hundred different productions, and they could all be great – this woman can take as many different incarnations. Nothing can destroy the music – or the *Traviata* legend.

NJ: You say this with great feeling!

HF: It would be wrong to say about this opera that you shouldn't do this or that: it's entertainment, not sacred.

NJ: What's your advice to someone coming to the role for the first time?

HF: Do it their way! I spent a year learning the role in Italian with my singing teacher, finding where it lay in my voice. It's a long role which requires a lot of stamina, and when you come to rehearse it you must be so confident vocally that it can almost be taken for granted. And secondly, put it away and come back to it. The ability to convey an intensity of emotion through the colours of the voice comes with maturity. So now, five years on, having had a baby and sung heavier roles like Butterfly, I should like to return to *Traviata* and see how I can bring different things to it. This role always demands more.

*Act One designed by Stefanos Lazaridis for David Pountney's 1988
ENO production, conducted by Mark Elder. The women of the streets
celebrated the triumph of the fallen woman in the scene of debauchery
below. The elaborate table decoration would become the controversial
hay-field of the country idyll of Act Two. (photo: Clive Barda)*

Ivan Turgenev
from On the Eve, *1859*

Translated by Constance Garnett, 1895

They were giving an opera of Verdi's, which though, honestly speaking, rather vulgar, has already succeeded in making the round of all European theatres, an opera, well-known among Russians, *La Traviata*. The season in Venice was over, and none of the singers rose above the level of mediocrity; every one shouted to the best of their abilities. The part of Violetta was performed by an artist, of no renown, and judging by the cool reception given her by the public, not a favourite, but she was not destitute of talent. She was a young, and not very pretty, black-eyed girl with an unequal and already overstrained voice. Her dress was ill-chosen and naïvely gaudy; her hair was hidden in a red net, her dress of faded blue satin was too tight for her, and thick Swedish gloves reached up to her sharp elbows. Indeed, how could she, the daughter of some Bergamese shepherd, know how Parisian *dames aux camélias* dress! And she did not understand how to move on the stage; but there was much truth and artless simplicity in her acting, and she sang with that passion of expression and rhythm which is only vouchsafed to Italians. Elena and Insarov were sitting alone together in a dark box close to the stage; the mirthful mood which had come upon them in the academy *delle Belle Arti* had not yet passed off. When the father of the unhappy young man who had fallen into the snares of the enchantress came on to the stage in a yellow frock-coat and a dishevelled white wig, opened his mouth awry, and losing his presence of mind before he had begun, only brought out a faint bass *tremolo*, they almost burst into laughter . . . But Violetta's acting impressed them.

'They hardly clap at that poor girl at all,' said Elena, 'but I like her a thousand times better than some conceited second-rate celebrity who would grimace and attitudinise all the while for effect. This girl seems as though it were all in earnest; look, she pays no attention to the public.'

Insarov bent over the edge of the box and looked attentively at Violetta.

'Yes,' he commented, 'she is in earnest; she's on the brink of the grave herself.'

Elena was mute.

The third act began. The curtain rose – Elena shuddered at the sight of the bed, the drawn curtains, the glass of medicine, the shaded lamps. She recalled the near past. 'What of the future? What of the present?' flashed across her mind. As though in response to her thought, the artist's mimic cough on the stage was answered in the box by the hoarse, terribly real cough of Insarov. Elena stole a glance at him, and at once gave her features a calm and untroubled expression; Insarov understood her, and he began himself to smile, and softly to hum the tune of the song.

But he was soon quiet. Violetta's acting became steadily better, and freer. She had thrown aside everything subsidiary, everything superfluous, and *found herself*; a rare, a lofty delight for an artist! She had suddenly crossed the limit, which it is impossible to define, beyond which is the abiding place of beauty. The audience was thrilled and astonished. The plain girl with the broken voice began to get a hold on it, to master it. And the singer's voice even did not sound broken now; it had gained mellowness and strength. Alfredo made his entrance; Violetta's cry of happiness almost raised that storm in the audience known as *fanatismo*, beside which all the applause of our northern audiences is nothing. A brief interval passed – and again the audience were in transports. The duet began, the best thing in the opera, in which the composer has succeeded in expressing all the pathos of the senseless waste of youth, the final struggle of despairing, helpless love. Caught up and carried along by the general sympathy, with tears of artistic delight and real suffering in her eyes, the singer let herself be borne along on the wave of passion within her; her face was transfigured, and in the presence of the threatening signs of fast approaching death, the words: '*Lasciarmi vivere – morir sì giovane*' (let me live – to die so young!) burst from her in such a tempest of prayer rising to heaven, that the whole theatre shook with frenzied applause and shouts of delight . . .

Their little room looked out on to the lagoon, which stretches from the *Riva dei Schiavoni* to the Giudecca. Almost facing their hotel rose the slender tower of S. George; high against the sky on the right shone the golden dome of the Doges' palace; and, decked like a bride, stood the loveliest of the churches, the *Redentore* of Palladio; on the left were the black masts and rigging of ships, the funnels of steamers; a half-furled sail hung in one place like a great wing, and the flags scarcely stirred. Insarov sat down at the window, but Elena did not let him admire the view for long; he seemed suddenly feverish, he was overcome by consuming weakness. She put him to bed, and, waiting till he had fallen asleep, she returned to the window. Oh, how still and kindly was the night, what dove-like softness breathed in the deep-blue air! Every suffering, every sorrow surely must be soothed to slumber under that clear sky, under that pure, holy light! 'O God,' thought Elena, 'why must there be death, why is there separation, and disease and tears? or else, why this beauty, this sweet feeling of hope, this soothing sense of an abiding refuge, an unchanging support, an everlasting protection? What is the meaning of this smiling, blessing sky; this happy, sleeping earth? Can it be that all that is only in us, and that outside us is eternal cold and silence? Can it be that we are alone . . . alone . . . and there, on all sides, in all those unattainable depths and abysses – nothing is akin to us; all, all is strange and apart from us? Why, then, have we this desire for, this delight in prayer?' (*Morir sì giovane* was echoing in her heart) . . . 'Is this impossible, then, to propitiate, to avert, to save . . . O God! is it impossible to believe in miracles?' She dropped her head on to her clasped hands. 'Enough,' she whispered. 'Indeed enough! I have been happy not for moments only, not for hours, not for whole days even, but for whole weeks together. And what right had I to happiness?' She felt terror at the thought of her happiness. 'What, if that cannot be?' she thought. 'What, if it is not granted for nothing? Why, it has been heaven . . . and we are mortals, poor sinful mortals . . . *Morir sì giovane*. Oh, cruel omen, away! It's not only for me his life is needed!

'But what, if it is a punishment,' she thought again; 'what, if we must now pay the penalty of our guilt in full? My conscience was silent, it is silent now, but is that a proof of innocence? O God, can we be so guilty! Canst Thou who hast created this night, this sky, wish to punish us for having loved each other? If it be so, if he has sinned, if I have sinned,' she added with involuntary force, 'grant that he, O God, grant that we both, may die at least a noble, glorious death – there, on the plains of his country, not here in this dark room.

'And the grief of my poor, lonely mother?' she asked herself, and was bewildered, and could find no answer to her question. Elena did not know that every man's happiness is built on the unhappiness of another, that even his advantage, his comfort, like a statue needs a pedestal, the disadvantage, the discomfort of others.